SIN & SURRENDER

THE LOCK&KEY MC ROMANCE SERIES
BOOK 12

CAT PORTER

DIRECTORY OF MOTORCYCLE CLUBS

THE FLAMES OF HELL - ELK, NEBRASKA
Finger & Lenore
Drac & Krystal
Catch & Nina
Cueball
Minty
Pick
Lindy

THE ONE-EYED JACKS - MEAGER, SOUTH DAKOTA
Kicker & Mary Lynn
Butler & Tania
Boner & Jill
Lock & Grace
Trick & Nicole
Dready
Bear
Dawes
Jordy
Willy
Wreck (deceased)
Dig (deceased)
Jump (deceased)

THE BROKEN BLADES (NOW DEFUNCT) - NEBRASKA
Zed (deceased) & Angel
Notch (deceased)
Thor (deceased)
Raptor
Minty
Pick & Emmy (deceased) & Lindy

"Life's random hits may have
brought us pain, but they also
gave us rare beauty,
rare to lost souls like us."

- Grace

PROLOGUE

WES

Nothing prepares you for your motorcycle flying out from under you, the whizz of bullets tearing past you. Hell raining down on you.

Nothing.

You grow up hearing about it, marveling at what the sensation of shooting back at an enemy must be like.

And then, one day…

On the road, a smooth road, on a perfect, sunny, blue sky day,

Feeling humbled and grateful, your bike's engine thundering in your veins.

In a flash, it all turns ugly.

Insane.

Pops explode in the air. I lose control of my bike. I'm spinning out, and I hold the fuck on and tumble over when the time is right. Smoke and heat rise, engulfing me. Pain explodes, a burning sensation ripping over me. But I must act fast, and finally, I'm using that gun my father taught me how to use. Using it for real, not aiming at cans and bottles out in the woods.

Why is this happening?

Doesn't matter, it is.

I'm covering Butler, he's covering me. Shouts, panic, my pulse pounding, my blood roaring. I'm focused, adrenaline pumping through every cell in my body. I look back, but Butler isn't there. I call out, but he doesn't answer.

I run.

He's motionless on the ground, and I scream his name.

His bright blue eyes are dull and lifeless in the impossible glare of the sun. Those eyes fade, he fades, and I shout his name to the sky. But nothing, nothing brings him back.

My gun clatters to the asphalt.

"Wes!" Lindy calls out my name, and a piece of my heart jumps. Hope.

But she sounds so far away. My knees buckle, and I fall to the ground next to Butler.

Sirens, sirens, sirens blare.

This is the nightmare I keep having. It comes, it goes, and I shove it away, but it seeps back inside me like a dark stain I can never fully scrub off, an odor I can't escape.

The grief of my father's death hovers over me still. Most of all, the guilt, the regret for things I can never change. And then, in the aftermath, the shame of my actions, the horror of what I might have done for the glory of revenge had it not been for Butler.

That was years ago. I want to live again in the light I once took for granted. I can't say I remember what that's like.

And now, through the smoke, in the heat of the flames that surround me, Lindy screams out my name again in that very same horror and helplessness I've known before. Yet she is full of passion, full of defiance, and her call ignites me to stay the course. To fight. Because fight we must. Or we die.

Crossed purposes. Broken destinies. Wild ambitions. Impulsive choices and lies, so many twisted blood-filled lies led us here.

Lindy's voice, full of rage and agony, determination and desperation, breaks those chains, breaks my heart, and yet, fills it with purpose.

Lindy…

I push back, and my bleeding body surges one last time. My hand finally closes over the gun and squeezes the trigger.

ONE

A BIG, round, orangey-bronzed butt, sticking out of a tiny thong with long, fake-tanned legs, a faded T that Dad wore yesterday, dyed blonde hair in a messy knot, and long, pointy, dotted with rhinestones acrylic nails which were tapping on my refrigerator door.

Not what I expected to see when I walked into my house.

And she was humming, this stranger, this woman I didn't know. Not a care in her fucking world as she scoured the fridge.

My jaw tightened, my teeth gritting together. Not today. Why the fuck today?

I slammed the kitchen door behind me and threw my bag on the table. "Can I help you with something?"

With a shriek, the female twirled around, eyes wide, mouth open. "Who the hell are you?"

"This is my house. That's my fridge. Get the fuck out."

"Are you Pick's old lady?" Her eyebrows hopped up on her forehead as she pressed her bare legs together.

"I'm his daughter, fuckwit."

"Oh." Her shoulders dropped as she let out a short laugh, her hand still on the fridge door. "Hi."

"Out. Now."

"He said I could—"

"NOW!"

She leaped out of the kitchen, running into the hallway toward the bedrooms, and I slammed the fridge door closed.

Dad's bike wasn't out front. He'd probably left early and let her hang out. Mistake. How could he trust these women in our house on their own?

Mom's house.

My head ached. I lit a cigarette from the pack tossed on the table and let out a long stream of smoke. I didn't even like smoking that much, but sometimes nothing else would do.

What a morning.

After my usual overnight hell shift at the diner, I got into my car and it wouldn't start. Not even a sound. Nothing. Wasn't much of a surprise. The past few months, the Challenger had been having more problems and more often than usual. The guys at the club would repair it, but the last time I was told: *"There's not much more we can do, hon. You got to take her for a total overhaul if you wanna keep driving this thing, and that's gonna cost..."*

This thing had been my mother's car. Her dream car that Dad had given her on her birthday way back when. The Challenger was a badass, and I would not give up on her. No way. Not ever. When she gave me no signs of life after my shift this morning, I asked for a ride home from a local customer who I knew. Then I walked into my kitchen...

"Taking way too long!" I raised my voice so she could hear it in the bedroom.

"All right already!" Ms. Badly Self-Tanned marched into the kitchen, shoes in hand, braless boobs bouncing in a magenta lycra mini dress she tugged down over her thighs. I'd bet she didn't know that color was magenta. She probably called it purply-red or wine. She grabbed hold of a kitchen chair as she shoved a foot in a high-heeled, gold you-know-you-wanna-fuck-me sandal. "I don't have a car. I need to call a—"

"Don't give a flying fuck. OUT."

She shot me a nasty look as she hobbled quickly out the door, leaving a trail of old booze and sickly sweet perfume behind her.

I blew out another exhale, the haze of smoke visible in the morning light that engulfed the room. I always liked the kitchen in the morning, but not at the moment. The ashtray on the table was full, and I dropped my cigarette in the empty beer can next to it. I locked the kitchen door. Made sure the front door was locked. It wasn't. Dad had left the house unsecured. Terrific.

He always used to be so careful about security. He had to be. He was a member of the Flames of Hell MC of Elk, Nebraska. Securing the castle was his jam, and from day one, he and Mom had taught me the rules to live by. But since Mom died seven years ago, he'd become scattered. He'd also started partying harder than ever, which was understandable, I got it, but lately, he'd been bringing women home. Home to *their* bed.

I should get over it like I supposed he had. No. I knew better, I knew my dad. He was trying, but on the inside, he was a gaping wound. He and I both.

But today …

Today, all this left a bitter taste on my tongue.

Today was Mom's birthday.

Dad and I didn't discuss these holidays or anniversaries, or bring them up in any way. Not anymore. We tiptoed around them. We knew they existed, but we tread gently.

Back in the good ol' days, there were surprise breakfasts, balloons and silly gifts, a dinner out, a decorated cake, frosting on faces. Most of all, loud laughter. Tight hugs.

Now there was only a tired, musty house that stank of strangers stampeding through it. Stank of loneliness and hurt. After my one and only vicious experience at love, and then Mom's illness blowing up and her death soon after, any other girl in my position would have gone off the deep end and gone wild.

Not me.

I kept my eye on the future. On one day getting out of this small town in Nebraska—out of Nebraska. On doing the work I loved full-time and maybe getting away from club life. I was born into club life, but a different club. A club that the Flames of Hell had destroyed.

The Broken Blades had been on the slippery road of self-destruction for a while and finally imploded, while other clubs, the Flames and the One-Eyed Jacks in South Dakota, gleefully added gasoline to that fire.

My father had been forced to join the Flames or be killed. He joined up. Going through that transition had been hell on wheels for all of us. In the end, only Dad and one other Blade had survived, and they'd done what they had to do to stay alive, to be good Flames.

I emptied the ashtray in the garbage. For me, Dad and Mom moving here to Flames-world had felt like being dragged into a different country where everyone looked at you with scorn and mistrust, like we were illegal immigrants who were out to take their jobs away from them. Dad bent over backward to prove himself to his new "brothers," and Mom had played nice with all the old ladies, as did I. It remained uneasy for a long time, and I hated it.

I was almost sixteen when it happened, my heart freshly broken, my mood permanently soured. Mom had warned me: *"You got to try harder, Lindy. We didn't expect things to go down the way they did, but they did, and this is what we got. The Flames are a solid club. We're lucky. This is good. Be grateful, I am."*

Grateful. Good. Lucky.

Now Mom was gone, and five nights a week I worked the late shift at the diner on the outskirts of town by the highway. It paid better than the day shift, so it was worth it to me. I'd have most of the day free to run errands, clean up, maybe cook, create my makeup looks and post them on IG, and, if I was lucky, work on a client at the local salon where I freelanced under the table.

With Dad, it was feast or famine, so at least I knew that my steady paycheck could pay the basic bills on time, and that gave me some peace of mind. My tips allowed me to occasionally splurge on clothes or jewelry, and my beloved makeup. But most of all the past year, my cash went to trying to fix my car. My gaze shot to the framed photo on the living room cabinet of Mom behind the wheel of her Challenger. Her shades on, her huge grin unmistakable. In his Blades cut, Dad leaned against the car grinning, with four-year-old me in his arms.

I dragged myself down the hallway to my room and spotted a ripped condom wrapper on the floor. Lately, when I'd get back from work, I'd often find party leftovers like this around the house—empty bottles of booze, drug paraphernalia, cigarette packs, dirty glasses and dishes, pizza boxes. But today was the first time I'd found a human leftover. Grabbing the empty wrapper, I crumpled it.

Maybe he didn't give a fuck anymore. Or maybe he realized he needed something and he was hunting for it, whatever it was.

I was twenty-three years old, and I knew how it all worked. Certainly, I no longer had fairy tale stars in my eyes about boys, men, sex, and I didn't trust the shit that came out of men's mouths. It usually boiled down to them wanting to get down your pants and get off, and they'd say and do anything to get it done.

Tossing my phone on my bed, I headed for the bathroom where I threw away the foil packet in the garbage, yanked off my clothes, and took a hot shower. Drying off in my room, my phone buzzed, lighting up with a text. Dad.

Where are u? Been calling.

I was in the shower.

R u home?

Yes

Thought you were working til noon.

That's tomorrow. U left something behind this morning. BIG behind.

Renee.

IDGAF what her name is

LINDY

Will u be back tonight?

I'm on a run to Wyoming. Leaving SD now. Be gone for a few days maybe more.

What? Since when?

Last minute thing.

My chest caved in, and my heart sank. I'd been looking forward to being with him tonight. Tonight of *all* nights. Every year on Mom's birthday we'd make dinner together, eat, watch TV, even go out for a beer. Oh fucking well.

OK

I'll text u when I get there

Ride safe

Luv u

Luv u 2

Luv u 3!!!

The corners of my lips pushed up and my muscles eased. Our sign-off from when he'd gotten me my first phone as a kid. He'd message me from the road, and I loved it. We'd send each other silly GIFs and emojis all the time. And whenever he'd sign off, it was always with that exact exchange. Even now, seeing it on the screen lightened the heaviness in my heart.

Tossing my phone back on my bed, I got dressed in my favorite pink sweatpants and a white T-shirt. In the kitchen, I cleaned up and made myself a tea to settle my stomach. In the living room, I plopped on the sofa and turned on YouTube.

I scanned my favorite beauty YouTubers' latest videos and landed on the one I'd been waiting for from my favorite professional makeup artist—a review of a new blue-purple metallic eye shadow palette that was releasing this week from a top indie brand. Nestling into the big pillows on the couch, I watched her use the palette on herself. The purples and blues drifted in front of me. My eyelids sank. Her voice drifted.

———

"LINDY. LINDY! HEY? LINDY!"

"Jesus, is she okay?"

"Lindy! Goddammit…"

I unglued my eyes. My throat constricted, and something hot fisted in my chest.

"Thank fuck."

I blinked. Four hulking men in leather stood over me. "What the hell?" I sprang from the couch. They grabbed me, and I twisted.

"Lindy, it's us!"

My body drooped in the guy's hold as my eyes focused on

him. Catch, an officer of the Flames of Hell who was a good bud of Dad's. I liked his old lady Nina a lot and babysat their kid on the regular. "Catch? Why are you here? What's going on?"

"Thank fuck you're okay."

"We've been trying to call you. Where the fuck is your phone?" said Minty, anger lacing his sharp voice. Minty was a Broken Blade who had become a Flame with Dad. I'd known him since I was born. He was close to Dad's age, and I'd always felt comfortable with him. Minty was a whiff of home, of the good ol' days. He always looked out for me around the MC like I was his kid.

Goosebumps raced over my skin. "W-what's going on?"

"Phone was in the kitchen." Cueball held my iPhone in his hand, his lips pressed together. Taking my phone, I glanced at my screen. A zillion calls from Minty and Catch had gone unanswered. "What's going on, you guys?"

"Hon, take a seat." The lines of Catch's face were stiff, and my pulse bopped in my veins. Clearing his throat, he planted himself on the coffee table opposite me, running a big hand through his shaggy hair. "We got a problem. Your dad's missing."

"Missing?" The blood drained from my face. The room zoomed around me. "No way. Can't be. I...I just talked to him."

Catch's eyes flared. "When?"

"When I came home."

"When was that? It's after three o'clock now."

"It is? Shit." My neck ached as if to remind me I'd fallen asleep on a bad angle on the sofa. "This morning, when I got home from the diner, he texted me. It was about nine thirty I think. He said he was in South Dakota heading for Wyoming."

"Only Pick never showed up for the meet in Wyoming."

"He always shows," I said.

"Exactly."

I took in all the grim faces. My chest constricted. "What about his bike? You have a tracker thing on his Harley, don't you?"

"The tracker is dead. That's what got me—"

My mouth dried. "What does this mean?" I went from face to face. Faces I'd known for the past eight years since my dad had become a Flame, one of the oldest and most feared clubs in the country.

"Honey, relax," said Minty.

This cannot be happening!

"Fucking tell me!" I screamed.

Catch pulled in a breath. "We think Pick got taken."

"You mean kidnapped? No way. He's too smart for that. What do you know so far?"

"We got nothing so far." Catch dragged the side of his hand across his mouth.

"Maybe he got into an accident and he's alone in some ditch and nobody's found him yet!"

"We're looking." Catch stood up. "Now we got to get you outta here. Pack some stuff and let's go."

"Go? Go where?"

"We're taking you to the club until we figure this shit out. You can't stay here alone." His hand squeezed my shoulder. "Come on."

"Wait!" My blood rushed through my veins as I hit "Dad" on my phone, my insides tightening at the sound of the ringtone. Everyone's eyes were on me as I listened. Waited. Hoped. We all did.

Straight to voicemail.

Shooting up from the sofa, my jaw tight, I went to my room. Through the blur, I grabbed at clothes and stuffed them into my only suitcase.

They wanted me safe? What a fucking joke. I hadn't felt safe in years. Not since I was a naive girl. I stuffed a small duffel bag with my makeup essentials and filled a tote bag with my boots and sneakers. I grabbed my heavy leather jacket, and the stuff was immediately taken from my hands. In the living room, I snatched the framed photo of me and Mom and Dad with her car.

"My car is still at the diner. It wouldn't start this morning," I sputtered.

"We'll take care of it, don't worry." Standing outside on the front stoop, Minty gestured for me to get out of the house.

My eyes blinked in the harsh August sun outside on the dried front lawn. The guys were on their bikes, their engines rumbling. A neighbor walking his dog glared at us as he picked up his pace.

"Lock up the house, Lindy," said Catch.

Breathless, I shoved my key in the front door, my fingers cold and numb. The *slide* and *cling* of the lock sent a shiver through me. Would Dad and I ever come back here?

Daddy, where are you?

Catch threw an arm over my shoulders, pulling me close as he walked me to his bike on the curb. "This sucks, Lind, but I got to ask—he say or do anything odd to you lately? Anything that was off?"

My head jerked back. "What are you trying to say, Catch? That he was into something dirty, something behind your backs?"

"Whoa, girl. I didn't—"

"Loyalty is my father's middle name. The club is his life."

"I know. I do not doubt that. We're trying to figure this shit out."

"Has someone been after him?" I asked. "After the club?"

"Lindy…" A smirk flashed over this face as he got on his bike.

"Stupid question." Someone was always gunning for the Flames of Hell. I shoved my arms through the sleeves of my jacket. "When I came home from work this morning, there was this woman here. He'd brought her home for the night and then he left and let her hang out 'til she was ready to leave. I saw her in the kitchen and booted her out."

"You get a name?"

"You weren't together partying somewhere last night like always?"

"I was home with my boy. It was Nina's night out."

"He said her name was…Robin? Let me check…" I went to Dad's text on my phone. "Renee."

"That's something."

Minty and Cueball took off down the street, the roar of their engines ripping through the air. As I got on the back of Catch's bike, I cast a final glance at the house with the dried brown leaves filling up the trim, the cracked siding, the broken cement walkway sprouting weeds. It was a small ramshackle thing we rented, but it had been home since we'd moved to Elk when Dad had become a Flame of Hell. When Mom was still alive.

I adjusted myself on the saddle. Lately, this house had been less of a home and more of a cruel reminder, an emotional burden, a dank cave, but I hadn't wanted to let go of it. Not yet. It was all we had left.

Catch's engine exploded underneath us, and my fingers dug into his middle. The bike shot forward, and we took off down the road like a rocket. I turned my head, my insides twisting.

Behind me, our house disappeared.

TWO

LINDY

EVERYONE STARED at me as I walked through the Flames courtyard and into the clubhouse. Stared at me in that same way again. Pity mixed with a jigger of anger, a cold cocktail that slithered through my veins as I followed Catch, chin high as if we'd come off a battlefield and had survived heavy losses. But my heart dragged down through my chest like a lead weight.

Catch motioned for me to sit on one of the sofas in the lounge while he disappeared behind a wall to where the President's office was located.

I went over to the bar where some of the girls were cleaning up. "Hey, is there any coffee? If not, I can make it myself."

"Sure thing," said the blonde who looked much younger than me. "Got a fresh pot. How do you take it?"

"I got it, thanks."

She passed me the mug with coffee and I inhaled the life-giving smell. Frowning at the packets of cheap powdered creamer they always had here, I gulped the stiff black brew.

Minty came up alongside me and poured himself a cup.

"Hi, Minty. Can I get you anything?" the blonde asked with a stewardess smile.

"Get lost," he muttered, and she took off. "Lindy, you okay?"

"What the hell's going on, Minty? Was he kidnapped? Or maybe he was in an accident and we don't know. Are they calling hospitals?"

"They're looking." He shot me a glance, his jaw tightening as his hand tightly gripped his coffee mug.

My back straightened. "What are you thinking? You know something?"

"Thinking it's not a coincidence that Pick went off the grid in our old territory."

He meant Broken Blades territory. My stomach dropped, my teeth gnashing at my lip.

Keeping his gaze on his coffee cup, Minty inched closer to me. "They're gonna ask you what you know. You don't know nothing, Lind. You don't remember shit. You were a kid back then anyhow. Anything said between you and your dad is personal stuff."

I took another sip of coffee, its hot, ashy bitterness filled my mouth and slid down my throat. "Is there something specific you don't want me telling them?"

He knocked back a gulp of coffee like it was tequila. "Don't give them anything you don't have to."

"But, Minty—"

"Lindy?" My name boomed through the space, and my breath cut. Drac, the VP, stood with his hands on his waist, filling the archway that led to the main offices. He motioned for me to come over. Setting my mug down, I sucked in a deep breath and walked over to him. His huge hand landed on my shoulder. "Glad you're okay and you're here."

"Thanks. Me too."

"Finger wants to see you." He steered me into the President's large office, my heart pounding in my chest. I'd never been in here before, let alone for an audience with the President. Finger sat at his desk, body tense, irritation etched across his scarred face. Catch was slumped in a chair.

"Have a seat, Lindy," growled Finger's voice. It used to make me jump and shiver, that scoured voice of his, rough and scratchy from some battle injury in his early days in the club. Now I was used to it. I took the seat next to Catch. Drac leaned against a wall by the desk.

I told them about my morning, Renee, Dad's text. "Then I fell asleep on the couch watching TV. Next thing I know Catch and the guys are waking me up. I tried calling him, but it went straight to voicemail."

"Call him now."

I took out my phone and hit Dad's name. Again, voicemail. I shook my head.

"Describe this woman you found in your house," said Finger.

I described Renee.

"That don't sound like any chick I saw last night when we were at the bar," said Drac. "I saw him with all the usual girls, drinking, playing pool, but none of them was her."

"Were you with him the whole night?" I asked.

"Nah, I cut out early."

"Go on, Lindy." Finger raised his chin.

"When I got home, she was going through the fridge and didn't seem to be in any rush. Seemed like a typical morning-after situation. She wasn't ripping through the drawers looking for something to steal."

"Did she have a car or…"

"She said she didn't have a car and needed to call a cab or a friend or something, but I didn't want to hear it and I kicked her out."

"We'll work on tracking this woman down. In the meantime, you're staying here."

"Here at the club?"

"Need to keep you safe until we know what we're dealing with, and then—"

"And then?"

"Got to wait and see."

"Is anyone calling hospitals in case he got into an accident or something?"

"We're on it. Nothing yet," said Catch.

"Is there someone who's been after Dad? I know you're not going to tell me, but has he been involved in something that put him specifically in danger? He's only a foot soldier–"

"What do you mean by that?" Drac crossed his arms.

"That he's not an officer. So why would he be targeted, kidnapped, or taken down unless whoever's out there is going to start tipping Flames one after the other, starting at the bottom rung of the long ladder."

"Maybe they're tipping former Blades." Finger's eyes narrowed over me. "Can you think of any reason why?"

My spine tingled, and my heart thudded in my chest. "You guys could answer that better than me."

"You were with the Broken Blades for a long time, Lindy. Nothing comes to mind?"

"One thing. The Blades' only enemies were the Flames of Hell, and look how that turned out."

Drac blew out a long breath and Catch shot me a sharp look. A warning. Finger leaned forward on his desk like a banker about to tell me he would deny me my request for a loan. "Only one Blade went unaccounted for. One."

I squirmed in the hard wood chair. "Raptor?"

"What do you know about him?"

"I can't say I remember him much. In the last few years of the Blades, he was never around. Always out on mysterious runs on his own."

"Your Dad mention him at all lately?"

"He'd mentioned that Raptor was involved with that Jacks mess after it happened a few months ago, but that was it. He doesn't bring up club stuff with me. We haven't talked too much lately anyhow." I swallowed hard, regret shooting pricks over my skin like a sharp needle. "He works a lot, I work a lot."

"You don't even talk about memories of the old days?" asked Finger.

He was fishing.

My back straightened. "My father isn't the nostalgic type. Especially since my mom got sick. He's all about getting on with things without a fuss, getting the job that needs to get done, done."

"And Pick always gets the job done," muttered Catch, his lips twisting. He was worried.

"What are we doing to find him?" I asked, forcing my voice to sound brighter, positive as I steered the conversation away from "the old days."

Finger drew up in his heavy chair. "We're working on it." Something in his tone was dull and dismissive.

"You are? Or it doesn't matter because he's a former Blade."

"Lindy!" Catch barked.

Unruffled, Finger tilted his head. "Pick is a Flame, and all my brothers matter to me. Each and every one of them." His stern, raw voice barreled through my chest like a power drill.

"I'm sorry, I didn't mean anything by that. I'm tired, I'm freaking out…he could be dead somewhere, alone…"

"We're on this, Lindy," said Finger. "In the meantime, you're going to stay here, where we can keep you safe."

"What makes you think I'm in danger?"

"I like to cover all my bases. In this instance, you are one of those bases."

One of them? Who else? Minty? They didn't trust us and they wanted to keep an eye on us—on me. Could Dad possibly be involved in something crooked?

"I get it," I replied. "No one's been in touch to say they have him and want a ransom? Or made any threats?"

"Nope. Nothing. It's like he disappeared into thin air."

I slumped against the chair, my jaw going slack.

"I'm not going to sugarcoat this for you," Finger said. "You're not a kid anymore."

"No, I'm not. And I appreciate it, Finger. I do." I sat up. "How about this—why don't we put me out there."

"Out there where? And why the hell would we do that?"

"Maybe whoever it is would try to contact me? That's what we want, isn't it? For whoever it is to make some kind of move?"

Catch smirked. "That was my idea, but—"

"And you got shot down for good reason," said Drac. "Honey, come on."

"Why not? What else do we have right now?" I said.

All the men took in a collective breath.

Catch leaned into me. "You sure, Lind?"

"I want my dad back, and I want to do something to help. Anything."

Catch crossed his long outstretched legs, a deep grin on his face.

I diverted my gaze back to Finger. He was the one I had to convince. "Please let me help. Like you said, I'm not a kid anymore." No one said a word. They only stared at me. "Geez, I didn't say I'd go undercover as a hooker or something."

"Say what?" exclaimed Drac, his eyes wide and white. The freaked out dad.

"Fucking hell, this girl!" Catch let out a piercing laugh, clapping his hands together. "Who's been watching too many cop shows from the 80s?"

"Me and Dad. They're our favorites." Grinning, I held onto Finger's grim stare through Drac and Catch's laughter and rumblings. "I'll stay here at the club, so it's not obvious, but I keep working at the diner, while you all are in the background, looking out, looking for a sign."

Catch clapped his hands together. "Prez, I could—"

"No." Wincing, Finger leaned back in his chair, his gaze shooting to a wall. Silence prevailed. The President was thinking.

I took in a tight breath as we waited. Catch lifted his chin at me, like he approved.

"There's a better way," said Finger, his voice now low.

"There is? What way?" I asked.

"You live with me and my old lady. 'Course I need to clear it with her first."

I blinked, my pulse stuttering. "With you and Lenore?"

"I need to clear it with her first, but yeah."

"With you and Lenore *in Meager*?"

His formidable brow scrunched. "That's where we live."

No. No. No. No. No.

Not Meager, South Dakota.

Not Meager, not ever. EVER.

My brain flipped, my stomach heaved. Meager meant one thing.

One person.

The one person in this world I never wanted to lay eyes on again.

"Oh, man, that's good. That is so good…" murmured Catch. "Lindy lives under the protection of the Prez. Makes total sense. Young sad girl on her own, blah, blah, blah."

"And it's Jacks territory. We'll have them on her too." Grinning, Drac chewed more fiercely on the toothpick between his teeth.

"Exactly," said Finger.

My heart thudded heavily in my chest, dragging me down with it.

Drac, Catch, and Finger talked, discussed, planned, their words bouncing off the walls, off me but only the words *Meager, South Dakota* drummed in my head like the drums of war. The very mention of that town sent icy prickles around my neck, squeezing like a hangman's rope.

"Great, huh, Lind?" Catch beamed at me.

"Great," I replied with a quick grin. I could handle it. I'd do anything for Dad. Dad was all I had left in this shitty world.

Is that the only reason?

My legs pressed together. I knew I'd see Wes again one day. I guess that one day was now.

"Lindy?" Finger's gruff voice knocked me free of my dark musings.

I wiped my messy hair back from my face. "Yes?"

"I already got a man on Lenore every day in Meager at her store. We'll add more men to watch both of you along with the Jacks."

"Will I be working at Lenore's store?"

"That would make sense. This girl she had there part-time quit and she's been looking for someone. But like I said, got to clear it with her first."

"Of course. Let her know I've got experience dealing with customers, working a cash register, organizing product, doing inventory."

"I'll tell her. I'm sure being in Meager and working with her would be more appetizing to you than sitting around here all day every day."

"Sure would—no offense." I shot him a grin so he knew I was pleased. And I was. Not having to work at that diner anymore would be amazing, and not having to be stuck here at the Flames clubhouse which was a barricaded bastion of alpha maleness gone wild would be a huge relief.

I liked Lenore a lot. She'd known my mom, of course. She and Drac's old lady, Krystal, would visit Mom regularly when things got bad, and they'd both been there for me when Mom had died. Lenore owned a lingerie store in Meager, a far cry from the diner. But living with Lenore and Finger? The President of the Flames? That might take some getting used to.

Living with anyone outside of Dad felt strange to me. I liked my routine, and being on my own, doing my own thing without answering to anybody, and, most importantly, having my privacy. I was an only child after all. But this idea was miles better than being stuck here at the MC drowning in testosterone and at best doing nothing but cleaning up after the men.

I took in the faces drilling into me. They were concerned, but they were also counting on me. Like I was counting on them.

My lips tipped up into a smile. "Sounds good, gentlemen. Thank you, Finger."

"You good, sweetheart?" Drac slung an arm around my shoulders.

"For now. Thanks for asking, Drac."

"Everyone out," growled Finger. "Got to call my old lady."

THREE

WES

"WES!"

I turned my head at the sound of my name booming through the tunes playing on my earbuds. Jill stood in front of the Rusted Heart, the art gallery and antique store she managed here in town, her toddler in her arms. Jill was an old lady in my dad's MC. She was married to Boner, the Sergeant at Arms of the One-Eyed Jacks.

I clicked off my music. "Hey, hey, what's up, Jill?"

Her long, curly, strawberry-blonde hair was pulled up in a knot on the top of her head, and her usually pale face was streaked with red. "I've been calling your mom, but she hasn't answered her phone."

"She had a bunch of appointments in Rapid today. Everything okay?"

"I have this very important Zoom call in less than ten minutes, and my babysitter fell through. Wes, I am begging you, begging, could you please take Nic for a little bit?"

"Oh...uh..."

I had just gotten off work at the tattoo shop down the block, but was on my way to a last minute booty call around the corner. Nothing like juicing up your afternoon with sex before you headed to your second part-time job of the day.

"Could you, Wes? Please?" Jill shifted Nic onto her other hip.

"Sure. I'll take him."

Jill was in a bind and I wanted to help. Even if my mom and I were no longer an official part of the Jacks club, we were still family. And family always helped each other.

"It should be no more than an hour, is that okay?"

"That's fine." I texted Marina, letting her know my plans had changed, and I wouldn't be coming over.

"Great! He's a bull in a china shop today, and there's no way." Jill handed me her son.

"We'll go to the Grand. Or maybe sugar isn't a good idea?" My phone buzzed, and I glanced at it. Marina had texted back angry emojis. I tucked my phone into my back pocket.

"Whatever you want, Wes. You can handle it. I'll reimburse you for all damages incurred."

"I got this, Jill."

"Wessss!" Nic's face lit up, and he slapped a tiny hand on the side of my face.

"Hey, little man, ready for some adventures on Clay Street?"

"Yah!"

"We'll be back in an hour plus. We'll be up and down Clay, so you can find us. You've got my number, and I've got yours."

"Thanks, Wes. You're my superhero."

"Yeah, that's me."

Jill dashed back into the Rusted Heart, and I put Nic on the ground and took hold of his hand. "We going to walk like big boys today?"

"I'm a big boy!" He hopped on his toes, the green eyes he inherited from his dad flashing.

"Let's do it." Holding his tiny hand in mine, we slowly

walked down Clay, stopping at stores to kill time, trying to get him tired. I lifted him in my arms so he could see the display of the colorful fruit and vegetables at the Organic Co-op, and he made a face when I pointed out the robust broccoli set up to look like a forest.

"Yuck."

"Yuck is right. You hungry?"

Pouting, Nick shook his head furiously. "No broccoli, noooooo."

"No way. Gross. I was thinking of a cupcake. Or a donut?"

"Chocklik. Please."

"You know where we have to go now, don't you?"

"The Grand!"

"Bingo." Adjusting him on my hip, I waited for the cars to pass, and I crossed the street to the next block. We entered our local gourmet coffee shop, and I ordered a double espresso for me, frothy chocolate milk for Nic, and a huge chocolate cupcake. Luckily, one of the small sofas with a table was available in a corner by the front window. I put him on the sofa and showed him a new game on my phone that I was sure he'd be into.

"Oooh!" He tapped on the screen, his eyes round and huge. Engagement achieved.

With an arm slung around Nic, I leaned back on the comfy sofa and sipped my coffee.

"Hey, Wes."

My gaze lifted. Julie, my sometimes hook-up over the past month, stood there with a big smile on her face.

"Hey, Julie, what's up?"

"Saw you and thought I'd pop over and say hi."

"Hi."

Her tongue lashed at her lip. "Turns out I'm not working at the Bay Leaf tonight. Our shifts got switched up at the last minute, and I thought…"

My gaze darted to Nic. "Thought what?"

"Maybe I'd see you at Pete's tonight? We could hang out... you know..." She let out a small laugh as she moved in closer to me, her hand landing on the sofa by my shoulder.

I swirled the remaining coffee in my cup. Clearly, Julie hadn't got the memo.

Two times was my limit and then I was done, because any more than that things got unclear. And for me, things were always clear. I'd moved on like I always did. So moved on that I'd had sex with a coworker of Julie's at the restaurant the night before.

I'd arrived at the Bay Leaf early to pick up my take-home order, and as I waited at the bar, one of the waitresses and I got to flirting and ended up fucking in a bathroom stall.

My gaze darted around the busy café. "I'm not going out tonight."

"You're not? Well, I'll be at Pete's late if you change your mind. And I'll be working tomorrow night. You could swing by the Bay Leaf for a drink?"

"Julie, not going to happen."

Her eyes narrowed and her playful grin had vanished. "Why not?"

"Because it's not."

"But, Wes—"

"It's not." I drained my cup as my gaze flicked out the front window to Clay Street. I choked on the hot brew.

No. Fucking. Way.

My lungs slammed into my ribs and fire raced up my throat. Was I hallucinating? Nope. I'd recognize her anywhere, even though it had been years since I'd last seen her.

It was *her*.

Lindy.

My greatest regret from the shadiest moment of my life. The unexpected bright in my darkest time.

Lindy in Meager?

"Wes?" Julie's irritated voice interrupted my swirl of thoughts and emotions. "What do you mean *it's not*?"

I absently put my coffee cup on the table, knocking over Nic's chocolate milk, but grabbed his glass in time.

Julie let out a gasp. "Here, let me—"

"I got it." Blowing out a breath, I mopped at the chocolate milk puddle with my napkin.

Dammit, I couldn't resist. I glanced at Lindy again. She swept the sidewalk in front of Lenore's Lace, the local lingerie boutique owned by Lenore, a Flame of Hell old lady and the president's wife, who was also my best friend's mother and one of my mom's closest friends.

Lindy's dad was a Flame. Was she working at Lenore's? Was she not living in Nebraska anymore, but here? Here in Meager? My pulse thudded in my ears. How did I not know this? I hadn't been paying much attention to much of anything lately, had I?

"Wes? Are you even listening to me?"

I balled up the wet napkin and tossed it on the table. "I got to run."

"But I'm talking to you!"

"I have to go." Wiping my hands, I stood from the table.

"Asshole!" Shooting me a glare, Julie stalked off.

I ran my hand through Nic's thick mop of dark hair. "Little dude, we have to leave."

"Huh?" Nic looked up at me, his face covered in chocolate smudges and multi-colored sprinkles. Giving me my phone back, he grabbed the last piece of cupcake in the dish before him.

"Let's get you cleaned up." I wiped down my phone, and with the last napkin, wiped at his face and hands as best I could. Picking him up I glanced outside the window.

Yep, she was still there. Still there. Not an illusion. Lindy was real.

Nic and I hustled out of the crowded Grand. I was on a mission. We made our way up Clay, charging across the street toward Lenore's Lace.

Lindy wore tight ripped jeans, black combat boots, and a loose purple T-shirt with an open neck, revealing a valley of pale skin. Her body was curvier than I remembered. She was no longer that fifteen-year-old girl whose innocent smiles and eager touches had been etched in my memory, haunting me for years. She had to be twenty-three now. Yep, all woman.

The last time I'd seen Lindy was four years ago when I'd gone down to Nebraska with Butler, the VP of the One-Eyed Jacks, to deliver a custom detailed bike to Drac, the VP of the Flames of Hell.

After we'd finished up at their clubhouse, we'd stopped at a diner to grab a burger before we got back on the road, and there she was working the register, taller and thinner than the last time I'd seen her. She took her time with each customer—she knew them, and they liked her.

It was crowded, and I waited in line to pay, my stomach churning the closer I got to the front. Finally, it was my turn, and I swallowed hard as I stepped up to the counter.

"Hey, Lindy," fell from my mouth, and at that moment her smile morphed into a harsh glare, which seared me like raw meat on a hot grill. She held my gaze for one awful, silent moment, then handed off my check to another girl and walked away. Not a word.

That had been brutal. The memory still brutal. But what the hell had I expected? I deserved it for the lies, the pretense, for concocting evil plans for her and attempting to carry them out. For never having come clean.

Once upon a time, she'd had a huge crush on me. A crush that suited my purposes. A crush that I'd fed with attention and promises. And kisses. Plenty of kisses.

They were fucking good kisses. Amazing kisses.

A dude in a Jacks cut approached Lindy. It was Dawes. He smiled at her, tossed his blond curls, and puffed up his chest as he leaned in closer and said something. She laughed, her head falling back. He took the broom from her and slid his shades off his face. With a sly smile, she backed up, opened the door of the store, and he followed her inside, closing the door behind them.

Fucking Dawes, the hot stud of the Jacks. *Goddammit.*

Charging forward, I finally reached the door and went into the shop.

"Ooooh!" murmured Nic in my arms the second we got inside.

Yeah, great, I'd brought a little boy into a shop full of colorful lacy bras and panties and corsets–and let's not forget the sex toys filling the shelves in the far corner.

Lindy and Dawes were laughing over a pile of panties. They both raised their heads. Her face tightened at the sight of me. She glared at me again, but this time, she didn't look away. She didn't walk away.

Is that good? Bad? No fucking clue.

Her cold gaze raked over me like a fine-tooth metal comb intent on pain. *Not so good.*

A tiny gold hoop pierced her nose, and her hair was no longer that soft-red layered with chestnut, but, a bold, screaming scarlet, twisted up in a scarf, the ends dyed black and falling free.

She was another Lindy. An older, wiser, edgier Lindy who didn't back away.

And didn't smile. At least not at me. Her cat-lined eyes glinted at me like a tiger's, and my skin heated.

"Hey." I raised my chin as I moved toward the center of the small shop.

"Hey, Wes, what's up? Hey, Nic." Dawes squeezed Nic's arm, and Nic smiled at him as his hand stretched out and grabbed a red bra from a small hanger.

I grabbed the bra from Nic as Dawes turned back to Lindy and put his flirt on in full fucking gear once more. She laughed, a hearty laugh. Full and rich.

A memory whipped through me, straightening my spine. Lindy on the back of my bike, holding onto me, that rich laugh of hers in my ear, her body one with mine as we zipped around a turn.

I glared at the two of them through a tree of panties. She was flirting back with Dawes but in a sharp way. Not fawning over him. Not impressed, but listening, and enjoying it on some level. She was handling him, and he had no clue.

"This might be a while, Wes." Dawes glanced at me over his shoulder. "Maybe you should come back later."

"I got plenty of time." I settled on the small yellow sofa in the center of the store, Nic heaving a satisfied sigh in my lap.

"She might like this one," said Lindy, holding up a crotchless panty.

"I definitely like it." Dawes felt up the material as he licked his lips. "Not sure if that's her color, but it sure would look ah-mazing on you." A dark laugh spilled from his throat. "You like wearing these, Lindy?"

Oh, for fuck's sake.

She ignored his comment and only held up another color. Her gaze met mine. I remained calm, amused. She averted her gaze quickly.

My foot tapped on the floor at the tediousness of Dawes's come-ons. She toyed with him but continued not to bite. A message dinged on my phone. Mom.

I need to see you. I'm at the house. Please come over.

I typed back. *OK. In a bit.*

My gaze shifted back to Lindy, and she shot me a sharp look. Was I making her uneasy? Uneasy in a good way?

A cell phone rang, and Dawes grunted as he grabbed his phone from his cut. "Got to take this. See ya, Lindy."

"Bye." Lindy folded the lingerie up into neat squares pressing her hands over it. She didn't even glance at him as he walked out the door.

I got up, adjusting Nic's weight on my hip. What was I going to say? No idea. My mouth was as dry as a pack of cotton balls. "Hey, Lindy."

Her eyes flicked up at me, but she said nothing, only her chin lifted.

My heart drummed in my chest. "Been a long time."

Her lips twisted and an eyebrow shot up.

Smack. Nic's hand landed on the side of my face. A hand covered in slimy, sweet-smelling goop.

"Dude, where'd you get the cupcake from?" I muttered.

"My pocket," Nic replied. "Want some?"

Lindy offered Nic a smile. "What's your name?"

Nic's eyes widened but he didn't answer.

"This is Nic." I wiped at the goop on my face, but I only made more of a mess.

"Hey, Nic," she said. Nic studied Lindy carefully, stuffing all his fingers in his mouth, sucking on them. He was mesmerized, same as me. Her gaze met mine once more, a gaze less cold. "He's cute. You're a mess."

Oh, in more ways than one, baby.

I swiped at the chocolate filling still clinging to the edge of my stubbly jaw. "He must have stashed a piece and I didn't notice."

Of course, I hadn't noticed. All my attention had been focused on getting to Lindy.

Laying his head against my chest, Nic stared at Lindy and let out a sigh, his eyes closing, his body slumping against me.

"He's crashing now." Lindy reached under the desk and handed me a wad of wet wipes. "I always keep these handy."

"Perfect. Thanks." I wiped my face.

She took another wipe and dabbed at Nic's chubby cheek as he slept against my chest. Leaning in close, the warm scent of vanilla and spice invaded my senses like a rush, the heat of her body blazing up at me. The curve of her breasts peaked from the top of her loose shirt, and something inside me twisted and pulsed.

Her serious gaze flitted from Nic to me, her face streaked with red. "Congratulations."

"For what?" I crumpled a wipe into a ball.

She handed me another wipe. "Your son. He's beautiful."

"What? Oh, no, no. No."

"No?" She blinked, her head dipping.

"He's not my son. Nic's dad is a One-Eyed Jack. You know Jill over at the Rusted Heart? She had to get on a Zoom call and needed help, so I—"

"Oh." Her cheeks flared with color, her back straightened. "Jill. Right." She shifted her weight. "I thought you—"

"God no. No."

She bit her lip as her gaze returned to Nic. "Nic's a baby Jack, huh?" Her voice had softened considerably, and my insides relaxed at the sound.

"Yep."

"He's a cutie."

"He is." We both stared at Nic. Was it easier than looking at each other?

"So you're a manny?"

"A what?"

"A man nanny."

"I'm no nanny manny whatever the fu—" Chopping off the curse at my lips, I blew out a huff of air instead.

"It wasn't an insult."

"And you…you're working here?"

"I am."

"I didn't realize."

"Why should you? Unless you're a regular customer of Lenore's Lace. Are you?"

My eyes narrowed at her. "Aside from Meager being my hometown, I work a couple blocks down at the tattoo shop and spend loads of time at the Grand as well. I'm up and down Clay all the time, and I haven't noticed you here or anywhere in town until now."

"Uh-huh." She moved away from the counter to the opposite end of the small store, tucking half the stack of panties into a drawer. Was I boring her? Or was she working hard to let me know she didn't give a rat's ass about seeing me again?

Message received. But fuck that, not giving up.

I followed her. "You still living in Nebraska?"

"No."

"You're living here in Meager?"

"Mmm." She rounded the counter and put the rest of the panties she'd shown Dawes back on display on a little round table.

"Since when?"

"Since when do I owe you personal information?"

"Suddenly you're here in my town working, and all I'm asking is if you live here too."

A hand slid up the luscious curve of her hip, resting there as she cast me a cold look. "Gee, Wes, being interviewed by you is super exciting and all, but I have work to do for Lenore before she gets back."

Lindy abrupt, sharp. A different Lindy than the girl I'd known before. She continued messing with shit in the store, keeping her distance from me.

Only I wasn't going anywhere. "You look different since the last time I saw you."

Her lips tipped into a tight grin. "And you look the same."

The blood backed up in my veins at her salty tone, her insinuation, the opaque look in her eyes. The gray truth fisted me in the gut and twisted there like a rigid bolt.

She was right.

Eight years later I was still wearing my jeans and hoodie combo—the same boots, in fact. Only my hair was longer, even more in my face if that were possible. I took in a tight breath. What did I have to show for the past eight years? Me in my twenty-fifth year of life?

Not a fuck of a lot.

I cleared my throat. "Maybe. But even though a lot has stayed the same, a lot has changed."

"For me, everything's changed." She went behind the small cashier counter. "Everything."

"Lindy, I know I don't deserve much of anything from you, and I get that—"

"You do? Wow. Should I be impressed? Grateful?"

I let out a strained chuckle. "No, definitely not impressed." Nic was now a dead weight against my chest, in my arms, all of it a dead weight. "I should get Nic back to his mom. It was good to see you."

"Oh, come off it."

"It's the truth."

Her eyebrows quirked. "The truth?" A hand went to her middle. "Wow, you actually said that?"

I moved toward her. "Lindy, I am so sorry that—"

"Save it." She raised a hand between us, blocking my movement closer to her, blocking my intentions. "I'm over it. I grew up, moved on, and I don't waste my time on bullshit from the past, or on bullshit artists in the present."

A sting raced through my veins at her words. The hammering of my pulse told me what had been festering in my blood and bones for years: I wanted her to believe that I regretted my actions. That I knew it was horrible of me. "It's not bullshit. I—"

"Whatever you have to say is bullshit."

She was bitterly angry with me, and she had every right to be. But I couldn't leave it alone. Hell, that's what had gotten me into this with Lindy in the first place—my burning need to leave no stone unturned in my quest to revenge my dad's murder, even if it meant seducing a fifteen-year-old girl because she was the daughter of a member of the rival MC everyone assumed had killed my dad.

I'd been a scorpion running loose, poisoned claws wrapped around Lindy, ready to strike. My only guiding principles had been *sting, crush, destroy.*

Thanks to Butler's intervention, I hadn't taken it that far with her. And then she and her dad ended up saving me and Butler from an assassination attempt by another biker who had a personal beef with Butler. Crazy. Incredible. So damn humbling. Scared the shit out of me then, and thanks to the joy of occasional nightmares, still fucked with me now.

I'd been grateful and deluged with guilt all at once. A high-octane cocktail in my veins at the age of seventeen. Guilt at what I could have done to her had overwhelmed me, and I was horrified at myself, at what could have been. What I would have been. A monster. But that shit was in my blood, wasn't it? My destiny had bared its fangs to me at the age of seventeen, stopping me dead in my tracks.

And before I'd had the chance to come clean with her, she'd found out the truth from someone else. That stung. But hell, of course, it had stung her way more, and way worse. And her now shooting me a cold, seething look was well deserved.

The revelation of my lies and planned cruelty had obviously had its effect on Lindy. Gone was the sparkling young girl with the thousand-watt smile who believed in me, who beamed at the sight of me. The girl who eagerly kissed me, whispered my name, sighed in my neck. The Lindy who held me tight, laughing loudly as she rode on the back of my bike. My jaw clenched. I'd crushed that bright and replaced it with shadows, bitterness, and anger.

And hate.

I'd been her first boyfriend, first love, *first liar*. I'd been the ruthless predator—looting with smiles, stealing with kisses, lying with touches full of promise, pleasure, possibility.

So foul.

So determined to hurt their club, make them pay for Dad's murder. I'd torched their businesses, I'd robbed them, and Lindy was going to be the cherry on that cake, the ultimate theft. An awful analogy, but it was so fucking true.

"Lindy, please give me a chance."

"Why should I?"

Her eyes were cold glass again, and that cold coated my chest like freezer burn. I swallowed hard past the jagged rubble. "Could we maybe get together and—"

"Seriously?"

"I want to talk. We need to—"

"We don't need to do anything. I know what you want. You want to feel better." Her eyes shifted quickly to Nic, who was fast asleep. "Fuck you and what you want, Wes," she whispered roughly, a whisper that clawed at me, a whisper eight years in the making. "Fuck. You." Her face had reddened. Her lips trembled, and she pressed them together. It wasn't triumph that stamped her delicate features. It was anger spiked with sadness. Sadness spiked with anger.

"Lindy—"

"Get out!" Clenching her jaw, she marched to the front door and opened it. "Do not come back again or I'm going to tell Lenore and Finger you're bothering me. Or maybe I'll tell them the whole story. The whole nasty truth. That would go over real big with them, don't you think?"

"Are you living at Finger and Lenore's?"

"How are you out of the loop on this? Why didn't they tell you?" Her gaze darted to my jacket. "You're not a One-Eyed Jack?"

"No."

She blinked, eyes wide. "You didn't join your dad's club? Why not?"

"That's my business," I spit out.

"Whoa there."

"Is that why Dawes was hanging out here today? Are the Jacks keeping an eye on you? Protecting you?"

A smile sliced her lips. "Dawes likes me. I like him. You know how that goes, don't you?"

"Lindy, tell me."

"It's Flames business." She crossed her arms, her lips twitching. "I can't discuss it with a civilian." Her voice dripped with disdain. With scorn.

Nic let out a tiny cry in his sleep, and she pulled the door open for me. I tracked out of the store, my arms tightening around Nic's limp body. I got him back to the Rusted Heart and into Jill's grateful arms.

Heading back toward my bike down Clay, I spotted Dawes ahead of me. "Dawes, wait up!"

"Hey. You and Nicky get your bra shopping done?" He chuckled.

"What's going on with Lindy?"

"What do you mean?"

"Why is she in Meager, living with Lenore and Finger?"

"You were just with her. You didn't ask her?" His lips twitched. "Or she wouldn't tell you?"

"Dawes, come on."

"You two know each other?"

"We go back."

"And still she wouldn't tell you? Interesting."

"What's going on?"

"She's under Finger's protection, that's all. It's temporary."

"I figured, but why?"

"Dude, you know better. This is club business, so you gotta back off."

"Fuck off. What happened?"

A grin flickered over his lips. "I gotta go pick up some coffees for the guys, and I'm running late."

"You're only late 'cause you took your time flirting with her at Lenore's."

"You know me, can't help myself when it comes to a pretty girl. And they can't help themselves with me either." He slapped at the side of my face.

I grit my teeth, the urge to punch him zapping through me as I swatted his hand away. "Not her, man. Back off."

"Easy. That's up to the lady, isn't it?" Dawes turned around and sauntered back down Clay toward the Grand.

I got out my keys. *Lindy duty?* Adrenaline rushed through my veins. A new kind of adrenaline. I was going to find out what the hell was going on with the Flames, and then I was going to make things right between me and Lindy.

I promise you that, Lindy.

FOUR

LINDY

WES STALKED out of the store and down the street, the little boy asleep in his arms. I let out a huge, shaky breath and slumped back against the door. The breath I'd been holding since I spotted him with the toddler earlier was now a spiraling ache.

I'd assumed the boy was his son. They seemed so *right* together. And even though a sharp tug had cut through my insides at the sight of them, at the thought of Wes having a child, being married, being happy with another woman, something warm had flickered through me as well.

It was still there. No matter what I'd done over the past years to stop it. The second he'd walked into the shop, he'd sucked all the air out of the space, out of my lungs.

Since the moment Finger had told me I'd be living in Meager, the one thing foremost in my brain was that I'd have to see Wes again. For four years I'd managed not to lay eyes on him, to not be reminded of his villainy and my stupidity, my humiliation. And the crumbling of a precious dream.

My dream had been a silly fairy tale, a sham. A scam. But I

was no longer that little girl who worshipped at his altar. If that's what he'd hoped for he was wrong. Arrogant jerk.

"You look different."

He noticed. He'd taken me in inch by inch when I first spotted him, which had given me some sort of pleasure. Had I offended him when I said he looked the same? But it was the truth. He'd practically stuttered for words, even lost his balance. That, too, had pleased me.

I'd heard he'd gone off to college, and it had to be four years since he'd graduated, but I couldn't say he looked any different for it. Then again, what had I expected to see? A smoother, more sophisticated Wes? A suit and tie? And he hadn't even joined his dad's club?

A tremble went through me. He was the Wes I remembered. The Wes who made my insides melt with a look, with the feel of his hand sliding over mine, taking it in his. I'd never forgotten that feeling.

My Wes.

Shut up! He's not your anything. Never was. It was all an act. All a lie.

He still had that same boy-next-door smile with a cryptic edge that made you want to kiss him and get under there, in there, be in on his secrets which promised to be dangerous and dangerously hot. Weren't you the lucky one if he let you?

That same saunter, his beautiful thick hair, those full chiseled lips that always looked like they were ready to smirk, ready to seduce, ready to...

My fingers went to my lips. Years later his kisses still lingered no matter how hard I'd tried to obliterate the memories. My body remembered.

I pushed away from the door and got back to work. Those brooding blue eyes that swallowed me whole hadn't changed either. This time, luckily, I'd been able to swim out of their indigo abyss. My heart pounded in my chest. *This time.* This was only the first time I'd seen him since I got here a few days ago.

There'd be plenty more times, but the dreaded first time was now over.

Wes. My big crush. My first boyfriend. My first love who'd obliterated my heart and soul just as it had begun to beat for real.

Everything that had come out of that boy's gorgeous, sexy mouth had been nothing but a blood-laced lie. Every touch of his warm hand, a teasing seduction rooted in hate and revenge.

I'd found out the truth later, and it was then I vowed I'd never be vulnerable to another man again. Not ever. The realization that I meant nothing—no, *less* than nothing to him the whole time had been so humiliating, so devastating. How could I have been so stupid?

I refolded the lacy halters for the third time, my hands pressing down on the silky pile. I was no longer that kid who believed a smooth-talking hottie on a motorcycle with a heavy, gleaming gaze that burned a hole through every cell in my body and ignited a blaze deep inside me.

Nope.

Instead, I'd made a career of taking from guys whenever I was in the mood, then walking away. One of the waitresses I worked with at the diner was always dreaming she'd meet a guy who would whisk her away from her humdrum life. That was a bull crap fairytale little girls were programmed to believe— someday we'd be chosen, we'd be saved by The One, a white knight, a handsome prince, a gray-suited billionaire, and he'd sweep us away to a perfect paradise.

Total baloney.

Little girls had to grow up fast and learn how to take care of themselves, learn how to watch out for assholes. I did.

My hand smoothed down my chest and settled on my middle where my insides had finally stopped tossing. Now it was over, this thing I'd been dreading since I'd left Nebraska. We'd seen each other. We'd talked. I'd told him to fuck off.

I checked the clock on the wall. Lenore would be here any minute, and I still had to redo the front display.

As I took off the lace robe from the steel cut-out mannequin in the bay window, an engine exploded loudly, and my gaze shot up. Wes riding a big vintage Harley, his jawline sharp, long muscular legs taut. In an explosive roar, man and machine picked up speed and tore down the road.

I let out a shaky breath that fogged up the front window. I'd lied to Wes.

He *was* different now. Hotter and sexier. No longer that boy, but a man. Taller, more muscular, more wicked…*more everything*.

And he melted my insides more than ever before.

FIVE

LINDY

"Ooooh."

"Mmm." Lenore's finger swatched a cherry pink color down the inside of her arm. It started delicate, but with each press of the powder, it became richer.

We sat at her kitchen table, the remnants of our take-home Italian dinner having been pushed to the opposite side of the table while we looked at lab samples of blush together.

Lenore swatched more blush colors on her arm. A deep, rich berry-brown and a peachy-melon color. I picked up the cherry pink one. The lab's packaging was thin, no-frills plastic. "Could I swatch?"

"Of course. I'd love your opinion."

I pressed my finger into the product. "How is it I've never known about your makeup line?"

"I haven't been consistent with it. I have so many ideas, but not enough time or hands. I have the fragrance oils, the bath salts, and candles, and the makeup started with a finishing powder in a compact, which I have made in small batches. It keeps selling out, and I never have to advertise it. But I've been wanting to do a blush and a lipstick for so long, I finally went ahead with the blush, and these are the first samples from the lab."

"So exciting."

"Isn't it?" She giggled, and so did I. We were co-conspirators indulging in a secret delight. Lenore seemed more like a girl my age in this moment than a woman my mother's age. Her unusual blue-green eyes gleamed at me, and my face heated under her scrutiny. "What is it?"

"This is the first time I've seen you genuinely smile." Her hand brushed my arm, and my back straightened. Was she going to dish out an it's-okay-to-talk-and-let-it-all-out line now? Lenore lined up all the blushes. "Nothing like makeup."

I burst out into laughter, my body shaking. "I think I have more makeup than I do clothes. Crazy, huh?"

Lenore leaned into me. "Lindy, it's me you're talking to." She let out a small laugh. "Same here, girl. If it brightens you up, if it's what you love, if it satisfies—yes, please. Give me more."

"That's exactly how I feel."

"Yes to makeup, makeup brushes, tattoos, and, of course, fabulous underthings. They all simply make my heart sing, no matter what. And each one never fails to make me feel good about me, about life. Always has. All these delights have been a form of therapy to me. A playful place, a safe place. Me taking care of me."

A whoosh rushed through my system at her words. "It's that way for me too." I cleared my throat. "What's your plan with the makeup now? Are you going to come out with a whole line? Are you going to set up an online shop or only sell at the store?"

"I came out with the powder compact a few years ago and it did very nicely. I'm not making any kind of money off of it, but so far it pays for itself. I replenish the stock in small batches. It's a blurring-setting powder in several shades. I want to expand the color range for many more skin tones and be able to have constant stock in the store, but I'm a one-woman show and not ready to handle all that it would require, let alone an online store."

"But you'd like to?" I grabbed the darker blush color.

"I'd like to." She smiled. "I want to see how the blushes do, and then a lipstick…I'm not in a rush. No need to be. I want to do things right."

I smudged at the swatch of dark berry cocoa on my arm. "This is so silky. And the pigmentation is there but not overwhelming. It's buildable, which I think is the best for blush. I like this formula. It's so smooth."

"You're talking like a makeup artist. I love it."

"That's what I want to be when I grow up." I let out a dry laugh.

"Fantastic. You should do it."

"I've taken a few masterclasses, and I did a summer program in Lincoln a couple of years ago, and I recently started freelancing at the hair salon in Elk, but I want to get my license."

"I had no idea. You absolutely should."

A flutter in my belly tickled my insides. I never did this, shared my stuff, but Lenore was different. She understood. Sharing this with her was a shot of feel-good confidence in my veins. I took out my phone, hit my Instagram, and slid my phone in front of her.

Lenore honed in on my account and swept through pics. Pics of me modeling my looks. Intense looks. Simple fresh looks. Strange looks, strangely beautiful to me.

"You did all these?"

"Hmm." I pointed to other posts. "These are a couple of friends of mine who I did for Halloween last year, and that bride was a friend of a friend. This girl was going to her prom…"

"Lindy, they're beautiful. And you're gorgeous."

"Nothing like makeup."

She raised her head in a sharp, quick movement, and met my gaze. "*You* are beautiful with or without the makeup, and these photos show me the passion in you. Am I right?"

I only nodded.

"You have a tremendous sense of color and you're not afraid of it. You can be restrained and delicate, and you're not afraid of being bold." She put my phone on the table. "Very talented."

"That is the best compliment ever, especially coming from you, Lenore."

"Does anyone know?"

"My dad knows. He helped me pay for the classes I took, and with staying in Lincoln that summer. I don't talk about it much."

"Why not?"

"It's special to me. My happy place."

She clasped my hand, and my pulse jumped. "I understand. That's the best thing, and you found yours. When I was your age, designing and sewing clothes was that passion for me. Something I learned from my grandmother. It saved my life over and over again." Her tone was colored with emotion, and on some kind of instinct, my other hand covered hers.

"I caught the makeup fascination from my mom," I said. "We never had much money, but even at a discount dollar store, she'd find cool eyeshadows, all sorts of brushes. She'd mix stuff together, try different looks, different colors. See what she liked, and what she didn't, and improvise. There were no rules, and she enjoyed the whole process. It was fun for her, and fun for me to watch, to shop with her, unwrap the goodies, play with them."

"All those colorful pots and compacts," murmured Lenore.

I grinned. "The packaging, the textures, the effect on your skin, the fluffy brushes in all sorts of sizes and shapes. It's a fun world to lose yourself in, and the result is that you can be whatever you want and create that for yourself."

Her grip on my hand tightened. "Would you be interested in helping me with the makeup line?"

My heart jumped in my chest. "Really?"

"I need help, and you obviously know what you're doing, and you deeply love it. I need to test things out on women your age as well as women my age. I have the old ladies here in Meager giving me their beta test opinions, and a couple of the dancers at the local strip club, which has been great because they need a formula that will last."

"That's a lot of data to keep track of."

"And my time is limited. I have custom lingerie that I'm always working on, which is important to me. And, of course, there's the club, my home. My man. I feel like I have to race to keep up, and I fucking hate that feeling, especially when I need to make the absolute right decisions. I need you, Lindy."

My brain stuttered. "You need me…"

"Is that a yes?"

"It's a hell yes." I let out a laugh.

"Good." Letting go of my hand, she slid back in her chair. "Every time I've seen you around the club you were never all glammed up."

"I always kept things basic for working at the diner and especially when I'd have to go to the club."

"You work for Lenore's Lace now. Glam it up."

Giggles spilled from my lips. "Yes, ma'am."

"How about you test these blushes this week? Keep track of each color, when you put it on, and with what kind of brush and application technique you use. Check-in times for how it's lasting on your skin. Use them over all kinds of foundation—powder, liquid, cream, stick—which I assume you have?"

"I have it all."

"And on bare skin too. We want to know all the things—blending, texture, longevity."

"I'll spreadsheet it."

"Fantastic. Make me one too, and at the end of the week, we'll compare notes. I'll let the old ladies know that they need to fill out the questionnaire I sent them and get them back to us."

"Sounds good."

"We can make a party of it. Finger is going to be out of town next weekend, so girls' night is on." She smacked her palms on the table, and my eyes shot to the beautiful tattoos she had on top of her hands.

Lenore was tattooed everywhere, which I found intriguing.

"I love your tattoos. They're an amazing collection."

"Thank you. This has been many, many years in the making. Another form of me making me, and me feeling good about me. Do you have any?"

"A couple. One for my mom, and another for a … a boyfriend gone bad."

"Oh, sorry to hear that."

"A life lesson. Never doing that again."

"Never doing what exactly?" She stacked the blushes back in the small box. "Having a boyfriend?"

"Pretty much."

"It'd be a shame to deprive yourself of a good man and deprive men of your beauty inside and out, sweetheart. Now you're smarter, I'm guessing you know more of what you want, what's important to you, than you did back then. And you're stronger for it. Never say never. Trust me. You never know what life will fling at you." She closed the box and slid it to me.

"That's for damn sure." My fingertips tapped on the box. "I know I sound negative."

"A bit." Lenore let out a laugh.

"Maybe one day I'll find someone who makes me happy the way my parents were happy together. I still remember those good times. Those memories still warm me up inside," my voice had become a whisper.

She touched my arm. "That's good. That's a real blessing that you had that. What a wonderful inspiration."

"My mom liked you, Lenore. I wanted you to know that. She'd told me how, when we got to the Flames, you made her feel comfortable from the very beginning. You were generous and kind, and that meant a lot to her."

"I knew it had to be hard on her and your dad, transitioning into a new club after all that went down. I liked Emmy. Loved her dry sense of humor."

"Me too. I miss that." I fiddled with the flaps of the small cardboard shipping box. "There are no guarantees about anything in this life, are there?"

"No. But you can choose to live in opportunity and positive energy."

"Mmm." I grabbed the dinner containers and brought them to the sink to rinse out for recycling.

"Your bad boy sent you reeling, huh?"

"Guys always seem to think they can take advantage of us, but I don't play that game. I want things on my terms. I'm super cautious now, which is a good thing."

"It's good to be aware and to protect yourself. But if you ever really like someone, you shouldn't let anything stop you from swimming in those waters. For a long while, I'd convinced myself that being alone was the best thing for me. I controlled everything where men were concerned, and it felt great. Clean sharp boundaries. Freedom from emotions, freedom from expectations."

"No mess." I stuffed the small cardboard boxes into the recycling bin under the sink.

"But if I looked under the surface of all that freedom, I wasn't truly satisfied. Because at the core of it was the burning knowledge that there was only one man for me. My first love was my forever love, and if I couldn't have him, I didn't want anybody. I couldn't go there. Couldn't pretend. I think you know what I'm talking about, don't you?"

Something pinched in my chest. I knew exactly what she meant because it was exactly how I felt deep, deep down. "I do."

"I was around your age when I'd gotten caught up in a bad situation with a man and then another. I met Finger, he helped me get out, and along the way, we fell in love. Some very crazy shit went down, and we had to keep things under wraps. It was really difficult and dangerous to be together. Then he got arrested and sent to prison, and I found out I was pregnant. I was still on the run, and I gave up the baby for adoption so she'd be safe."

"Zoë."

"Zoë." She grinned. "I took off, got myself a new name, created a new life, and years later, I ended up marrying someone else."

"Beck's dad?" Lenore had a son with her first husband. A son who was now a famous rockstar.

"Eric was a good guy, but…"

I sat back down at the table. "Doomed from the start."

"From the start. My heart was branded with someone else's name and always would be. Years later, when Finger and I crossed paths again, I wasn't open to a relationship with anybody, but he kept insisting."

"Oh boy…Finger insisting?" Letting out a laugh, I pretended to shiver.

Her features softened. "He was right. There was no reason not to be together anymore, no reason to be in shutdown mode. My biggest dream came true better than I ever imagined."

"I'm so happy you got that second chance, Lenore. Happy for both of you."

"Me too. It could happen for you too. I don't mean a second chance with that guy, but you're so young, Lindy. You could have your happy ever after. If you want it, you can make it happen."

"Sounds like a fairy tale."

"Let me remind you that Snow White and Cinderella, among others, all went through very tough times before they triumphed and found a good guy." She touched my arm. "It's smart to be careful, and I'm proud of you for standing up for yourself, but you don't have to be alone to prove a point."

"I guess I never saw it that way."

"All I'm saying is be open to the possibilities. They always come from unexpected places and in unexpected ways." She went to the sink, wet and soaped up a small microfiber towel, and wiped down the table. "I noticed Dawes has been paying lots of attention to you."

"He's only flirting with me because I'm the shiny new girl in town, and he can't help himself."

She laughed. "You've got him pinned."

"He's good-looking and a real charmer, but I'm not here to have myself a good time. Dating a Jack is a complication I don't need, and I don't think our clubs need it either. I wouldn't want to create any problems over nothing."

"That's smart. But your feelings, your wants and desires, whatever they are, are not nothing. You deserve the things you want. You deserve to have the man you want."

My face heated. "I do, huh?"

"Of course. You need to believe it." She rinsed out the towel.

My vision blurred. What the hell? I'd stopped crying years ago. Talking to Lenore like this, the same way I'd talk with my mom, both of them strong women who understood the way my heart beat. That damned heart that still ached. Still yearned for one boy.

That boy was a man now.

Over the years, I'd carefully built my walls and marked my boundaries. But being in Meager, seeing Wes earlier today, talking frankly with Lenore, those walls, no matter how thick, how high, were quaking.

SIX

WES

"I HAVE NEWS." Mom's lips slid up into a grin as I entered the kitchen of our house.

"You're pregnant?"

"Wes! For God's sake…"

I laughed. "Couldn't resist."

Mom had a new boyfriend. Well, Ronny wasn't new. Even though they'd been dating since Dad died eight years ago, and had been living together here at our house and his place in Deadwood for the past four, to me, Ronny was still the "new boyfriend."

She was happier than she'd been the last few years of Dad's life. There was something bubbly and at ease about her, whereas before she'd been more…on edge. On edge all the fucking time.

I grabbed the carton of orange juice from the fridge and drank.

"Wes, take a glass."

I kept drinking like she knew I would.

She leaned back against the kitchen counter, arms stretched

out, her long, manicured fingernails tapping on the surface. "The house got sold."

My eyes bulged. "It did? That didn't take long. You got the asking price or—"

"Better."

"Better?"

"Three different families wanted the house. There was a bidding war, and we accepted the highest one, of course."

"That's terrific."

"Like I told you, you're getting half, so now there's more than we'd hoped. And that house Ronny and I liked? Our bid got accepted this morning."

"Perfect timing." I wiped at my mouth.

"I'm very excited about how it all worked out."

"I'm happy for you, Mom."

"Thank you, baby. Don't forget, we have the anniversary party for the shop coming up."

"How could I forget? I work there and it's all you talk about."

"I want to make sure you'll be there."

"Of course, I'll be there."

Mom was a terrific store manager and a people person. Back in the day, she'd even whipped the One-Eyed Jacks' strip club into shape when the men had gotten sloppy with it. Now, without a motorcycle club to reign over alongside her old man, the prez, she'd transferred all that energy into her and Ronny's project: a branch of his famous Deadwood tattoo shop, Trash Ink, here in Meager. A true shared project. Recently the shop underwent a renovation under Mom's direction and business had picked up even more since.

"It's a lot of change all at once," she murmured. "Which was something I was never a fan of, but I'm loving it. Feels good to do new things, to move forward."

Her feeling good was obvious. She was beaming from every pore. I'd never seen her like that with Dad. I knew she loved him. She worked hard at making it work. One time she'd said to me, *"I love him like crazy."* That had fascinated me. Made me curious as to what that "crazy" felt like, what that was. A frenzy of turmoil like she and Dad seemed to be? Or a whirlwind of passion and craving that defied practical logic?

After I'd realized all the shit Dad had put her through, I knew "loving like crazy" was a fucking mistake. Lindy's cold, tense face from earlier burst into my sightline, and I swept it away with another slug of orange juice.

As I'd grown up, I realized Dad didn't give Mom much of the attention and affection she craved from him. Yeah, he depended on her, needed her to be his rock, and she loved that, she needed that too. But I began to figure out that the scales in their relationship were always tipped in his favor.

With Ronny, she seemed genuinely content. No more complaining to her friends, no more bitter side remarks or cursing to herself, cursing him. And she and Ronny rarely argued. Sure they had disagreements and hot debates, but gone were the famed Jump and Alicia blow-out battles of yesteryear. That was a whole lot of fucking crazy in my book. I drained the juice carton.

Mom let out a satisfied sigh. "I'm finally ready to let go of this house. It's time, for both of us, I feel that. To let go of—"

"Let go of Dad?" I tossed the empty carton in the recycling. "I fucking did that a long time ago."

"Did you?"

"What's that supposed to mean?"

"I think you're hanging onto a ghost. To either make yourself feel better or…"

"Or?"

"To make yourself feel bad."

"Ma, don't psychoanalyze me."

"I'm telling you what I see. I'm your mother. I know you like nobody else. When I say "letting go," I don't mean cutting your dad out of your heart and your mind or forgetting our memories here in this house as a family. I'm not. I cherish those memories. We built a good life here."

"Our one and only home."

"Your dad and I didn't have a perfect relationship, no news there. But nothing and no one is perfect. Jump was who he was and lived that unapologetically. He loved you and me as much as he knew how. Maybe he didn't show his love the way I wanted him to, and that hurt. It sucked. But I knew he loved us and that's the truth, no matter all the shit he got himself into." She swept a lock of hair from my eyes. "Your father adored you, and nothing can change that. Not ever."

Yeah, no matter how hard I've tried.

"It's been eight years, baby. He'd want you to get on with your life, to be happy with whatever you do."

"He sure was good at that, wasn't he? Plowing ahead, doing whatever he wanted, no guilt, no regrets."

"Are you getting on with your life?"

"I'm getting on with it every day, Ma. Life's great, thanks."

"Is it? College was rough on you. The timing…"

"You disappointed I didn't bring home straight A's?"

"Oh, Wes. I only expected you to be responsible and enthusiastic. It was supposed to be the time of your life, but you were dealing with so much that had happened only weeks before. First Dad, and then you and Butler almost getting killed. I really thought that you getting away from here in the aftermath of all that hell was the best thing."

I took in a deep breath. "I did graduate." I gestured at my diploma in Graphic Design that she'd immediately framed and hung on the living room wall.

"You did, and I'm proud of you for seeing it through, no matter how tough it was."

"No matter what my GPA was?"

She planted a kiss on my cheek. "Proud mom here."

"I am currently using my college skills in two jobs."

"You sure are." She grinned at me.

School seemed like a lifetime ago. A blur.

I'd gotten into Arizona State on a partial football scholarship. It was a dream come true. But when Dad had gotten killed the summer after I'd graduated high school, and then weeks later I survived a shootout on the road meant to kill Butler, who I was riding with, that dream started to crumble.

Everything crumbled.

I'd barely paid attention in class and paid more attention to having a good time. But even that "good time" always proved empty. I'd go through periods of I-don't-give-a-fuck and then dive into bouts of what-the-fuck-am-I-doing, then I'd put in the effort and pull through. Then I'd screw it up all over again, and round and round I'd go.

And my passion for football? Petered out fast. Unlike my classmates, in the last few months of senior year, I didn't look for a job, I didn't interview. All I wanted was to get back to Meager. And that's what I did.

My gaze trailed out the kitchen window to the big backyard that had been my childhood kingdom. "This house was always full of people. The Jacks coming over to eat or watch a game, or you and the old ladies making cocktails in this blender—" I patted the old blender standing on the counter and Mom laughed. "So many birthday parties and barbecues. Us kids running around. Full of laughs and noise and music." My breath caught in my chest. "Full of all of us."

Mom joined me against the counter. "Being an army brat, my family never lived in any one house or town for longer than a couple of years at most. When your dad and I bought this house, I was so excited, so determined to make it a real home for us."

"You did, Ma. You did great."

She leaned her head against me. "We did it together."

I wrapped an arm around her shoulders. "You deserve your fresh start. I'm glad you and Ronny got your new place."

"Me too. And now a new family is going to make this house theirs and make their memories. Do me a favor—" She patted me on the chest. "Make time this week to clean out your room, and see what you want to keep."

I blew out a huff of air. "Let me jot that down in my calendar."

"Don't groan, I made it easy for you. I brought up stuff of yours I found in the basement and the attic. I haven't gone through your closet, that's for you to do. Let me show you." She led me up the stairs to my old room.

I hadn't been in here for a while. Once she'd signed with a realtor, Mom had changed shit around the house and made my room look like a young boy lived there. She knew how to sell the cozy family home vibe.

My old football and dirt bike trophies were on the dresser, whereas I'd stowed them in a box in the attic when I'd left for Arizona. There was a pile of books on the desk, novels I'd read in junior high. Even a mason jar with freshly sharpened pencils and a couple of pens. A new quilt on the bed, not my old faded blue one.

My gaze snagged on my Star Wars poster on the wall that I'd taken down when I hit high school. Hadn't seen that in ages. Luke Skywalker, lightsaber in hand, looking to prove himself. Looking for his Jedi dad.

How's that going for you, Luke?

And on the other wall, my framed poster of The Flash. A vintage poster of my favorite superhero Dad had found for me on a run to California when I was little. He was my favorite because Dad used to call me "Flash."

As a little kid, I was hyper, always running around, could never sit still. Then Dad introduced me to dirt biking and motorcycles, and I fell in love and thereafter zoomed with purpose.

Three jumbo garbage bags stood in the center of the room along with a couple of crates filled with stuffed animals, board games, baseball and football gear, and old car and motorcycle magazines. A sour taste filled my mouth. With a flick of the hand, what had been was now bundled, re-arranged, and classi-fied into garbage, giveaways, or maybes.

Although, I was the one who'd abandoned ship first by moving into an apartment in town once I started working, now the ship was leaving port and moving on.

My hand dug through my hair. Mom had a point. Had I moved on?

"I've been decluttering slowly since I put the house on the market, but now we have a closing deadline, so I'd like you to take care of this by the end of the week please."

"You don't mess around, Alicia."

"Do I ever?"

"Never."

My lungs squeezed together. I had to get out of here. "Got to go." I zipped up my hoodie and left the room.

"When are you coming back to get this done?" Mom's voice followed me down the staircase.

I pulled open the front door.

"Wes!"

SEVEN

ON A BREAK from my paint detailing job at Eagle Wings, I charged into the One-Eyed Jacks clubhouse next door. This had been my second home since the day I was born, and now I worked here part-time as well as at Trash Ink.

"Hey, Wes, what's up?" asked Jordy, a new prospect, a kid I'd known from elementary school.

"All good, man. You seen Butler?"

"He's in with the Prez." He gestured toward Kicker's office.

As if on cue, Butler, the VP, stepped out of the President's office, closing the door behind him. His face broke into a smile at the sight of me. "Hey."

"Hey B, I wanted to ask you something if you've got a moment?" I walked alongside him back into the central lounge area.

"Sure—have a seat in my office." Chuckling, he went behind the bar and poured himself a club soda. "What's up?"

I sat on a stool. "I saw Lindy, Pick's daughter, in town today. She's working at Lenore's Lace. She was real cagey about why she's here in Meager, and I got the impression something's going down with the Flames, but she wouldn't tell me. I saw Dawes hovering too. What's going on?"

"Wes—"

"I know. I'm not a member of the club, I'm not this, I'm not that, but Lindy's in trouble, and I want to know what's going on."

His brow furrowed deeply. "And once you know, you plan on doing something about it?"

"So something is going on. If Lindy and Pick are in trouble, I'm not going to sit back and do nothing to help. They saved our lives."

"They sure did." Rounding the bar he sat down on the stool next to me. "There's nothing you can do except be a friend to Lindy while she's here."

"If she's living with Lenore and Finger, she must need protecting. Where are her parents? This is me you're talking to, B. I need to know."

"Wes, I cannot have you running off, doing shit—"

"I'm not that kid anymore. I got it then and I get it now. I'm worried about her. Like you said, I want to be a friend."

Eyeing me, Butler crunched on the ice in his glass. "Uh-huh."

"Give me the basics."

"Pick is missing. He was on a run from Nebraska through South Dakota to Wyoming and has not been heard from since he left South Dakota for Wyoming."

"Missing or taken?"

"Not sure yet."

"A rival club?"

"Wes."

"So she's here under Finger's protection? But playing it 'normal.'"

"As she's here in our territory, we're watching over her too."

"What about her mom? Why wouldn't Lindy be in lockdown at their club? Shouldn't she—"

"We going to sit here and question Finger's judgment? She's

working at Lenore's Lace with Lenore and living at their house under their protection."

"You think whoever it is would try to get to her?"

"I would put nothing past these motherfuckers."

"So you know who it is?"

"We don't know anything yet. But if he got taken…" Holding my gaze, his eyes shuttered as he drank.

"You think someone's sending a message or they're out for Flames blood?"

Heaving a rough sigh, Butler put his empty glass on the bar top. "So you saw Lindy? How'd that go?"

"Saw her earlier today at Lenore's store. I was surprised to see her."

"How did she take seeing you?"

"Not thrilled, but I'm going to work on that."

He arched an eyebrow. "Oh yeah?"

"Yeah."

"Wes, now may not be a good time."

"Why not? Like you said, she needs a friend."

"A friend, yeah."

"She comes to Meager under these shitty circumstances, doesn't know anyone, but she knows you and me. Her whole world has crashed around her overnight. I want to be supportive."

"Supportive is good. But tread lightly."

"Don't worry, she already let me have it."

He let out a short laugh. "Terrific."

"Yeah, it was real fun."

"One step at a time. It's been years, and you've both done a lot of growing up. Don't expect her to be that same girl you twirled around your fingers years ago. You got me?"

"She's not the same girl, and I don't want to twirl her around my fingers."

"Fresh start. The two of you can get to know each other all over again with no assumptions based in the dark past."

"You might have a hard time convincing her of that."

"Patience." He tilted his head. "And no expectations either, you got that?"

My hands raised in surrender. "No expectations here. Absolutely none."

"Mmhm." Swirling the last of the ice in his glass, he eyed me.

I never lied to Butler. But just now?

I lied.

EIGHT

LINDY

Tania, Butler's old lady raised her shot glass in the air. "Here's to our men holding down the fort!"

We were celebrating Ladies Night at Dead Ringers, a classic old-time saloon which was located in between Meager and Rapid, and was a known biker hangout from the seventies. My dad had been here many times with the Flames and had often mentioned it to me.

We all raised our glasses as Tania continued, "And it's great to have you here with us, Lindy. Part of the woman fam."

"That's my girl!" shouted out Nina, Catch's wife. I clinked her glass with mine.

"Yeah!" said Lenore.

All the ladies cheered and drank. Grace, Jill, Tania, Mary Lynn, Nicole, Nina, Krystal, and Lenore.

"Thank you." I raised my now empty glass at Tania. I couldn't believe Tania was Catch's sister. They were total opposites. Tania, who owned the Rusted Heart, the art gallery and antiques shop in Meager, was sophisticated and articulate, while

Catch was the classic jaded bad boy from the wrong side of the tracks.

From the get-go, Catch had told Tania to have an eye out for me, and when Lenore had introduced us on my first day in Meager at the store, Tania had swept me up in a big hug, which had come as a shock to me. I'd noticed all the One-Eyed Jacks old ladies were tight and very affectionate with each other.

The Flames were a bigger club, and their old ladies were separated into cliques, like high school, so I appreciated this different, positive energy that was obvious with the Jacks women. I liked it. Had my mom experienced this kind of sisterhood with her fellow Blades old ladies back in the day?

And even though Lenore was Queen Bee of another club, she was a part of this sisterhood like Nina seemed to be, Krystal too. Families overlapped. Families woven together.

Electric guitars blared as couples filled the dance floor. I spotted a group of Flames at a table in the corner. They had their eyes on us as they partied. The security gig was on. Minty was with them, and he stared at me as he drank. I lifted my chin in salute, and he nodded and turned away.

At another table were a couple of One-Eyed Jacks, including Dawes, who winked at me as he drank from his beer bottle. I gave him a quick smile and turned back to my newly arrived gin and tonic.

There were lots of bikers here tonight partying, but house rules decreed that wearing your club colors was forbidden so that the joint didn't turn into a battleground, but it was easy for me to tell who were the civilians and who were the bikers.

"We need more nachos!" shouted Nina next to me. "Where's our server?" She and I scanned the cavernous bar for the tall blonde, and my gaze snagged on a hot man at the bar. He seemed familiar. That sharp jawline, that teasing grin…my insides curled with heat. But that hair was distinctly unfamiliar…

My mouth fell open.

It was Wes, and he'd gotten a haircut.

No more long hair falling to his shoulders, in his eyes. Nope. He had some kind of Viking do, shaved on the sides with a long, thick patch on top that fell over one side of his face. I blinked, my blood rushing through my veins.

In combination with his sculpted cheekbones, perfect eyebrows, and those mesmerizing dark blue eyes, his new haircut gave him a full-blown edginess, an edginess that he always had, but held on the back burner.

Not anymore.

My mouth dried. Now that unique Wes intensity was front and center. And white hot.

I gulped down my gin and tonic. *Holy fuck. So fucking hot.*

Sparks and fizzles popped inside me, heat simmering through my flesh like a gas burner that got lit and blazed away on high. My legs pressed together. This was what real attraction felt like. Not that tickle I got whenever Dawes paid me attention.

My lips pressed together. I could not allow Wes to enter my lust zone now.

Wes was a no-brainer. Off-limits. Outlawed. Illegal.

I glanced back over at Wes leaning against the bar in a devil-may-care-cool-cowboy or undercover assassin kind of way, licking his lips as he studied his liquor, swirling it in his glass.

Kill me now.

The cute bartender in the tiny yellow halter top with the amazing cleavage leaned over and said something to him, and he perked up, giving her his full attention. They both burst into laughter and high-fived each other. She refilled his glass as they kept talking. I tore my attention away from them, the heels of my boots digging into the floor.

"Having fun, honey?" Lenore leaned into me.

"Yes, yes, I am. Great way to celebrate the new blush." I had created that spreadsheet template and emailed it to all the Jacks ladies and the three dancers at the Tingle, and the data had come in quickly. "It's great meeting everyone."

"We get together regularly, but it's extra fun to have you with us."

"You have great friends here, Lenore."

"These women are very special to me. I want you to know that you can count on any of them if you ever need something. Anything at all. Even if it's only to listen."

"I'm getting that feeling."

Don't do it. Don't do it.

I did it.

My gaze turned to Wes again like he was a magnet and I was helpless in the presence of his atomic particles. My jaw tightened. Of course, now he was with another girl. A beautiful woman with long dark blond hair hugged him. They laughed and talked excitedly and then they hugged again, squeezing each other tight. A happy reunion.

With an arm slung around her shoulders like he'd done it a million times before and it was second nature for him and his arm, they turned and ordered from the bartender. The woman lifted on her tip-toes and planted a kiss on his cheek. Giggling, she rubbed at his face. Was she removing her lipstick from his skin? How considerate, sweet. Intimate. What a good girlfriend. My fingers tightened around my glass.

Wes had a girlfriend. Of course, he did. A handsome, sexy dude like Wes with the perfect smile, the perfect body?

It hadn't occurred to me because I was too blinded by my emotions, by the shock of seeing him again, but here at the bar of Dead Ringers was reality playing out in live 3D. No denying that.

They got their drinks, clinked their shot glasses, and knocked them back. Talked, laughed.

A hot sting stabbed my chest. Wes in a relationship. I took in a painful breath. That was good, wasn't it? I didn't have to worry about dealing with him at all.

Sure was.

"You want to switch to beer, Lindy?" Nina held the big pitcher next to me.

"Perfect!" I replied, and Nina poured out a beer in a draft glass. Grabbing it, I sucked down the cold brew, but it did nothing to ease the fire burning my throat, blazing through my insides.

Stupid me, I had assumed he was almost flirting with me yesterday. Dying for my attention. But he wasn't. He was expressing his lame regrets for yesteryear and sympathy for my present plight.

This was a relief, wasn't it? Sure it was. Meager was now a worry-free zone. I didn't have to give any more energy to thinking about Wes. Not at all.

Wes was taken—*I mean, taken care of!*

Wes was somebody else's—*I mean, somebody else's problem!*

Wes was not mine. Gah—*not my problem!*

I was free. Freeeeeee. Yup. I sucked down the beer. I was all about being free, wasn't I? Absolutely. Hooray. Hallelujah. Glory be.

"Hey, Lindy, wanna dance?" Dawes leaned down and grinned at me, a hand on my chair. My interior radar went into overdrive, hunting for flutters, tremors, shivers, pulsations.

NADA.

I shot him a huge grin. "You bet."

"Dawes is an amazing dancer, you lucky girl!" Nicole shouted out.

"That so?" My grin deepened as I rose from my chair. "Show me what you got."

"Oh, I will, sweetheart." Winking at me as he took my hand in his, Dawes chuckled as he led me to the wooden dance floor and swept me up in his arms, pulling me close to his body. We moved to the loud music under the red and blue spotlights in the cavernous dark saloon. Nicole was right. Dawes was a terrific dancer.

"I don't think I've danced like this since middle school." I laughed.

"Don't you have places like this in Nebraska?"

"Sure we do, but I've only been a couple of times."

"Let's make this memorable..." His arm tightened around my middle, our bodies pressed together, and we swung to the music on the crowded floor underneath the swirl of colored lights. He moved quickly in tune to the beat. I loosened up at last, to the music, to Dawes's fluid moves, letting the buzz of alcohol melt away the incessant stream of thoughts crowding my head.

The colored lights changed their tempo. A different song had blown up on the speakers. A blur of movement flared around me, and my body jerked.

"Hey, got to cut in. This is our song."

"Jesus, dude!"

I was in Wes's arms and he spun us away from Dawes, his hand pressing into my back, keeping me close.

"We don't have a song!" I shouted over the music, attempting to pull back. Impossible.

"It could be this one, don't you think?"

The band played a rocking version of Warren Zeiders' "Sin So Sweet."

"Really?"

"I was going to ask you to dance, but I knew you'd say no. Don't worry about Dawes." Wes's hand slid down my lower back to the curve of my rear, and my muscles tightened. I spotted Dawes in the crowd dancing with a statuesque brunette, a grin on his face.

The intensity of Wes's grip on my body deepened, and my skin heated. The friction of our bodies brought my attention back to the wonder of Wes. The wonder I'd spent half an hour attempting to deny.

"You got a haircut."

"One of the artists at the shop cuts hair and she did this for me. She's been after me for a while—"

"I'll bet."

He chuckled. "After me to let her cut it."

"So what made you give in now?"

"When you told me I looked the same, I realized you were right. I could use a change, step outside my box. This is a start."

"That's good."

"You like it?"

"No."

He only laughed as he moved us over the dance floor.

"What are you doing here tonight?" I asked.

"Dead Ringers is a hotspot. Everyone comes here. Now that you're in Meager, our paths are bound to cross all the time." He leaned down close to my face, his overgrown stubble rubbing against my cheek. Leather and a mossy wood scent filled my nostrils. Dammit, he even smelled good, miles away from that Old Spice he used to wear to impress me years ago. "Are we supposed to ignore each other?"

"Why not?"

"Waste of time."

I pulled my head away from his and, as I straightened, I spotted his girlfriend. She scanned the crowd. He'd dumped her and grabbed me for a dance? *Jerk.*

A few yards past her, my gaze snagged on Minty who was staring straight at me, his face tight. He lifted his chin, and raised his eyebrows, his head slanting to my left, and I glanced in that direction. A neon sign for the bathrooms glowed over a hallway. I gave him a chin lift in return.

Did he know something about Dad?

Wes held me even closer now, my chest smashed against his hard wall of a torso. The friction between us as we moved to the music intensified. That feeling of liking being in his arms began to overwhelm my senses.

I sucked in a breath. "Your girlfriend's looking for you. Are you trying to make her jealous by dancing with me? Nice move."

"What? What are you talking about?"

The crowd exploded into cheers and applause. The band's set was done, and Wes's grip on me finally loosened. I peeled myself off of him. "Bye now." I darted off.

"Lindy! Lindy!" His voice rose behind me as I slid through the crowd and headed to the bathrooms.

I recognized Minty and his long ponytail up ahead of me in the dimly lit hallway outlined with colored LED lighting. He shoved at a door and light spilled out into the hall. Grabbing my arm, he pulled me in after him. The antiseptic odor of the large accessible bathroom filled my nose as the bright fluorescent lighting made me blink.

"Minty, what's going on?"

His face was etched in a deep scowl, and the hair on the back of my neck stood on end. Minty reached behind me and, letting out a gruff snarl, locked the door.

NINE

LINDY

"What's going on, Minty?"

"I came along with the brothers who are here to watch you and Lenore tonight because Finger wanted me to check in with you."

"Check in with me?"

"Make sure you're okay. He knows we go back, that me and your dad are close, so you'd feel comfortable talking if anything was up, anything was bothering you."

"Great. He realizes I keep things tight, does he?"

"He realizes a lot of things, that one. You doing okay? Any problems with the Jacks? They treating you good?"

"Everything's good. Lenore's been great. I work with her at her store, and things at her and Finger's house are comfortable. Every day, the Jacks keep an eye on us, and our guys do too. It's been fine, no issues."

"Mmm. Good." He rubbed a thumb along his temple, a habit he'd always had when he had something on his mind that was troubling him.

"What's going on at the club? Have you guys figured out

who has Dad? Have you heard from anybody? No one's told me anything."

"What did they ask you when they brought you in to see Finger?"

"If Dad had said anything unusual lately, or did anything out of the ordinary, which he hasn't, so I said no. Then Finger asked if Dad ever gets nostalgic about the old days."

His dark eyes flared. "See? They think he took off on his own, like he's ditching."

"Why would he do that and not tell me? Leave me behind?"

"He wouldn't tell you to keep you safe, Lind."

"That sure wouldn't keep me safe from the Flames, would it? Doesn't make sense to me. That's not him. He wouldn't leave like that. I don't believe it. Like I told Finger, all the Blades are either dead or with the Flames so—"

"Jesus, you got to watch your mouth, Lindy."

I only shrugged.

"Me and your Dad are the only Blades left. But Raptor's the only Blade not dead and not a Flame, and he's out there somewhere. To Raptor, me and your dad are fucking traitors. They ask you about him?"

"They asked if Dad ever talked about him, but like you said, I didn't say much of anything."

His brow furrowed. "Has Pick been talking about him?"

"He bitched about him a couple times when that thing with Trick, the One-Eyed Jack, happened."

"Everyone's been looking for him since then. Us, the feds."

"What's up with that guy, Minty? I know he and Dad were close in the early days."

"Fuck, did you tell Finger that?"

"No, of course not."

He pressed his lips together in a grimace, his gaze darting around the bathroom. He was uptight. "Yeah...him and your dad were real close," he muttered, his tone bitter.

"What's that supposed to mean?"

"Nothing." His thumb went to his temple once more. He rubbed at his eyes.

"You okay? You don't look so good."

"What if it is Raptor?"

"What do you mean?"

"What if your dad took off with him? What if they're planning something?"

"Planning what? A Broken Blades comeback? Are you fucking kidding me?"

"Hush!" His mustache twitched. "I'm not kidding you."

My jaw dropped open. "The Blades blowing up was awful and the roughest thing ever for all of us, but there can't be a chance in hell that the Blades could rise again."

"Why not?" he bit out, and my head jerked back. Was it the odd tone of his voice? The coiled tension in his body? I couldn't figure out if he was all for a comeback or if the idea terrified him.

Minty shifted his weight. "What if Raptor's got some new band of brothers and he's ready to make some kinda move?"

My heart shriveled in my chest. "You think Dad would do that? Really? He's been so committed to the Flames. To making this work, since day one."

"Your dad's a good soldier, Lindy, but he's a Blade through and through. That won't ever change for us."

"Is that what Finger thinks?" My voice croaked, echoing in the tiled bathroom.

"Who knows what he really thinks of us? I'm just throwing shit out there. Got nobody to talk to about this, can't trust nobody. I got all these fucking ideas whirling, twirling in my head. I'm going crazy over here."

"I get that. Me too. But you need to chill out, Minty. We're Flames. You can't be acting all funny and strange now. For all our sakes you got to stay cool. Finger's a smart man, all his men are. If you think they're not watching you now..."

"I know they are," he gritted out, his eyes flaring at me. "Don't think they ain't watching you too. And I don't mean only to protect you." His seething voice drilled into my chest like a burning hot poker.

Stepping back from him, I glanced at myself in the mirror over the sink and pushed my unruly hair away from my hot face. "I need to get back out there. If you find out anything, let me know, okay?"

"I will. You do the same. You take care, Lindy."

"You too." My hand shook as I unlocked the bathroom door, and I took in a breath to steady myself as I tracked through the hallway.

Back out in the dark saloon, I let myself get engulfed by the thick sea of people dancing, drinking, and laughing under the moving, brightly-colored lights. But I couldn't hear their laughter or the music blaring. All I heard was Minty's *"Why not?"* repeating in my head on a loop. All I could see were his dark eyes filled with worry and panic and questions, so many questions. An ache sprang over my skull. Somehow I made it back to our table with a relaxed smile planted on my face.

"There she is," Lenore said.

"There was a line at the bathroom."

In my seat was a striking platinum blonde woman about Lenore's age, who grinned at me. "So good to see you again, Lindy. Welcome to Meager." She took my hands in hers and squeezed them. She looked familiar. I'd met her before but there was something else—

"We met once before years ago, but I'm sure you don't remember me. I barely recognize you. How you've grown up. You're a stunner."

"Isn't she?" said Lenore.

I bit my lip. "Thank you. I know we've met before, but I—"

"I'm Alicia, Wes's mom."

I froze. *Wes's mom!*

"You and your dad saved my son along with Tania's man, Butler? We talked at the hospital that day?"

"I remember. Good to see you again, Alicia."

"Hello ladies!" Wes's voice burst from behind me, and my gaze shot up at him as all the women greeted him loudly.

"Shit, your hair," exclaimed Alicia. "You look amazing, honey."

"Thank you."

"You look FINE!" shouted out Grace, raising her beer in his direction.

"Thanks, Grace." He blew her a kiss.

Alicia touched Wes's arm. "Honey, you remember Lindy?"

"Of course I do." He held my gaze, and a flare of heat smoldered up my spine. "Never forgot her."

"Look at the two of you, all grown up now." Alicia grinned. "You're making me feel old."

"You old? Never," laughed Mary Lynn.

"Truth," I agreed.

Alicia leaned into me. "Sorry to hear about what's going on. Your dad was always a fighter. I got faith."

"Did you know my dad other than from that day in the hospital?"

"There was a time when Wes's dad and I used to hang out a lot with Zed and his old lady, so we knew the club."

"You were close with Uncle Zed and Angel?"

"We were." Her eyes lit up and she let out a short laugh. "Those were good times."

"Did you know my mom?"

"Sure, I met her. Sweet lady, great sense of humor." She grabbed my hand. "So sorry for your loss, Lindy."

"Thank you. I appreciate it."

Wes's brow furrowed.

"I'm glad you're here with Lenore and Finger. If you need anything, any time of day or night, Wes and I are here for you. Aren't we, Wes?"

"We sure are." His eyes gleamed at me, two orbs of blue fire. "Anything. Any time."

Lenore screeched, and we all turned toward her. Someone

had two arms wrapped around her shoulders, squeezing her tight. It was Wes's girlfriend. Lenore jumped up. "What are you doing here?"

"I wanted to surprise you."

"You did!" They hugged. "How long are you in town for?"

"Three days. My shoot got delayed, so I wanted to come home. Wes told me everyone would be here tonight, so I thought it'd be fun."

Lenore threw an arm around Wes's girlfriend's shoulder. "Let me introduce you to Lindy, my houseguest. Lindy, this is my daughter-in-law, Violet."

My eyes widened. This was Violet? Violet, who was married to Lenore's son, Beck, the amazing guitarist in the rock band Freefall? She was Beck's wife, not Wes's girlfriend.

Of course, Lenore had told me about Beck and Violet. But the framed wedding photo that I'd briefly glanced at was from a couple of years ago, and tonight I hadn't recognized her.

Of course, you didn't. You were blinded by jealousy!

"Good to meet you, Violet."

"Great to meet you, too, Lindy. I've heard a lot about you."

"You have?" I glanced at Lenore, who shook her head.

"From Wes," said Violet. "I'm glad you're here and safe."

"Thank you."

"Lindy, you want to hang out with us?" Wes's lips curled into a smirky grin.

"I'm going to stick around here. Another time. Thanks."

He dipped his head. "We'll leave you wild ladies to your party."

"What are you up to tonight?" asked Alicia.

"It's Friday night, Mother. You know me, on the prowl." His eyes widened like he was being facetious, laying it on thick for his mom's benefit, for all the ladies. For me.

"And I'm here to make him look even more tempting than he already is." Violet shoved his shoulder. "Like I've been doing since elementary school."

"Go get 'em, tiger," shouted out Mary Lynn.

Waving at us, Wes and Violet melted in the crowd. Alicia let out a throaty laugh. "I love teasing my son."

"I think he likes teasing you, too," I murmured.

"Oh, he does."

"Let him have his fun," said Nina.

"He has plenty of fun. It's relationships he's allergic to."

"Is he?" I took a gulp of warm beer.

"Not one single relationship. Just—"

My throat tightened. "Fun?"

"And that's all fine and good, but it's time he got on with it."

"Can't tell him what to do. He's a grown man now, Mamma," remarked Grace, and the ladies laughed in agreement.

"He certainly is…" The amusement had vanished from Alicia's voice. "That's why he's got to figure this shit out for himself and sooner rather than later, 'cause later may be too late."

TEN

LINDY

As I LOCKED up Lenore's Lace, I spotted the Flames prospect down the street, watching me. I'd texted him earlier to let him know I'd be going to the tattoo shop down the block. Lenore was there having work done, and I'd meet her there and we'd go home together.

I learned the other night at Dead Ringers that Trash Ink was owned by Wes's mom and her boyfriend, Ronny. My dad had gotten work done at Ronny's shop in Deadwood not too long ago. Meager's Trash Ink was on a corner with a wall of windows, so you had a great view of the goings on inside. The place was full.

"Hey, how can I help you?" A green-haired girl with loads of piercings along both ears and in her nose smiled at me from the front desk.

"Hi. I'm supposed to meet Lenore here."

"Are you Lindy?"

"That's me."

She grinned. "I'm Rachel. Lenore told me you'd be coming.

She should be finishing in another twenty minutes or so. Can I get you something to drink while you wait?"

"I'm good, thanks. Could I ask you about making an appointment for myself?"

"You bet. What do you need done?"

"I have a tattoo that never got finished, and it also needs improving."

"Do you know what kind of design you want?"

"I do, yes."

"Great, half the battle. There's an opening at the end of this week, or there's next Wednesday. When would you like to come in?"

"Come in for what?"

My heart stopped at the sound of Wes's voice. I raised my head. There he was, behind the reception desk area, leaning against a wall, muscular tattooed arms visible from his cut-off T, and those gorgeous blue eyes of his narrowing at me.

"What are you doing here?" I asked.

"I work here."

"Oh. Right."

"Hi, Wes," chirped one of the teenage girls seated in the waiting area behind me. He lifted his chin in her direction, and his attention immediately returned to me.

Rachel rolled her eyes. "He's good for business. Thank God he's talented."

We both laughed as Wes came over to the counter. "You need work done on an existing tat?"

"I do."

"Why don't I take a look?"

"Reminder, you have an appointment in twenty minutes," said Rachel.

"I know. This won't take long."

Rachel glanced at the large clock on the wall. "Lindy, you up for Wes taking a look and doing a preliminary sketch?"

"Um. Sure."

"Follow me," said Wes. My heart pounded in my chest as I followed Wes into a back room. "You have a lot of tattoos?" He gestured at the lounger chair and lit the big lamp that towered overhead, the rest of the room in darkness. He pulled on black latex gloves, snapping them on his large hands. Hands that soon would be touching me.

My pulse thrummed. "Only two. For now. I'd really like more, but I haven't had the chance."

"So where is this tattoo?"

I kicked off my Hi-Tops. "On my inner thigh."

His eyebrows jumped and his jaw clenched.

Holding his intense gaze, the blood rushed in my veins as I unbuttoned my jeans and peeled them down my legs. He remained still.

Turning around, I picked up my jeans and folded them across the arm of the lounger. A growl rose behind me, and I grinned to myself. I'd given him a full-on view of my ass in my new thong panties. Luckily, today I was wearing one of Lenore's luxury band designs in a bright turquoise color, and not one of my simple cotton undies. I hopped on the lounger.

"Show me." His voice was positively stony.

I spread my legs, and my fingertip traced around the design on my upper inner left thigh.

"What's the issue?" Touching my leg, he leaned in to inspect the artwork, and my breath cut. Wes touched me, his touch barely a trace, and yet it burned over my flesh as his hot breath fanned my delicate skin.

"*Hell No*," he repeated the words on the design. His fingertips pushed gently on my leg to get a full view of the artwork. Beneath the words "Hell No" was a demon's fiery red eyes. "Not very welcoming, is it?" he muttered.

"Not meant to be."

"When did you get this?"

"Eight years ago."

His gaze darted up at me.

"Did it because of you," I said. "But now I want to fix it. Make it…welcoming."

"Oh yeah?" His lips pressed into a firm line.

"I'd like a friendlier message to all who may enter."

"You got plans, huh?"

"Open to possibilities."

"Mmm." His neck stiffened. "Any idea on how you'd like to make this harsh warning welcoming and friendly?"

"I want a Hell Yes underneath the Hell No and a tongue on the bottom of that, licking at the YES."

"A tongue licking?"

"Something that drips of anticipation and temptation."

His jaw muscles flexed. "Uh-huh. And which kind of vibe are you going for in particular? Enter at your own risk or come on in, y'all?"

I shot him a smirk. "Enter at your own risk."

"Got it." His lips curling, he ripped off one glove. "Keep your legs open like this while I sketch out an idea." He tilted the spotlight over my tattoo and grabbed a sketchbook and a pencil. His hand flew over the paper, and his eyebrows scrunched as he glanced at my tat and back to his sketch and back to my tat.

Despite the air conditioning, my flesh prickled with heat. I was on display, his artwork in the making. Even though the padded lounger was perfectly comfortable, my muscles remained tense, my back rigid, my chest tight.

An ache spiraled through me as he worked. I was the object of his creativity, a creativity that hummed between us.

"How about this?" He handed me the sketchbook as I sat up.

A lasciviously long red tongue beckoned from the bottom of the Hell Yes addition. The new letters were scripted in gold, not red like the Hell No. Blue roses and thorny vines wrapped around the letters. The tongue had a few drops of blood falling where it had been pricked by the thorns. My lips parted. It was utterly beautiful.

"What do you think?"

"It's perfect."

"Yeah?"

"You're very good."

"Thanks. I figure…" He leaned in closer, and a shudder went through me, the warmth of his body positively palpable. My hands gripped the sides of the lounger to keep steady, my nails digging into the vinyl. "Right here we could do more vine work —" His gloved fingers traced and stroked my upper thigh, all the way up. Heat hurtled through me as his stroke took my breath away and aroused every cell in my body. "A thorny vine that would lead straight to your pussy."

I hissed in air at the sound of that word easily passing his lips. An electrical current raged in the room around us, between us.

"Maintains the warning theme, yet breaks out an invitation all at once. But it's a dangerous invitation." His breathing had gotten heavy, hard.

My breathing had gotten heavy. "Mmm."

"That's what you want, isn't it?" The darkness in the room had become velvety and thick.

"Uh uh." I swallowed hard, but it did nothing to ease the massive swell of cement in my chest or relieve the knot of heat between my legs.

His knuckles brushed against the uppermost part of my thigh, and my clit swelled and throbbed under his simple and brief touch. My muscles ached as I tried hard to hold myself steady and not waver, not move an inch. I prayed my undies would not get visibly wet because, dammit, I was getting wet. I could feel it.

"Lindy?" His voice was hoarse. "You want it?"

My chest squeezed painfully, I could barely breathe. *YES YES, I WANT IT. I WANT YOU.* "Uh…I…"

His tongue slid out and lashed his upper lip once more. "You want the vine around your thigh? You like that idea?" His thumb absently stroked my leg.

A small moan escaped my throat. "I like it. Very much."

"Me too." Releasing me, he wrote something on his sketch. "Think about if you want to do something on the other leg too." His arm lifted swiftly and he snapped the light off, pushing back from me like a doctor having finished his study of the patient. He ripped off the latex glove, a jarring sound that sheared through me.

Sliding off the lounger, I quickly yanked up my jeans. I grabbed my sneakers, my fingers fumbling as I fought to tie my laces.

That intense heat between us was still there. For me, like it always had been. He didn't look up but remained focused on his sketch. Did he feel it? Was he fighting it too, or enjoying it and playing it cool? Or simply being professional?

"Make an appointment and we'll get it done."

Professional and good at playing it cool. How the heck would I survive him inking my thigh for fuck's sake?

"I will." I charged out the door, my heart banging in my chest.

What did I get myself into now?

ELEVEN

WES

"Dude, you look like a million bucks. A million *grunge* bucks." Beck clapped a hand on my shoulder as Violet smoothed down the back of the black French designer suit jacket I'd put on.

Beck had surprised us all and landed in town late last night. They'd insisted I come over today and hang out with them for lunch before they had to get back on a plane for L.A.

"What do you think?" Violet peeked over my shoulder, checking out my reflection in the big mirror in their bedroom at their beautiful house, Whisperwind.

"I...I don't know what to think." I stared back at the sleek Euro dude in the mirror.

"He's at a loss for words, babe. We have a winner," Violet shouted out to her husband.

"It's cut so perfectly like it was made for you." Beck grinned.

"I don't know about the belt..." I loosened it and began taking it off.

"Leave the belt!" They both snapped at me, and Violet fastened it up again.

"Guys, when am I ever going to wear this?" I glanced at

Beck. "Your wedding was the only truly formal occasion I've been to in my adult life."

"Wes—" Beck packed his small suitcase. "You need to have a basic black suit in your closet."

Smirking, I let out a dramatic groan. "You are your mother's son, aren't you?"

"She taught me everything I know, and now I get to style you, bro."

Violet poked me in the ribs. "My man has a great eye and good instincts. Has he ever let you down?"

I smoothed a hand down the seductive fabric of the jacket. "Never."

Beck had given me tons of clothes over the years. Clothing that he'd gotten as gifts from designers, or stuff he'd bought me on his travels all over the world on his many concert tours. Stuff he knew I'd like—amazing leather jackets, crazy expensive jeans and cargo pants that were incredible quality, top of the line athletic shoes, designer leather backpacks and messenger bags and man bags, one of a kind graphic tees. Cashmere scarves and hats, even a thick, mohair black coat last winter that I had to admit was a godsend in the polar wind we enjoyed in the Black Hills in winter.

"You can always wear the jacket with jeans too," said Violet. "But oh, these trousers…this slim cut looks so good on your long legs. The fabric falls beautifully, and that cuff…"

"I don't think I've ever used the word 'trousers' before."

Beck laughed. "There's a first time for everything."

Violet locked her small suitcase and rolled it to the door. "I'm going to order us lunch so we have plenty of time to eat before our driver gets here. Burritos or barbecue?"

"Burritos," Beck and I shouted out.

"Got it." Violet gave Beck a quick kiss and left the room.

"Thanks, man, I really like it." I took off the jacket.

"I'm glad." Beck hung it back on the plush hanger. "You sure about the boots?" He gestured at the row of Italian handmade boots that were his favorite. After all, he was a model for the brand.

"No way, glam boy, but I love that you keep trying." We both laughed. "I'll stick to my biker boots and the western boots I've had since high school." I took off the trousers and got my own clothes back on, a casual T-shirt and faded jeans. The Wes I knew stared at me from the mirror once again.

Beck carefully arranged the suit in its fancy garment bag. "What's with the haircut? I thought I'd never see the day that you'd chop off your locks." He zipped up the garment bag.

"You don't like it?" I got up close to the mirror and smoothed back my hair.

"I love it, looks great on you, already told you that. But I'm impressed. What made you do it? Or is the better question *who* made you do it?" He eyed me, a grin curling his lips. "Violet updated me about Lindy being in Meager." Beck and Violet knew all about my and Lindy's history.

"When I first saw her in town she made a comment that I hadn't changed since she saw me last, which was when I was seventeen."

"Ouch."

"She was right."

"Maybe you want to try the boots after all?"

"No."

"You got it bad, huh?" Laughing, he grabbed a couple pairs of the boots and brought them to his massive walk-in closet and stashed them on a shelf.

I brought him the other two pairs. "And it's rapidly getting worse."

Choosing a thin cotton sweater from another shelf, Beck pulled it over his head. "I'd bet it only feels bad because it's intense and you're not sure what to do about it. That should tell you something."

"Like what?"

Beck pushed his hair back from his face. "Like you give a damn about what she thinks of you."

"I do give a damn. I give a lot of damns. Plenty of damns."

How many times had I replayed touching her bare tattooed leg from the other day? Countless. Being so close to her in a small dark space had taken my breath away. Seeing that nasty tat she'd gotten by her pussy? That had made my pulse hammer in my chest. I'd done a number on her, and I wanted to fix that. Not only fix it…I wanted another chance with her, didn't I?

Well, working on her tattoo over the next few weeks would certainly keep us in ultra-close proximity. The memory of her beachy perfume, the feel of her silky skin, the slight jump of her body when I'd touched her. My dick had been pounding in my jeans like a starving maniac.

Beck opened a drawer and picked out a heavy stainless steel watch. "Flirting, fooling around, that's easy, but the other…"

"We've got history between us, and she's not making it easy. But I deserve what she dishes out."

"She matters to you."

I gently swatted at the necklaces that hung on a jewelry stand on the dresser island. "She does." Following Beck back into the bedroom, my gaze darted out the massive window to the grand backyard and its sapphire blue tiled swimming pool, the fancy loungers, Beck's recording studio shed, and all the trees and flowers they'd planted which had made the property positively lush.

Beck had bought this old Queen Anne style house for Violet which, in fact, one of her ancestors had built in the nineteenth century. Whisperwind was one of the first and only grand mansions of Meager from the town's early days. Together they had restored and transformed this vintage house into their family home. Fresh and vibrant and all their own.

Earlier, over coffee, they'd told me that they wanted to get pregnant. The two of them had been on a wild rollercoaster ride to get to this solid bright place they were at today. Violet and I had been close friends since kindergarten and from the moment Beck and I had met in our early teens when his mother had moved to Meager, we'd been good buds. I liked to think I had played a role in the two of them getting together.

Seeing my two best friends so content, so in sync, settled on their own terms, was satisfying, yet, I had to admit, gnawed at me. Could it be possible for me too? None of this had ever appealed to me, or maybe, more to the point, *I hadn't allowed it* to appeal to me.

I blew out a breath. "Beck, I don't want to fuck this up."

"You won't. You're a good person, Wes, with the biggest heart." He handed me the garment bag. "Go easy, but along with that, make yourself clear so there's no bullshit, no time wasted or missed opportunities. Make it clear that you genuinely like her, that you care. Get that on the table early."

"And then what?"

"Keep proving it to her." He grabbed his suitcase and a leather tote bag, and I took Violet's suitcase, and we headed down the stairs. "There's nothing like genuine truth in action. Melts hearts and sets souls on fire."

"What a wise poet you've become, Lanier."

Beck's gleaming eyes met mine. "I'm a man in wild crazy love."

TWELVE

WES

A⊤ OUR OLD HOUSE, I'd gone through the bags of my stuff that my mother had put aside for me. Stuffed animals, board games, gadgets, decks of cards, Legos, and baseball caps all hurtled me down memory lane.

Sticking out of a crate were my old ice skates from my brief stint in ice hockey. Next to that crate stood a bulging shopping bag filled with high school and college logo sweatshirts and sweatpants.

For years, I'd pointed out to Mom that she wasn't doing much to get on with a new path in life, for still hanging onto this house even though she was with Ronny. He'd never really moved in, either. Something inside her didn't want to give it up. But she'd finally done it, cutting those old attachments that no longer served her. I was proud of her.

Now this room was ready to be filled by another kid. Or, who knows, maybe a cranky mother-in-law. This room where I'd danced around to great music blaring from my stereo. Played my video games. Plastered so many posters on the wall of my favorite dirt bike and Moto champions, rock bands and movie heroes.

My glance went to my old twin bed that I'd often used as a trampoline as a kid. First time I fooled around with a girl was on that bed. My desk where I'd studied for so many tests, distracted myself with doodling, constructed a model train that won me an award, put together so many projects for school, and sketched when I was feeling frustrated, moody.

I scratched at that old Harley-Davidson sticker on the bottom corner of the mirror over the dresser, but it was still as stubborn as ever. My gaze settled on my reflection, the stuffed bags and crates in the background. Nothing I wanted to save. Nothing I was nostalgic about. I was done here.

I went through the dresser drawers one last time. Empty. My desk drawers. I pulled out the right side. Empty. Pulled out the left, and a rolling sound rattled across the wood. A Hot Wheels. "Fuckkk." Not any Hot Wheels, but one of my top faves, the red Ferrari F50 Spider that had come out before I was born.

My father used to buy them for me all the time, starting from when I was a toddler. Instead of candy or fast food as a treat, he'd bring me a new Hot Wheels, any time and for no reason at all. Or as a present from a run. When I was little, I used to think that a Hot Wheels from anywhere outside of South Dakota was the coolest thing. As if they were different. I had a massive collection.

That's what was missing. My Hot Wheels. My gaze shot to my closet. *The Man Stash.*

In the back of my closet was a hiding place my father had built when I was maybe ten years old. Mom had been out of town at the time. It had been mine and Dad's secret. He had a metal lockbox in there, and I had my older and precious Hot Wheels carefully layered in a big shoe box. Dad had said that was our special place where they'd be safe, where no one knew about them except for him and me.

When I was thirteen, I'd gotten my hands on a porn magazine and I'd stashed it in there until I'd gotten bored with it and gave it to my friend, Zac. I didn't think I'd opened the stash since.

My closet was unusually deep and was L shaped which was where the secret panel was. Now there were no coats and piles of shoes and boots or stacked shoe boxes in my way, making me feel like I was in an endless dark forest. Now the slight indentation in the wall was visible to me.

My fingers rounded over the long seam past the corner of the L, then the bump. I shoved, shoved again, and it finally gave way.

Using my cell phone's flashlight, I trained it on the hollow in the wall. There it was, the cherry red cardboard box with my Hot Wheels collection inside. My treasure chest. Taking it out, I set it on the floor and shined my phone light in the small dark space again. A big metal box was visible. Dad's lockbox.

I took it out. Heavy and still locked. Dad always carried a huge mess of keys on him. For the house, his vehicles and bikes, the club. Everything was on there. And I knew where it was.

I darted down the stairs to the entry way of the house. Willy, the eldest One-Eyed Jack, was a carpenter, and years ago he'd made this wood slab console table as a gift for my parents' anniversary. Glancing down the hall to the kitchen, where my mother was cleaning up for the night, I gently pulled on the wrought iron handle of the one large drawer where we kept pens, measuring tapes, keys, new batteries, lighters, rolling papers.

"Honey, everything okay?" Mom called out from the kitchen. "You need help?"

"Nope. All good." I shuffled through the full, deep drawer. Finally, there it was. The red and silver J keyring along with Dad's favorite skull and Harley logo key rings attached to it. Sure, it was a ton of keys, but odds were good the lockbox key was one of them.

Back in my room, I tried every key that might fit, and

finally…*click*. I blew out a breath and opened the box. But there was no gun, or knife like I'd expected. Eight spiral notebooks, and underneath them, aluminum foil wrapped packages which could only be one thing. I ripped one open. Cash.

Hundreds, fifties, twenties stacked in neat bundles. A lot of bundles. I knew my parents used to keep cash in the house in an old ugly lamp in the living room. Sitting on the floor, I leafed through the notebooks, the oldest dated over twenty years ago.

Each line was filled on each page. Dollar amounts. A tally of guns, rifles, automatic weapons, and chemicals. Where they'd been acquired, for how much, who was buying, the prices. Dates of transport. Names of contacts on the routes. Biker road names I didn't recognize. All in Dad's tight, clean handwriting.

I went through the other notebooks. More of the same through the years.

I chewed on my lip. Dad was old school, had never been very tech-minded, so using a spreadsheet or keeping files on a USB stick had never been his bag. Years ago, when Dready had upgraded all the systems at the club, Dad had grumbled endlessly about the expense as well as now having to keep track of passwords and codes.

In the oldest notebooks, the one name featured over and over again was Zed. One of the last presidents of the Broken Blades before their club had been ripped apart by the Flames and the feds.

The other night at Dead Ringers, Mom had mentioned that she and Dad hung out with Zed and his old lady a lot. And Lindy had referred to him as "Uncle Zed," so he and Pick must have been tight.

Had Dad and the Blades been involved in some secret underground business for years? Why would he keep these notebooks here?

So Mom wouldn't find them.

So the Jacks wouldn't find them.

So if anything ever happened to him, only his son would

know. He'd depended on his son taking the cash, destroying the evidence, and keeping his secret.

My chest caved. He'd made me his co-conspirator.

"Don't tell your mom. This is a men's only vault, okay, Flash? It'll be our man stash. Just you and me. Put whatever you want in here. Stuff that's sacred to you."

"Sacred?" I'd repeated the exotic word.

"Something so special you want to keep it safe, keep it just for you."

Sacred. Secret. Special. Just for me…my Hot Wheels!

I'd only nodded my head, hanging on his every word, and done like he said.

I skimmed through each notebook, my insides tightening. Some gigs were over a month apart, others several months plus, others over a year in between. Business was inconsistent but steady. After the fifth notebook, Zed's name wasn't listed, but other names were. Names I didn't recognize.

I went through the last notebook. The final entry was dated a week before Dad's murder. A cold prickle raced over my neck. Death was the only thing that could stop Dad, and stop him it did.

I tucked the notebooks and the cash back in the lockbox, and the lockbox in a thick black garbage bag. I threw in some CDs and the box of Hot Wheels on top and tied the bag. I grabbed my old Snoopy, who was staring at me from the pile of sweatshirts, and shoved him on top of the bag so I'd remember to take it to my apartment tonight and not confuse it with the other bags for donation. I headed for the kitchen.

"How's it going up there?" Mom closed the dishwasher.

I grabbed a bottle of beer from the fridge. "I think I'm done."

"Terrific. Find anything interesting?"

"Snoopy, remember him?"

"Of course I do. You loved him so much when you were little, always walking around the house holding him. Even when you ate at your highchair, he had to be with you. I've washed him so many times, and yet he survived intact."

"He sure did." I sat down at the table. "Were there any other stashes in the house other than the lamp in the living room?"

"That was it. Sometimes I'd keep a Tupperware in the freezer, but haven't done that in a long, long time." She let out a short laugh as she straightened her kitchen towels in a drawer.

Nope, she still didn't know.

I wiped at my mouth. "I wanted to ask you, the other night at Dead Ringers you and Lindy were talking about a Zed and an Angel that you and Dad used to hang out with?"

Her face brightened. "Zed was the prez of the Broken Blades, and Angel was his old lady. The four of us were good friends. We used to party together a lot. It was fun to have that sort of friendship between clubs. We'd organize runs together, meet up at bars. Go to their clubhouse, and they'd come here. We had a lot of fun…while it lasted."

"Why did it end?"

"Poor ol' Zed had a massive heart attack out of the blue and died. Then his VP, that fuckwad Notch, became president and everything changed. He didn't like a lot of Zed's policies, plus he had a stick up his ass with the Jacks. That was the end of the good vibes and the good times between our clubs. It got so bad that all lines of communication and good faith broke off. Your dad was really upset about it."

"So he and Zed had been tight?"

"They were. Why?"

"Kinda cool, all this history." I drained my beer bottle. "You and Dad knew Lindy's parents back then?"

Mom filled a glass with water and joined me at the table. "We knew them, but we didn't hang out with them much. Something about Lindy reminds me of her mom."

"Oh yeah?" I'd met Lindy's mother once. She'd caught us fooling around in their backyard late one night but didn't raise a fuss. Luckily, Pick had been out of town at the time or I might not have made it out of that backyard alive.

Mom continued, "Emmy had this sweet country girl feel

about her, which had made an impression on me—obviously, because I still remember. Lindy has that too—a genuine smile and eyes that light up and sparkle when she's listening to you. Shame she died the way she did."

"She died?" My chest tightened. "When? How?"

"It was your freshman year at college. Around Christmas. Lenore told me she got diagnosed with some kind of cancer, and within a couple months or so, she was gone. Can you imagine?"

"She didn't go to a doctor or get treatment—"

"You think they had that kind of health insurance?" Her lips twisted. "I don't know the details. All I know is she went real quick, and it was a shock to everybody over there. Pick was a mess and Lindy...awful. She's an only child like you. All that grief and loss when a girl needs her mom the most."

"What do you mean?"

"Lenore had told me Lindy had just turned sixteen."

"Right..." My thumbnail scratched at the wet label on the beer bottle.

"That's when you start fighting your parents for independence, but down deep, a girl needs her mom to deal with boy shit—plain ol' life shit—to make the right decisions for herself, because suddenly, they're so many to make. Lindy was in that wild, fucked-up spot between girl and woman, where everything feels exciting, confusing, demanding, and extreme all at once. You're ready to stand up to the world, be your own woman, but you don't have your footing yet." She let out a dry laugh. "Been there."

"You ran away from home at sixteen."

"I sure did."

A flush of heat radiated over my chest and up my throat. *Holy fuck.* I'd betrayed Lindy, lied to her, and blown her off, and then her dad was forced to flip over to a new club, the enemy's club. And in the next breath, her mother gets sick and dies. Her whole world had imploded.

An innocent girl who hadn't deserved any of this. Any of it.

And I'd been the first stick of dynamite to go off in those harrowing explosions she'd suffered. Of course Lindy had changed, gotten hard. Of course.

If only I…

My pulse picked up steam. Now, again, she was suffering loss. Her father missing, not knowing where he was, if he was even alive, and being forced to live in a new town with strangers.

I could help her now. I wanted to. I would. Would she let me?

"I was thinking…" My mother's voice brought me back to the kitchen. "I have loads of pictures from back when we used to hang out with the Broken Blades. I always took pictures on the runs, at the parties."

I chuckled. "The Kodak that would never die."

"That camera was nothing special, but it never quit on me, and even more importantly, survived all those trips and parties. I haven't packed the photo albums yet. I'll find them."

"I'm sure Lindy would enjoy seeing them. I would too."

Her eyes narrowed at me. "I thought you and Lindy were friends back then?"

"We were."

"You didn't know about her mom dying?"

I brushed a hand over my mouth. "We didn't stay in touch after I left for school."

She let out a long sigh. "Think of what they went through. Pick's club gets blown apart, Notch, their prez, gets killed, and everything the Blades owned gets picked over by the Feds and taken over by the Flames—who Notch hated with a passion, by the way."

"Did all the Blades agree to become Flames? They voted on it?"

Mom's brow furrowed. "No time for a vote. I think some of them, like Pick, joined the Flames on the spot. Finger must have given all those men an ultimatum: death or become a Flame. At least that's how I imagined it because that's how it had to be."

"And the Blades who didn't agree to join…"

"Disappeared." Mom got up from the table and put her glass in the dishwasher. "And on the heels of all that chaos, as Pick's trying to prove himself at a new club, which must have been a total bitch, he finds out his wife is sick."

My fingers throttled the neck of my beer bottle. "Now for Lindy to have her Dad taken…"

"Awful." Mom took the empty bottle from me and tossed it in the recycling bin. "That girl must have balls of steel by now. She seems to have a good head on her shoulders, and I'm glad she has Lenore and Finger. She needs good, strong people in her corner now. Real friends she can count on."

"She does."

She has me.

Mom wiped her hands on a kitchen towel. "I have to get going. Ronny's waiting for me to join him for a late dinner in Deadwood, then we're going to stay at his place."

We hugged goodbye, and she left, her car zipping out of the driveway onto the road. I locked the front door and heaved a breath. An ache pounded through my head with all the information I'd soaked in.

My gaze landed on a framed photo which sat on the top of an open packing box in the hallway. I picked it up. Me, Mom, and Dad were at a Jacks barbecue at the chapter in Colorado back when Dad first became president. I had to have been about three years old at the time. He held me in his arms, and I wore a tiny leather jacket, tiny black boots, and my fingers were in my mouth. Mom leaned against Dad. The three of us grinning. Happy. The future ours for the taking.

I put the photo back in the box with other framed photos Mom had stuffed in there and headed up to my room. My closet door stood open.

Dad had left a trail of foul fumes behind him.

Could it be true? Had he been some kind of traitor to his club with this Zed? Those fumes lodged in my throat, blocking the flow of air. *No way. No fucking way.*

But a bunch of notebooks and wads of cash told a different story. Snoopy smirked at me from his perch on the bag filled with the remains of my father's black ambitions and betrayal. Money had never before felt so meaningless to me or so noxious. Sour roiled in my stomach. My chest ached.

Back downstairs in the living room, I grabbed the lone bottle of whiskey, ripped it open, and gulped. I caught my reflection in the mirror over the fireplace.

I was my father's son, wasn't I? Betrayal and lies and twisted deeds were in our blood. Nothing could wash that away. Nothing.

I drank, and the fiery liquor blazed down my throat, but it didn't numb the burn of my sordid truth.

THIRTEEN

LINDY

I RANG Alicia's front door bell, and within moments the door flew open. My breath cut at the sight of Wes. His hair was messed up, a muscle twitching along his jaw. Had I interrupted something?

At the sight of me a dark eyebrow shot up as his watery eyes widened for a split second. A lazy laugh that sounded almost bitter erupted from him, sending a chill over my skin. "Ah. Perfect timing." His voice was unusually husky, growly even. His body seemed to waver.

My spine straightened. Something was wrong.

I raised the Lenore's Lace shopping bag in my hand. "Alicia ordered this from Lenore, and it came in late today, so I'm dropping it off on my way home. Is she here?"

"Nope."

"Oh. Okay. Sorry to bother you. My mistake."

My Jacks prospect had dropped me off at Lenore and Finger's, but after he left, I'd decided to take Alicia's bag over to her house, which was only two blocks away. Lenore had planned on dropping it off herself, but she'd gotten a last minute hair salon appointment, so I'd taken the bag.

I knew it was a risk to go on my own, without telling anyone, but I gave into the temptation. I craved taking a simple walk outside, doing something, *anything* other than go from the store to the house to the store to the house. And what did I get for this impetuous decision of mine?

Wes. Sexy Wes. Wes alone, and in a strange, dark mood.

"Here—" I shoved the shopping bag in his chest as I stepped back down the stone stairs. He didn't even attempt to grab the bag, and it dropped to the floor.

His body wavered again and he propped himself up against the doorjamb.

My gaze landed on a whiskey bottle in his hand. "You okay?"

"Better than ever."

I glanced past him into the dark house. Empty beer bottles were lined up on the kitchen counter in the distance, giving off a green glow from a small light in the kitchen, the only light on in the house. "Am I interrupting a party?"

"Party for one." A biting smirk swerved over his lips. "Want to make it a party for two?"

Something was definitely off. "I should go." I turned away to head down the walkway.

"Hey, Blade girl, hold up!"

I swiveled around. "Excuse me?"

"I need to ask you something. Something about your club."

"That club doesn't exist anymore, and I've got nothing else to say about it."

"Lindy! Please…don't go!"

The urgent ache in his voice stopped me. There was desperation there, sadness. I knew them well. I returned to the front steps. "What's wrong, Wes?" I lowered my voice. "What's going on?"

He rubbed a hand across his broad chest, his taut arm

muscles flexing. "I found something, and I need you to help me figure it out. Please."

"What is it?"

"Something of my dad's," he whispered. "It's got to do with the Blades. Please, Lindy."

My teeth dragged across my lip, and I stepped inside the house. A flare of warmth from his body rolled over me like a thick, heavy wave from which there was no escape. Locking the front door, he glanced down at the shopping bag at our feet. "Lingerie?"

"Bingo." Grabbing the bag, I set it down at the foot of the staircase. I gestured at the bottle in his hand. "Alicia went out for the night and you're partying it up alone at the house?"

His features twisted. "I haven't lived here in years."

"Oh."

"My mom sold the house and I came by to clean out my old stuff."

"Nostalgia hitting hard?"

He wiped at his mouth, teetering. "Other things are harder."

"Like what?"

"Did your dad ever cheat on your mom?"

"It kind of goes with the biker territory, doesn't it?"

He tilted his head. "So he did and you're cool with it?"

"I didn't say that. I don't know for sure, but I only have good memories of my parents together—they laughed a lot, were always affectionate with each other. Enjoyed being together. They didn't fight much or get nasty, at least in front of me. They never seemed unhappy."

"Lucky girl." He raised the bottle in my direction and drank. "In this house, there was a shit ton of yelling and arguing. Loads of anger. Mountains of resentment."

So his nostalgia was the bitter kind. "That must have been rough on you. I'm sorry."

"The last year before my dad died was the roughest. I was sixteen-seventeen, I understood what he was up to, and I understood how it affected my mother. I saw it, felt it, and I started hating him for it. Then, poof, he was gone. You know what that's like too, don't you?" His fingers went to the side of my face, brushing my skin.

"I do," I whispered, my insides fluttering at his touch in the dim light, at the rawness in his voice. "So…what did you find?"

"It's in my room." He climbed the staircase and I followed him, holding onto the banister in the darkness. On the second floor, we entered a bedroom where the light was already on.

A small Snoopy stuffed toy stuck out of a black plastic bag on the floor, and I plucked him off the bag. "I love Snoopy. I lost mine on one of our many moves. Never got over it." My fingers squeezed Snoopy's soft curved torso.

"You can have him."

"Are you sure?"

"He's all yours."

"Thanks." I glanced around the room. "This room has been frozen in little boy Wes time."

"My mom redecorated when she started showing the house to potential buyers to encourage the family vibe."

"Smart move." I sat on the quilt covered twin bed. "Did you used to bring girls here?"

"Sometimes. If my parents were out."

I put Snoopy on the desk. "You never brought me here."

"You were different." He took my hand, and a soft heat billowed up my arm.

"Because I was the fake relationship that you kept a secret from your family?" I took my hand back. "Imagine if your parents knew you were dating me, a Broken Blade? And you never told me that your daddy was the president of the Jacks, did you?"

"I did not."

"That girl I saw you with after? Did you fuck her here?"

His eyes narrowed. "What girl, when?"

"After us." I let out a dry laugh. "But there were so many

girls, weren't there? How could you possibly remember one out of the many?" I took in a breath. "A few weeks after you got shot at, there was a music festival in Deadwood. I was there with a couple of friends. I saw you with your arms wrapped around this cute blonde cheerleader type. Like you were in a heavy relationship. Blew my mind. Stupid me hadn't realized we were officially broken up, that it was over." I dug my heels into the carpeted floor. "I hadn't even seen you there until Zac pointed you out to me."

"Yeah, Zac…" He took another gulp of whiskey. "I remember. I was trying to forget you that night."

"How sweet. Did you forget me while you were screwing her?"

"I didn't screw her, and I never forgot you," he bit out.

"Be still my heart, you fucking liar."

"I certainly was a smooth fucking liar back then. Lying to you, to myself, to everybody around me. After my dad got killed, after us and the shooting, I was trying to pretend I could pick up the pieces that were left of me and keep on keeping on."

"You only considered your pieces, not mine."

"True." He sat on the floor opposite me, his body sagging. "I hope you can forgive me for that. For all of it."

"Zac told me everything that night."

His eyes lifted to meet mine. Heavy, glassy. "He did, and he made sure I knew that he'd told you everything. I was so angry."

"That your secret was out? That your intended victim heard all about the plan to share her with his pal, to use drugs if need be? And then after, drop her like trash."

His jaw tensed. "I didn't realize the consequences of what I'd set out to do. I only knew that striking out seemed like a solution, like I was achieving something."

"And I was going to be your virgin sacrifice roadkill in the name of outlaw justice." I grabbed the bottle from his lax grip. "Here's to you, big man."

His head jerked back as if my words had stung him. "Unforgivable, I know." He wiped his hands down his face. "I felt no one was doing anything to find my dad's killer. The word was that the Blades were responsible, and I was desperate to hurt them any way I could. I stole from them, torched their junkyard. Using you was another part of that revenge."

His truthful words hung in the room, giving off smoke like glowing embers in the night. It was logical this plan of a broken teenager who was grieving his father. I got it. That kind of cold, churning black ocean of bottomless grief that threatened to pull you under in its tide every day and crush you as you sank. I knew that ocean. I'd been paddling in it for years.

"I should have come clean to you right away, Lindy, especially after you and your dad saved me and Butler on the road. Jesus, I'll never forget that. That's in here." He tapped on his chest.

"I'll never forget it either."

"It's eaten me up inside ever since, what I tried to do to you," he whispered, his voice an ache. "I want to believe I'm not that fucking monster."

My shoulders fell. "I don't think you're a monster."

The scent of the sweet liquor on his breath, coupled with man and something like spicy wood, hit me in my already melty center. I cleared my throat. "You told me you found something that you needed my help with? What is it?"

He sat up on his haunches, his hand cradling the side of my face, and I shivered at his touch, at the sadness filling his eyes. "I wanted to avenge my dad's murder no matter what, no matter who I crushed, even myself. But he wasn't worth it."

"Why wasn't he worth it?"

He let go of me and a sigh dragged from his lips as he stood up. "He wasn't only a cheater, but a fucking traitor to his own brothers. I was going through all this old stuff today when I remembered my dad had a hidden compartment in my closet. It was our secret. We had a stash point in the living room, but my mom didn't know about this one."

"We had stash points too."

The edges of his lips curled into a slight grin. "Goes with the territory, eh?" he quoted me. "I haven't opened it in years. Tonight, I did. And I found these."

He went to the bag where Snoopy had been and pulled out a lockbox, opened it, and took out a pile of spiral notebooks, handing me one. "Take a look."

I flipped it open. A tally of names, figures, a count of weapons and chemical ingredients bought, sold, traded filled the pages. "Accounting for different jobs?"

"Look at the names."

I let out a gasp, my finger tracing over Uncle Zed's name written in black ink all down the page.

"These are jobs my dad and Zed were running together. My dad was club president, and yet look what he was doing with another club. Cutting deals, making cash for himself."

"Are you sure the Jacks didn't know about it?" I grabbed another notebook and leafed through it. Jump and Zed. Jump and Zed. "This doesn't necessarily make Jump disloyal to his club or Zed to his."

"Then why did my dad stash these here and not at the club safe? Nah, Lind, this fits his profile."

"What profile is that?"

"Always looking out for number one," he spit out. He was stewing in this discovery. In what it implied, and maybe worse, what it confirmed. A grimace flashed across his face.

I closed the notebook. "Zed and Jump were both presidents. Maybe what they were doing was for the good of their clubs? Laying some kind of groundwork, making contacts for some big future project? I know that my dad really respected Zed as his prez. Always said he was a solid brother and a great leader. He was devastated when he died."

"When Zed died, this didn't die." He handed me another notebook. "You're a Blade. Take a look, see if you recognize any other names. The first five notebooks are all Zed and my dad. But the others have other names."

I leafed through the fifth notebook. Toward the end of July the Zed notations stopped. I remember it was summer when Zed had died. I'd been eleven or twelve when it happened, and the heat and humidity had been brutal at his epic funeral. Holding onto my mother's hand as we stood in the thick of the massive noisy crowd, sweating, tired, thirsty, dizzy. Everyone so upset. It had been horrible.

Beck handed me another notebook. The first transaction listed was dated late September that same year with the name Thor.

"Thor was a Blade," I murmured. "Zed's Treasurer. Dad used to call him Money Man. He got killed in the takeover." I opened the next notebook. My breath balled up in my chest, my pulse jerking at the sight of that name.

"What is it?" Wes sat down on the bed next to me, the mattress dipping. His warm fingers brushed the hair from my face, and sparks prickled over my flesh, bringing me back to the here and now. "Lind, you okay?"

I swallowed hard. "It's Raptor."

"That name sounded familiar to me, but…" Wes looked at the notebook with me, his gaze following my fingertip tracing the entries. Pages of transactions with Raptor's name. "Who is he?"

"Raptor and my dad were best friends. They'd come into the Blades together as prospects. Raptor later became Zed's Sergeant at Arms."

"So maybe he knew what Zed and my dad were up to and took over after Zed died?"

"Seems that way." I sat up straighter, trying to inch away from the warm wall of hard muscle that was Wes, strong Wes, comforting Wes, hot Wes, that was distracting me. "My dad always said that after Uncle Zed died everything had changed at the club, not only because their new president, Notch, was kinda nuts and completely swerved the Blades' allegiances around causing havoc. But after Zed died, things weren't the same between Dad and Raptor. Raptor had allied himself with Notch and had iced Dad out."

"Survival."

"But my dad was an officer too. He was Road Captain, but Notch only kept his VP and Sergeant at Arms real close."

Wes scanned the page, opened other notebooks. "Judging from the dates, my dad and Raptor were running shit up until Dad got killed. Raptor's a Flame now, like your dad?"

"No."

"He's dead?"

"He's the only one who got away. He's been a renegade nomad of sorts. The Flames and the Jacks have been after him for a while. Why don't you know this?"

"My mom and I aren't part of the club anymore, we're not in the loop."

"Why aren't you a One-Eyed Jack?"

"Am I supposed to follow in my daddy's footsteps?" he shot back, his voice a dark sneer that made my heart stop. There was raw pain in that voice, in those beautiful blue eyes that had now darkened.

My hand went to his thigh, and his muscles tightened under my touch. "You don't have to do anything you don't want to do."

"Sorry." His jaw muscles flexed.

"It's okay."

He let out a heavy breath. "Tell me more about Raptor. If you want, that is."

"He has this insane tattoo from his throat down to his chest of a dinosaur's open mouth, fangs and all. I still remember how it gave me shivers when I first saw it, and I was in elementary school then." I let out a breath. "When the Blades got destroyed, Raptor refused to join the Flames, and he took off before they could kill him. Disappeared for years. Word was he'd become a nomad for the Smoking Guns."

"He affiliated himself with the Flames' number one enemy? Did Raptor stay in touch with your dad all these years?"

Raptor might have taken my dad, but I can't tell him that, can I?

My fingers curled tightly into the notebook. "They'd gone their separate ways years before the Blades fell apart."

"Now everyone's after him because he never came to heel?"

"I don't know all the details, but my dad said Raptor had been running a human trafficking operation with a Smoking Guns president and some gang or mafia organization. A few months ago, that Smoking Guns president got arrested—"

"That I heard about. Dog, right? It was in the news, and Trick and Nicole had something to do with that."

"They did. But Raptor managed to disappear again."

"Maybe there's something in these notebooks that can tell us more about Raptor. If he picked up the reins after Zed died, he and my dad must have had a solid infrastructure that worked and, more importantly, stayed under the radar."

"Good point," I murmured. "How about I make us coffee and we go over the notebooks?"

"Sounds good."

We went to the kitchen, and I made us coffee with the Keurig on the counter as he cleaned up the empty beer bottles. Sitting at the table, Wes and I combed through each notebook.

"I keep seeing the word 'dip'," Wes said. "And dip is capitalized. What the hell is that?"

My pulse flickered. "Let me see." I leaned over, and he showed me the entries.

"Does that mean anything to you?"

"When I was little, my dad used to take us to this open field where the guys would race around on their bikes. They'd found it off an old hiking path over the Nebraska border into Wyoming. They liked it because there was a hill, and at the bottom there was a dip in the earth, a kind of basin. And depending on the weather, it would get real dusty or real muddy. Either way, everyone loved it. An amusement park for the big kids. And in the winter snow? Best sledding hill ever. It was fun.

"There was an old shack at the top of the hill, wasn't much of anything. A tiny wood house built by some wilderness loner dude. This old man. We'd bring him food and clothes, blankets, and drugs in exchange for us coming and making a ruckus once a month or so.

"He liked lollipops. I remember that because my mom made me give him mine the first time I met him and I'd gotten upset. But the lollipop got this little boy smile out of him. Same smile that dropping acid with the men brought out in him too."

"Creepy."

"It was. After that, Mom used to bring him a bagful of lollipops every time. I remember he had a trap door in the floor and he'd store weird end of the world stuff in there along with the lollipops. They'd always send a club girl in there to fuck him, and everyone would laugh at the noise they'd make."

"Nice."

"Then he died, but we kept going out there."

What had Minty said? That he didn't think it was a coincidence that Dad had disappeared in Blades territory? I sank back onto the kitchen chair. The Dip was in our old territory—over the Wyoming border where dad was last heard from.

Biting the inside of my cheek, I went back over the notebooks I had and went down the list.

"What is it, Lind?"

"Jump and Raptor kept using the Dip. Even more than with Zed."

"Then it's a perfect off-the-grid location. Do the Flames know about it?"

"I don't know, but I do know that, for my dad, the Dip was sacred Broken Blades territory, and I doubt he would have offered it up to the Flames, you know what I mean?"

"Sacred, huh?" A wicked smirk flickered over his lips again. "I get it. The Flames had taken everything from his club, taken out his brothers. Why would Pick hand anything over to them like some freebie on a silver platter?" He took in a deep breath. "So that makes the Dip a good place for Raptor to lay low all these years, to keep using it." He closed the notebook, his face lighting up. "I'll tell the Jacks about the Dip."

My body jerked. "What? Why?"

"What do you mean why? Raptor could be there. Sounds like they haven't had a solid lead on him in a long time. This could be it."

"You can't do that."

"Why not? What's wrong?"

"Because…" I stuttered. My heart stuttered.

"What is it?"

"Wes…"

"Tell me. I want to help you find your father, don't you believe me?"

"I do believe you."

His eyes widened. "Holy shit. You think your dad could be there with Raptor?"

My face streaked with heat, and I pressed my lips together.

"Lindy?"

"I don't know what to think! I've been in the dark since I found out he was missing. But I need to consider the possibility that maybe he went off grid with Raptor." I swallowed hard. "But it doesn't make sense to me. He's worked so hard to settle in as a Flame, to be accepted, to prove his loyalty. And I know him, I know he feels good about that, so, no, I can't believe that he would go off with that guy, disappear, and not tell me, not give me some kind of heads up, something…"

"Sounds like a huge risk, but the brotherhood runs deep, doesn't it? If that's what Pick did, he'd keep you out of it to keep you clean."

My chest caved in, and my shoulders sank. "I don't know

what to think, Wes. All I know is that I miss him. That I hope he's still alive wherever he is." My breath hiccuped in my chest.

Wes pulled me into his arms and rubbed my back. I sighed deeply, my face buried in his rippling chest. His clean scent of wood and warm skin filled my senses, and my muscles eased one by one. It felt good, so good to be held by him, comforted, but I couldn't break down now.

Wes kissed the top of my head. "You remember where the Dip is?"

"I could find it."

"If what we have in these notebooks is something to go on... I want to help you find your dad."

"You would help me?"

"You two saved my life and Butler's."

My fingers pushed against his chest. "You don't owe me, Wes."

His hands cradled my face, keeping me close. "I don't want you to lose your dad." His raw voice drilled a hole in my wretched heart. He had a hole too, didn't he? "I could have lost Butler that day too. Thank God I didn't."

"You two are real close?"

His hold on me relaxed. "We are. Something changed that day in Deadwood, on that road, and I'm glad it did."

He'd lost his dad but gained another father figure, a mentor. "You're lucky."

"I know I am." His fingers brushed back that lock of my hair that always fell in my eyes, and a delicious shudder went off inside me as we held each other's gazes. Intense, heated.

The need to help him overwhelmed me. I wanted to, he needed this. He needed me. "Here's an idea: Why don't you show Butler the notebooks that have Zed listed. See how he reacts. Find out if he knew about their gig. That's what you want, isn't it? To know what your dad was really up to?"

"I need to know." His jaw tightened once more. He believed the worst of his dad and it was killing him inside.

And I hated seeing it. It was why he got drunk tonight, wasn't it?

"Your dad took advantage of a business opportunity with a friend and kept it going because it was a moneymaker. Who would say no to that? You don't know if he shared it with the Jacks or not, if it was some strategy thing with Zed for the future. Discussing it with Butler would give you the answer. But…" I touched his arm.

"But what?"

"If this is news to Butler, would he flip out and tell everyone? That would suck."

"I don't think he would. He'd let it lie."

"Either way, your father's reputation as President would remain intact with the club. Wes, you've got nothing to lose and a whole lot to learn."

He met my gaze. "You're right."

"Go for it. Find out what you can. And I'll go to the Dip."

"You're not going there alone!"

"I don't want to put my dad's reputation with Finger in jeopardy. He's worked so hard to be a part of the Flames, you have no idea. First I need to see for myself if he's there or not. Then I'll tell the Flames about it. "

"Hold up. I won't tell Butler about the Dip. I'll only show him the Zed notebooks, see if he knows anything. Then you and me will go to the Dip together."

"Really?"

"Really."

Warmth flowed through my chest at his confirmation of helping me. "If my dad is there with Raptor, he might have been forced into it, blackmailed by him somehow. I need to be sure. Either the Flames still don't know anything or they're not telling me what they know." I let out a breath. "To them I'm the girl. The Blade girl."

"You're not a girl anymore, Lind." There was something smoky in his voice. Maybe it was the booze. His gleaming gaze burned right through me, burned through my veins, my heart, igniting everything I'd felt for him since the last time I'd seen him as that girl. *His girl.*

"I kicked that girl to the curb a while back." Darting up from the table, I picked up our coffee mugs and brought them to the sink.

"Thanks to me?"

Rinsing off the mugs quickly, I shoved them in the dishwasher. "Did you even like me? Were you even attracted to me or was it all fake? I'd like to know. I want the truth whatever it is. Because I liked you. I wanted you, but I'd made that obvious, didn't I?" I slammed the dishwasher door shut. "You were special to me, and I'd wanted you to be..." I bit my lip, stopping the words, my face heating.

What the hell had gotten into me?

He sat up straighter. "Wanted me to be what?"

"Nothing." I ripped a paper towel off the roll and wiped my hands.

His lips curled as he pushed back his chair, and it scraped loudly on the floor. "Lindy. What did you want me to be?" Facing me, he planted his hands on the counter. The demanding urgency in his voice lit a match through my veins, igniting something bolder inside me.

Go on, let him know how deep it went.

"I wanted you to be my first."

His eyes widened in the silence. In a burst of movement, he lunged around the counter and grabbed me, his mouth crushing mine as my lungs constricted.

Wes kissed me like a desert traveler and I was his oasis. His tongue drove deep with need, a fierce need that matched my own. The firm muscles of his arms held me tight as his hips pressed against mine.

But, oh, that taste. *His taste.*

Those intense sensations I hadn't felt in centuries surged inside me. This was no memory, but a potent, intoxicating cocktail of this-is-for-real. I was engulfed on a tidal wave of Wes, out of myself, and into the heart of an explosive and violent storm.

My arms pressed around him. I reveled in the feel of him, the intensity of his kiss. A kiss that branded and claimed and demanded. Back then it had all been fake. But was it fake now? Ignited by guilt? Or was it only whiskey and hormones?

My body went rigid, and I shoved at him. "You don't deserve me."

"No, I don't." He brought me back into his chest. "But I'm showing you…"

I shoved again. "Showing me what? What *you* want?"

A noise tore from his chest. "Showing you how I feel about you."

My fingernails dug into his arms. "When you targeted me, kissing me and touching me must have been a real tedious chore for you, but you did it for the good of the mission, right?"

"I liked you, Lindy. You were all innocence and enthusiasm about life. Passionate about diving in headfirst to whatever it was you wanted. You were genuine. Everything I wasn't. Everything I didn't know."

"But you kept your eyes on the prize, didn't you? Nothing got in your way, until Butler did."

"I was real goal oriented then."

I twisted in his grip. "You're not now?"

"Now I'm just getting by," his voice rasped, ragged and bruised, fisting in my heart.

My hand reached up and stroked his warm, stubbly cheek. His eyelids sank as he leaned into my touch, a low noise escaping his lips, a raw, vulnerable sound. The same raw that filled my soul.

"Wes?"

His eyes blinked open.

"Is leaving this house behind hard for you?"

His ringed fingers slid over my hand and took it in his. "I didn't think it would be, but the little boy in me, the one who took the family fairy tale for granted, always thought this house would be here for him forever. No matter what, this house was a sure thing."

I squeezed his hand. "My dad and I are still living in the house where my mom got sick and died. And you know what? Now that I'm not there, I realize it's been sucking the life out of me. Out of my dad too. I never wanted to let it go because it meant letting her go, letting go of the way we used to be as a family. But what the hell's the point? She's not there anymore."

He curled my hand in his. "And she never will be again."

I blew out a breath, blew out all those child fears of letting go, of what if. "Like your dad isn't here anymore and never will be again." The two of us stared at our hands clasped together. I shifted my weight. "Your mom has gotten on with her life in a big wonderful way, and that's fantastic."

"It is. I'm happy for her. How about Pick?"

"This year, for the first time, he started bringing women to the house instead of keeping it at the club. But I don't know if that means he's letting go and trying to start over or if he's floundering even more, given up."

"And you?" He took my other hand in his. "You getting on with your life?"

"Just getting by," I repeated his words on a whisper.

Our gazes locked once more and something powerful and loud hummed in the room, throbbing around us. Need, want, desire.

Recognition.

My arms flew around his neck, and I smashed my mouth against his.

FOURTEEN

WES

WE KISSED, tongues twisting, sliding, searching. Her hands dug in my hair, holding me close. Electricity surged through me as we kissed, our bodies pressing, needing. A bolt of current tore through my veins, sending a tremor through my core.

I didn't only need. I needed Lindy.

She stiffened in my arms. "Wes…we should slow down."

"Why?"

"We've been drinking…"

"I know damn well what I'm doing." My hands slid over her hips, dug into her fantastic ass, pressing her against my stiff cock. I let out a groan. "I want you, Lind. I want to be inside you."

"You're horny, and I happen to be here." She wiggled out of my hold, and I let her go.

"It's you, Lind. It's you." A confession from the bottom of my soul. "Can't get you out of my head. Can't stop thinking about you. Hell, I've never stopped thinking about you. About what could've been."

"Then it's guilt on the rocks with a stiff shot of hormones."

"You're wrong." My chest expanded with the idea, with the feeling. With the truth. "I wanted you then. I want you more now."

She pursed her lips, her eyes flashing. Was she in a panic? "This is your big opportunity to make yourself feel better? A few orgasms and we're all good, right?"

"I'm gonna give you way more than a few."

"Wes…" Her body visibly stiffened.

I crossed the distance between us, and my hands slid around her face, pulling her close. This time, she didn't fight me. "The attraction was always there, and now it's…fucking over-whelming."

"Probably because…because we never had sex. It's a holdover. A fascination." She bit her lip. Did she regret her little outburst?

Her admission.

My thumb stroked over those soft, silky lips. Lips I wanted on my body, on my cock. "Maybe we'll get over it if we do it."

Her eyes widened. "Have sex?"

"Have sex." I gently brushed her lips with mine, and she let out a tiny gasp.

"That's a real enticing proposition when you put it like that."

My hands slid down her sides, and something like a growl escaped my chest. "You think it'll be a disappointing experience? You won't want more of me?"

"More of you or just your cock?"

"Ouch."

She patted my ass. "Relax, big boy. It's just sex."

Just sex. The thought of her getting off with other guys over the years had my pulse drumming in my veins. Not that I'd been a monk, but… "Listen to you, Ms. Jaded, Ms. Been-There-Done-That."

"Are you trying to slut-shame me because you're not getting what you want?"

I let out a loud laugh, raising my hands in the air. "Fuck no, not me. I've been there done that. Over and over again." I smoothed a hand down my chest to steady myself under her tense scrutiny. She liked being in control, having the upper hand, didn't she?

Lindy's chin noticeably lifted. Challenge mode. "Let's do it. Get it over with."

My breath hitched as the blood rushed through me, stiffening my balls.

She grinned. A brittle grin. "You've got this whole house to yourself tonight. We can pretend we're in high school again and do it on your boy bed. Kind of hot, don't you think?"

"Very hot." I licked at my lips.

Was she for real or making fun? Time to find out.

I grabbed her hand and we charged up the stairs back to my room. Her ass landed on the bed. I ripped off my T, threw off my jeans and my boxer briefs. Without moving a muscle, she took me in from head to toe, and heat licked at my flesh with every stroke of her intense gaze.

She got up and took off her clothes but left her bra and panties on. A low groan escaped my throat as I took in her gorgeous body, my heart slamming in my chest. She'd developed into a fine, fine woman from the teenager I remembered. Sensual, sexy curves, and that pale skin as creamy as ever, begging me to lick every inch.

Something pinched in my chest. I'd never seen her naked before, or even like this in her underwear. In the past our fooling around had always happened with us mostly dressed and in the dark in my car, and had consisted of me fingering her, her jerking me off, or us dry humping. A fury of fingers slipping past waistbands, sliding under shirts, tugging at buckles, snapping at buttons.

One night in her backyard, I'd gone down on her, the one and only time, and she'd come hard as she cried out my name. She'd been so surprised by it, and so elated. A next level orgasm. After, she wouldn't let go of me and curled up in my arms on that rickety, reclining lawn chair. Her genuine reaction had softened something in my chest. I'd felt a shift between us that night, and so had she.

But it was a shift I hadn't expected and hadn't planned on.

We'd decided to have sex for the first time the following week in Deadwood, where we had tickets to go to a rock concert. I'd taken money from the family stash for a hotel room and food and booze. Lindy was elated because her mom was going on some old ladies weekend to a casino resort, and her dad was going to be out of town on club business. Perfect timing.

Zac was supposed to bring this girl he was seeing and get shit for the four of us to get high, but instead, he'd showed up in Deadwood without his girl and not with Ecstasy but with roofies. He'd planned on having sex with Lindy by slipping her drugs at some point. That had been our original idea when I'd first hatched this revenge scheme, but as the weeks wore on, the plan had begun to make me sick to my stomach. I'd decided against it.

But Zac didn't agree with me, so he thought he'd force my hand. We'd argued that whole afternoon once we met up in town. *"You've come so far, dude, don't drop the ball now. This is the perfect plan. Don't be a pussy. She's just some girl."* But then Butler showed up and stopped it all.

Now, I'd been graced with a second chance with Lindy. Now, her gaze burned over my body as she moved toward me. Would she bite me? Kiss me? Whatever she fucking wanted. My heart pounded uncontrollably as she got closer … *and closer.*

Her cool hands settled on my arms. "I realized something."

The walls of the small bedroom closed in on me. Her breath fanned my flesh, and I swallowed hard. "What's that?"

"Never got to see you naked before," she whispered.

"Was thinking the same thing…"

Her tongue lashed at my chest.

"Fuck…" I moaned, my flesh on fire.

Her fingertips touched the scars on my left pec and across my abs. "What are these scars from?"

"When Butler and I got shot at, I wiped out on my bike. Got skinned."

Her lips parted, and keeping her gaze on mine, she licked the scars slowly, gently. My balls tightened, my blood pounding in my veins.

"Get on the bed and lie down," she ordered. Adrenaline blew through me as I did what she said. She climbed on top of me, settling between my legs. Her soft fingers closed over my stiff cock and stroked. Stroked up and down and around. She knew what she was doing.

"Lind…" My back arched off the mattress, my every muscle tightening.

"And I never got to do this…" Her tongue darted over my swollen, already wet tip, around and around. My hands dug in her thick hair, and I let out a moan. She dove, her mouth taking in my shaft.

"Goddamn…"

Lindy had me in her hot, silky, wet mouth. My heart charged in my chest with nowhere to go. Her eyes flashed up at me as she took me deeper down her slick throat.

I blanked. No words. None.

Wet and hot and tight. She sucked swiftly, firmly, a hand at my balls. I was at her mercy and I loved it. Her head bobbed over me, and my fingers dug through her silky hair, my loud grunts filling the room as her tits, bursting in lace, brushed my thighs, her muscles straining as she worked me.

She pulled and tugged, slid and pressed, her one hand now stroking my balls. I groaned loudly with every long suck. Helpless, powerless. I was gone. Spinning in heaven.

The pleasure grew, intensified, and my hips pumped against her face, my eyes shutting tight. My back arched. "Lindy!" The pressure had my eyes roll in the back of my head as my hips rocked and thrust. I exploded yet her suction got even tighter, slicker, her rhythm quick and intense. She swallowed everything I had to give, and with her fingers wrapped around my base, she eased to an insane slow slide.

"Lindy, shit...Lindy..." I grabbed her arms, hoisted her up my body, and took her mouth. My hand cupped her ass, keeping her on top of me. "So fucking good. I want you bad, Lind." My fingers slid under the thin material of her panties. Her breath cut as I dipped into her wet. "Fuck yes..."

My fingers stroked around her swollen-for-me clit, and she cried out against my lips, her body squirming, her fingernails digging into my flesh. "You feel so good, Lind. So good...so fucking wet..." My brain cells rearranged themselves over and over and over with every moan I drew out of her. "Want to be inside you so bad, so fucking bad...want you coming on my—" I froze. "Dammit! I don't have a condom!"

She blinked, her body tightening. "Oh. That's okay..."

"No, it's not. Fuck!"

"It's okay." She tried to disentangle herself from me, but I flipped her onto her back.

This wasn't over.

"Wes?"

"You know what I never got to do back then?"

"What?" she whispered.

As I kneaded her tits, I licked a curvy trail between them, down her torso to the top of her panty. Her body quivered, her stomach clenching. My tongue nudged at the thin, satin waistband. "We were always fooling around in the dark somewhere, weren't we?"

She let out a short laugh. "Always in the dark."

My fingers dug into her hips. "Never got to see your pussy."

Her mouth moved as if to speak, but nothing came out. Lindy's eyes widened as my fingertips slid along the band, under it, along her skin, nudging the fabric down. My mouth watered, and my balls throbbed, my cock hardening again as she trembled. I tugged her panty past the curve of her hips, and she let out a cry as my tongue licked a trail down her flesh…

A ring tone I didn't recognize blew up, and we both froze. Her gaze shot to my desk, to the alarm clock. "Shit! It can't be that late!" She scrambled from under me, tumbling off the bed.

"What the hell?"

Grabbing her jeans, she fished out her phone. "Dammit!" she muttered, answering the call. "Hey, Dawes." She winced as she used a perky tone of voice. "I'm fine. Everything's good. I'm at Alicia's house. I had to drop something off for her. Wes is here, we got to talking, and I lost track of time…I should've called, I'm sorry. I know, I know…You're right. Everything's cool. Okay, okay. Bye." Tossing her phone on the dresser, she pulled her jeans up her legs. "Dawes is coming over."

"No, no…I'll bring you home." I sat up, and the bed seemed to swerve underneath me. "Whoa." I blinked, my vision blurry.

"You're drunk." She threw her clothes on quickly, hopping up and down, biting her lip. Standing in front of the dresser mirror, she quickly smoothed out her hair.

Steadying myself on an inhale, I pulled up my jeans, not bothering with my boxer briefs. A heavy knock erupted on the front door. The front bell rang repeatedly. "Dang, he's eager."

"He's worried. I didn't check in when I was supposed to."

"You got distracted by my beautiful cock."

"Shut up." She shoved her feet into her All Stars as I moved to the doorway with her. "No, no, no. You stay here."

"You don't want him to know that we were—"

"Wes! Get some sleep, and tomorrow go find Butler and ask him. Let me know what he says."

"Yes ma'am." My hand cupped her chin. "Kiss me goodbye."

"No." She darted past me.

She came to a halt in the dark hallway, turned, and marched back toward me.

"Changed your mind, huh?"

"No." She brushed past me into my room and grabbed Snoopy from the dresser.

I leaned against the doorjamb and her gaze snagged on mine. Darting at me, she raised up on her toes and brushed my mouth with her swollen lips. I remained still, holding my breath, holding the feeling of her silky skin against mine, her taste, her scent all over me.

"Call me." She was gone, her quick footsteps stamping down the stairs.

The front door swung open. Voices. The door slammed. Engines.

Slowly, I headed downstairs and locked the front door. In the dark, my head sank against the thick wood as images of Lindy taking off her clothes, taking me in hand, taking me in her mouth, collided through me, setting off another spiraling ache through my entire body, making my balls heavy. I replayed every moment of us in that bed. Her desire and determination to make me come washed through me.

On a moan, I smoothed a hand over my stiffening cock. I couldn't wait to make Lindy moan, moan my fucking name.

FIFTEEN

WES

"Thanks for meeting me."

"Always got time for you, Wes. Thanks for the coffee." Butler raised his decaf latte and drank.

I cleared my throat as I pressed my hands over the five notebooks on the table before us, my double espresso staring at me, untouched. It was late morning and the Meager Grand wasn't crowded. We were alone at a table in a far corner.

"I hear Alicia sold the house?"

"She did."

"How do you feel about that?"

"I'm cool with it. It's time. She doesn't need it, and I don't want it. And the cash will be real nice to have."

He grinned. "You got plans for it?"

"Not yet, no."

Setting his mug down, he leaned forward on the table. "What's up?"

"I found something of my dad's at the house and I wanted to ask you about it." I passed him the first notebook. "I found these notebooks in a secret hiding place he'd made in my closet years ago. Said it was only for us. He always kept a lockbox in there. I opened it and found these."

Butler opened the notebook and scanned each page, flipped pages. His big shoulders went rigid, his jaw tightened. His broad chest expanded with a breath.

I leaned in closer to him. "Did you know about this?"

"That he was running a side hustle with another club for years?" he spit out.

And the answer is NO.

I knocked back my coffee.

He closed the notebook. "Did your mother know about this?"

"I don't think so, and I haven't told her. She never knew about the hidden compartment he built in my closet. But I asked her about Zed, and she had all sorts of stories of how she and Dad were close to him and his old lady. Partying together, hanging out, going on runs."

"That's right, that's how it was with them." He rubbed a hand across his forehead, his gaze stony.

"What's wrong?" My heart thudded in my chest.

"This explains a fuck of a lot." He pressed his hands down over the cover of the notebook.

"Like what?"

"Back in the day, Dig, Grace's first husband, was VP when your dad was Sergeant at Arms. Dig had all these creative ideas about us forming alliances to strengthen our territory and our trade in our area. For him that meant hooking up with a powerful ally."

"The Flames of Hell."

"At the time, Finger was VP of the Flames, and Dig had set up a meet with him to open the lines of communication, offer to do them a few good turns, build trust. Back then, the Flames were supreme lone rangers. No allies, no nothing, only pure one percenters full steam ahead and fuck you if you even dared glance their way.

"It was a hot idea, exciting—to most of us. But Jump? Hated

it. Flew off the handle about it. Threatening Dig to stay away from Finger. None of us could explain it, his extreme reaction over and over again for years."

"Did Dig go ahead anyhow?"

"He tried, but shit fell apart at the last minute, and it didn't work out then. Jump was thrilled, and he kept shoving it in his face way after the fact."

"Pure Dad."

Butler folded his hands together over the notebook. "But, years later, years after Dig got killed, I felt that idea was more important than ever, and so, when I went nomad for our national, I contacted Finger, did some work for him that I shouldn't have, but I wanted to prove to him that I was trustworthy and useful while still being a Jack. I tried to show him it would be a good deal for the Flames too."

"Did he bite?"

"Slowly, we forged a relationship. We needed the Flames on our side because the Smoking Guns were coming for all of us. And when I got back to Meager, I wanted to bring that opportunity to the table, and that's what I did."

Butler had been exiled for a few years after he'd let his drug addiction get the best of him.

"How did Dad react?"

"Blew up at me. Of course he wasn't happy about taking me back in the first place."

"He didn't trust you anymore."

"Jump was pretty damned absolute when he mistrusted someone. Nothing was going to change his mind. Could have been a small thing from years back, but he always remembered it and would find a way to use it against you even a hundred years later." He slapped a hand on the notebooks, his back going straight. "Man, you don't need to hear this. I shouldn't be talking shit about your father to you."

"I want the truth, Butler. We all knew he was a selfish prick, my mom before everybody else. I learned it the hard way." I leaned over the table and whispered, "Nothing and nobody mattered as much as what he wanted. Not even his club. That I can't wrap my head around, and I never will." I gulped the last of my coffee. Ice-cold. "What do these notebooks tell you?"

"That the reason he was so anti-Flames and anti-Finger was because of his secret alliance with Zed. Zed's club and the Flames were enemies, so any proposed alliance with the Flames would have threatened that special relationship and any potential plans those two may have been cooking for the future.

"When your dad became president, his number one principle was that any kind of alliance was a bad thing. That we didn't need anybody. But times were changing fast, businesses were changing, and it became a major pinch point for him. He blew a lot of smoke about it and we could never figure out why."

"Now you know."

A growl left Butlers' throat. "Wasn't some philosophy about the purity of the brotherhood. He was filling his own pockets."

My fingers slid up and down my coffee cup. "It's funny how when I was so hell-bent on getting justice for Dad, you told me I could've ruined his reputation, blackened his whole life's work with the shit I was up to," my voice seethed. "Seems like he's done that all on his own."

Butler's sharp gaze drilled into mine, drilling way down into my gut. "You understand loyalty."

"Damn straight I do." My gaze trailed out the window. "After Zed died, the Blades blew up, right?"

"Six months later, give or take." He tilted his head. "These were the only notebooks?"

"Yep." My pulse pounded in my head as I fingered my empty coffee cup, my one leg jittering under the table.

"There was nothing else in that lockbox?"

"A couple of knives, a few hundred bucks," I lied again, my shoulders stiffening. "You going to tell the men about this?"

"No point. But I'll tell Boner. He deserves to know. You okay with that?"

"Yeah."

"I'm glad you showed this to me. No matter what, there's nothing better than knowing the truth, even after all these years. I'm glad I know."

I put the notebooks in my backpack. "In the end, Dig's original vision became reality, and you made that happen."

Butler winked at me. He was trying to be cool for my benefit, but it was the way he let out a breath, moved his gaze to the window, curled his lips, that I knew deep in my gut that this news had upset him.

I zipped up my backpack. "I realize you can't tell me much, but any news on Pick? Where he might be? Who's got him? If he's alive?"

"Nothing yet."

"Unbelievable."

"Speaking of, I heard from Dawes that Lindy was at your house last night?" Butler's forehead creased.

"My mom had ordered something from Lenore, and Lindy dropped it off when I was there." I shrugged. "We ended up talking, catching up."

"All caught up now?"

"I guess."

"You guess?"

"I'm still not her favorite person, but we were able to … communicate."

"Communicate?" Gripping his mug, he slid it back and forth across the table absently. "That's good."

"Things are real rough for her with her dad missing. I didn't know her mom had passed away after they got to the Flames."

"Shit, that's more than rough."

I slid the strap of my backpack on my shoulder. "I got to get to the tattoo shop."

He stood up from the table. "How's that going?"

"It's going good. Real good." We left the Grand and stood on the sidewalk out front.

"I'll say it again, you want to prospect for the Jacks, you're in."

"B—after this little discovery…"

Butler grabbed my arm. "Wes, what Jump did, how he behaved, has nothing to do with you. Nothing at all. You hear me?"

I shot him a lame grin. "See ya." I walked off toward the shop.

"Wes!"

I didn't agree. And I didn't think I ever would.

SIXTEEN

LINDY

NEED TO SEE YOU

Wes's text sent an electric shiver through my body.

Need.

I bit my lip.

And I need to lick you.

Need to bite you.

Need to kiss you.

Need to...

It had been two nights ago that I was at his house, that we'd made confessions, that we'd fooled around. And since then, the sensations of Wes kissing me, touching me, his long, hard, velvet length filling my mouth, his salty taste, the sounds he made as his gorgeous muscular body writhed and jerked in pleasure, his fingers fisting my hair, had kept me breathless and aching all day.

When he'd shouted out that he didn't have a condom, it was as if a freezing ice bath had been thrown at me, and I'd snapped out of the haze of desire and shot back to reality.

How could I have let it get this far?

I'd figured I should test the waters, to see if I was still attracted to him in that visceral way I always had been or not. And if that attraction no longer existed, my stubborn resentment had simply clouded my judgement all this time. What a relief it would be.

I failed that test miserably.

Or had I passed with flying colors?

Gah!

The attraction was even more fierce, the chemistry between us even more powerful than I remembered. My cheeks stung with the vivid memory.

My body had hit overload with the two of us simply standing there almost naked, staring at each other, not even touching. And then when we finally touched, overwhelm hit me like a tidal wave. I only wanted more.

I'd licked his perfect chest and taken him in my mouth. And the way he'd reacted–throbbing, hissing, moaning for me–had me transfixed on making him come. He came, and I tasted him for the first time. I loved it. Loved it so much.

Too much.

My phone pinged with another text.

Lindy? You there???

I'm home. Come over

Lenore and Finger wouldn't be home for another hour and a half at least. Every Thursday afternoon they'd meet at Pete's Tavern in town for drinks before they came home for dinner. Perfect timing. Wes would stop by and tell me how things went with Butler, what he found out, and then he'd have to leave. No possibility of any touching, kissing, tasting, coming…

Yep. Great idea.

I caught my gaze in the mirror. I'd been playing with the new

Lenore blush, and then, of course, an hour later I had a full face of makeup on along with some false eyelash pieces that filled out my own lashes. I'd layered powder, highlight, more blush, more bronzer…I'd gone all out.

I glanced at the time on my phone. Wes was probably getting off work from either Eagle Wings or Trash Ink. Either way, I'd have plenty of time to get all this makeup off my face before he arrived. I grabbed a cotton round and the bottle of Micellar water.

Something hit the window, and I let out a gasp. Had a bird crashed into the glass? I ran to the window. My heart skipped a beat. Wes stood on the backyard patio, waving at me, hoodie over his head as if he'd snuck undercover into the fenced backyard. He probably had.

My Meager Romeo.

I shoved open the window. "What the heck are you doing?"

"Never threw stones at your window before."

My breath caught. He used the same phrase I'd used the other night when I'd…

A grin slashed his face, and my insides twisted. The provocative bad boy making dirty promises. "Stay there, I'll be down in a sec."

"I love it when you dish out orders."

"Wes!" My lungs crushing together, I rushed down to the kitchen and unlocked the patio doors. His eyebrows lifted, his head jerked back, his lips parted. "What are you staring at? Come in already." I pulled on his arm, and he stumbled inside as he twisted around.

"You…you…"

"What?" I locked the glass doors behind me.

"You're gorgeous."

I rolled my eyes. "You men are so easy. A bit of greasepaint or a little bikini and you're falling all over yourselves."

"No, Lind, seriously." He grabbed my upper arm as I brushed past him. "You look amazing. I mean, you always look amazing, but this is… out of this world glamorous but you." As his thumb rubbed my arm, his eyes scrunched up, and he released his firm hold on me.

"Thank you." My mouth had gone totally dry.

He lifted his chin. "You getting ready to go out for a big night on the town?"

"Yeah, the limo's on its way."

His brow scrunched. "What?"

"Joke." I gestured at my face. "I did this for fun. It's…a hobby of mine."

He stroked the side of my cheek. "You sure are good at it."

I swallowed hard at the gentle stroke of his warm fingers. "It's what I love to do more than anything else. Like riding a motorcycle is for you, maybe? Or drawing and painting?"

"Right on both counts. Nothing like it."

"It excites me and keeps me centered. I lose myself in it, but find myself at the same time." My cheeks heated at my confession.

A genuine smile lit up his face, softening his jaw. "That's exactly what it's like, yeah."

"I'd love to make a career out of it, but I haven't quite gotten that off the ground yet. I used to post looks on Instagram, but I had to put my account on private since I got here."

"Like a beauty influencer?"

"I wouldn't say that. "

"Show me."

I picked up my phone, brought up my IG, and gave him the phone.

He scrolled, his eyes widening. "Goddamn, woman. This is insane."

"Thank you." My voice had gone soft. He gave me back my phone and our fingers brushed together, the contact sending sparks up my arm, making my back straighten.

His lips tipped up. "Will you accept my follow if I make a request?"

"Maybe."

We both laughed, and silence fell between us as we continued the mutual staring. His gaze dropped to my lips, and I took in a deep breath. "So..." I shifted my weight. "What's up?"

He ran a hand through the crop of hair on top of his head. "I talked to Butler. I showed him the Zed notebooks. I wanted to tell you about it."

"What did he say?"

"He was playing it cool, but he was upset. He told me that from the very beginning, before my dad was even president, he was very anti-Flames and anti-Finger. Constantly putting up roadblocks to any sort of communication or cooperation between the clubs that Butler and another brother were trying to get off the ground for the good of the club. They'd fight about it, but he'd never give any kind of explanation. When Butler saw the notebooks it all started to make sense to him."

"Oh boy. Was he real upset? Did he feel that your dad was a traitor?"

"He kept it tight for my sake. We were at the Grand in public too. But it was obvious to me that it upset him. Butler confirmed that Dad had never told anyone about it, so it wasn't part of some awesome plan for the future of the two clubs but for his own pockets.

"All Butler knew was that the Jacks and the Blades had never worked together, only did the odd charity run, partied—mostly in the Zed era as he and Dad were tight—but no business collaborations. He asked me if there were any more notebooks past Zed's death, and I lied to him. Said no."

"That's all right. He knows the core truth now, that's what's important. How long it went on for is frosting on the cake."

His gaze fell to his boots. "Fucking ten-layer cake."

"Is he going to tell everyone?"

"Only Boner."

"That's good."

"But I'll know. He and Boner will know." His jaw tightened in that way that told me he was conflicted. Irritated. Upset.

"Wes, you think no other brother in any other club does this sort of thing? Come on. It's rough passing up an opportunity to make a tax-free buck. Things are tough out there. Or maybe your dad got off on the thrill of it. On the forbidden. On taking that risk and getting away with it."

"Yes to all of the above."

"Was your dad an adrenaline junkie too?"

He let out a dark laugh. "He was a junkie on lots of fronts—riding, power, sex."

I leaned a hand against the counter. "Did you inherit those cravings, junior?"

"Is that what you think?" His voice sharpened, his eyes narrowed at me. "Is that what you think of me?"

I'd hit a major nerve.

"I don't think that of you, Wes. It was a bad joke. I'm sorry." I curled my fingers into his T-shirt. "But that's what you think, isn't it?"

"You don't know anything about it." He stiffened, his gaze darting to the window.

"I know you."

"Yeah, me, the guy who played you. There you go. See?" He raised his hands in the air as if I'd proven his point.

"Stop it."

"That's the cold truth."

"But that's not who *you* are. You're not your dad, you're not Jump. And you're not responsible for him or his legacy with the club, be it good or be it sullied. Tell me you believe that."

His features tightened. "I can't…"

I took in a breath, my chest filling with purpose. I had to say it. It was the truth, and he needed it, and I would offer it to him. "You know what?"

"What?" he said sharply.

"I forgive you."

His gaze snagged on mine. A teeming dark-blue sea I could drown in, but Wes was the one drowning, and I would throw him a lifeline.

"I forgive you, Wes. And you need to forgive yourself."

"I don't deserve—"

My fingers went to his lips. "I. Forgive. You."

His hand closed over mine and he gently kissed it. "Thank you," he whispered.

I hugged him, and his arms pulled me in tight. "I have regrets with my dad too," I murmured into his chest. "I wasn't the nicest daughter the last few months. Always pointing out where I thought he was going wrong. Never satisfied with anything, always frustrated. Now he's missing. In danger. And I don't want it to end here. It can't." My lips pressed together to halt the tide of messy emotions rising in my throat. "He's all I have left, Wes, and I don't want to lose him. I can't." There was a tremor in my voice, and his arms squeezed me even tighter. I buried my face in his soft hoodie, in the hard protective wall of his chest, his steady heartbeat drumming in my ear.

His lips brushed the top of my head. "You're not going to lose him," he whispered.

Our breathing synced as my body nestled deeper into his. I began to breathe normally again.

His hands rubbed my back. "It feels good to talk to you like this, Lind. I don't share real shit with many people. I can count the times on one hand."

"Me neither." My teeth scraped my lip.

"With you, it's different." He stroked my hair down to the side of my face.

"I feel that too." I peeked up at him, and that tight pressure in my chest intensified. "Wes…"

Cupping my face, his lips brushed mine, kissing me gently. Around us, the world's spinning slowed and blurred, and my blood sang in my veins. Everything about this kiss was beautiful. A yearning answered, an ache soothed, a hurt relieved. We kissed like we had all the time to explore, to share.

I wanted to share with Wes.

My tongue dove, and everything swirled, and I held onto him, onto us, while it did. His hands slid down my back, over my hips to my ass, pulling me into him, into his hardness, his need. I reveled in the knowledge of it, in the feel of his firm body, his heat and desire fusing with mine.

His heart beating with mine.

"You feel so good…" He lifted me up in his arms, and my legs snaked around his waist. He put me on the counter, his hands sliding under my cropped T-shirt as he let out a groan, sending electric sparks over my skin. I trembled as if it were the first time he was touching me, a touch that blazed and incited a riot inside me. His hand cupped a breast and stroked. "Lindy…" he sighed against my lips

The heels of my feet dug into Wes's ass as he took my mouth, claiming, possessing. His hand roughly kneaded my breast. "So beautiful…" Groaning, he picked me up off the counter and we turned. He lost his balance and tipped me against the refrigerator. The water and ice dispenser erupted in that jerky grinding sound, and ice cubes spewed onto my bare skin. I let out a shriek, clinging to him.

We laughed, but didn't stop kissing, which only made our hunger bolder. My fingers raked through his hair as he adjusted me in his hold. I liked being held by him. I was on fire, and all the ice and cold water in the world couldn't put out these flames. "Wes…"

"Lindy…tell me. Tell me what you want, and I'll give it to you…" His hand gripped my ass cheek.

My heart pounded in my chest. "I want—"

"What the hell's going on?" a rough voice boomed, and my fingernails dug into his flesh, my gaze shooting over Wes's shoulder. A big, dark shadow loomed over us in the kitchen, blocking all the sunlight.

"Shit!" I yelped, springing out of Wes's arms.

"That all you got to say, young lady?" growled Finger.

SEVENTEEN

WES

A SHAMED SCHOOLBOY, that was me. I shrunk three sizes in one second.

Lindy sprang a foot away from me. Cool air stung my skin where she once was pressed against me.

I cleared my throat. "Finger, we were just—"

"Oh, I know exactly what you were *just*...." He tossed his keys on the kitchen table, and they clattered loudly on the wood. I winced.

Genuine truth in action, Beck had said.

Here we fucking go.

"Finger, could we talk? You and me?" I held my breath, and Lindy did a double take at me, at Finger, back at me, her eyes widening as she tugged on the edge of her T-shirt.

Finger's brow creased. "You and me?"

My chest tightened. "You and me."

I got a deeper furrowing of his brow and a snarl curling his lips for a response. He was a wild west outlaw and I was the young punk unworthy of his time.

"I-I'm going to get out of this makeup," Lindy said.

"You do that," muttered Finger, his fierce gaze lasering a hole through me.

"See you, Lind," I said without looking at her.

"Bye." She left the room, her bare feet padding in the distance.

Finger curled his maimed hands around the top of a kitchen chair. "Am I going to need a beer for this conversation or a whiskey?"

"Both."

"You grab the beers, I'll pour the whiskey." He moved to a cabinet and took out a bottle of liquor, while I went to the fridge and grabbed two cans of beer. Setting a tumbler of whiskey before me, Finger sat down at the table, and I took a seat opposite him. He knocked back a swallow of the liquor. "What do you got for me? Been a long day."

"Me and Lindy—"

"There is no you and Lindy."

"There *was*."

"Say again?"

I cleared my throat. "Years ago, Lindy and I were seeing each other."

"And how old were you? Twelve?"

"It was after my dad got killed. When the Broken Blades were still the Broken Blades. I was seventeen, and she was almost sixteen."

"*Almost*?" His jaw visibly tightened. "Did her father know?"

"No."

He let out an ominous, low noise, his metallic eyes narrowing at me. Grabbing a beer, he ripped it open and took a slug. "Go on. Because I'm feeling there's a story here, and it ain't only about teen angst."

I took a swallow of the whiskey. "I came up with a plan to get revenge for my dad's murder. I started ripping shit off from the Blade's junkyard, throwing explosives. Minor shit that caused a big hassle."

A crooked grin flared over his features. "That was you?"

"That was me. But then I came up with a grander plan." I drank down more of the smooth liquor, and a trail of sweet fire flew down my throat, to my belly, making my back straighten. "I targeted the daughter of a Blade—Lindy. I thought what better way to get back at the bastards who murdered my father at his own club."

"I better not hear what I'm thinking."

"You won't. It didn't happen. Butler figured it out and snapped me out of my delusional fog."

He tipped his head. "Delusional fog?"

My mouth dried. "I'd gotten obsessed with striking back, and striking out was the only thing that felt good. Like I was doing something important. I thought the Flames and the Jacks weren't doing enough to find out who'd done it, like it didn't matter to anybody. For me it wasn't about politics or business. My father had been assassinated on his own turf, and I wanted justice for him. For the Jacks."

His jaw tightened, and his heavy gaze went to the whiskey he swirled in his glass. "Frustrated, angry, powerless, and abandoned all at once."

Shifting in my chair, I blinked at his perfect articulation of my clusterfuck of emotions. He knew what that felt like, didn't he?

He poured more whiskey for me and I drank, the booze searing my throat. "What made it shitty was, at the time that he got killed, my dad and I were barely talking. My mom had kicked him out of the house, couldn't take his cheating anymore. And I was glad 'cause I was over his bullshit too."

We drank in silence, the late afternoon light waning in the kitchen changing the colors and tone of everything as if I were in an orange-purple dreamscape and not here, in reality, spilling my guts to Finger in his kitchen.

I took a sip of the cold beer to clear my throat. "It's strange talking about this with you 'cause everyone knows my dad was no fan of yours."

"And I was no fan of his." His gaze was now even, controlled, only the muscle along his jaw pulsed once, twice. "But that's got nothing to do with you, Wes. Or with you and me." He lifted his glass in salute and drank.

I did the same. "I appreciate that." My pulse eased its tight, quick rhythm at last.

Finger swiped a hand across his chin. "My dad was no saint either. Definitely no hero to his club. He stood up for me in the ways he could, but I always wanted more from him."

"Yeah." I licked the whiskey off my lip. "Always more."

"My dad cheated on his wife with my mother. His wife and their kids wanted nothing to do with me, but he came back for me, saved me from a bad situation, and brought me to his MC. I grew up at the clubhouse, not with him at his house. Still, it was a way better situation. At the MC I was eating, going to school. I was safe.

"Did I want more from him? Fuck yeah, I did. Every time I saw him. Every time I didn't see him. Did I get it? No. Did I have to suck it up? I sucked it up. We spent some time together, and it was priceless to me. He was a simple man, and yet the things I learned from him have helped me over the years in intricate ways."

"What happened to him, if you don't mind me asking?"

"I was a little younger than you are now when I got kidnapped by the Smoking Guns. He had a heart attack when he heard. Didn't make it."

"That must have been rough on you when you got out."

"Changed everything. In an instant, all those little boy hopes I'd been hanging onto for so long vanished."

"Little boy hopes...yeah..." I knocked back more whiskey.

He downed another shot. "That's when I knew that all I had was me. That I could stand up on my legs and claim what I wanted for myself. And I wanted better, I knew there was better out there for me, and I couldn't sit tight and hope no more. I had to go get it."

"I hear that."

"I figured whatever my father had given me—his practical smarts, his puny measures of love and support, even his inability to be the man I wanted him to be—that's what I had. And I finally, finally felt thankful for what I had and for him. All that became a bridge from disappointment to opportunity."

"And you crossed that bridge?"

He let out a short laugh. "I did, literally. This old narrow iron suspension bridge over the Missouri. Never forget it. Crossed over it on my bike to a new life on my own."

"You made peace with him. With yourself." I stared into my whiskey. "With all of it."

"What is it, Wes?"

"I found out some new stuff about my dad, and it's reeling me back into all that old shit all over again. That anger, that resentment. Making me question everything, making me…" I pressed my lips together. "I thought I'd put all that to rest."

"Or you've only been pushing it down, out of sight? Trust me, Wes, I get bitterness and revenge. I do. It's fueled me over the decades, but it doesn't own me. Not anymore. That anger and revenge still boiling inside you?"

"That I laid to rest. The men responsible for his death got served justice thanks to you and Butler, and I'm good with that."

He brought the whiskey to his lips and drained his glass. "Then what's boiling inside you? Something is."

"Regret," tumbled from my lips, and my insides quaked at the truth that hurtled from my soul.

He leaned back in his chair. "You need to make a change, son —and I'm not talking about the paint color on your bike, or moving to another town. Or some pretty girl. I'm talking core, deep down. And no one can do that for you but you."

I dug a hand in my hair. "I think seeing Lindy again reminded me of the shitty choices I'd made, of all the crazy back then, and how I've done nothing much about moving forward since. She sees it. My mom. Butler too. I know I don't ever want to be that cruel, selfish asshole blinded by anger, or the guy who's laying low because of doubts and regrets."

"Wes—" A raw urgency in his growly voice had my muscles tightening at attention. "Make your bridge out of what your father gave you along with your own vision 'cause that's what you got. May be good, may be dark, doesn't matter. Bright spot, your mother is a hell of a strong, straightforward woman, and you got Butler and the Jacks in your corner. All of that is the truth of who you are, and that's powerful. You want better? Use it and cross that bridge."

"I do want better. For me. And for Lindy."

He cleared his throat and his back straightened. He seemed even taller. "Lindy's dad isn't around, so I'm going to step up here. She's a good kid who's had to do a hell of a lot of growing up real fast over the years. Responsible, tough on the outside, and a good girl on the inside. Doesn't play games, was never one of the reckless young ones you had to keep your eye on."

"That's not Lindy, never was."

He tapped a finger on the table. "Lindy is under my protection now. I'm responsible for her, and I take that responsibility very seriously. Which means you do not fuck with her."

My pulse jerked. "I'm not fucking with her."

"But you did fuck with her once."

"I did. Now I want to help her."

"By seducing her in the two minutes that she's been in Meager?"

My face flared with heat. "Uh…Lindy and I…"

"Lindy and you WHAT?" His lips curled into that harsh snarl and his thick brows jumped on his face.

"Lindy and I got chemistry. Always have. But now it's different…now it's—"

"It's what?"

"Brutally honest."

Ain't that the fucking truth?

His lips twisted under his mustache. He didn't expect that

reply, and I didn't either. Finger drew himself up taller. "Right now, Lindy needs to be focused and clear-headed, not distracted by chemistry with a smooth-talking boy who only wants one thing from her."

"I'm not a boy, and that's not what this is." I raised my voice.

His head tilted. "Then what the fuck did I walk in on, Wes?"

"Us getting carried away…with our chemistry."

He broke out into loud peals of hoarse, raw laughter. I grit my teeth, the heels of my boots digging into the floor. "Ah, Wes, I know what it is to burn for a woman, and I know what it is to have a hunger for revenge burn in your veins. They can be two sides of the same fucking coin."

"This is about helping a good woman I owe so much to, a woman who deserves her father back safe and sound. A woman who is suffering. I care about Lindy." I sucked in a breath. "That same day in Deadwood, when Butler figured it all out and shook sense into me, those two men came for us on the road, and Lindy and Pick showed up and saved our hides."

He dragged his fingers through his long beard. "That was when Butler had his heart attack?"

"He'd collapsed on the ground after all the shooting was done. Jesus, I'll never forget it. Pick doing CPR on him, Lindy calling 9-1-1. I…I…fucking lost it." My voice had gotten lower.

"You'd just lost your dad, for fuck's sake." That tense muscle along his jaw flexed again.

I swallowed the last of the cold beer, my grip tightening around the damp can. "I was so grateful my dad and his brothers taught me how to use a gun and that I had it on me that day, and so grateful that Butler survived, that Pick shot them down. In all that dark insanity, there was a flicker of light, and that light was Lindy."

"Your guardian angel. Your angel of mercy."

"She was, yes," My back straightened. "A true angel of mercy. And that gave me this new sense of hope that I've never forgotten." I scrunched the metal can. "And even more fucking guilt." How had I finally expressed what I'd been feeling, and to Finger of all people on this planet? I met his gaze and swallowed hard past the stubborn knot of emotion still stuck in my throat. "And now, she's going through this hell? I have to help her."

"You feel obligated."

"I *need* to help her. I want to."

He leaned back from the table, studying me, and my pulse loudly banged in my veins under the weight of that heavy glare. In the tense silence, acid poured into every nook and cranny of my being.

"Finger, me and Lindy…it isn't only some attraction I can't get enough of. It is that too, but—"

Finger's lips curved. "Wes, you ever been in love before?"

"No."

"Hits you like a train. A train that keeps rolling over you and hurtles you down the track along with it. You got no choice in the matter."

I let out a nervous laugh. "Sounds like you know what you're talking about."

"I do know." That crooked grin broke across his lips once more. "Still on that train. Never want to get off."

EIGHTEEN

LINDY

MY HEART JAMMED in my chest, and I clamped a hand over my mouth, stifling the cry that welled there as I huddled in the hallway.

The last thing I ever thought I'd witness was Wes and Finger having a heart-to-heart conversation. Wes confessing his sins, and the two of them discussing their less-than-stellar experiences with their dads. Discussing me.

Wes's feelings for me.

Brutally honest chemistry

I need to help her. I want to.

His words vibrated through me.

In all that dark insanity, there was a flicker of light, and that light was Lindy.

Wes truly cared. About Dad. About me. About *us.*

Holy. Shit.

Even his voice had gone fragile as he spoke with Finger. Earnest, full of yearning and heartache.

The chemistry between us was brutally real. The fire between us ignited so easily. If Finger had walked in a minute later, he would've found us on the way to my bedroom.

Loud, long scraping of the kitchen chairs across the tiled floor filled the air, and my spine straightened against the wall. Manly mumbling. The front door opened in that squeaky way it had when it reached its arc limit. Wes was leaving. I hightailed it up the stairs to my room.

Sitting down at the small desk covered with cosmetics, I stared at my reflection. Wetting a cotton round with Micellar water, I dragged it across my skin. The foundation, the eyeshadow, the eyeliner, concealer, contour, bronzer, blush, powder vanished with every swipe. I let out a breath as I took in my bare face in the mirror. No masks, no veils. No bravado. No camouflage.

Only me.

The me I could share with Wes.

When Finger had walked in on us, Wes hadn't muttered some dumb excuse or lie and taken off. He'd requested a sit down to state his case, and I'd been rendered speechless. Blown away.

There was something old-fashioned and gentlemanly about it that made my pulse pick up speed. And so fucking brave, too.

Wes had bared his soul to Finger of all people. He wanted to prove to him that he wasn't flirting with me or taking advantage but that he and I had a history—which he didn't gloss over either. Wes stated his case of sincere regret and genuine sincerity to the judge, and Finger honored his effort with respect. He'd listened, even shown interest in Wes.

From the get-go, Finger had waded in like a protective father would. Goosebumps prickled over my flesh all over again, like when I'd heard his accusations, his demand for explanations from Wes. My eyes filled with water, and my chest whirled with warmth. I had support. I had people around me who cared about me and showed it.

I'd never felt comfortable with Finger and the Flames. Mom

and Dad and I were Blades, and we never expected that would change, not ever. And yet everything had changed for us in a snap, like a tornado that blows through your town overnight and destroys every single house leaving nothing but rubble behind. That's life's random chaos, of our lives especially, and we dealt with it, we adapted, or we died. Over and over again.

My phone beeped. A text from Wes.

All good. Talk soon :)

That flutter went off in my chest again, but this time it twirled and gently floated through me. I sent him back a bunch of smile emojis.

Now it was my turn to face the daddy music. I smoothed my hair back into a tight knot and headed to the kitchen.

Finger glanced at me as he put a bottle of whiskey in a cabinet.

"Finger, I'm sorry about what you walked in on before." My skin heated like a forest fire in August. "That wasn't appropriate."

"I appreciate the sentiment." He closed the cabinet. "You two seeing each other now?"

I grabbed the glasses from the table and put them in the dishwasher. "We're spending time together."

"As long as you like spending time with him."

"I do."

He wiped his hands on a towel and tossed it on the counter. "Wes told me all about your past relationship and assured me that on this go-round his intentions are not false." He tucked the two empty beer cans into the recycling bin. "But it's up to you."

"Thank you for standing up for me." I went to the sink, wet the microfiber towel and added a bit of dish soap, and wiped down the table. "I also wanted you to know that I'm grateful to you and Lenore for having me at your home. I don't take it for granted and would never take advantage of your generosity."

He dipped his head as he curled his fingers in his beard. "Got to admit, it was fun seeing the panicked look on Wes's face when I confronted him about what he was up to with you. I missed out on the Dad thing, so I enjoyed it." A smirk slashed his lips, and I let out a laugh.

The sound of Lenore's car rolling up the driveway had us turning. The front door blew open, and Lenore and Zoë burst into the kitchen.

"Hey, there are my girls," Finger exclaimed.

Zoë rammed straight into Finger's chest and hugged him. "Hi."

"Zo." His arms were tight around his daughter, and he kissed the top of her head. The child he and Lenore didn't get the chance to raise. The daughter they both adored.

Lenore had told me the whole story. With the Smoking Guns on her trail, she had found out she was pregnant and then Finger had gotten arrested and sent to prison. The second she'd found out that their unborn baby had Down Syndrome, she'd made the heartbreaking decision to give her up so that she'd be safe and have the healthcare she needed.

Tania had helped her find a new home for the baby, and that home happened to be in Pine Needle, the next town over from Meager. Many years later, that had brought Lenore to move to Meager. Once Finger and Lenore got back together, she told Finger about Zoë, and they were able to forge a relationship with her and her adoptive parents.

"Zoë's staying for dinner tonight." Lenore threw off her embroidered jean jacket and kissed her husband. They both gave each other a deep, warm grin.

I clapped my hands together. "Great news because it's home-made pizza night. I got lots of pepperoni and mozzarella yesterday."

"My favorite!" shouted out Zoë.

"Mine too," I said.

"Lindy, after pizza can we do makeup?" Zoë's cheeks flushed

pink as she waited for my reply, and Finger let out a hoarse laugh, shaking his head.

"Of course we can."

———

Zoë, Lenore, and I made the pizzas while Finger fielded phone calls on his cell phone in the living room. His responses on the calls were a series of grunts and cryptic phrases, so I had no idea if any of these calls were about my dad.

We ate, cleaned up, and then I took Zoë to my room so that I could give her a makeover. She was fascinated by all the products I had. She touched almost every single bottle, container, compact, and brush. Each one was a great exotic mystery and source of delight to her.

"How about shimmery blue eyes?" I said. "What do you think?"

"Shimmery, yes."

"And bright pink on your cheeks?"

Her eyes bugged out. "Lenore's new blush?"

"Here it is…" I opened the package with dramatic flair, and she let out a sigh of wonder as she admired the bright pink blush. "And we could try this new glow serum primer and a highlighter too if you want? You want to get your glow on, Zoë?"

"I want all the glow."

"Sit here, please, Miss." I patted the armchair, and she sat. I set up my small ring light to see what I was doing and to give Zoë the social media influencer feel, which I knew she loved. She sat up straighter and, leaning toward the mirror, peered at her reflection from every angle possible. I dabbed the glow serum primer on her skin.

"Lenore said you don't have a sister or a brother."

"That's right."

"I used to not have a brother. Now I have Beck." She pointed at the poster on the wall of Beck and his rock band, Freefall, onstage at a concert in Berlin last year. "I love my brother. I'm so glad that he and Violet have their own house here. It's so pretty, like a great big dollhouse. I go swimming in their pool, and we cook together in their big kitchen. I'm good at stirring sauces."

"That sounds amazing."

"Are you sad that you don't have a brother or sister?"

"I can't say that I am because I don't know what it's like to have a brother or sister, so I don't miss it. You see what I mean?"

She nodded. "You and me can be sisters. And then Violet can be your sister too and Beck could be your brother. If you want?"

"That sounds nice." I blended the contour on the edge of her forehead with a soft, dense brush. "I already feel like we're sisters. Here I am staying in your room."

"Which used to be Beck's room. See? We're all connected."

"We are. And you and me and Lenore do chores together, play with makeup together. Go shopping. Like mommies and daughters and sisters do." Something caught in my chest and fisted there. "I like that a lot." I swallowed hard as I blended the contour under her cheekbones.

"Where's your mommy, Lindy?"

"My mommy died." I switched to using a damp beauty blender sponge.

Her lips parted, and her small hand reached out and touched my arm. "You miss her?"

"I do, very much." Blinking, I turned away and busied myself with choosing a blush brush.

"You used to do makeup with her?"

"We did. She loved makeup too. We did makeovers on each other all the time." My heart expanded with the memories as I dabbed excess blush powder on the back of my hand. "You're so lucky you have two mommies."

She grinned deeply. "And two daddies."

"That's a lot of hugs all the time, Zoë."

"When does your daddy come home from his trip? Finger

goes on lots of business trips too. I guess this time your daddy went far, far away?"

"Mm-hmm." Sucking in a breath, I focused all my energy on gently patting the blush on her cheek, otherwise, I would burst.

"He'll be back soon," Zoë said softly.

"He sure will." I shot her a quick smile as I grabbed the highlighter compact.

He will. He will. He will.

Earlier today at the store, I'd called Minty and played it like I'd called to say hello.

"Sorry I haven't checked in with you sooner, Minty. Everything's still new to me here. I'm keeping busy, but I've been out of it. I've been such a dip lately, you know what I mean?

I'd heard his breath catch over the line, then a split-second pause before he smoothly replied: *"Yeah, Lindy-loo, no worries. Good to hear from you."*

My eyes had shut tight at his words, a sting racing through my veins. He'd used my parents' nickname for me, a nickname that the Blades would call me when I was a little girl, the only little girl at the club at the time, among the sons of the families. Dad and Minty had stopped calling me Lindy-loo a long, long time ago.

Minty had gotten the message about the Dip.

"And when your daddy comes back, he'll bring you back a present!" Zoe's enthusiastic declaration brought me back to the here and now.

I let out a tight laugh as I dabbed highlighter on her upper cheek. "You're right. He always does. Last year, he went to Idaho and brought me back this necklace." I pointed to the silver charm hanging from a chain around my neck that I never took off.

"An angel? So pretty! Her wings are soooo big."

"I love that about her. She can fly high and protect everyone she loves." I patted finishing powder under her eyes and over her cheeks, around her nose.

"So Wes came over before?" Zoë glanced at me and closed her eyes again as I brushed her skin.

Finger had mentioned it to Lenore over dinner, and she and Zoë had stared at me, expecting a story, but instead of talking, I'd only nodded and shoved a slice of pepperoni with olives and extra cheese in my mouth.

"He did."

"Wes is cute."

"He is."

"Do you like him? You know—*like, like*?"

"Wes and I have been friends for a long time. Since we were in high school."

Her eyes popped open. "Were you boyfriend and girlfriend?"

"We were, for a little bit."

Her face lit up. "Wow."

"It's nice to see him again now that we're all grown up."

Her eyes widened. "You're boyfriend and girlfriend again?"

"We're friends."

She slumped in the chair. "Awww…"

"What's wrong?"

"If you were together once, why can't you be together again? Now?"

"Zo, things change, people change, they want different things. Sometimes it's better to go your separate ways."

Her lips parted. "But where do all those feelings go? How do they go away? You don't like him anymore? How can you not like him?" She raised her voice. "He's so handsome and funny and—"

"Zoë, shhh. It's okay." I rubbed her arm, and her shoulders dropped, her lips twisted. "I like him, and he likes me. And we'll see what happens."

The smile sweeping her face filled my soul, and I let out a laugh.

"Eyeshadow time. Close your eyes for me a sec." She closed them, and with my finger I gently dabbed a sparkly blue cream eyeshadow on her eyelids. Her lips pulled into a stiff line, and her cheeks puffed. Zoë was working hard to stay still for me.

"Okay, open." We both studied her reflection in the mirror.

"Oooo." She leaned her head against mine, hugging me tightly. A gesture of joy, of gratitude. Of intimacy.

Where do all those feelings go?

I wrapped my arm around her tightly. "Can I tell you a secret, Zoë?"

"What secret?" Her voice squeaked.

"You have to be quiet, and you can't tell anyone. It's between you and me only."

"I promise."

"My feelings for Wes never went away, never stopped." I tapped my chest over my angel necklace. "They're in here."

"See?" She gently touched the angel charm like it was precious to her too. "Those feelings stay, if they're true." Her arms shot up in the air. "Yay!"

"Shh."

"Shh." She giggled uncontrollably, and so did I.

Using my soft makeup remover cloth, I swiped at the residual smudges at the edge of her eyes. "You think that's a good thing?"

"Oh yes, it is. Can I tell you something now?" She motioned with her hand for me to come closer, and I leaned into her. "Wes goes out with girls who are pretty and all that, but I can tell they aren't special to him, like Violet is to Beck, like Lenore is to Finger. Like Mommy is to Daddy. I can tell. He probably just likes to kiss them and stuff."

"Zoë!" I burst out into laughter, even though images of Wes kissing other girls made my insides pinch together.

"Beck and Violet always tell Wes that he deserves a good woman," said Zoë.

"He does."

"You're a good woman, Lindy."

"Thank you, honey."

"Beck found Violet, and now it's Wes's turn. You're good and pretty and smart. And you're already his friend *and* his girlfriend. And now you're here, and you're part of our family, see?" She tilted her head at me. "One big perfect circle."

My heart thundered in my chest at her easy assessment. Zoë, this gentle vibrant soul who believed in true love and a loving family. Who believed in "perfect."

I believed that once too, Zoë. I want to again.

I hugged her, and she sighed. "I like having a sister."

"Me too," I whispered, emotion filling my voice. I showed her the container filled with lipsticks and lip glosses. "What lipstick should we go for tonight?" I chose one. "What about this peachy nude? It's been going viral on TikTok."

She waved it away, shaking her head emphatically. "I want Lenore's new dark red lipstick." A sample of the new shade had arrived today and Lenore had showed it to Zoë after dinner.

"You wild girl. Are you sure?"

Zoë nodded her head emphatically. "I want to look glamorous and hot like my sister."

NINETEEN

LINDY

"Lindy? That you?"

I stopped moving, my grip tightening on the window wiper in my hand. I'd never forget that voice. Ever.

Zac, Wes's friend from the old days, stood there gawking at me as I cleaned the windows of Lenore's Lace before opening. I glanced at him. He wore a jacket and shirt and tie with khakis and loafers. And that flippant smirk of his. "What are you doing here?"

I wiped the window dry in long strokes. "Working."

"Here in Meager? At the lingerie store? You modeling here or…"

"Are you modeling?" I sprayed cleaner on the next section of glass. Unfortunately, he didn't move away, didn't walk past. My muscles tightened under his inspection.

He let out a too-loud laugh. "I'm an accountant now. I work at a company in Rapid—"

"Don't care."

"You look…amazing."

"You sound amazed."

He let out a short laugh. "I am. Full of amazement and awe." His voice drawled. The arrogant shit was flirting with me.

"You're full of crap, and I'm real busy. Good-bye."

"Aw come on, don't be cold with me, Lindy. We used to be friends, didn't we?"

"No, we were never friends."

Grinning, he sauntered in closer to me. "We should go out sometime, catch up, hang out."

"Why would I do that? I don't like you. Never have."

He chuckled, almost shrugged, his hand wiping down his navy blue tie. "Liking" each other didn't matter. What he was after, as ever, was to get laid.

He cleared his throat. "After that night, I called you so many times, but you never called me back."

I wiped down the window in long strokes.

"I wanted to make sure you were okay."

"Fuck off. You lit the match and walked away laughing."

"That's not the way it was. I laid out the truth about Wes at your feet. You saw him that night with his girlfriend. You wouldn't believe me, so I had to show you. That must have been some shock, but you don't have to take it out on the messenger. Wes is the one who blew up your world, not me. I was honest with you—" His hand flattened against his chest.

"Honest? You had a big plan for us that day in Deadwood, didn't you?"

"Come on, that was…boys being boys."

I stilled, my lungs crushing together. "Of course, you said that."

He pointed a finger at me. "After he blew you off without a word, I was the one being understanding. Wes was the cold-hearted liar."

Fierce winds gathered in my chest, whipping together into a tornado. "You offering me revenge sex after I saw him with that girl was you being understanding?"

"It was an opportunity to get him but good, but no reply…" A grin twitched his lips.

My fingers tightened around the neck of the liquid cleaner bottle. "I missed out, huh?"

"Fuck yeah you did. But we could have some real fun now." His teeth dragged against his bottom lip. "You don't look like that spooked virgin anymore, so—"

I lunged at him, the bottle soaring, my fist flying, landing on his face. He howled as pain exploded through my hand. The plastic bottle spun on the sidewalk at my feet.

An arm snapped around my waist, hauling me backward. "Hey!" shouted Bear, the huge One-Eyed Jack who was my protector of the day.

"What the fuck is wrong with you?" Zac's hand covered his eye as he gasped for air, coughing. "You crazy bitch!"

"You've always been nothing but a cheap bully!" I launched at him again, but got heaved and landed in someone else's grip. Wes.

"Who the hell is this joker?" growled Bear, his hand on Zac's chest, holding him back.

"Who the fuck are you?" Zac screeched, hopping on his toes. "Don't touch me! I'll sue you for assault." Zac blinked at me and Wes, his face splotched with red, his tie crooked. "Are you two together again?"

"You still talking?" ground out Wes.

"Stay away from us, you rotten piece of shit." My hands cuffed Wes's arm, which remained firm around my middle. Steady and sturdy. I pressed into the wall of his body, and his grip on me tightened.

Bear let go of Zac. "Keep moving."

Wiping at his mouth, Zac glared at me. "You're nothing but a trashy cu—"

Wes lunged at him, a hand at his shirt collar, pulling, twisting, shaking him. Bear stepped back and caught me with his heavy arm.

"Not one word more, you fuck. Not. One," shouted Wes. "Do not even look at her. Not ever. You hear me?" Lips curling, he shoved him, and Zac stumbled back. "Move the fuck on, man!"

"Don't talk to either one of them again, you hear?" Bear growled at Zac. "Now move!"

"Fucking low-life white trash bikers."

"Who you calling white trash, asshole?" I yelled.

"All of you! And him—" his voice seething, he gestured at Wes. "Sure, now he's playing the white knight, but he's nothing but a pussy! Tried to back out of our plan at the last minute, 'cause he felt bad. Fucking idiot, ruined everything. Would've been so good. We were going to pop all your cherries, Lindy. I was—"

Wes flew, his arm swinging. In a flash, Bear grabbed him back with one hand and shoved at Zac with his other. "Shut your foul mouth, you little fuck!" He shook Zac like a sack of beans.

My lungs squeezed tightly in my chest. Wes had changed his mind. Wes had said no. He'd said no.

Zac smoothed back his hair and adjusted his waistband, an ugly scowl searing his bruised face. "You two deserve each other, you know that?"

Ignoring Zac, my arm slid around Wes's torso, and he pulled me in tightly alongside his body. Casting us a final acidic glare as he spouted curses under his breath, Zac tracked down the sidewalk, shaking his head.

"What a fucking shit," muttered Bear.

Wes pressed me deeper into his side. "You okay?"

My gaze locked on his like a magnet, and heat blasted through my veins. Wes was no longer the legend in my teenage mind—not the knight in shining armor, not the ruthless villain. He was a man. A man who felt passionately and deeply, a man who made mistakes and bore regrets. The man I craved.

My hands went to his jaw, and raising up on my toes, I brushed my lips against his, and a moan uncoiled in his throat, matching mine. We held each other, kissing fiercely, kissing gently.

There on Clay Street in broad daylight, in the heart of Meager, we kissed like it was the beginning of something new, something that would last forever.

Only in my world, nothing lasted forever.

TWENTY

LINDY

"Thank you, Susanne. You enjoy it." Lenore handed the woman the purple Lenore's Lace shopping bag.

"Oh, I will."

When she'd come into the store earlier, Susanne had told us that she had been saving money for several months to be able to buy the lacy nightgown she'd fallen in love with, and along with a nice discount from Lenore, it was finally hers. A divorcée in her early forties, Susanne had recently remarried, and to her high school boyfriend. The joy and satisfaction on her face were obvious.

"Thank you, Lenore. My first purchase from your boutique. Won't be my last."

I opened the door for her. "Goodbye, Susanne."

"Bye, Lindy, thanks."

As she stepped outside, my gaze landed across the street on my and Lenore's Flames of Hell protector of the week, Cueball. Bald with big, dark aviator shades hiding his eyes, he stood sipping on a soda and smoking a cig like he had been all morning, slumped against a wall. He lifted his chin at me, and I nodded back.

I returned to the back corner of the shop, where I'd been setting up a new display of lingerie robes for the past half an hour.

The front bell on the door rang, and I turned my head. Jimmy, our courier delivery guy from Rapid. "Hello, my fair ladies!" he sang out as he entered the shop with a box in hand.

"Hey you," said Lenore, grinning from behind the cash register where she was going over paperwork.

"Hi, Jimmy." I dropped what I was doing and moved through the shop toward him.

Jimmy and I had become pals since I'd arrived in Meager as we frequently got packages at the store.

"Today, I got a little something for you, Lindy." He held up the small square box. Had to be the new multi-chrome eyeliners that I'd ordered with express shipping from one of my favorite indie brands.

"Hooray!" I let out a laugh as I signed the digital screen on his handheld device, and he gave me the box. "Thank you."

"You bet. Good day, ladies."

"Bye, Jimmy," Lenore and I both chimed as he headed out the door and crashed into Wes, who entered the shop. My skin heated at the sight of him filling the doorway, towering over Jimmy.

Wes put a hand on the older man's shoulder. "Hey, Jimmy, sorry."

"Aw, Wes, you're so eager to see the ladies that you're not watching where you're going?"

"Something like that." Wes laughed as he stepped aside for Jimmy to exit. "Have a good one."

"You too." Jimmy left.

"Hey there. How can I help you today?" I asked. "Perhaps you'd be interested in our new line of mens' pajamas?"

"Sell it, girl," laughed Lenore.

"No pajamas today. But I was curious about your thong underwear?" Grinning, he winked at me, and my insides twisted with heat. "Kidding. I got off work from the shop, and before I headed to the club for my shift at Eagle Wings, I thought I'd drop by and… say hi."

I grinned back at him. A goony grin, my heartbeat jumping wildly. "Hi."

"You good since seeing asswipe this morning?"

"I'm good."

"Good."

We both laughed softly.

He tapped on the box in my hands. "Jimmy brought you a package?"

"I was about to open it."

"Is it more thong underwear?"

"I don't need anymore. I've got a great selection already."

"You do, huh?"

"I do. This has to be some makeup I ordered."

"Allow me—" he pulled out a Swiss Army knife that was attached to his keys, and taking the box from me, slashed at the tape on the seams. "There you go."

"Thank you kindly, sir." Taking the box, I peeled open the flaps. Paper was stuffed inside, and a bleach odor rose from it. A prickle raced around my neck as I pulled back the flap with the address label. My name and this address in handwritten block letters. No return address. My pulse picked up as I opened the flaps again and plucked the paper stuffing out of the way. My stomach flew up my throat and jammed there. My heart stopped. I froze.

Everything froze.

No.

No.

NO.

Acid flooded my mouth, my insides jerked, and sinking to the floor, I retched.

"Lindy?" Wes's shout came from far away. "Lindy!"

A low, keening sound pulled from me. A biting cold liquid crept through my veins. Everything blurred, everything except for the image of—

"Daddy…"

Wes lifted me up from the floor and leaned my back against the love seat. "Lind? It's okay. I'm right here." His gaze hardened as he pried the box from my ice-cold hand. "Jesus Christ."

"Holy shit," Lenore exclaimed from somewhere above me.

"Lenore, call your Flame outside," said Wes.

My body shuddered, cold prickles racing over my flesh. Mind blank. Numb.

I was being lifted and settled on the loveseat. "Feet up 'til the dizziness passes." Wes wiped the damp hair from my face.

The room tilted again. "Daddy…Daddy…"

"It's okay, baby. Hang on for me."

In the distance, I heard Lenore talking, but I could barely make out the words. Only the image of my father's cut-off middle finger in that box flared through me over and over and over again.

They cut my father's finger off.

His middle finger. Just like Finger.

This had to be the Smoking Guns. The same club that had kidnapped Finger a long time ago and tortured him, cutting off both his middle fingers. The Guns and the Flames had been enemies since the early 70s.

My brain functioned like an out of whack factory machine. The Flames had taken over the Broken Blades out from under the Smoking Guns, and now my father was caught in the fucking crosshairs of their legendary and unrelenting symphony of animosity. Were they using Dad to send Finger a message of hate and scorn and revenge?

Now we knew what happened to Dad. We finally knew.

The door flew open. "What the fuck?" Cueball locked the door behind him.

I shielded my eyes from the afternoon sun pouring through the front display window as if I was a vampire who agonized in the light. I was cold everywhere, so cold.

Lenore handed him the box and tapped on her phone again. "Baby?" She'd called Finger.

Wes handed me an open water bottle, and I only stared at it. He brought it to my lips and tipped it. I gulped down the cool water, so hard, so fast, that a lot of it spewed from the sides of my mouth, streaming down my shirt. I brought it to my forehead. "We gotta find him. We gotta find him."

"We will, sweetheart." His voice had softened and the gentleness of it, of him, flooded my veins.

Cueball returned to me. "Sorry, Lindy, but I got to ask—you sure it's his?"

"I'm sure." I gritted out, my stomach rolling. "My mother's name is tatted on the side."

"Ah, shit." Cueball's phone rang, and my body tightened at the loud, jarring sound.

Bringing my knees to my chest, I hugged myself. "He got that tattoo when I was born. And he got my name inked on his other middle finger."

Wes sat down next to me and took me in his arms.

Cueball's and Lenore's voices blended into a cacophony of terse words, firing away in the small store, ricocheting around me.

A bang erupted on the front door, and Cueball darted over, unlocking it. An angry One-Eyed Jack flew into the shop, long dark hair flying. Boner. He glanced at me as Cueball led him to the desk and he examined that foul box of evil.

Lenore came over to me, a hand on my cheek. "Honey, you doing okay?"

"This has got the Smoking Guns written all over it, doesn't it?"

"Yeah."

"I've been called back in to the Flames." Cueball eyed Lenore. "Plans are being made."

"You go on, man," said Boner. "I'm here to take Lindy to the Jacks clubhouse."

"You are?" Wes stood.

I wiped at my face. "What? Why?"

"I'm going to Nebraska with Cueball. I need to be with my old man," Lenore said. "You can come with us or stay with the Jacks?"

"Lindy..." Wes's hand pressed into my back.

I swallowed past the dry dirt in my throat. Again, everything was changing quickly, rapidly, at a breathless pace, and I was racing to keep up. "Where does our prez want me?" I asked Lenore.

A small smile tugged on her lips. "Here with the Jacks while our men do what they got to do."

"I'll go to the Jacks then."

Lenore darted to the counter and swiftly packed her tote bag. "I'll call Mary Lynn and Tania and let them know you'll be there."

"Okay." My heart sped up in my chest, watching her prepare to clear out. "How long will I have to stay there?"

"We gotta see how this plays out, Lindy." Boner's jaw tightened. "Get your stuff, let's go."

Wes held out his hand and I took it. I got my jean jacket from the back and my oversized suede hobo bag, a precious hand-me-down from Lenore.

Grabbing me, Lenore gave me a fierce hug. My senses seeped in her aromatic fragrance, committing it to memory because that scent was about all the new goodness in my life. A new friend, a good job, new home. An older woman I could confide in, laugh with, learn from. "Text me when you're settled in over there, okay, Lindy?"

"I will. You text me when you get to the clubhouse."

Her warm hand cradled the side of my face. "I will, honey.

We got this. Wes, you look out for my girl."

"I will," replied Wes, his voice steely as he took my hand in his again and led me out the door.

Outside, the sun's glare had me wincing, and I fished out my sunglasses and put them on. Lenore locked up the shop and she and Cueball, who held the fucking box from hell, charged across the street.

"I'm parked at the end of the block," said Boner. "Where are you, Wes? I'm guessing you want to take Lindy."

"You bet I do. My bike's down here on the corner. I'll follow you."

I moved like a freshly-created zombie between the two men. Stumbling and ungainly, struggling to make sense of the outside world. Shouts and laughter raced around us on the sidewalk and had me cringing. Mothers strolling with baby carriages, teenage girls on their cell phones, laughing. Wes slid his arm around me, pulling me in close to his side.

"Meet me at the light." Boner gestured at the lone traffic light in Meager and kept walking toward his bike.

"Got it," said Wes as we turned the corner. He took my bag from my stiff grip and packed it in a saddlebag on his bike. His eyes narrowed at me. "You good to ride, Lind?"

Lifting my chin, I took in a deep breath as I slid on my jacket. "Always good to ride."

———

I'D NEVER BEEN to the One-Eyed Jacks clubhouse before, which was on a property tucked in the woods northwest of Meager. The crisp scent of the evergreens filled my senses as we rode through a new gate over a winding road which finally opened to a wide clearing. Wes pulled up to a renovated old factory with vintage Depression era touches enclosed by a high fence in the distance. Loads of bikes and vehicles filled the parking lot. The famed Eagle Wings Detailing & Repair shop where Wes also worked stood on the other end of the property from the clubhouse.

As Wes shut down his bike, I detached the helmet and rubbed at my blurry eyes. I had entered Jacksland where Wes had grown up. Something stung inside my chest. He was lucky. He'd never had to move with his club from rickety abandoned houses and motels to shoddy warehouses, from one crappy town to the next, sometimes wondering when his next meal would be as he grew up. That's how it had been for the Blades in my early years. Later, they'd finally settled down and had even acquired their own property, and their own on-the-books business. But all of that was gone with the damn wind now, wasn't it?

The ride here had been refreshing and reviving, but as I steadied my feet on the ground once more, I felt more like I'd stepped off a space ship and onto an alien planet. Above me, the club's logo of the skull with his gleaming eye glared at me, and my pulse thudded in my neck, that chill creeping over my flesh once more, swallowing me.

Boner waited for us at the main entrance. What lay in there for me? Panic seized me, and my legs froze.

"Lindy?" Wes had his hands on my shoulders and shook me gently. "Lind? You okay?"

That forbidding and ominous Jacks skull gleamed down at me. Watching me. Warning me. I buried my face in Wes's chest, my nails digging into his leather jacket. "Don't let me go."

TWENTY-ONE

WES

"I GOT YOU, Lind. I got you."

I bound her with my body, squeezing her tight with everything I was. My hand dug in her hair, and the fruity scent of her shampoo filled my senses. A sweet, bright, innocent scent, so odd in the circumstances. But that was the Lindy I knew, wasn't it? I brushed the top of her head with a kiss. *I'll never let you go, Lind.* My resolve to protect her, be her refuge, fueled my veins.

Boner, arms crossed, waited for us at the entrance.

"You're safe here, Lind. I promise," I whispered in her ear. "Let me take you inside."

"Can you stay?" Her eyes peeked up at me, her voice fragile. "Can you stay here with me?"

My heart jacked in my chest. She wanted me to stay with her. "Of course I will." We followed Boner inside. My phone beeped in the back of my jeans. I read the text and slid my phone back in my pocket. "Lenore talked to my mom, and she'll be coming over later to bring you stuff you might need," I said to her as we entered the main lounge. "So don't worry about any of that now."

"That's nice," she murmured on a tight exhale.

"I'll be back." Boner headed to the office, and I steered Lindy over to the long bar in the empty central lounge, guiding her to a bar stool. Her face was pale, her lips too.

I shot behind the bar. "What can I get you? We got everything here, from coffee to bourbon."

"No booze, not yet. Is there iced tea?"

"Coming up." I grabbed two bottles of lemon iced tea from the refrigerator and led her to a sofa. We drank, and I put a hand on her leg and squeezed. "Better?"

"Mmm."

Butler came out from the back offices with Boner, and the two of them stood over us. Butler's gaze shot from Lindy to me and Lindy. I knew what he was thinking. *What the hell are you doing?* And I didn't give a fuck. Lindy was hurting.

Butler crossed his arms. "Lindy, until we know what the Flames' plans are and whatever that is goes down, you'll stay here with us, so we can ensure your safety."

"Okay," Lindy replied.

"Sorry I can't be more specific, but when we do find out more, you'll be the first to know."

"Promise?"

"I promise, yeah." Butler lifted his chin in my direction. "And you? What are you up to?"

"I was on my way here for work, but popped by Lenore's Lace to say hi to Lindy, and that was when she got the delivery. Brought her here with Boner." My voice came off a little short and tight, and Butler's brow furrowed at my tone.

A grin slashed Boner's lips as he patted Butler on the arm. "You got this, don't you?"

"I got it all right."

"Welcome to the One-Eyed Jacks, Lindy," said Boner.

"Thanks, Boner," she said softly, and he left the lounge.

Butler cleared his throat. "So."

"So." I put my empty iced tea bottle on the table to my side with a clank as I met Butler's stiff gaze. "Can I get you an iced tea?"

"No thanks." Butler's jaw flexed. "You two hanging out again?"

"Yep." I slid an arm around Lindy's shoulders, and she leaned into me.

Butler let out a breath. "Yep."

"Is there a problem?" Lindy asked, her voice weary.

"Not at all." Butler shifted his weight.

Oh man, we were getting the parental examination of our status and intentions.

"It's nice to see the two of you friends again after all these years," Butler said.

Lindy attempted a small smile as she shot me a WTF-is-going-on look.

"Lindy, we got a room for you if you want to go there and relax or…something." Butler shot me a look, his tone colored with grim.

I sat up. "Which room?"

"Seven."

"Got it." I took Lindy's hand, her warm fingers curling around mine and we rose from the sofa. "I'll be staying here too until Lindy gets the all clear."

"Jesus," muttered Butler.

"I'm not leaving her on her own with you assholes."

Butler's eyebrows furrowed. "Respect, young one."

"My apologies. Still staying." I led Lindy away from Butler toward the hallway for the bedrooms.

"Hey! Did you ask Lindy if she wanted you to stay?"

Lindy squeezed my hand and tugged on my arm, stopping me in my tracks. "I want him to stay," she said. "If that's okay?"

"Entirely up to you," replied Butler.

Her gaze met mine and it bore a hole through me. Steady and resolute. "I'd like him to stay."

Butler only dipped his head in reply.

"We good now?" I asked him.

"All good." Butler's face looked as stony as an eagle's. "Let Lock know what's going on, okay? Your shift already started." He headed outside.

"What was that about?" she whispered.

"He's being a dad, I guess."

"To you or me?"

I chuckled. "To both of us. Maybe I'll get another talking to later on."

Her attention went to our hands clasped together. "That's kinda nice."

I let out a breath. "It is."

"He cares."

"He does." I cleared my throat. "Let's go check out your penthouse suite, shall we?" I showed her to the room and opened the door. "Deluxe all the way, huh?"

We entered the small room. She placed her handbag on the simple wood dresser as she glanced at the queen sized bed. "Are the sheets clean, you think?" She let out a short laugh.

"The girls make sure everything is in top shape at all times."

"There are club girls here too, huh? The Flames have five or six of them. I think there's even a waiting list to be one."

"Here they only got two, Shannon and Lucy. Lucy works at Eagle Wings too. We should find them and introduce you." We both stared at the bed with its faded green bedspread and two puffy pillows, the pine headboard. My jaw tightened as my brain raced with images of me and Lindy on that bed. On that bed all night long curled up in each other, touching each other, moving together, making noise together...

My balls tightened. "I'm starving, how about you?"

She cleared her throat. "Me too."

———

Before we headed to the kitchen, Lindy and I went next door to Eagle Wings. We stepped into the bay area where the men were working on bikes.

"This place is legendary," Lindy said. "I've heard my dad and a lot of the Flames talk about it. They're in awe." Her gaze darted to all the vintage gas station signs, road signs, framed paintings of eagles, and the variety of American memorabilia that filled the walls. "How long have you been working here?"

"Since high school—cleaning up, that sort of thing, but then I started working with Lock, who's an amazing artist, on paint detailing, which has been a hell of an experience. Helped me figure out what I wanted to study in college,"

"What did you major in?"

"Graphic design. Got to say, wouldn't have happened without Butler and Lock on top of me from day one."

She stopped in her tracks, her eyes lighting up. "You're actually using what you studied at college in both your jobs? Jobs you actually like? Do you realize how lucky you are to have Lock and the guys here *and* Ronny and Trash Ink? Most people, I'd say 99%, never get to work in the profession they truly like and are good at. That's the dream. Not to mention have good mentors who genuinely care about them and their development."

I took in the two Harleys standing before us on which I'd done touch up work the past few weeks. The incredible Trans Am in the exterior bay whose detailing Lock and I had been brainstorming together. My chest swelled. "I am lucky."

"Hey, man."

I swiveled at the sound of Tricky's voice. "Hey Tricky, this is Lindy."

"Hey, Lindy. Pick's daughter, right?"

"That's me."

"Good to meet you—of course not under these circumstances." He and Lindy shook hands.

Lock, his long black hair up in a ponytail, moved through the bikes toward us. "There you are." His gaze flicked over Lindy, and her back straightened.

I introduced them. Lindy's hand shot out at Lock and took it on a grin. "Wes was just telling me how much he loves working here."

"Oh yeah?" He chuckled. "It'd be nice if he'd show up on time…"

"That's my fault. Today at least."

"Lindy's staying at the clubhouse until further notice. Boner and I brought her over. I'd like to help her settle in."

"Good man." Trick slapped my shoulder.

"Sorry to hear that, Lindy," murmured Lock, crossing his arms.

"If it's cool with you, I'll be in super early tomorrow morning to finish up on the two bikes."

"Make sure you do, because they need to be finished by noon."

"He'll be here," said Lindy.

"You need anything, Lindy, we're here. And usually my old lady Grace is in the office, but she left to pick up our son from school."

"Thank you."

Back in the clubhouse we headed to the kitchen, where we made ham and cheese sandwiches and ate at the long counter. I found a small bag of barbecue chips and we shared them as Shannon and Lucy came in. I introduced them to Lindy, and the girls started meal prepping for dinner as we talked.

"Baked ziti with meat sauce is on the menu tonight. You guys good with that?" asked Shannon.

"Awesome," I said.

"Sounds terrific," said Lindy. "Can I help you with—"

"We got this," said Lucy. "You get yourself settled in."

"Let me know what I can do," said Lindy.

"We will, thanks." Shannon shot her a smile.

Lindy and I played a round of pool with Dawes and Bear when the familiar sound of heels clapping on concrete had me turning.

"Hey, everybody!" my mother's voice boomed through the lounge, and everyone brightened as if the sun had broken through a cloudy sky.

"There's my number one girl." Bear grabbed Mom in a big hug, and she giggled, patting him on the back.

"How you doing, honey?"

"I'm good. You look fine, as evahhh."

"Why, thank you." Mom's eyes gleamed as she put down two big shopping bags. She missed this, being the club First Lady. The men still treated her special, which shot warmth through my veins. I liked that for her because I knew that it meant a great deal to my mother and always would. "We going to see y'all at the party at the shop tomorrow night?"

"Wouldn't miss it," said Bear.

They'd better not or she'd never let them forget it.

"Hey, Mom." I gave her a kiss on the cheek.

"Hi, baby." She launched at Lindy, hugging her. "I'm so sorry you're going through this, Lindy. How are you holding up?"

"I'm hanging in there."

"I have keys to Lenore's house so after she called me I went over and got some of your stuff. I hope you don't mind."

"Not at all. I appreciate it."

"I thought you'd like your own stuff rather than—"

"You were right." Lindy took a shopping bag, and I took the second one.

"I brought you the big cosmetics bag you had on the desk. I figured those were your daily go-to items."

Lindy smiled, the lines of her face easing. "They are, thanks."

"I also got you a bunch of mini water bottles and snacks for you to keep in your room. Hydration and chocolate are both very important."

"I totally agree."

"I wasn't sure what you liked, so I got a little bit of everything."

"Alicia, thank you."

"And I have a little surprise for you. I'd mentioned to Wes that I had photographs of the good ol' days when the Jacks would hang out with the Blades, and I found them." Mom pulled out a thick photo album from the tote bag on her arm. "This was from a weekend run where we'd camped out in the woods and there was a live concert. Lot of clubs were there, even the Flames of Hell. I thought you might enjoy seeing them."

Lindy's eyes popped open wide like she'd heard she'd won the lottery. "Alicia, thank you so much. This means a lot to me." Her eyes filled with water.

Something pinched in my chest. "Way to go, Mom."

"Keep in mind, it was over two decades ago, and things were a little wild back then. But I suppose that's relative…" Mom let out one of her wicked throaty laughs.

I chuckled. "Oh, this should be fun."

"I figure you're both club kids and over eighteen so you can handle it." She gave Lindy the album. "Are the girls making food or should I order something for you?"

"Everything's covered, Ma. We're cool."

Her eyebrows jolted. "Are you staying here? Because I don't want Lindy alone. She needs friends with her."

"I'm staying."

"Good." *I love this*, her firm voice told me as her gaze shot from me to Lindy, her face beaming with satisfaction. "Oh, and Lindy—being a mom here—don't forget to check in with Lenore. She's glad you're here, but worried about how you're doing. Have you called her since you got here?"

Lindy let out a gasp, her eyes widening. "Dang, I forgot. I'll do that now." She handed me the photo album and moved away from us as she tapped on her phone. "Lenore?"

An eyebrow arching, Mom moved closer to me.

I braced. "Mother, don't say it."

"Be good to her."

My back straightened. For the first time ever, Mom didn't recite her usual refrain of *You like her? I like her. She's pretty. Is this going somewhere?*

"Lindy deserves the best, Mom, not *good*."

A proud smile lit up my mother's gorgeous face and she hugged me, planting a kiss on my cheek. "Love you, baby—and I like her. Very much."

"I knew there was no escaping. Love you too, Mom. And thanks for finding these photos. Perfect timing."

"You're still coming to the party tomorrow? You have to be there."

"I wouldn't miss it."

"Good. You two need anything, any time, call me, call Ronny. Don't hesitate."

"Will do."

She blew me a kiss, and waving goodbye at Lindy, who was still on the phone, sashayed out of the lounge toward the exit. Bear caught up with her, throwing an arm around her shoulders, their laughter echoing from the hallway.

Lindy was still on the phone with Lenore, so I took the shopping bags and the photo album to her room. As I stepped back into the lounge, Shannon called out: "Dinner's on!"

Lindy and I went into the kitchen, along with the handful of guys who were around. Lindy already knew the men because they'd all taken turns guarding her around town, and everyone greeted her warmly. They all knew what had happened. Lindy played with her food but soon ate most of the pasta on her plate.

"Hey, Wes, that girl who works at Ronny's, the new one with the long black hair?" Dready asked.

"Jet?"

"Yeah, Jet." His face relaxed. "What's her deal? She got a man?"

"Not that I know of, but she goes out almost every night of

the week. Doesn't miss a beat. Better put your running shoes on."

"Will do." Dready winked at me.

"Speaking of—" I crunched on the ice from my soda. "You guys are coming to the party at the shop tomorrow night, right?"

"You bet," replied Bear.

"Course we are. We support our local businesses," said Dready. "Ronny's always done our tats way before he opened the shop in Meager. Plus, it's Alicia. No-brainer."

"Lenore had mentioned the party," said Lindy. "We were going to go."

"Lenore is our number one client and always comes to these shindigs of Mom's." I refilled Lindy's glass with water. "Guys, if the whole club's coming, can't Lindy come with?"

"We could make it work." Bear eyed Lindy. "But you up for a party, hon?"

Lindy's gaze snagged on mine, her teeth biting her luscious lower lip. "I'd like to go."

Bear put down his fork. "We'll all go to the party together, and then a few of us can come back early with Lindy. Of course, you're welcome to join us, Wes." He winked at me, and everyone laughed.

"Gee, thanks."

"It's a cocktail party, huh?" Jordy opened a bottle of beer. "That mean snacks are included?"

"Snacks, not a meal. You know my mom, every party detail is thought out. She's expecting a big crowd, so you can't be scarfing down all the food."

Everyone laughed, Lindy too.

We finished eating, and the girls, Jordy, Lindy, and I cleaned up. After, we headed to the lounge, where music played.

"I think I'd like that drink now." Lindy climbed onto a bar stool.

"You got it." I darted behind the bar and raised a whiskey bottle at her.

"Yes, please."

I poured out two glasses. "To clubhouse-ing."

Lindy let out a laugh and clinked my glass. "To clubhouse-ing." She swallowed down a gulp and shot me a soft grin. Warmth filled my veins at the sight. Although today had been insanely stressful for her, she now seemed somewhat at ease. She deserved to be.

Raising my glass at her, I drank. "Speaking of clubhouse-ing…." Bringing my fingers to my lips, I let out a sharp whistle. "Yo! Who wants a drink?"

The orders came in fast. I got the drinks ready, and Lindy served them to everyone, insisting Shannon and Lucy relax with the guys.

Lindy made colorful cocktail concoctions for Shannon and Lucy, complete with umbrellas that she'd found while digging through the shelves behind the bar. She served them up on a tray like the experienced waitress she was, and Shannon and Lucy shrieked with delight.

Jordy lowered the lights in the lounge, and I wiped down the bar. With a big grin on her rosy face that made my insides light up, Lindy returned and sat on a stool opposite me. "Everyone's good. For now at least." She slid her glass towards me. "Hit me again, barkeep."

I refilled both our glasses with whiskey and we drank, silence falling between us. I leaned over on the bar. "How you holding up, Lind? We haven't had a chance to talk yet—if you want to, that is. These assholes are fucking crazy to have sent you—"

"They're fucking crazy assholes all right." She leaned her head on a hand. "Feuds between clubs never die, do they?"

"Runs deep between the Flames and the Smoking Guns. From the beginning of time kind of deep."

She took another swallow. "After their president got arrested, we've all been waiting for some kind of retaliation, but I never thought it would involve my dad."

Dready entered the lounge from the offices and came over to

us. "Hey, got word that the Flames are on their way to Kansas City to the Guns clubhouse."

I put down my drink. "Fuck."

"Yeah."

Lindy let out a breath. "Thanks for letting us know."

"Sure thing." Dready joined the party again.

Lindy's gaze darted around the lounge. Dawes had arrived, and he and Bear were focused on the television in the corner as they drank and smoked. A car race was on the big screen TV and the men no doubt had bets going. Lucy climbed onto Dready's lap. The acrid smell of cigarettes and weed wafted around the vast room.

"Lind, you want something stronger?"

She returned her gaze to mine, her tongue skimming her bottom lip. "I have an idea…"

"What's that?" I refilled my glass and drank.

"Now would be the perfect time for us to go to the Dip."

The booze reversed its trajectory in my mouth, and I sputtered and coughed. "How do you figure that?" I wiped at my lips.

She leaned over the counter, handing me napkins. My gaze automatically shot to her breasts, which threatened to spill out of the low-cut V-neck of her T-shirt. I strained to unglue myself from the enticing sight. "We go there, and whatever we find, we'll let the Flames know. Now that they're going to Kansas City, saves time for everyone all around, don't you think?" She chewed on her lip. *More like chomping at the bit.*

She was anxious, and she wanted this done. I got that, I did. The Reaper's fucking clock was ticking loudly in her head, especially now that she'd seen a mangled piece of her father's body. He was being tortured. He was suffering. What piece of him would be next? What piece of her soul would shrivel next?

"Think about it—" she whispered, her back straightening. "Kansas City is at least nine hours from the Flames clubhouse, and the Dip is less than a couple of hours away from Meager. By the time they get down there, do whatever they have planned… then they'll need to eat, sleep, ride back —"

"Lindy, hang on…"

She leaned in even closer. "Raptor could still be using the Dip to hide or stash shit. It's worth checking it out, don't you think?"

"You're on lockdown, young lady, remember that?"

"So?"

I let out a loud laugh. "There she is, my little fucking Flame."

"A Flame with the heart of a Broken Blade." She drained her glass, her eyes gleaming at me in the dark, piercing my chest like daggers.

"Here's the thing, little Flame, you and I both have got to be at that party at the tattoo shop tomorrow night or everyone's going to know that something's up, especially my mother, who will sound the alarm. It would be understandable if you didn't go to the party, but I've got to be there."

Moans and groans rose from the lounge, and our attention shifted to the source. Lucy straddled Dready's lap on a sofa in a corner, the two of them kissing deeply, a votive candle glimmering its dim light around their forms that moved in the shadows. Lucy pulled back from him and peeled her shirt off, and he snapped off her bra, releasing her bare tits. He kneaded them, kissing them as she moaned softly.

Lindy's gaze fixated on the couple, and I slugged back another whisky. "Hey, Lind, you want to get out of here? Why don't we take a walk on the grounds? I could show you the—"

"I'm good." She grabbed the whiskey bottle and poured herself another, her gaze darting back to Dready, who was sucking on Lucy's tits while she ground her body against his, her hands in his long hair.

Turning back to me, Lindy grinned as she clinked her glass against mine. "To club life."

"To club life." I came around the bar and sat on the stool next to her.

"Being the little girl at the Broken Blades, I got shielded from all the partying, but when we got to the Flames I was older and managed to see a few things. Being a guy, I'm sure you saw a lot."

I shrugged, my pulse throbbing in my veins at Lucy's low moans. I rubbed the side of my neck. "Not so much. But there was this one time Zac and I were in middle school, and we hid in the woods in the back when there was this huge party going on."

She giggled. "Oh no."

"Oh yes." I drank. "Was real exciting, up until I recognized my dad going at it with three women."

Lindy let out a gasp.

"Zac thought it was a real hoot, but I didn't."

"Of course not."

"It all clicked for me that night. That's when everything started making sense. I realized my mom was getting way less than she deserved. And what I finally got was that she knew it, she knew what was going on, which was why she fought him all the time. Yet through her disappointment, she still hoped. But after that, I gave up hope. Things fell into place and started falling apart for me."

"Is that why you haven't joined the club?"

"Part of the reason."

"What's the other part? Because from what I'm seeing, they love you. Even though your dad's gone, they still consider you and your mom part of the family. You're so lucky you still have—"

"My dad was club president since before I started walking. It was everything to him. He spent almost all of his time here or on the road. I understood it, respected it, but yeah, it sucked. As I got older we hung out more, argued more, and then he got killed here on club property." I took in a deep breath. "This place reeks of him. Reeks of a whole lot of —"

She clasped my arm. "A whole lot of good, don't you think? Commitment to the brotherhood, loyalty?"

"Oh babe, yeah..." I let out a dark chuckle. "Loyalty was at the top of Jump's list."

Her warm hand slid down to mine, and she gently stroked my fingers. "Wes, I get it," she whispered roughly, her voice blasting through my insides like a molten flow of lava.

My fingers tightened over her warm ones. "I know you do," I whispered back. "And I like that you do."

"Me too."

Tugging on her hand, I pulled her off the stool, and she stood in between my legs, her body pressed against mine. My mouth brushed her silky lips and they parted for me. Our tongues dove and slid. The sweet, warm dazzle of the liquor mingled with her taste and set my blood on fire. My hands cuffed her neck, bringing her in closer, holding her tight, and she let out a small cry that went straight to my balls. She cried out again, and I swallowed that moan.

Her lips nuzzled my cheek. "I have another idea," she whispered against my ear. Taking my hand, she led me to a small sofa against a wall where we sat down.

"W-what's that?" I adjusted my jeans around my stiff cock.

"We're both going to the party, and Bear said I'd have to come back early, which works in our favor."

"How?"

"Once we come back here early, we'll need a believable reason to be left alone and not be disturbed so once they come back from partying and go to sleep, we leave."

Lust had taken over my senses, and my brain wasn't computing. "Where are you going with this?"

"Tonight we need to set up the reason to be left alone and undisturbed."

"The reason being..."

"That we're both very into each other and eager to fuck."

My pulse jagged like a shot of high voltage adrenaline in my veins at the sound of that word from her lips. "To *fuck*?"

"We have to make sure they believe what we're up to in my

room. Otherwise, you'd be in another room on your own and they'd be checking up on me."

My heart galloped painfully in my chest as it fought the booze in my system.

Lindy wrapped an arm around mine, her breasts pressed into my side, her lips brushing my cheek, my ear, sending tingles over my skin. "It's perfect. Whoever comes back here with us will be partying, and we'll head straight to my room because—"

"Fucking." My breathing deepened.

Her hand squeezed my leg. "And later, once the others get back here, they won't bother us because they'll assume we're—"

"Fucking." My chest squeezed together painfully. "Lindy…"

"It'll be real late by then. And once they fall asleep, we leave for the Dip. And since it's not too far away, we can be back here before dawn and sleep in, which would be normal because they'll think we had a long wild night and a hot morning too. Good, huh?"

I was Adam being beguiled by Eve.

She slid an arm around my shoulders, her fruity scent shifting around us as her soft lips brushed the side of my face. "So tonight we should set the stage and play up the fact that we're…"

"Fucking?" I grit out.

"And tomorrow morning, we can play up being hot for each other too. Then, at the party tomorrow night, they won't think it's unusual that we're glued to each other and into getting back here early to—"

"Fuck."

"All night long." She let out a short laugh as her other hand slid across my chest. "See? It's perfect. It won't be a surprise to anyone. We already made an impression on Boner, Butler, and your mom. Even Bear."

"You noticed that, huh?"

"Mmm. And after dinner, when we were cleaning up,

Shannon and Lucy were asking me about us and I was a bit cagey, but…"

"But what?"

"I let them know that we have it going on."

"You laid the groundwork already?"

"I figured—"

I cuffed her wrist, stopping her hands wandering down my torso. "Do we have it going on or …"

Her eyebrows peaked. "We haven't been playing Legos, Wes, have we? You came in my mouth, didn't you?"

My brain locked on her words, reliving all the stroking and kissing that we'd shared like a video running on loop. "I sure did." I bit her bottom lip, and she let out a gasp.

Her fingers brushed her swollen lip. "So all we have to do is play it up good tonight so they have a clear picture of us together from now on."

"Hold on. You want us to fake our real, here? Isn't faking done the other way around?"

"All I'm saying is that we amp things up for our audience. Drive the point home."

"Put on a show?"

Her hand squeezed my thigh, and my muscles jumped. "Wes, I'm being strategic and methodical here."

Strategic and methodical?

My neck went rigid. While Lindy was an army general swiftly planning her strategy, I was sitting here with a throbbing dick and a spiraling ache in my chest that wouldn't quit. Taking in the pleased jut of her jaw, the eagerness in her voice, a basic truth smashed over me like a wave of ice-cold water.

I wanted her, and not only her body to ease my cranked up high. I wanted Lindy.

All of Lindy.

Not to put on a show.

Not to amp up for an audience.

I wanted Lindy for me. For *us*.

Faking it is what I'd done with her all those years ago. Hell, that's what I'd done on some level with all the women I'd slept with.

Now, after this short time of getting to know each other again, getting along, and being way the fuck into each other, on the cusp of starting something new and real, Lindy and I were going to *fake it for an audience*?

Newsflash, Lindy: I don't have to fake anything.

Did she?

Maybe this was a convenient way for her to toy with me and dump me? Get her revenge for the past while she worked her strategy? Quite a master plan.

I blew out a huff of air. The booze was fucking with my head. I'd never doubted the chemistry or the signals between me and a girl before, not ever. What the fuck was happening to me?

Lindy, that's what.

I cared about *Lindy's* signals. *Lindy's* chemistry.

She brushed the hair back from my face, my body electrifying at the simple contact. I'd prove to her that what we had was real, that there was no denying it, no faking it. I wanted her to know that this was genuine for me. My fingers tightly clamped over hers, and her eyes widened. How would she handle my strategy?

Game on. At least for a little while.

I heaved her onto my lap, and she let out a sharp gasp, her cheeks flushing, her fingernails digging into my shoulders. "How's this?" My tongue lashed at the seam of her lips.

"Uh…" She squirmed in my lap, eyes wide. "Great start."

My fingers slid down her throat to her chest, and her breath audibly cut as I cupped a breast. On a tiny gasp, she took my mouth, her hands sliding around my neck as her tongue dove against mine.

The general was most certainly all in and taking charge.

Our tongues slid and tangled as her fingers raked through

my hair. I let out a groan at the fiery sensations engulfing my body. Gripping her ass, I shifted her even closer.

We kissed and groped, and sparks flew around us, the heat of our bodies, the need for more friction, melding us together. Enthusiasm and desire and hunger drowned out the television, drowned out everyone's voices, the cheering, even the bumpy feel of the shitty sofa under us.

But not the needling fear that all this to Lindy might be more fake than real.

TWENTY-TWO

LINDY

WES SLID a hand down the back of my jeans, past my panty, and cupped my ass cheek. I let out a moan at the illicit contact, his skin cool against mine as he roughly palmed my flesh. His lips found my throat, and sparks went off all over my body. Shifting me on his lap, he held me closer. More friction, more intensity.

More *everything*.

My muscles melted. I was molten, on fire, and alive in a whole new way. I tensed for a moment at the sound of boots tromping by, at laughter in the distance, the rip of a bag of potato chips. Wes groaned, and the raw sound blocked out the world and I dove back into the fire.

Fooling around with Wes in the club lounge with people there was exciting. Wes and I were doing what our parents and all the other members had done a zillion times in the past. What little we'd witnessed, but what we always knew went on.

Now we were doing it. Well, kind of. Was kissing and groping in the club lounge "wild"? Not really, in the scheme of MC life, but who cared? Hell, we had a room here all to ourselves tonight.

Tonight. Would tonight be THE night? Was this a good idea?

Wes's grip on me was like steel. A little firmer, tighter, rougher than it had been other times. As if he wasn't relaxed. Was it my imagination or had he gotten annoyed when I'd proposed my strategy? Now he was roaring off like a motorcycle in full throttle, leaving smoke in its wake, its explosive thundering demanding attention.

I pulled back from him. "Why don't we slow down a little?"

"Shouldn't we keep going?" His hands rubbed my ass, grinding my body over his erection. "Fuck, you feel good."

My clit throbbed in response, as my nails dug into his shoulders. "I don't plan on getting naked out here in front of everyone if that's what you mean."

"Not that. But you want to make it look real, don't you?" His hands spanned my waist and squeezed, stroking upwards, landing on my breasts, his thumbs grazing my nipples. "So they're convinced that we fuck?"

My lips tightened at his remark. There was something cold and clipped about his tone of voice. But what did I expect? That was exactly what I'd asked of him, *let's put on a sex show*, wasn't it? My pulse drummed in my neck. Was I excited or in a panic?

His fingers wiped the hair back from my face and my insides fluttered. A tender move. Possessive. Cupping the back of my head, he pulled me in and took my mouth once more. Demanding and rough, he stormed. Controlled. Laid siege.

My plan made perfect sense. While the Flames went to Kansas City to confront the Smoking Guns, why not go to the Dip and see for myself if there was any trace of Dad having been there? And if we found evidence of Raptor using the place, that would be a huge win for everybody.

Even though it was likely Dad had been taken by the Smoking Guns in a revenge move, something inside me felt that maybe Minty was right, maybe Dad was with Raptor. And even though I hoped it wasn't true, I wasn't sure. Most importantly, I needed to find out in a way that protected my father.

Wes pulled down the edge of my shirt and nipped on the top of my breast, sending flames straight between my legs. However, with this plan, I was pushing me and Wes into fifth gear. He certainly was going for the gusto. But did I want to move forward with him, with us, on a pretense and not…

I wanted authentic, genuine feeling this time, didn't I? That's what I'd always wanted, and it was happening, but now—dammit, why did this have to be complicated?

Because circumstances. Because Wes.

"Hey, kids, go get a room somewhere!" Bear's voice boomed, and I stiffened. Loud laughter rolled through the lounge. Bear had Shannon on his lap, who winked at me, sticking out her tongue.

Play your part! I shot her a tight grin right back.

"Why didn't I think of that?" Wes replied loudly as he rose from the sofa, his hands on my ass.

"Whoa!" I yelped loudly on purpose and gripped his shoulders tighter. Wes smacked my ass, and my nipples hardened painfully against his chest. This strategy of mine was going to kill me, wasn't it?

"Nighty-night, you guys," Shannon giggled.

"Don't be too loud, kiddies!" Bear roared with laughter.

"Yeah, we need our beauty sleep." Dawes glanced at us as he chewed on potato chips.

"Aw, leave them alone." Lucy settled on the floor between Dready's legs.

Wes took us down the dark hallway, me bouncing in his grip with his long, quick strides, the sound of his heavy breathing echoing in my ears. He was excited. My heart galloped as if it had been injected with two dozen energy drinks. I was excited too.

He put me down in front of the door, and I opened it. He locked it behind him and grabbed me again and kissed me.

My hands went to his chest and pressed, and somehow I

managed to pull back from his fantastic mouth. I gulped in air. "Mission accomplished."

"Why stop? Feels good, doesn't it? Been a long day, let's keep on feeling good…"

My brain blanked at his words, at the seductive quality of his voice in the darkness that wrapped around me like the finest silk, melting me as it furled around me. He took my lips again.

I couldn't stop, didn't want to stop, I wanted…"Wes—"

Lifting me, he laid me back on the bed, which creaked and squeaked underneath us. He ripped off his T-shirt, and a helpless moan escaped my throat at the sight of his gorgeous chest in the dim light filling the room from the outside lights. Contoured muscles, defined pecs, necklaces, tattoos. He brought my hands to his middle. "Touch me."

Gladly!

He let out a groan as my hands raced over his chest, exploring every inch of his gorgeous flesh, his scars, every smooth, hard plain and curve of the most beautiful man I'd ever known. My hands slid down his sleek back into his jeans, past his boxer briefs, to his incredible sculpted ass. On a guttural moan, he bent over me, his lips making a fiery trail down my throat.

He would be the death of me.

Once upon a time, he had been.

But now? Now, Wes was killing me in a whole new way. He deepened the kiss, a moan rumbling in his chest.

This was happening. This was real. Was this a good thing like this? I couldn't breathe. Couldn't think. I was on a twisty slide, plummeting downwards into a dark, velvet abyss.

"Back in the day we never had a bed, huh?" I murmured.

"Never."

"We were always fooling around in a car or a truck, in my backyard, always waiting for someone to catch us."

"Your mom caught us once."

"She did."

"We're not kids anymore," he gritted out as he nuzzled my breasts over my T-shirt.

"Not anymore, no." My fingers shifted through the beautiful thick hair that remained from his haircut.

"In fact, they just applauded for us out there."

My legs twisted, the swelling in my clit unbearable. The bedroom door was locked, the outside world having bestowed its approval for us to have wild, loud sex all night long.

Having sex with Wes, taking our time, being entangled with his naked body, touching, stroking, exploring, kissing, and being kissed EVERYWHERE by him—wasn't that the dream? No limits. Yes, it fucking was…

His fingers slid under my T-shirt and cupped my breasts. "Beautiful…"

I gasped. "Wes, slow down…"

"Slow is good…" He kissed my cheek gently, his fingers going to the hem of my tee and lifting it. My breath constricted, I wanted nothing more than our bodies touching skin to skin. To taste his warmth, to taste him again. *But—*

He cupped my breasts over the satin bra. "Gorgeous." My nipples ached for his mouth. My entire body ached, need blooming deep inside me. Pushing up my shirt, he tugged down the sleek fabric of my bra and nipped at my flesh. His teeth grazed a nipple, his tongue lavished me with wet strokes and I let out a whimper. His fingers drifted to the strap at my back.

"Wes, wait."

He stopped, his gaze snagging on mine. "You okay?"

"Yeah…it's…um…"

"Strategy for the audience is over so you're done?" His index finger traced a lazy circle around a nipple and my body quivered. "You teasing me?"

My lips pressed together. How many times had I been accused of being a tease?

Hundreds. Because it had been the truth.

And each time it had made me laugh as I'd thrown my

clothes back on and walked out the door. But not now. Not with Wes.

"I'm not teasing you, I just…"

His tongue licked at his swollen bottom lip, his chest heaving, his thick hair mussed. Lust incarnate. His fingers tightened around my nipple, tugging, delivering a fiery ache that blew up deep in my core. A sword against flesh. I cried out, my back arching, and he let out a hiss as his tongue padded over my sore nipple. "Mmm…did I get too amped up for you, Lindy? Guess I got into my role."

"You were terrific."

"But?"

I sat up, adjusting my bra. "But what?"

"Are you scared?"

"Scared of what? Your dick?"

He laughed softly. "You want my dick bad. Maybe you're scared of what's happening between us. It's easy to put on a show like we just proved." His lips tipped up. "I think you feel safe faking it, being in control of a situation."

My body stilled. He'd figured me out, and hearing that truth from his lips stung. A truth I'd never dared articulate to myself. My strategy with men the last few years had been get what you want and walk away.

Having a real relationship with Wes? Finally being intimate with him? Scared the living daylights out of me.

He leaned in closer, his breath a warm, rough whisper on my sensitive skin. "I haven't been faking tonight. Have you? I need to know."

No words came.

He took my hand and laid my palm over his damp, warm chest where his heart beat hard. "You feel that, Lindy? I'm all in. I'm not faking. And I know what I don't want."

"What's that?" I whispered.

"I don't want a strategy fuck, and I don't want to get laid for the fuck of it. Not for our first time together. If I wanted to get laid for the fuck of it, I could leave here right now, go to Pete's, and make it happen within fifteen minutes tops."

"Bravo you." I moved to get off the bed.

He grabbed my arm, stopping me, and held on tight. "But I don't want to. What we have *means* something to me. Something big." His eyes narrowed, and suddenly it was as if I were under a lone spotlight on a dark stage. "What are you not telling me, Lindy?"

I pulled up my fallen bra strap. "What are you talking about?"

"We all lie in little ways and big ways, especially to ourselves. Which kind of lie you telling right now? And is it me you're lying to or yourself?" A noise rumbled in his throat as his warm hand stole around my neck. "Why, baby?" His forehead sliding against mine, his voice a sigh. "Why you fighting this?"

TWENTY-THREE

LINDY

Wes was right.

There was no reason to fight anymore, was there? I was so used to fighting. But here, now, me and Wes together like this, was the dream coming true at long, long last. And I could embrace it. Embrace him.

My hand went to the side of his face. "I don't want to fight anymore." I brought my lips to his and kissed him gently. He remained still. My lips brushed his, my tongue sought entry. Finally, he opened for me. Union.

On a growl, his body surged against mine and our kiss deepened. Raw and hungry. Tearing off my T-shirt, he brought me down on the mattress again, his weight settling on me, my legs twisted around his hips as my clit throbbed against his body. Kisses seared my throat, my chest.

This was the night. Finally.

Kissing, we shifted on the bed, and a sharp pain burst in my flesh. "Ouch!"

"What is it? You okay?" He shot up.

"Something jabbed my back..." I reached out, and my hand

slapped over a book. "It's the photo album." My hand pressed down on the vinyl cover.

He let out a soft laugh and fell back on the bed. "Ah, right. I tossed it there before dinner."

It was good to hear him laugh. I wiped my hair behind my ears. "Would you mind if we looked at the photos?"

Turning on his side, he rested his head on his hand. "Sure, let's do it. I've been dying to check them out since my mom gave them to you."

"Me too." My shoulders eased.

He scooped up my T-shirt from the floor and held it out to me. "Thanks." I grabbed it on a small grin.

"I'm going to turn on the lamp. Watch your eyes."

"Okay." Turning around, I put my shirt back on and stretched out. Dim light glowed in the room. The quilt was crumpled, and I smoothed it out.

Wes ran a hand through his messy hair. "My mother mentioned chocolate, didn't she?"

"God, yes. Where's that shopping bag?" I spotted the bags and grabbed two bottles of water as well as a bag of chocolate Kisses. Wes and I climbed back on the bed, peeling open candy and munching with the album between us like two kids having found a secret treasure in the middle of the night.

Ease shot through me. Any other guy, the ones in my experience, would be crabbing about wanting to get off. But not Wes. He was not only generous and kind, but he knew how important this was to me, and that mattered to him. I also knew that it was important to him too, to see these old pics of his parents in probably happier times, and I liked that it was meaningful to him like it was for me.

He caught me grinning at him. "What is it?"

"Nothing."

"What is it?"

"I like that we can share this together."

"Me too," he whispered.

I opened the album. Each page had four photos inserted into four slots. The Jacks and the Broken Blades were on a run together. Each club's bikes were lined up on the road, and each biker had his old lady with him. They were all waving at the camera or shooting the finger, grins on their faces.

"There's Alicia." I pointed to a shot of the long haired platinum blonde with smokey eye makeup and a petite thin body standing up on a chopper. She wore a bikini top and very short denim cutoffs and boots. Both her arms were up in the air as a man drove the bike, his beard and long braid of hair flying. The two of them laughing.

A smile curved Wes's lips. "Mommy and Daddy."

"They look like they belong on that bike together."

His eyes were glued to the photo. "You're right. They do." His tone was wistful, soft.

"Damn, he's some alpha hot man." I giggled.

Wes shot me a look. "You say that like it's unusual. Like you're surprised."

"I did not."

"You don't think I inherited that quality from him?"

"Umm…"

His jaw tightened, and his brow furrowed. I put a hand on his arm. "You're a different kind of alpha hot man. Not gruff and rough all over like Jump. You're more alpha around the edges. And when you get poked–watch the fuck out."

Wes grinned at me, a sly careful-you're-asking-for-it grin that made my pulse tick up like crazy. Chuckling, he flipped a page. More of Alicia and Jump hugging in group photos of the One-Eyed Jacks. Wes's forehead creased as he probably remembered faces, placed people that didn't seem immediately recognizable. There was one of Alicia kissing Jump as he held her up in his arms, as if he'd won her in a contest, best prize ever. Dudes stood around them cheering and holding up beer bottles.

"Your parents had lots of fun together."

"They did." He stared at the photo, chewing his lip.

I leaned my shoulder into his. "It's nice, huh?"

Our gazes met. "It is."

"I'm guessing you've never seen this album before?" I asked.

"First time. There are others. My mom loved taking photos for the club, of her and her friends. Souvenirs of golden times."

"I sure am grateful she did."

Something about Wes's face remained wistful, sad.

I turned the page, and my breath cut. Broken Blades of yesteryear. "Here we go…" My pulse picked up at the familiar faces, our logo on their cuts. "Here's Minty. He's a Flame now." I let out a laugh. "And still rocking this same handlebar mustache. And this is Notch." I pointed to the skinny black-haired biker, who looked like he needed a shower and had just gotten kicked out of a heavy metal band after a long, ugly night.

"Yikes."

"This is Zed, who was president before him, and his old lady, Angel." I scanned the photos on that page, pouring over every face. My gaze froze over a photo of two big, burly men laughing, their arms slung around each other, giving the photographer the finger. "This is my dad and Raptor."

"Whoa…there's that tattoo on his throat and chest you told me about."

"Impressive, huh?"

"Mmm. Dad and Zed with their bikes," Wes murmured as he took out the photo to look at it closely.

"That's your bike now, right?"

"I have it."

"Looks the same. I would have thought that by now you'd have painted it yourself with something different." He ignored my remark as he tucked the photo back in the album. I continued, "I have my mom's old car, it's a vintage Challenger, and one day I'm going to give her the all-star treatment."

"A Challenger? Cool."

"Sure is."

He pointed at a photo of Zed and his Dad. "Zed's bike is outrageous. Those handlebars…"

"Zed's dad had been a Blade too. That chopper had been his."

"Amazing." Wes turned the page, and my heart jumped. "Lind, is that your mom?" He pointed to the photo of Mom and Dad. "You look just like her."

"That's what they tell me." My voice came out quiet. "When I was little, I looked more like my dad, but the older I get, the more my mom comes out in me. At least that's what Dad says. He says, 'Thank God 'cause I've got an ugly mug, baby.' But he's not ugly, at least I don't think so."

"No, he's not. Rough, yes, but not ugly." Wes nudged me with his body, and I let out a small laugh. "My mother was right."

I met his bright gaze. "About what? What did Alicia say?"

"She said she'd only chatted with your mom a few times but there was something real genuine about her. Like an innocent country girl. You got that genuine too, Lindy."

My whole body lit up with his words, the fierce way he looked at me. His gaze shot to my mouth, and I couldn't resist. I pressed my lips softly against his.

He grinned. "Did she have your sassy mouth?"

"She sure did." I let out a laugh, and we both went back to the photo album. More pics of the old ladies of both clubs. Alicia and Angel showing off their bodies in low-cut, sopping wet, white T-shirts in what was most probably the aftermath of a wet T-shirt contest. "Hot babes," I murmured.

"Oh yeah." Wes let out a laugh.

My gaze scanned the familiar Blades faces from my childhood, my heart squeezing that this moment in time had been captured. An icy prickle flared over my skin. This club, this family of mine, was no more and would never be again.

Another page. Couples kissing, Jacks leaning back against their bikes, laying down on the ground by their Harleys amidst a zillion empty bottles and cans of beer. My gaze landed on a pic of a handsome, dark blond guy, bare-chested in a Jacks cut with a young brunette at his side. They were both beaming, his long tattooed arm slung around her shoulders, bottles in their hands, drunk on love, drunk on each other. My finger tapped on the picture. "Why does she seem familiar?"

"That's Grace and her first husband. He was a brother too. Got killed a few weeks before I was born."

"Oh no."

"She was pregnant at the time, like my mom was with me. But Grace ended up losing her baby."

My hands shot to my mouth. "That's awful."

Wes turned the page. More Broken Blades. I took in each photograph slowly, carefully, my gaze pouring over every detail, every nuance as if I were drinking a fine wine, savoring its scent and every layer of flavor.

Notch dancing with a topless girl who seemed underage young. Angel having a laugh with Jump as she handed him a beer. Raptor kissing a woman in a deep, animal kind of way. Wes chuckled. "There's some alpha hot man action for you."

"What a lucky lady," I murmured. Raptor held the woman up high in his arms, his huge muscles bulging. Her long cowboy booted legs were wrapped around his waist. My lungs crushed together in my chest. "Holy shit…"

"What is it? What's wrong?"

"That's…" My breath cut.

"That's your mom!"

I brought the photo album closer to the lamp. That page was full of pics of Mom with Raptor and him with his hands on her. His mouth on her. His hands on her hips. On her bikini clad tits, her grinning. Their tongues out and touching. Another with my mother slung over his shoulder, her long hair flying, his hand on her ass like a cave man who owned her, and her raking her nails on his back as she laughed. My heart pounded in my chest. That ringing laugh of hers I loved so much went off in my head.

Wes flipped to the next page. "Jesus, look—"

My parents posing with Raptor. The two men had their arms around Mom, one around her waist, the other over her shoulders. Both men possessive and yet perfectly at ease. And the look on Mom's face? Defiant and pleased. "Holy fuck, they were a threesome. Holy fuck." Adrenaline washed through me like a bolt of lighting.

Wes flipped pages back and forth. "This was way before you were born…"

I pushed my hair back from my face as I studied the photos. "We were a normal mom and dad and kid family. I didn't see any sharing or menage shit going on, but what the fuck did I know?" My voice had gotten louder. "The three of them could've been bonking at the clubhouse while I was at school or at softball practice or—"

His hands cradled my face. "Lind, Lindy, it's okay."

My skin heated. "It's not okay! How could I not know?"

"Maybe they didn't want you to know."

"But…but…"

"Breathe. Come on. Breathe. Look at me, come on…that's it."

I took in a deep breath and let it out, focusing on Wes's warm hand on the back of my suddenly clammy neck, on his steady deep-blue gaze.

"Let's take this from the beginning," he said softly. "You said you remember your dad and Raptor being good friends?"

"That's what I remember from when I was little. But I don't remember him coming over, hanging out with us at home ever."

"You remember them fighting or falling out?"

"No."

"Did you ever get a vibe around the club that they hated each other? Or your mom didn't like him?"

"No, none of that. I don't remember my parents ever talking bad about him. Or talking about him much at all. If they talked about the club at home, they'd gossip about Notch and his old lady fighting all the time. It was always a drama about Notch screwing young girls. Or his extreme point of view versus Zed's. That I remember, but nothing about Raptor. Anyhow, Raptor wasn't around too much. He would go on lots of special jobs for National or secret jobs for the club."

Wes let out a huff of air. "Maybe he was also doing those jobs with Zed and my dad."

"Maybe. I remember when Uncle Zed died and Notch became president, Raptor and Dad became officers, and then Raptor was around more."

"Was he ever at your house with your mom, when your dad wasn't home?"

"He never came over. And I'd remember because he always creeped me out a little. Had a way of staring that made me uncomfortable. Plus he was…larger than life." My teeth scraped my lip as my brain sifted through images and memories and clips of conversations. "How could I not know?"

Wes closed the photo album. "It's late, and you've had a fucking long and crazy day and night, and now you're upset again and that's not good. You need to relax. Let's put this away and get some sleep."

"Wait—" Grabbing the album, I flipped it open to the page where the pics of the three of them were. They looked comfy together. Happy together.

On fire together.

"Lindy, you're upset—"

"Wes, I'm not upset. I mean, I'm not upset because I'm shocked morally. I'm upset because what I assumed was true all my life was not true. There was a whole other life going on right in front of me and I never realized. That's the shock."

"I get it, believe me."

My gaze snagged on his, and something in my chest heated. "I know you do."

"Lie down." He took the photo album from me and put it on the desk.

"What? Why?"

"So I can take off your shoes and you can relax, that's why."

"You don't have to—"

"Lindy. Let me do something for you."

Other than kiss me, touch me, lick me, make me come?

I laid down and Wes unlaced my hi-tops and slid them off my feet. His hands rubbed my arches. My body sank into the mattress. "Feels so good…" I groaned as he kept rubbing.

"You said your parents were happy together, and I'm 100% sure that's true."

"Are you trying to make me feel better? 'Cause I don't know what's true or not at this moment."

"What I'm saying is as kids we know."

Grabbing the album again, I flipped to the page of another pic of Jump and Alicia that had caught my eye earlier. Alicia riding piggyback on Jump, the two of them laughing. I showed it to him. "That looks real happy to me. Do you remember this kind of happy when you were little?"

Releasing my feet, he climbed up on the bed next to me and took in the photo. "I do. It's good to see, really is. But this is what I'm saying—as the years wore on, and once I got older and could compute my parents' shit, they were not truly happy together anymore, not like this. By the time I hit middle school, so much resentment and anger had lodged between them like dried thorns and weeds, and that rotted and kept on building and building and got as thick and hard as cement. That I could feel. I didn't understand it, but I knew it was there. That unease. That resentment. All this to say if it was bad between your mom and dad, you would've felt it on some level." His fingers stroked my chest. "You would've known in here."

My breathing picked up at his tone, his touch, his heavy gaze. His wisdom. "You're right. I would've known."

He laid down next to me and took out the photo of my parents and Raptor. "They look happy together, don't they?"

"They do. Very happy."

"Now that's some alpha hot," he whispered.

"It is." I giggled.

Wes put the album on the dresser next to the bed along with the photo, kicked off his boots, and laid down next to me on a sigh. "Maybe in the beginning, when your dad and Raptor first joined the club, the three of them were together, but then for some reason they stopped. Maybe something happened or—"

I turned over to face him. "Maybe I'm the *something* that happened. She got pregnant and Raptor wasn't into being a dad and doing the whole family thing. Or Mom decided with a baby in the mix, she didn't want to have a three-way situation anymore. Or she wanted a kid and he didn't, so she and Dad–"

"Lindy–"

"Or maybe the club had a problem with it? Or Zed?"

"Lindy."

"But that doesn't make much sense, does it?"

Launching at me, he took my mouth and bit down on my lip, and I gasped, blinked as the sting of pain raced over my flesh. I gripped his arms, his taut muscles flexing. "Babe, stop."

My eyes fluttered, and my heartbeat twitched at the way his voice pleaded and demanded, at the way he kept kissing me. "Stop what? Wondering? I can't. I want to know." His lips took mine once more, and I tore myself away. "Dammit, Wes, stop kissing me. I can't think."

"Good." His tongue dove into my mouth again, and I melted, I heated. Flared. Floated.

I pushed him away. "Wes!"

On a chuckle, his head fell back against the pillow. "Here's the bottom line—you love your mom and dad any less 'cause you know this about them?"

"No." I laid down next to him and let out a breath.

"There you go." He took my hand.

My hand squeezed his. "I miss them so much."

"I know you do," he whispered back, and the ache in my heart only grew deeper. He took me in his arms and held me.

"So much." A cry spilled from my lips as water filled my eyes. I cried, burying my wet face in his chest.

"Baby, the only one who can tell you the truth is your dad. Only Pick."

I nodded, words beyond me. Emotions tangled in my brain, tears in my throat threatening to drown me. "If we ever find him. If he's still alive." I shut my eyes against the wave of horrible reality threatening to assault me all over again and burrowed deeper into Wes.

"We're going to find him." He kissed my forehead. "We're going to find him and bring him home. I promise." His chest rumbled with that strident word as his big hands stroked my back.

His steady heartbeat thrummed under me, and I breathed in his warm scent. Arousal and refuge. Sighing, I fell into the deepest sleep ever.

TWENTY-FOUR

WES

THE SOFT LIGHT of the sun breaking through the shades of the room at the MC had me groaning, twisting away, but I didn't get far as Lindy was wrapped around me.

I grinned. In the middle of the night I'd gotten out of bed and stripped my clothes off, leaving only my boxer briefs on. I'd climbed back in and spooned Lindy from behind, but in her sleep, she'd immediately turned around and nestled herself in my chest once more.

Lindy, curled up in my embrace, filled me with something that I couldn't quite figure out but I liked how it felt. Genuine and solid.

I ran my fingers gently through her mass of red and black hair. She usually wore it up, twisted in scarves or interesting thick bands, but now, feeling it tumble in long waves down her back, just for me, made my breath deepen.

My lips brushed her forehead, and her body squirmed against mine. Ah damn, my morning wood was only getting more intense with her luscious body firmly pressed against me. Carefully, slowly, I reached out for my phone on the edge of the desk and checked the time. I needed to get ready for work soon, which luckily was next door.

Sensing my movement, Lindy's body tensed and her head lifted. "Wes?" Her eyes blinked.

"Good morning." I stroked her back.

"Morning." She stretched out, and her hair fell in her face, a small groan escaping her lips. My grunge goddess. Her gaze ran down my body, and a prickle of heat needled my flesh. Her eyebrows lifted. "You took your clothes off?" She blinked at my clothes on a heap on the floor.

I stroked a hand across my chest. "I got hot. We fell asleep wrapped around each other."

"Sorry."

"Wasn't a bother. Just…"

"Just?"

"A lot of heat." My hand went to my bulging cock as I let out a dark chuckle. My hand lazily stroked my shaft. Her eyes widened. At my audacity? My shameless lust?

I slid down my boxers a couple of inches, and my grateful shaft was freed. On a hiss, I fisted him and pulled slowly. My jaw slackened as I grew harder, longer.

She let out a small noise as her fingers absently stroked my pecs, laying a silky trail down my abs as she held my gaze.

I licked at my lips. "When we were together at my mom's house, we got interrupted when Dawes called." My voice came out rough.

She only nodded, her fingers racing back up over my pecs.

"Never got to see your pussy."

She drew in a tight breath, her teeth scraping her bottom lip.

"Show me, Lind."

Getting up, she took off her jeans and her T-shirt. Her nipples had hardened into pebbles in her bra, and my jaw tensed. I wanted to rip that bra off with my teeth and sink my face between those full tits. Suck on them. Thrust my dick between them, my cum jetting all over her incredible breasts.

She went to take her panties off. "I want to do that." I held out my hand to her and she took it, climbing back into the bed, which sagged under our weight as she laid down. I rose up over her and licked at the waistband of her lacy underwear, my fingers curling into the fabric at her hips, nudging it lower, licking, nudging, her gasping, licking until a tiny strip of hair appeared.

"Oh yeah…" My mouth watered, my muscles tightened.

"Wes…" Her voice ached, her body twisted.

I ran the back of two of my fingers gently up her wet slit and she cried out, her legs tensing. Her nub was swollen, her flesh pink. "There you are," I murmured as my thumb gently brushed over her silky core. I blew air over her clit and she cried out, her head rolling on the mattress.

My tongue lashed through her, taunting her clit. Warm and sweet and musky. Something heavy slicked through me, towing me under.

I spread her legs as far as the panty would allow, which wasn't much, keeping it on her for tension. She fought it, her hips twisting, her pelvis curving up as I ran my knuckles over her, rotating them around her clit. "Wet and juicy," I murmured, holding on tight to the panty, keeping her still. My strokes became more intense.

"Oh God!'

My balls twitched, the roar of anticipation so acute it was painful. I licked her. "You taste so good, Lind." I dug my fingertips into her thighs. "Want to eat you." I licked at a thigh, her tattoo staring back at me. "You want that?"

She trembled in my hold, her breathing shallow. "Yes, yes…"

Ripping her panty off, I leaned over and said, "Want you on my face."

Her eyes flaring, she quickly lifted up as I laid down. Digging my fingers into her hips, I pulled her up on me, and her sweet pussy finally sank over my mouth.

Fuck yes. I lost myself in her.

She yelped loudly as my tongue lashed her, my teeth grazed, my lips suckled. Lindy ground down on me as I sucked, kissed, swirled around her clit, her silky flesh. Her gorgeous tits bounced in that fantastic bra. Reaching up, I tweaked a nipple and she cried out and clawed at my hand as I roughly kneaded her tit.

She rode me, rode the pleasure I gave her. Her moans got tighter, quicker. "Oh Wes…Wes..!" She grabbed the headboard. Her body tightened, and I teased and gave, my fingers digging into her ass cheeks. She exploded for me, on me, and I lapped at her, my hands sliding up her sweaty torso as she moaned, as she trembled.

Lindy collapsed into my arms, curled into my embrace. The two of us steaming, sweaty, out of breath. I wiped her damp hair back from her eyes, my fingers running down her wet throat. "You're so beautiful, Lind. So beautiful."

Bringing my mouth to hers, she kissed me deep. She wanted to taste herself on me. God, I fucking loved that. My hand went to the side of her face, keeping her close as our tongues danced and dove. Pushing the sheet away, she laid her head on my chest, the sound of our ragged quick breaths filling the room.

I let out a soft laugh. "Mission accomplished, huh?"

Her head lifted. "What do you mean?"

"That you got good and loud first thing in the morning. Now your strategy idea is complete."

Her face fell. "Did you think I was faking for the strategy?"

"That wasn't fake. You came in my mouth and it was so fucking hot."

She sat up. "Is that why you…was all this just now for show? To get me to…Oh, man…"

My pulse jerked in my neck, and I shot up. "That's not what I meant! What I meant was that we ended up getting done what you wanted with your idea."

Her lips smashed together, and her face was streaked with

red. She snapped up her T-shirt from the floor and yanked it on. "A+ for you, alpha hottie big man."

"Baby—"

"Don't call me that," her voice snapped as she scrambled off the bed.

"Listen to me, I wasn't faking anything just now. And I didn't do anything on purpose for the sake of a show or an audience." Launching out of the bed, I faced her, my eyes boring into hers. "I wanted this. I wanted you. I wanted you on my mouth, and I wanted to make you come. And that's the truth. Them out there hearing us? Cherry on the cake of the goddamn plan."

The redness in Lindy's cheeks deepened. "You're right." She averted her gaze. "I need to call Lenore and check in with her, and you should get to work. You shouldn't be late." She high-tailed it into the bathroom. The firm sound of that door shutting made my gut clench.

Lindy wanted me bad. Only, for some reason, she wasn't ready yet to fully admit it and dive in. Dive in to us.

I kicked at my jeans on the floor. I thought we'd come a long way. Was I wrong?

TWENTY-FIVE

LINDY

AFTER I GOT out of the shower, Wes was gone.

I kept myself busy all morning, helping Shannon and Lucy with a bunch of housekeeping chores around the clubhouse. I wasn't sure if I'd hear from him, but around midday, he texted that he'd come by to pick me up for the party at seven and to be ready.

A buzz filled my veins the rest of the afternoon like a wild electrical current over which I had no control. I remained mesmerized by the memories of this morning. The way he'd touched me. Kissed me. Reveled in me. His words, and the look in his eyes.

This morning I'd woken up with my body circled tight around Wes's, and it felt *good*. Then the sight of him stroking himself in bed, his thick cock stiffening in his hand, his eyes melting, made me lose my mind. I'd touched his warm skin, and I was gone, consumed. The things he'd said…

Desire for him had overwhelmed me.

He'd wanted to me to ride his face, and I didn't hesitate. I rode his face. I came. I came *so* hard. Then he'd held me and told me I was beautiful and my heart soared. But when he'd said "mission accomplished," I'd slammed back down to earth.

His remark sounded glib, but he was pointing out the practical, which was what he thought I wanted. Because that's what I'd told him I wanted

And when he'd jumped out of bed, looked me in the eye and stated his truth—a moment I will never forget in my entire life—I was blown away. *Brutal truth*, like he'd told Finger. Truth I'd always wanted.

Truth I needed to own up to one hundred percent.

Instead, I'd freaked out. Those years-old knee jerk defensive responses of mine still had me in their claws, and I'd ran into the bathroom.

After a late lunch with the girls, I went next door to see if Grace needed help in the Eagle Wings office. There was no hope of seeing Wes because I'd heard his bike take off over an hour ago.

I helped Grace answer phones and file paperwork and handle requests from the men in the shop and all kinds of deliveries. On the wall over the cabinet, I took in the photos of finished cars and bikes and their pleased owners, and lots of old photos of One-Eyed Jacks from years ago repairing their choppers in a simple shed with the sign "Wreck's Repair" hanging overhead. The humble beginnings of Eagle Wings.

Grace clicked off her phone. "Lindy, I'm so glad you showed up when you did. Thank you for pitching in. I'd just gotten on my phone for a meeting, and suddenly, the house phone blew up."

"I'm glad I could help." I closed a file folder and put it on top of the others on the cabinet.

She pushed her chair back from her desk and stretched her legs. "You hanging in there? I promise you both the Jacks and the Flames are doing their best to find your dad and bring him home."

"I know they are."

"It must be difficult for you to be here at another club."

"It is, a little."

"I saw that Wes brought you over yesterday. I'm glad you have him on your side at a time like this."

I shifted my weight, my skin heating.

Sitting up, Grace touched my arm. "Honey, I don't mean to put you on the spot."

"You're not. It's…uh…it's just…"

She grinned at me. "Complicated?"

I only let out a nervous laugh.

"When I was your age, I was going through a rough time with my family—actually, with my sister. My parents weren't around. I was alone and had to stay at the club for a bit too. I felt like the world was slipping out from under me."

"Exactly that." I sat on the chair by her desk.

"If it wasn't for one special guy, a Jack, who stood up for me, made sure I was safe, I don't know what would have happened to me. Made all the difference in the world knowing he was on my side. That I belonged." She let out a small laugh. "Then he changed my life forever."

"Was that your first husband? Wes showed me an old photo of the two of you."

"Mmm. It was only years later, when I came back to Meager, that I realized that we're the ones throwing roadblocks into the mix." I followed her gaze outside to where Lock was showing a newly refurbished motorcycle to the owner who'd come to pick it up. A smile lit up her features. "How we feel isn't a complication. It's the clear and true path."

My heart thudded in my chest as last night came roaring back to me. When Wes had declared that he couldn't fake it with me, I'd brushed him off because of my great plan, but he didn't let it go. *Maybe you're scared of what's happening between us. It's easy to put on a show. You feel safe faking it, don't you?* He was right. I did feel safe faking it. He'd battered at that castle wall I'd carefully built around my heart all these years.

I was scared of all this between us finally being real, being so good, because for so long it had been the impossible dream that I loved and loathed with equal fervor. In my mind, Wes had become my greatest mistake and my greatest failure.

After Wes, after my mom passing, I'd forced myself to control my emotions. Where men were concerned, I gave up on dreams and hopes and only expected games and lies.

Faking with men had become my new normal. Bold on the outside, faking it on the inside, and always getting myself out real quick. I'd been pleased with myself; I was in control and taking care of me.

But after Mom died I'd even faked with Dad, hadn't I? Never being honest about how truly upset I was, how frustrated, how much I needed him, because I didn't want to burden him. Instead, I soldiered on, like he did. But that didn't work for me, did it? It only frustrated me, and frankly, frustrated him, too.

Where had all this gotten me? Lonely. Bitter. Full of regret.

"It's already time to get a move on." Grace grabbed her handbag and her sunglasses. "Will we be seeing you at the party tonight, Lindy?"

My lips tipped up as I rose from the chair. "I'll be there."

———

"LINDY, YOU'RE AMAZING. THANK YOU." In the mirror, Shannon admired the eye makeup I'd applied on her. Shimmery duochrome purple eyeliner with more blue around the contour of her eyes, along with a pink wing at the sides. Tiny rhinestone-like glitter dotted her upper brow.

Lucy had red glittery eyeliner with a gold wing at the sides. Lucy hugged me. "I love it."

"My pleasure, believe me. I'm so glad you guys like it."

"You're fucking good at this," said Lucy.

I checked my face in the mirror. My metallic silver eyeliner looked good with the dark-red lip. I swooshed the highlighter brush across my cheekbones and my upper chest one last time. I was my casual but fancy self in tight black jeans, high-heeled boots, a lot of jewelry, a silky scarf wrapped around my hair, and of course, my makeup was top-notch glowy glam.

A knock came at the door. One of the prospects. "You guys ready? Time to scoot."

"We're ready." Lucy checked herself out in the mirror one last time.

Shouts and hoots exploded down the hallway, sharp whistles slicing through the air. "Yo, Lindy!" Bear's voice boomed. "Prince Charming is here!"

The girls grinned at me as we left my room, and I shot them back a smile. Only I wasn't truly feeling that smile. The tightening in my stomach as we headed down the hallway to the lounge told me how facing Wes after this morning's orgasmathon and slight tiff had me anxious.

"Lindyyyyy! Where are you?" Bear hollered.

The girls and I got to the lounge, and everyone moved aside like a sea parting for me. My breath lodged in my chest.

Wes stood on the opposite side of the lounge looking... fucking amazing. Black motorcycle boots, and lean black trousers that fit him so precisely. A printed dress shirt with a silver design on it, unbuttoned down his spectacular chest covered in his tattoos and several heavy silver necklaces. A perfectly-cut black jacket that matched the trousers. Silver and black rings on his fingers, and small silver hoops in both ears.

My body wavered, and my brain stuttered. My insides blazed, sending flames licking over every inch of my flesh.

His eyes narrowed as he took me in, those unforgettable lips of his now twisted. Lips that had been on me this morning. Lips I knew so well. Lips I craved.

Wes's cool gaze flicked over me from head to toe, sending chills racing over my heated flesh. I dug the stiletto heels of my boots into the floor as a hot vibrational hum blasted through me at full force. Only Wes, be he the rugged hoodie and jeans version or this cold edgy alpha (in an incredible sophisticated black suit!) version, had the power to make me melt, blush, tremble.

And come.

Alpha hot man, indeed. I swallowed hard, but it was no use, I couldn't steel myself against the magnificence that was this man, and I didn't want to anymore. Didn't have to. *No. More.*

Everyone stared at us. Grinning, waiting, a dizzying current buzzing around the lounge.

I lifted my chin. "Where's my corsage?"

Wes's eyes widened. "Your *what*?" Everyone burst into laughter.

A grin twitched over my lips. "It feels like you're picking me up for the prom."

Wes's lips tightened, but no grin. "The prom that never was, huh?"

Something in my chest pinched. He remembered. When we were seeing each other back in high school, Wes had promised to take me to my prom and to his. But it had all been a lie. A lie that I had counted on, daydreamed about. Spent hours fantasizing about.

But now, I could dream again.

My back straightened as I strode toward him with everyone silently watching us, my boots making a *dink dink* sound on the floor in the loaded silence. I got close, and Wes's chest expanded on a big inhale, his spicy woody cologne filled my senses. All man.

I slid my hand in his and smiled softly at him. "This is way better."

His gaze shot down to our joined hands. "Is it?" His voice was a hoarse whisper.

I squeezed his hand in mine. "Most definitely."

His jaw still tight, he met my gaze again. "You look beautiful."

"Thank you. You look fantastic. Handsome, in fact."

"Are you saying I'm not usually handsome?" He let loose a smile, which sent an electric jab through my suddenly wobbly insides.

"You're always cute—"

"Cute?" His lips twisted.

"And sexy and very hot. This is sophisticated and edgy handsome." I touched the edge of his black jacket and a familiar luxury French designer logo flashed at me from the inside. "Whoa. You're going all out on your clothes."

He let out a chuckle. "All of this was a gift from Beck. Didn't think I'd ever wear it, but here we are."

"I'm glad you did." My gaze raked down his chest and his long legs to his boots. "It's perfect on you, especially with your boots and all the silver." I fingered the wallet chain hanging from his pants.

Our gazes locked and held, and that internal hum got louder. *Mesmerized all right.*

"Let's roll out!" Bear's booming voice snapped me and Wes to rigid attention. Bear marched out of the clubhouse and we all followed.

Outside, Wes handed me a lid, and fastening it on, I climbed on the back of his bike like the proverbial ol' lady. This was my life. The life I knew. Only this time I wasn't my parents' kid on the sidelines anymore. I was *in* it.

Wes took off in the middle of the convoy of Harleys toward the center of town. I held on to him, a slow grin growing on my lips. Me and Wes. On a bike. Like years ago. But I wasn't that bright-eyed innocent, and Wes was no longer that angry rebel with the nefarious cause. Now we were adults making choices.

Adults shadowed with sadness and regrets but reaching for something better.

We glided over the winding road through the forested hills, riding in the center of the Jacks. My body leaned against Wes as he commandeered his Harley. The Jacks were not my father's brothers, yet I felt accepted, a member of their family somehow.

"*I belonged,*" Grace had said.

With Dad missing, I clung to those feelings of acceptance and comfortable, soaking them up through the intense vibration and roar of the chrome monster underneath us and the thundering of all the bikes surrounding us, soaking them up through Wes. As we zoomed over the blacktop my body curled around his.

The cool wind pummeled me, and the crisp air scented with resinous woods that were almost sweet filled me up. My gaze took in the cathedral of evergreens on the high hills surrounding us. Meager was so beautiful, so different from all the many remote Wyoming and Nebraska small towns of my past that had blurred into one quiet, dusty strip of aged stores and nondescript houses surrounded by farmland or flat, empty prairies. They had their own austere appeal, but this...

This was truly beautiful, stirring something new inside me.

The road descended, and suddenly the wall of forest broke and the peaks of buildings and roofs were finally visible. The sun set in the distance, its rich orange glow a ball of fire in the sky over the ridge of evergreens that enclosed Meager.

Slowing our speed, Wes got us onto Clay Street, and I sat up straighter. The old fashioned street lamps had just flicked on, brightening the street along with the lights glowing from every shop. There was traffic, vehicle and pedestrian. The town was crowded this evening with people strolling and window shopping on a breezy summer's evening. Cocktail hour at Pete's Tavern. Dinner time at the Bay Leaf.

And party time at the town's tattoo shop, Trash Ink, whose neon signs lit up the freshly-painted white brick building outside and in, along with multi-colored lights strung up on its corner location, creating a party space outside. I was sure Alicia must have had to wrangle town permission for that, and she'd gotten her way.

A crowd of boisterous people had already spilled out onto the street, rock music filling the air. The roaring blast of our motorcycles had everyone spinning around, smiling, waving, a few scowling. Luckily, we all found parking down the side streets. Locking down his bike, Wes took my hand and we charged up Clay with the Jacks crew. My pulse pounded along with our quick pace and with the feeling that Wes and I were on a date.

"By the way—" He slung an arm around my shoulder, pulling me close, and I let out a small gasp at the sudden movement. "I'm all set for tonight." He lowered his voice. "My truck is ready for us on the outskirts of the clubhouse."

"You're still into going?"

"Why wouldn't I be?" He kept his attention ahead, not meeting my gaze.

My hand went to his chest. "Thank you, Wes."

We got to the shop, and the people partying on the sidewalk turned and stared at us. A couple of women my age frowned, spotting Wes with his arm around me.

"I think your fan club is disappointed."

"They'll survive."

We cut our way through the crowd to get inside the shop.

"Wes! There he is!" Jams, a tattoo artist who worked on Lenore, darted over.

"Hey, man, you know, Lindy?"

"Hey, Lindy. You work for Lenore, right?" asked Jams. "I've seen you around."

"That's me. You do amazing work, Jams."

"Thanks." His grin deepened. "When are you coming over for some work?"

"I—"

"She's mine. Only I get to touch her skin."

My heart jerked in my chest, and Jams raised his hands in the air, his freckled face blushing. "Message received loud and clear, bro."

I forced a laugh to release the tension. Alpha Man mode had been engaged.

Jams handed us beers.

"Thanks. To the shop!" I raised my bottle.

"To the shop!" the men said.

I swallowed down a gulp. It had been so long since I'd been to any kind of party, and here I was with Wes. Definite date vibes. The teenage girl in me squealed and happy danced in delight.

I reminded myself not to drink much more. Sure, I'd love to catch a buzz to take my current edge off, but I didn't want to pay for that pleasure with sluggishness later on as tonight was game night.

I'd never heard back from Minty. Had he gone to the Dip already? Could he even get away from the clubhouse? I knew if I told him what I was planning he'd freak and find a way to stop me, so I didn't tell him.

Wes steered me through the crowd. "Let me introduce you to Ronny." Another group of young women's faces brightened at the sight of Wes then dimmed at the sight of me with Wes.

Alicia had her arms around a tall, robust, older man with longish hair pulled back in a ponytail, earrings along his one ear, tats swirling around his neck and down his chest, chains around his jeans. A blazer over a shop T-shirt.

"Sweetheart, hey." Alicia beamed at Wes and beamed light on me too. "Lindy, so good to see you, hon. You look fantastic. So good to see you here together." She hugged me.

Approval formally bestowed.

"Thanks, Alicia. Congratulations on the shop's anniversary. It looks incredible tonight."

"Thank you, hon."

"Hey, Ronny—" Wes touched the man's arm. "Want you to meet my girl, Lindy."

My heart expanded and squeezed all at once. *My girl.* Did he say that to make a show of being in a relationship, for the strategy? Maybe, but it damn well sounded good, landing straight in my chest and melting there. Felt good, too.

"Hey, Lindy." Ronny took my hand, and Alicia's smile got wider and brighter. "Great to meet you. Heard a lot about you."

"Great to meet you too, Ronny. I've been over here a few times with Lenore, but I never got to meet you. Congratulations on the store's anniversary, to both of you."

"Thank you. I want you to know, I'm praying and hoping your dad comes home real soon. That's got to be real rough on you. I've met your dad a number of times and he's one tough man."

"He sure is."

Ronny leaned in closer to me. "A man doesn't get his road name for an ice pick for nothing, now does he?"

"He certainly does not." I grinned. "Speaking of which, he loved how you improved on his original ice pick tat a few months ago. Your sense of detail is beyond."

His eyes lit up. "Thanks. Appreciate that."

Wes introduced me to Jet, a gorgeous raven-haired tattoo artist he worked with, and we hung out with her and Rachel. Jams came over and he took off with the girls to check on party supplies. Wes leaned into me. "You're not drinking your beer. Need a soda?"

"That'd be great, thanks."

Wes dove back into the crowd and headed for the drinks corner. As he waited for the bartender at the front reception desk, a woman chatted him up. She was gorgeous. Tall, athletic body. Great makeup. Maybe she was a dancer at the local strip club?

My stomach twisted as I remembered what Zoë had told me about Wes dating lots of pretty girls all the time. I'd bet Wes was a popular man over at the strip club. A handsome grin lit his face as she spoke, but the second he got our drinks, he disengaged and came right over.

I let out a laugh as he handed me my soda. "Thank you."

"What's so funny?"

"Everywhere you go, you've got a fan club."

He only shrugged and sipped his beer. No comeback.

"It's a sure sign," I said.

"Of what?"

"An Alpha hottie who leaves a potent scent trail behind him, leaving all in his wake swooning."

"You don't have to flirt with me, Lindy."

"What?" My shoulders tensed.

"I don't want any more misunderstandings between us. I made myself clear last night and this morning, but if that's not what you want, that's not what you want. So, this, now, tonight —" He wagged his index finger between us. "—is all about the strategy, right?"

My brow furrowed.

"That's what you said, isn't it? That's what you want?"

I only twisted my lips. Words jumbled in my brain.

"Excuse me?" He tilted his head. "What was that?"

"That is what I said, but–"

"I must admit, you're right."

"I am? About…"

"The strategy. Good call. I'm committed to the plan for later tonight, and I know you are too, so we need to see this through for that to work smoothly." Taking a long pull from his beer bottle, he pressed me in tight to his side. His hand lazed down the slope of my hip to my rear, sending blazes of fire over every inch of my body. His lips brushed the side of my face. "You smell good. Feel even better."

A shiver went through my middle. "You're enjoying this, aren't you?"

"I am, because I like being close to you, 'cause I'm feeling it." His lips brushed my temple. "We made it obvious to the club, now we got to do it for the whole town—" Turning me, he took my mouth.

My pulse jerked, my clit throbbed. "Wes—"

His tongue dove deep, a ringed hand sliding around my neck, keeping me close.

Holy. Shit.

"How was that?" he said against my lips.

"Huh? Oh." I swallowed hard. "That was g-good."

"Good? That's all you got for me?"

"Amazing."

His thumb rubbed across my swollen lips as a sly grin prickled over his features. I knew what was coming.

"Don't say it, Wes. Don't…"

"So amazing, *babe,*" he purred on a chuckle as he leaned back against the wall, his arm casually slung over my shoulders. "I get it now, Lindy. I do. It's easy for you to tease and take the reins. You dig that. You like the control."

I stilled. My face heated.

"You don't have to answer, because I know the answer. No one can threaten you in your bubble." He took my hand in his, gently brushing my skin with his soft, warm lips. A moan rose in my throat. "Funny thing though, Lind, that's usually a guy issue. Yet, you outdo us all."

I bowed my head. "So honored you think so, especially coming from Meager's most sought after young stud. All the sighing and fluttering of eyelashes in here has made me positively dizzy."

His lips tipped up. "Mmm. I should take credit for your tough as nails bubble. I'm the one who put that defense mode there, right?" That muscle along his jaw flexed.

"Wes, hi! Great to see you!" a young blonde chirped at his side.

He turned, his hand releasing me from its firm grip. "Hey, Debbie." His voice brightened, a smile forming on those sensual lips.

My lips.

My fingers curled into his fabulous French suit jacket, and with a tug, I swiveled him back toward me and took his mouth, my body surging against his. His hand cupped the back of my head as he moaned down my throat. I swallowed that moan like I'd swallowed his cum. With determination, with longing. Lust and hunger.

Wes was mine.

TWENTY-SIX

LINDY

ALL THE JACKS couples were here at the party tonight. Each old lady saying to me one variation or another of *"You and Wes are together? Wow!"*

I smiled at Tania, Grace, Mary Lynn, Nicole, and Jill, and blushed each time. Alicia didn't say a word. She only beamed her laser light of approval on me through her smile or a squeeze of her arm around my shoulders whenever we stood together.

Wes either kept an arm around my waist or an arm slung around my shoulders, always keeping me close. He introduced me to his clients, friends from high school, and a few of his fan girls–young ones, like Debbie, who I'd interrupted earlier by kissing Wes, and many women who were over fifty. They showed me the designs Wes had created and inked for them and shared the personal stories behind the images.

"Wes, Debbie's mermaid fairy is so beautiful."

"She came out good."

"More than good. More like incredible, glorious…"

"You liked it?"

"You're very talented."

"Thanks."

"Your clients genuinely like you. They trust you and your vision. You've given them something so special and unique. You must be real proud of that."

He pushed a lock of his hair back from his face. "I haven't really given it much thought. Not like that at least. I want them to feel comfortable and be 100% happy with the result. The key for me is the personal significance of the design they want. If I can make that come to life for them, and maybe make it even more special than they'd first imagined, that's a real good day."

There was that look on his face again. That innocent, kind, easygoing look. It wasn't naive. It simply was something pure—that was pure Wes. An appreciation of the simple truths. I took his hand in mine and squeezed. "You've created something good and lasting with your work. You give people joy. That is a beautiful thing. And it's important, too."

His gaze shifted to his boots and back to me. "Thanks."

I lifted up and pressed my lips against his cheek, and his breath audibly caught.

"Hey, Wes, help me bring out the cake?" Jams stood in front of us. "Sorry, guys. Alicia gave me the bat signal."

"There's cake too?" I said.

"It's a surprise for Ronny," said Jams.

"It's his birthday next week," said Wes. "So we thought it'd be fun to celebrate tonight with everyone here."

"That's a great idea."

"Be right back." Wes gave my arm a squeeze and took off with Jams toward the back of the shop.

I moved through the crowd toward the front. Dawes, from across the room, and Bear, on the sidewalk outside the main window where I stood, tracked my movements. It felt good knowing they were keeping an eye out. So far we hadn't heard a word from the Flames about their location or, for that matter, what their exact plan in Kansas City was, or if they'd found out new information in the meantime. At least no one had told me about it.

"Excuse me," I said to a woman, who stood in front of me talking loudly to a friend. She turned around, and I stopped in my tracks. Filling my vision was a face that shot flares through my veins like it had the first time.

The grin on her overly bronzed features morphed into a scowl. "What are *you* doing here?"

Renee, Dad's hook-up.

"I live here."

Her heavily outlined matte brown lips twisted into a smirk. "Aw, did your daddy kick you out for being such a bitch to me?"

"My father went missing that day, and I don't think that was a coincidence."

"Aren't you the Conspiracy Theory Karen? All we did was fuck."

I leaned into her, teeth bared. "Did you fuck him over too?"

"What are you talking about?"

"What are you doing here? You keeping an eye on me? Are you following me?"

"Why would I follow you after how you treated me? Are you nuts? You obviously got daddy issues, and that's your problem, honey. Not mine."

"Why are you here?" I crossed my arms.

"I got invited, that's why. I'm a steady client at all of Ronny's shops. A few years ago I even modeled for a couple store ads."

"What's going on?" A hand landed on my back. Alicia. "You two know each other?"

"She fucked my dad the night before he disappeared."

"Ah," quipped Alicia, completely nonplussed.

Eyes wide, Renee jerked her head back. "Alicia, she's—"

"You go on, Renee." Alicia gestured for her to leave us.

"Watch out for her. She's a loony tune." Renee swirled her finger in the air.

"Fuck off!" I bit out. People around us turned and stared.

Renee shot me the finger and strutted away.

"Lindy—"

Wes charged over. "What's going on? What did Renee say to you?"

"You know her?"

"She's a steady customer at the Deadwood shop," he replied.

"She's also a biker groupie," said Alicia. "Guess she's been over at the Flames?"

"I found her alone in my house the last morning, and I threw her out."

Alicia squeezed my shoulder. "Good for you, honey."

"She's the last one to have talked to him or seen him. Catch found her and talked to her, but he said she didn't seem to be lying or hiding anything. Seeing her here, now, after…"

"Bear knows her," Alicia said. "How about I have him talk to her?"

My shoulders eased. "That'd be great. Thanks." I grabbed her hand. "I'm sorry, Alicia. I don't want to create problems for you at your party. Lashing out at her like that was wrong. I'm so sorry."

She held my gaze. "You've got nothing to be sorry about, Lindy. Not a damn thing. Good for you for telling her like it is. Cake in two minutes." She winked at us and left.

Wes let out a breath. "Damn, woman, I walk away, and you get yourself into a cat fight."

"Wes…"

"I dig that about you, baby." He grinned. "Huge turn on."

"Stop."

"Stop telling you how you turn me on?"

"Not that." I laughed. "Stop calling me baby."

"It should be earned, huh?" He took my hand in his. "That must have been a shocker to see her here."

"It was."

His head slanted toward the window. "Check it out–Bear is on the move."

My gaze followed Wes's. Bear handed Renee a drink and led her outside on the sidewalk. Smiling huge, she trotted alongside him, a hand wrapped around his massive tattooed bicep. He was a charmster when he wanted to be, wasn't he? And Renee seemed to charm so damned easy.

My stomach pitched at the sight of her flirting, laughing loudly at whatever Bear said to her, a hand lightly touching his chest while she sipped on her straw. Had she flirted with Dad like that? Had she flirted with and screwed a whole string of bikers since she last saw Dad? Oh, what did it matter?

"Happy birthday to you!" A chorus of voices rose in the shop, bringing me out of my head. Wes and I joined in the singing, moving toward where Alicia and Ronny stood by the cake.

We applauded and cheered as Alicia gave Ronny a big juicy kiss. With his arm around his woman, Ronny expressed his thanks to everyone for supporting the shop and coming out tonight.

Wes leaned into me, the press of his hard wall of warmth against my body, his delicious spicy scent filling my senses made me wobbly. "We need head back to the MC."

Back to the MC.

Back to my room.

Only me and Wes in that room.

His hand slid over my ass, his gaze shooting to my mouth.

I cleared my throat. "We should."

"Let me get Dready—"

A woman with long, highlighted brown hair blocked Wes's way toward Dready. Danielle, the owner of the local hair salon. She was gorgeous, over forty-something, and a frequent customer at Lenore's Lace.

From what Lenore had told me, Danielle had been in a war with Alicia since Alicia had laid out an edict for all the old ladies to stop going to her salon for over a year due to some man snafu. But after that died down, Danielle had been caught in action with the former mayor by his then wife, Erica, the sweet woman who owned the Meager Grand. As Erica's daughter, Violet, was married to Lenore's son, Lenore didn't need to pick sides, and neither did the other old ladies. Again, Alicia had invoked pariah status.

My pulse ticked up as Danielle swept her glossy soft waves from her face, cocked an eyebrow, seemed to wink at Wes, and touched his shoulder as she laughed at something he said. Was she flirting with Wes or was it my always in-fourth-gear-and-thinking-the-worst imagination?

Her hand brushed his shoulder this time, a slow smile sweeping over her filled-in lips. No, she fucking was flirting with him. I'd bet every single one of Lenore's thousand tattoos that Danielle was into seducing Wes, not only to have a bite of that delicious young hot bod of his but to get back at Alicia.

I tracked over, and nestling in between them, slid my arm under Wes's jacket and around his waist as my other went to his bare chest and stroked. "Baby, I'm ready to get out of here. How about you?" My voice came out glazed and steamy, leaving no doubt as to my intentions.

Wes's tongue darted out and lashed at his full lip. *That wicked tongue.* I grinned at him, and he pulled me in closer. "Danielle, you know my girl, Lindy, don't you? She works at Lenore's."

Her gaze narrowed, and her bladed brows pinched together as she took me in. "Sure. Hi."

"Bye," I chirped, and I led Wes away from her.

"That was kinda fun." Wes chuckled.

"I thought so too."

We found Alicia and Ronny and said our goodbyes with big hugs. Slinging an arm around me, Wes guided me to the street outside. Tonight, each and every time he'd pulled one of these possessive moves—and there had been many—it made my insides twist and pulse and thrum. I loved it. I was finally enjoying it.

Outside, the evening chill raced over my skin. We bumped

into Butler and Tania, who were laughing with Boner and Jill on the corner. "Are you guys coming to Pete's with us?" asked Jill.

"Not tonight, we have to get back to the club." Wes pressed his body against mine, his hand dangling over my shoulder.

"Ohhhh." Tania grinned. "Alrighty."

Mission very much accomplished.

Butler's face tightened. "Go straight back to the MC. Do not stop anywhere, got that?"

"No stops," Wes affirmed.

"You're not going alone. Dready and the two prospects are going with you?" said Boner.

"They're coming out now."

"Keep our girl safe," said Tania, a hand on my arm.

"Night y'all," said Wes.

"Good night, everyone," I murmured.

With Dready and two prospects, we headed to the bikes. I took in big gulps of the fresh cold air as we walked down the well-lit side street where we'd parked earlier. But it did nothing to stop the rabid butterflies from twitching in my stomach. I blew out a breath. Was I nervous to be alone with Wes?

"You okay?" Wes handed me the helmet.

"Yeah. Sure." I took it, adjusting it on my head.

We took off, and my heart thudded in my chest. Dready was ahead of us, and two prospects rode behind us in the dark through the town. Up we climbed through the thick, silent woods.

We flew over the smooth road that Wes had grown up riding. I leaned into Wes's warm, firm body as he took a tight curve. Ease flooded through me as my hands pressed into his sides.

But the pounding of my heart wouldn't stop.

TWENTY-SEVEN

WES

WE FINALLY PULLED into the club, and Lindy and I got off the bike. As she handed me the lid, our gazes met in the gleam of the harsh overhead lamps in the yard.

We had achieved phase one and two of the plan: Make them believe we were together and return to the club early. Next up: Confirm they know we should definitely not be disturbed and then put our alarms on and get a few hours of sleep.

I checked my watch. 10pm. In five hours we'd be off. Slinging my arm around her shoulders, I gave her a quick kiss as we entered the clubhouse.

Dready grabbed a bottle of beer from the bar. "You guys want one?"

"Nah. We got some edibles to enjoy tonight," I lied, licking my bottom lip as I gave Lindy *the look*. My I'm-gonna-fuck-you-like-a-wild-monkey-all-night-long look.

A small giggle spilled from her lips. *Good girl.* "Who needs booze? Not us." Her voice came out seductive and sly, and it made my dick pulse in my jeans. I only chuckled.

Lindy reached up and planted a kiss on my mouth, her

fingers curling into my shirt, pulling me close as she sighed loudly. I let out a groan for effect, my hands squeezing her ass. "Let's grab some snacks for later."

"Good idea." Lindy moved past Dready behind the bar and grabbed bags of pretzels and potato chips.

I leaned on the bar. "Babe, there's chocolate pudding by the cola. Grab a couple, huh?"

"Oooo, yummmm…." Lindy flashed me a grin as she opened the bar fridge and took two pudding cups.

"Have a good night, you wild kids." Dready let out a laugh as he headed across the lounge toward the offices. The prospects eyed us as they flopped on the sofa in front of the television.

Lindy rounded the bar, and I grabbed her arm and reeled her in. I kissed her so the prospects would see and hear. Dropping the snacks on the floor, she let out a loud laugh followed by moans as I deepened the kiss.

"Let's go, baby." I smacked her ass.

We grabbed the food from the floor, and she laughed loudly as I chased her down the hall to her room.

Once inside, I locked the door behind us, and dumped the food on the dresser. Lindy toed off her boots. "They bought it, huh?"

"They bought it." I took off my jacket and hung it on the back of the chair. "We've got a few hours yet." I pulled off my boots. "I already set my alarm. Set yours too just in case. We should get some rest so that—"

"I don't want to."

"Don't want to what?" I said carefully in the dark.

"Get some rest."

My heart thudded in my chest. "What do you want, Lind?" My rough whisper seemed to make her breathe heavier.

She lunged at me, her tongue plundering my mouth. Demanding, searching. Fucking hungry.

Jesus.

"Lindy—" I peeled myself away from her. "We don't have to—"

Her fingers dug into my waist. "I want to."

I smoothed back the hair from her face. "What is it you want exactly?"

"I want you."

My head tilted. This was what I'd been waiting to hear, and yet...

She kissed me again, pulled back, kissed me again. I didn't move a muscle. She did all the work, all the exploring. Her hands spread over my chest and yanked up the ends of my dress shirt from inside my trousers. Her fingers fumbled at my belt. A hand cupped my hard erection over my trousers and squeezed.

Gritting my teeth, I grabbed her wrists, stopping her. "I can't do this. Not like this."

Her body stiffened, and her eyes widened. "Why not? You don't want—"

"We got the room, we set up the scenario, might as well?"

"No! It's not that." Her lips trembled. She seemed to shrink. "You don't want..."

"Oh, Lind..." I let out a deep groan as my forehead slid against hers. "I want you so fucking bad, so bad it hurts. But I can't pretend with you, or play a game with you. And I don't want to. I've been a master pretender with women ever since I can remember." My hands slid up her silky arms, and she shivered. I grabbed her hand and put it on my heaving chest, over my scars, over my heart. "You feel that? That's me wanting you, Lind. I'm feeling things I've never felt before."

I took in a breath and kept going. "I want to be clear and straight with you on this because I fucking hate mixed signals and misinterpretations, like yesterday. Hell yeah, I want to have sex with you, but because I want us to go that next level. I want us to be together for real and in all the ways. I don't want us to do this because we never did or because we're both here and horny."

I cradled her face. "Being inside you, coming inside you, would be that next level for me, not just getting off. You want to go there with me? Really be with me? 'Cause that's the only way you're getting my cock. I know I did you dirty, and I deserved every slap you've given me since that day and more. Things are different now. And I'm telling you, I want you in my life, and if we do this, it's a step on that road, in that direction. It's the fucking door opening."

Her lips parted, and her eyes widened. Speechless.

"Lind, I'm asking you again, what do you want?"

"I-I want you."

"That just your pussy talking?"

Her chest expanded. "All of me wants all of you." Her voice was clear and firm. "And I want you to know that I'm grateful you've been there for me since I got here."

"I don't want your gratitude."

"But I am grateful for you in my life, and you need to hear it. You being here for me at the Jacks, taking me to the Dip tonight, means everything to me. Everything." Her fingers dug into my sides. "I don't know what we'll find over there, but I know deep in my bones, that right this second, I want to stop time and go to that next level with you. I want us to open that door and go through it together." She swallowed hard. "I want you, Wes. I want you in my life. I want to be with you for real."

My heart banged out of my chest, and I snatched her up in my arms. We held each other—*held each other*. I brought her to the bed and took off her blouse. Her back arched, her body writhing on the mattress, hips twisting as I stroked her beautiful tits. I peeled back the lace cups of her bra and sucked on a nipple. Pure fucking heaven.

She wrapped her legs around my hips. "I want to feel you, Wes. I want to feel you everywhere. On me, in me…"

"You will, Lind." I unbuckled her big leather belt and peeled those tight jeans off her legs, tossing them to the floor.

She freed her hair from the scarf that bound it, and it tumbled in waves over the pillow. "Fill me up. Make me forget all the—"

I cuffed her wrists, her face inches from mine. "I'm not going to fuck you for the first time because you need to forget something, no matter how shitty things have been. I'm going to fuck you because you want me so damn bad you're going to cry and explode if you don't have my cock pounding you. And you're going to remember it for fucking ever. You feeling me?"

Her eyes widened, her lips fell open. "Oh my God."

"What?" I grit out.

Her tits arched closer to my chest. "My hot alpha rough guy." Her pelvis ground against mine. "Kiss me."

"No."

"What do you mean, no?"

"I'm gonna make you come first. Then, maybe, I'll let you kiss me."

She let out a loud whimper, her head falling back. "Hot alpha rough guy fury… I'm coming already…"

"Don't you dare." I tore her panties off her legs. "Want you coming on my mouth." A caveman impulse had me in its grip, her scent filling me like I was a wolf in hot pursuit of its prey. Gripping her thighs, I sank my face in her pussy in one quick, rough stroke, and she yelped loudly. So wet for me.

Digging her hands in my hair, Lindy lifted her hips against my face. She moaned and cried out. "Wes…oh, Wes!" She came.

I gripped her body tightly, my lips sucking, tongue swirling from her throbbing clit down to her ass, exploring every delicate wet inch of flesh. "Up," I ordered as I lifted her on all fours and bit her ass cheek. She cried out sharply, her arms wobbling as I slid two fingers into her pussy. "Do not move." I brought her pussy over my face, that Hell No tattoo daring me.

The tip of my tongue lashed her wet slit, and she gasped. "Ride me." She sank over my mouth, and I ate her, her hands gripping the headboard as she ground over me. Moaning in short, sharp cries, her body trembling, the bed screeching, she came again, and I lapped at her, my fingers gripping her thighs.

"Wes…"

"Keep it going…" I pinched and stroked and licked and squeezed. I smacked her damp inner thigh over that tattoo. *Fucking hell yes.* She was all mine to make scream, to beg, to come, to fuck. My fingers squeezed her swollen nub, pressing it.

"Oh my God!" Her body quivered in my grip.

"No, baby, you say my name." My fingers churned and slid. "Say it while you come for me."

Her jaw slackened as her body tightened around me. "Wes… Wes…WES!" She came again, and that throb kept pulsing through me. Her body slumped, and I flipped her over on the mattress.

Her eyes blinked up at me as I ripped off my clothes. Opening the drawer of the small night table, I grabbed the strip of condoms that I knew would be there, and ripped one open with my teeth. Her breathing picked up as she watched me fit it over my aching stiff dick already dripping at the tip.

I leaned over her and brushed her lips with mine as I spread her one leg with my knee and brought my aching cock to her slick opening, her fingernails raking my skin.

"Ah, Lindy, baby, finally…" I entered her, sliding inside slowly. Sleek and tight. She adjusted herself, tilting, making all sorts of innocent, illicit sounds, and moans. Her fingernails dug into my back as I thrust deeper. My body tightened. "Lind?"

"Keep going," her voice bit out in the dark.

I stopped moving.

"Wes! Keep going!"

"Lindy." I pulled out of her. "Have you ever—"

"Wes…"

"Tell me the truth."

She took in a breath. "This is my first time."

My brain exploded. "Lind?"

Her warm hands cupped my face. "Please keep going."

"But…Why? How?" I sat back on my haunches. "When we were together, you always wanted to. In fact, you insisted before I'd even had the chance to bring it up."

"Because I wanted *you*. And after, no one else came close. I tried, a couple of times, but I couldn't go through with it. You were it for me, Wes. Even when I hated you, it was always you. Only you."

My heart twisted painfully in my chest. Gently, I brushed her lips with mine. A sadness overwhelmed me with a new thought as I stroked her cheek. "You sure it was me, or were you punishing yourself all those years for having believed in me? I know you, Lind."

"Wes," she gritted out.

"Tell me. Tell me right now with my dick at your door. Doesn't get any more honest than this."

Her hands swept down my damp chest. "After you, I didn't want to be anyone's toy ever again, but I didn't want to settle either. Or just do it to do it. After my mom died, all those heavy dark emotions cemented together inside me. No matter how much I willed myself to keep hating you, no matter how much I clawed at my heart to get you out, it was always yours."

My vision blurred as a wave of heat washed through me, blood rushing through my veins. Every cell in my being ignited, ignited for this girl. *My girl.* I kissed her, tasting salty wet over her lips on her hot face. "I'm going to make you mine, baby. All mine."

"Make me yours, Wes. Make me yours…" Her voice ached in the dark as she pulled me back down on top of her.

My tongue lashed at her lips, trailed down her throat as she opened her legs for me. Her one leg wrapped around my hip as I got my dick at her entrance. I took her hand in mine and brought it to my cock. "Feel me go in you." She let out a cry as her fingers brushed my cock at her slit.

Rocking my hips, I thrust slowly, my cock burrowing inside her. I met the barrier again, but this time, kept moving. Kept thrusting. Her head knocked back, a long, low cry left her lips, and I froze. Had I hurt her?

"Yes, oh yes…" Her fingernails dug into my flesh as her pelvis tilted against mine, her other leg bending at my side. "Keep going."

There was nothing I wanted more than for her first time to be perfect. This was a gift beyond anything. A pure gift. On a quick breath, I rocked deeper, and my cock throbbed enclosed in her tight heat. A blast of light went off in my head, burst in my chest, burst through every muscle as I moved deeper inside her.

We found a gentle rhythm, a sensation unlike any other I'd ever experienced. It built, it grew, we pleaded, demanded. She clung to me, urging me on, taking me in.

Rocketing through me was one thought. *Sacred* ignited in my soul. *Purpose* flared through my veins.

A consecration of us.

Brutal truth was the most beautiful thing.

My heart thundered in my chest as we slid and ground against each other, throbbing, searching, exploring. I kept my eyes on her, wanted to watch her, be there with her, for her. "Lindy…" I slid my hand between our sweaty bodies and found her clit and stroked.

Her pelvis moved quicker, urging me on. Her breathing got deeper. "I feel you, Wes. I feel you." A searing whisper.

My lungs jammed together. "You're all I feel, baby."

Everything I was roared, and I lost all control. I hammered inside her, desperate for more, for more of us. Her body bucked with mine, the bed jerking against the floor. The air in the room was thick with sex, thick with the harsh sound of our ragged breaths and our flesh slapping together, the thud of the head-board banging against the wall.

I squeezed her swollen clit as I kept up the pace. "My pussy."

She groaned. "My cock," she said, her voice raw, her gaze never leaving mine, her full tits bouncing with my driving thrusts. Her body suddenly tensed and jerked in my hold, her raw helpless cries filling the small room.

Waves of pleasure slammed into me. "Lind…Lind…"

I slid down her sweaty, luscious body, my tongue padding her clit. Gripping her trembling thighs, I licked at the blood staining her flesh, *our blood,* staining that Hell No tattoo. *All mine.* Lapped at her cum, *our cum.*

The taste of us, of what we'd done, how far we'd come, us together, filled my mouth. Filled my soul. Filled a place in my heart that I'd never known existed.

Holding each other in the quiet darkness, we kissed slowly, our tongues, our lips sealing every promise our bodies had made.

Lindy was mine.

And I…

I *belonged* to her.

TWENTY-EIGHT

LINDY

THE ALARM HAD GONE OFF, and I darted to the bathroom and took a quick shower to get energized. Faded blood stained my inner thighs.

I'd had sex for the first time.

I'd had sex with Wes.

I caught my gaze in the mirror as I wrapped the towel around me and grinned at my reflection. Did I look different? I felt different.

Wes came into the bathroom, a lazy grin on his sleepy face. "Hey." He wrapped his arms around me from behind, and we both took in our reflection in the foggy mirror. "You good?"

"Very." I turned around in his arms and gave him a quick kiss. No time for indulging in much more right now.

In the room, I got dressed and pulled my hair back in a ponytail. As I tugged on my jeans, Wes came out of the bathroom naked, and my heart leaped in my chest. He was so fucking beautiful. And he was mine.

I could see him naked all the time from here on out…Who knew how this would go? Where we'd end up? All I knew for sure right this very moment was that I had no regrets. I was truly happy that we had happened. It was everything I'd ever wanted it to be. Rough, gentle, sweet, hungry. So satisfying in ways I'd never known satisfying to be. My heart squeezed as he pulled a long-sleeved thermal shirt over his lean, sculpted torso.

He ran his hands through his wet hair. "You ready, Lind?"

"Ready." I slid on my boots, and our gazes locked.

"Come here." He opened his arms, and I launched at him, pressing myself into his chest. "We got this."

"We got this." I stroked his back. "Thank you for doing this with me."

He pressed his lips against mine. Lips that I knew so well now, lips that I craved, lips that laid a trail of fire on my flesh over and over and over. Lips that were home.

Dragging my fingers through his silky wet hair, I hugged him and took in a final inhale, memorizing the warm scent of his throat, the feel of his body. I let go. "Let's do it."

Wes tugged a black beanie over his head. "Let's do it." We shut off our cell phones and put them in the dresser drawer. In his truck, Wes had two burner phones for us to use.

He unlocked the door, and needles prickled my skin with his careful turn of the bolt. If anyone heard us now…

I blew out a breath.

We exited the room, and I locked the door slowly with my key. I followed Wes down the hall. There were no sounds coming from any of the bedrooms or the lounge, and peeking to make sure no one was there, we darted through the lounge and headed down another hallway toward one of the back doors.

Wes dialed a code on the security pad of the metal door, and it opened. Taking my hand, he led me through, and we were outside. Three thirty-three in the morning and the black sky was full of stars, the air crisp and sweet. Squeezing my hand, Wes led me against the back wall of the building. He knew where the security cameras were, and we were, of course, avoiding them. "Now." We ran down toward the far fence.

My pulse pounded along with my lungs. Finally, Wes gestured and stopped at the end of the open field in the back of the clubhouse. "Now we climb over. Ready?"

He sprang over the fence in seconds, tossing himself on the other side. I climbed up, my heart hammering in my chest. I got to the top and twisted over, my fingers burning in the metal strips, my muscles throbbing. Taking in a deep breath, I scrambled down. Wes's hands met my back and he grabbed me.

We ran in the moonlight across the field, as if we were kids running away from home. Suddenly, Wes's truck took shape in the distance, its gleaming metal visible.

He unlocked the truck, and I climbed in the front seat next to him. As I put my seat belt on, I noticed a black backpack tucked on the floor behind his seat. The truck's engine rumbled to life, and we took off in the infinite darkness of the dense trees.

My back pressed against the padded seat. "I'm glad you know where you're going because I feel like we're lost in a forest."

"There's an old hiking trail a couple hundred yards down from here that people stopped using decades ago, and that's what the club uses to get to the back end of the property if they need to go under the radar to load and unload."

Finally, we got onto the dirt trail, and the truck jolted and bobbed along the rocky and uneven path, branches and dense greenery scraping and brushing the truck. My fingers dug into the upholstery of the seat, my attention focused on the sharply lit-up terrain in front of us. My shoulders eased. Finally, ahead of us, was blacktop.

"And away we go…" murmured Wes.

I forced my back to relax and settled against the cushioned seat as the truck picked up speed on the smooth road that took us to Route 385 toward Hot Springs. We got onto Highway 18 and headed out of the Black Hills toward Wyoming.

And into the unknown.

We had about an hour more until we got to the location. We

listened to the radio, and the new Freefall song came on. We chatted about Beck's new album coming out soon and the big national tour the band had planned for next spring as if it were just another day and we were out for a long scenic drive. Ha.

We crossed the border into Wyoming. That ease I'd been enjoying quickly evaporated from my body, and my insides screwed up tightly. One step closer.

Wes and I had gone over the location of the Dip on the map a number of times, but now, to be actually in the area? My fingers had become icy-cold, my breath shallower. The prospect of finding my dad was exciting yet filled me with dread at the thought of what state we'd find him.

If we'd find him.

If we'd find him alive.

And the real reason that he had disappeared *or* had been kidnapped.

My emotions couldn't keep track of it all.

Wes put his hand on my thigh and squeezed. Could he read my mind?

Within minutes, the navigation system told us we'd arrived. Adrenaline shot through me, pumping furiously into my veins. "Slow down a bit," I said. "I think this is where we need to veer left."

"Yep..." He turned, and the truck jerked forward, jostling, coming to a screeching halt that had my heart launching out of my chest. "Fuck!" Wes shouted.

"Wes? What the—"

Snarling, he slammed his hands on the wheel. "We left our phones behind because I knew they'd probably track us with them, but I didn't check my truck. Goddammit!" He bolted out of the truck, and I followed him. He slid his hands around the area of his front tire. He went to every tire and did the same. I turned on the flashlight of my burner phone to help him. He slid under the cab of the truck, and I angled the light so he could see.

The light caught a reflection of metal on the side of his chest. And a leather strap. Wes was carrying a gun.

His jaw tightened as he clawed at something. "Motherfuck!" He scrambled out from under the truck, a device in his hand, and my pulse banged in my neck at the sight. We were being watched. Wes threw it on the ground and smashed it with his boot.

"You think it was the Jacks?" I asked.

"Jacks, Flames, whoever has your dad? Who the fuck knows?" he bit out. "Let's go."

We got back into the truck and took off, our eyes trained ahead.

"There should be a fork in the road coming up," I said, my voice tight.

"There it is." Wes turned right on the fork and a long, narrow country road took us to the outskirts of the town of Rock River.

Only one tall, crooked road lamp provided light over the few blocks of stores, a cafe, and a gas station. "All these years and Rock River looks the same as I remember," I murmured, looking out my window. The adrenaline settled, leaving me supremely alert.

"We follow the road to the next town, but just before the entrance there should be an intersection, and we'll turn left."

"Got it." He knew all this, we'd gone over it so many times, but it kept me sane to say it and he went along with it. Wes kept his eyes on the road, his expression serious. How must he be feeling, knowing that his Dad had probably ridden through here many times doing business with the Blades?

We got to the intersection, a small almost inconsequential fork in a massive field. Wes made the turn onto the dirt road that cut through the field into nowhere. The road became rockier and more bumpy, filled with tall grasses and weeds.

Dimming his lights, he proceeded slowly. "Should be another three miles or so before we see that pathway on the left."

Keeping the speed of the truck under control, both his hands firmly gripped the steering wheel.

"There it is!" I spotted a worn road that had never been tarred over. Wes turned and proceeded even more slowly. "I think this is the beginning of the hill."

He slowed down even more. "I'll park somewhere over here and we'll walk the rest of the way." Wes swung around a grove of trees and we parked on the other side of them.

We got out, and I stretched to combat the tightness in every muscle. There was a chill in the air, and I pulled my jacket around me. Wes came around, locking the truck doors. "Take this."

"Your keys?"

"This is my second set."

"Why?"

"Just in case."

My chest caved in. "In case of what?"

"If something happens, if we go running, if we get separated. At least I'll know you'll be able to get to the truck and use it."

"I wouldn't leave without you."

"Lindy. Take. The. Keys."

My teeth dragged across my lip as I took the keys and shoved them in my pocket.

We walked into the darkness, the dry grasses crunching underfoot, an owl hooting somewhere close by. Wes had that black backpack slung on his back, and a prickle raced around my neck. "What's in the backpack?"

"Insurance." He took my hand and squeezed.

We trekked silently in the dark. The zillion and one stars overhead were bright, but of course, did little to illuminate the landscape. My vision strained to catch anything that was recognizable. We hiked on. A roar thundered in the distance.

A motorcycle.

We froze, my heart pounding loudly in my chest, my stomach churning and clenching. Could it be Raptor? My dad?

"Over here..." Wes pulled me to an overgrowth of bushes and grasses, our heavy breaths filling the air. Squatting down, we waited. The bike got closer and came to a stop, the engine shutting down. Footsteps, muttering. My muscles screamed. Quick marching through the dried grasses, sweeping through the brush. Closer. Closer. My breath burned in my chest as I raised up an inch. I had to see. Had to know.

The figure tracked past. I'd recognize that loping walk anywhere. On the back of his leather jacket was a bright red flame.

I shot up. "Minty?"

"What the fuck!" Wes launched at me, grabbing my jacket and hauling me back.

Minty stopped abruptly in the shadows and swiveled around. "Lindy? That you? What the hell are you doing here?"

"I came to see if Dad was here."

"Who's this?" he growled, gesturing at Wes.

"Wes is a friend. He's with the Jacks."

"You crazy?" He got in my face and turned to Wes. "Take her home, now!"

I got between them. "I never heard from you after I called you. I thought you would've come up here sooner to check it out."

"Been chomping at the bit to come here since you called me, but I couldn't take off with the way they were watching me. Now that most of the club is gone to Kansas City, I managed it."

"You and Dad ever tell the Flames about this place?"

Minty only cast a cold glance at Wes.

Wes shook his head. "Dude, I don't give a shit,"

His jaw tightening, Minty only lifted his chin in reply.

"Didn't think so," I said. "You been back here since?"

"Nah."

"We're here now, so—"

"Dammit, Lindy." Minty gripped my arm.

"Hey!" Wes shoved at him.

"It's okay, Wes." I pulled out of Minty's hold. "Three is better than two or one, don't you think?" I took Wes's hand. "Let's go."

"Jesus." Minty let out a ragged breath. "The hill's not far from here."

The three of us tracked on, and just as Minty had said, the terrain began to ascend, leading us on a curvy trail. We hiked through the grasses, our breathing loud. Suddenly, a narrow dirt footpath was visible. We were almost there.

The path brought us to a clearing. Just as I remembered it. A small wood cabin, only now it had a window, siding, and a thick roof that seemed durable and solid, not uneven and curvy like warped cardboard the way I remembered.

I squeezed Wes's hand. "Welcome to the Dip."

TWENTY-NINE

LINDY

THE THREE OF us scanned the clearing. "No sign of a vehicle or a bike," Wes whispered.

"Dad could still be in there."

"Sure could. You see any lights or cameras? I don't," whispered Minty.

"I don't," replied Wes. "But there could be tiny ones in the trees for all we know, and if he has an app, he'll see us. Then again, if he had an alarm system set and he's inside, it would have gone off already, right?"

"Terrific," Minty grumbled.

"I'm going to check out the periphery of the cabin," said Wes. "Stay with Minty."

"Wes—"

"Remember the keys. Don't stop, don't turn back, don't wait. Promise me."

My muscles tightened. "Promise."

Wes pressed his cold lips against mine, and he was gone.

"Kid might find something out there. "

"In the meantime, let's head to that window."

"I'll go. You stay here."

"For Pete's sake—" Crouching low, I darted forward. Minty came up behind me, the two of us tracking toward the lone square window on the side of the cabin. Our breaths were puffs in the cold night air. Raising up, I peeked through the glass. There was a shutter on the inside, and it was slightly open. My eyes strained in the dark, my pulse pounding. "I see something...a big mound on the floor," I whispered. "Could be him."

Minty lifted up and took a look through the window. "Fuck it." With his gloved hands, he took his gun out of his holster and butted the glass. It broke, cracked. He pushed at it and, shattering, it gave way.

The mound moved. A small groan.

Minty hoisted himself up and darted through the broken glass. "Pick?"

Taking off my jacket, I put it on the window sill and climbed through. My father's voice cried out, and my heart flew up my throat. "Daddy?"

"Lindy?"

My heart pounded wildly. "It's me." The cabin interior was icy cold, and I put my jacket back on.

"Good to see you, brother." Minty squatted down next to Dad as I patted Dad's chest, his shoulders, his arms. A bandage covered his left hand, and my insides twisted.

"Why the hell d'you bring Lindy with you?" Dad barked at Minty.

"You shitting me? I found her here!"

Straining, Dad leaned his head against the wall. "You got to leave, baby. Now."

"We're all going to leave together, Daddy."

"You gotta go. Both of you, go now!" The whites of his eyes glowed in the flashlight of the cell phone Minty had propped up by a chair. Minty whipped out a knife from his boot and cut the ties at Dad's ankles. He went to his back, and cut again, releasing his arms. Rolling over, Dad's body twisted slightly as he groaned.

"Dad, did Raptor do this to you? Was it him?"

"I'm telling you now, go, leave!" my father roared. He lifted up, stretching his arms out. The bandage was bloody and dirty. He yanked on Minty's jacket. "Brother, take her now, get out, the two of you! Leave me and go. He can't find her here. And he sure as hell can't find you."

"Fuck him. We're taking you with us, man."

"I'll just slow you down. I'm telling you, you gotta go!"

"Daddy, it's Raptor, isn't it?"

Grunting, he nodded.

We ignored Dad's pleas and helped him stand. Gulping in deep breaths, he stumbled and leaned against the wall. I darted to the door, and running my hands along the edge, found the bolts and released the locks.

"Listen to me—" Dad sputtered. "He went to go get supplies. Always does it in the middle of the night, then he's back before sunrise. There's no time."

I'd never heard my father talk like this before. Not ever. Obviously, he was strung out, exhausted, in pain, but he sounded *anxious*. He always stood up to threats, to challenges, to the dare of being dared. Roared back, fought back.

Not now.

Had Raptor double-crossed him? Or maybe Raptor just out and kidnapped him.

Minty's heavy gaze snagged on mine as he hitched an arm around one side of Dad. I darted over and took up the other side of him. With Dad weak, groaning, and stumbling between us, we finally made it to the door and down the two steps. "I've got a truck. We'll take him there," I gritted out. The three of us hobbled across the small clearing.

The distant roar of a motorcycle ripped through the quiet of the forest, and we froze. Dad pushed at me. "Run, go!"

"I won't leave you!"

The engine grew louder and louder.

"Minty, take her and go. That's an order."

Gripping Dad, I steadied myself. "Come on. We can do this."

"Lindy…"

I fisted Dad's shirt. "Come the fuck on!"

The three of us shuffled across the grasses, the tall trees around us rustling in a sudden cold breeze. An eerie warning. Dad grunted with every step, his feet dragging. A cold sweat prickled my skin. If only I had the iron muscles to match my iron will to haul Dad to the truck quicker. "Over here." I guided him toward where Minty, Wes, and I had entered the property.

Where was Wes?

Crunching and stomping sounds rose up behind us, and a shot exploded in the air. Minty howled, his body jerking and crumpling to the ground. My heart stopped.

"Don't fucking move!" a deep, harsh voice exploded, and my pulse jammed in my neck. Dad's grip on me tightened as we turned around.

Raptor stood before us, a towering beast of anger and muscle. Aiming a gun at me, he kicked at Minty, who cursed, blood seeping through his jeans from a gunshot to the thigh. "Saw that Flames cut, couldn't control myself. You know how I feel about traitors, don't you, brother?" Snarling, Raptor smashed his boot into Minty's chest.

Minty's agonized howl ripped through the dark.

THIRTY

LINDY

THE ODOR OF DRIED BLOOD, urine, and sawdust filled my nostrils.

Dad and I scrunched on the floor of the cabin against a wall, against each other. Minty was on the opposite wall facing us, his eyes struggled to stay open.

I prayed Wes was safe. If Raptor had seen him, he would have chased him down, shot at him, and then told us all about it. Wes was still out there in the woods, he had to be. I hung on to that thin sliver of hope as my back straightened against the coarsely textured wall.

Raptor finally sat himself down in a chair, a rifle at his side. Tilting his head, he studied me, and I steeled myself against the cold slime oozing through me. Should I have been trembling? Crying? Fuck that. Fuck him. I was finally here, face to face with this demon from the past, and right now Dad, Minty, Wes, and I were stuck beyond fuck.

"You came here with Minty?" Raptor asked me.

"I did."

Raptor pointed his rifle at me. "Don't even think about lying to me, Melinda."

My head jerked against the wall, a tight laugh escaping me. "You know my real name? No one knows it, except for my father."

"Your daddy and I go back a long way."

"I know you do." I took in a deep breath to keep my voice calm and even. "You, Dad, my mother."

"Huh…" His eyes narrowed at Dad, at me, a slight smirk shadowing his face. "What do you know?"

"The three of you were together."

My father let out a grunt.

Raptor pointed his rifle at Dad. "He told you?"

"Nobody told me. At the Jacks clubhouse, I happened to see some photos of the old days—the Blades and the Jacks partying on a run. Wasn't hard to figure out."

He let out a prickly laugh. "Old days, huh? Don't seem old and far away to me. Those were good days. The best."

"Am I your daughter?"

"Lindy!" Dad barked.

Raptor's eyes widened. "What's that?"

"You heard me."

A heady silence filled the already stifling room. Raptor only continued glaring at me, slightly amused, slightly annoyed. I wasn't sure which with the way his lips curled—*reptilian*.

"Well?" I pushed.

"Lindy…" Dad's body shook against mine.

"Shut the fuck up," Raptor's voice seethed. "She didn't ask you, did she?"

"Am I your daughter?" I raised my voice, my pulse jostling in my veins as if my next heartbeat depended on his answer. Did it?

A grimace etched Raptor's face. "I don't fucking know. None of us knew, and it sure didn't matter to them. They just went and did what they wanted."

"So it didn't matter to you?" I shot back, resenting the slight tremor in my voice.

He leaned over in the chair, seeming even bulkier than before, his forehead a ridge. I was annoying him. "Does it fucking matter? He raised you, didn't he?"

My chin lifted. "He did. He sure as hell did." My hand pressed over Dad's thigh, his muscle tightening under my grip.

"You didn't want a kid," Dad grit out. "Emmy did. So did I."

Raptor wiped at the side of his mouth. "You both knew I didn't want a kid. I'd told her that over and over. Made myself crystal clear. And what does she do? Gets knocked up anyhow."

"She did it all on her own, huh?" I bit out.

Raptor gestured at Dad. "This one over here stepped up."

"He married her, asshole."

"Feisty little one, huh?" His eyes narrowed at me. "Just like Emmy." My insides twisted at his uttering my mother's name with such warm nostalgia. "I came back from a long-term stint on an underground job and found a ring on her finger, you born, and the three of you all cozy."

Dad let out a grunt. "She found out she was pregnant after you left. She didn't want to get rid of it, and I didn't want her to."

Raptor let out a hiss of air. "None of us ever gave a shit about getting hitched, having kids, about any of it. Suddenly you all changed your tune, didn't you?"

"And you never forgave them for making decisions they had to make? For wanting other things?" I swallowed hard. "For moving on? Is that it?"

"You got that wrong, sweetheart. Emmy lay dying, and she begged me to forgive her."

"You fuck!" shouted Dad.

"What the hell are you talking about?" My fingernails dug into Dad's leg, my pulse jacking up. "You saw her then? How did—"

"'Course I saw her."

I blinked. "When? Where?"

"That hospital in Scottsbluff. I risked everything to be there. I was supposed to be in Texas, and instead, I was holed up watching the two of you, watching the hospital 24/7. Finally, late one night, you both left, and I went in." His eyes flashed. "She was glad to see me."

"Was she?" I muttered.

"Oh yeah." A small smile perked up his lips, and a dagger ripped up my spine. "Oh yeah," he repeated in a whisper, dragging out the word with relish as if he and Mom had some grand reunion hook-up in her hospital bed.

I grit my teeth. "And why would she beg you to forgive her?"

"Because she'd turned her back on me! For you. For him and their family—we already *were* a family, but suddenly, that didn't seem to matter no more."

My breathing had gotten louder. "And what did you tell her?"

"There she was dying, and she still loved me, still cared. So, yeah, I gave that to her. Forgiveness. Looming death makes you realize the futility of your lies."

"What lies?"

"She'd lied to herself that she was better off without me. She wasn't." He pointed the rifle at Dad again, and my breath cut. "She suffered on his watch. She died."

"She had cancer!"

"And I would have moved heaven and earth to get her the help she needed. Did he? No. No, he didn't."

"You don't know shit!" Dad growled.

"I know she didn't have to go like that, you fuck," said Raptor. "Not like that."

"Holy shit." I sat up taller. "You kidnapped Dad on her birthday. On her birthday…"

"That's right, Melinda."

"But she died almost seven years ago. If this is your revenge, why now?"

"You love fucking yapping, don't you?"

"I want answers," I shot back. Minty's ragged breaths grew louder as he made noises, warning noises I recognized. I ignored him. "You're also pissed off that he joined the Flames?" I asked.

"What kind of brother jumps ship in times of trouble? Pick and Minty took the easy way out," his voice sneered. "First chance they got, offered their asses for Finger to fuck."

"I had a family!" Dad yelled, gulping for air. "We'd just found out Emmy was sick. Who was going to support her and keep our little girl safe? What did you think I was going to do? Take off with you to fuck knows where for however long? Didn't mean I wasn't a worthy brother, a loyal Blade. But I was sinking in hard, cold shitty facts. Facts that you were denying."

"Fuck you say!"

"The Blades were done, the writing had been on the wall for a long time, and you refused to accept it." Dad's chest heaved. "That day, on that battlefield with the Flames, I accepted that fact and made a decision. I wasn't going to abandon Emmy and our girl for an idea that no longer was. They needed me, and I needed them."

My heart pounded at my father's emotional fervent words. Their fire filled up all the hollows in my veins, in my soul.

"I needed you!" Raptor said. "The Blades needed you."

"There were no Blades no more." Dad's head sank back against the wall. "You could afford to cling to that fairy tale. Not me."

"Our brotherhood was no fairy tale," shouted Raptor. "And neither was me and Emmy. It was me who'd brought you into our bed, motherfucker. You forgot that?"

I had to cut this argument off. "What do you want from Dad? Everyone's been looking for you, and now you ran out of options? That it? You need a way out, a way off the grid? You need money? We don't—"

"I already gave it to him," said Dad.

I swiveled toward my father. "What did you give him?"

Raptor stretched out his long legs. "Something that belonged to the Blades that only Pick knew about, that only he could get for me."

"What is it?"

Raptor wiped a hand across his forehead. "Back in the Blades' time, each one of us officers held the key to a different stash. Only we knew what it was and where it was so that if anything ever happened to it, there'd only be one person responsible for the fuck-up."

"That's how much Notch trusted his own brothers, huh?" I said. "What a president."

"You don't know the half of it," Dad muttered.

"The Flames killed the other officers, so their stashes are lost forever," said Raptor. "I'd already gone through mine—drugs, semi-automatic weapons. Pick's stash was the only one left, and I needed whatever the hell it was to sell, to bargain with."

"Because you need to forge new business relationships, right? Your reputation went up in smoke after the Feds came in and made everyone you'd ever worked with vulnerable. Who'd want to work with you again?"

A noise rumbled in Raptor's throat. "I had a hot business going, and it was destroyed by the Flames and the Jacks. I've been on the run for too long now, living by the skin of my teeth. A few months back, almost got caught in Chicago. Getting Pick's stash was vital."

"What was it?"

"A big stockpile of well-made brass knuckles. It had been one of our many side hustles back in the day. Always in high demand by clubs and gangs. But there was something else even sweeter—raw material for making explosives, the kinda shit you can't find easy no more." He let out a laugh. "Notch was a crazy fucker, but a smart one." He tapped the side of his head with a thick finger.

"You found your stash?" I asked Dad, and he only nodded.

"He found it all right. Now it's mine."

"Great. All good. Now you're done, and I can take him off your hands."

"You ain't going nowhere, Melinda."

"Why not? You got what you wanted, didn't you?" I swallowed down the bile that had been gathering in the back of my throat. "Now you can go disappear into the dust once more. We won't tell, for old time's sake. And after this, Dad and Minty will be forever mistrusted by the Flames, if not kicked out, which should make you real happy, right?"

He chuckled, a low sound from his chest. "Pick was only half my plan."

Half?

My breath burned in my chest as his hand brushed over the hunting knife holstered at his side. "You chopped off Dad's finger and sent it to me, not the Smoking Guns."

"The Flames are in Kansas City now, aren't they?"

An icy hand curled around my heart. "You got the Flames to leave. You created a surefire distraction for Finger, and more hostility between those two clubs."

He grinned slowly. A grin that seared my insides. "How's it been living under the devil's wing, Melinda?"

"Delightful." I gulped for air, but there wasn't any. "What's the other half of your big plan?"

"You."

THIRTY-ONE

LINDY

My heart thudded a rhythm of doom in my chest. "Me?"

"I was going to get rid of your dad tonight, then come to Meager to get you. But you came to me." A rumbling noise curled from his lips. "How did you know to come here to look for him?"

"Minty said Dad had disappeared in Blades territory, and I remembered we used to come here when I was little. How you were the one fixing up this house, saying how much you liked it, that it'd be useful one day."

His hand cupped the side of my face. Hot, damp, and callused. I jerked away from him, my insides shrinking. "That's my Blade girl. Remembers the good times of her club."

"I remember you gone most of the time."

He pushed me, and I stumbled back. "You think I wanted to be around the three of you? Worked out for me anyhow. My life took a profitable turn."

"What you always wanted," Dad said.

"You know what I want now?" Raptor's voice thundered,

and he grabbed me, crushing his mouth on mine.. Stars exploded in my eyes, I choked. My hands slapped and pushed and shoved against him, but this mountain of a man was a boulder, immovable, rigid as stone. A sharp sting flared through me and the copper taste of blood filled my mouth. He'd bit my lip.

"Let go of her, you crazy fuck!" shouted Dad.

Yanking me back toward the chair, Raptor blew the rifle in Dad's direction and an explosion went off by Dad's legs. I screamed.

"No!" Minty raged.

"This is how it's gonna go down." Raptor pulled me into his side. "You and me, baby, we're gonna fuck, and he's gonna watch and he's gonna listen." He pointed at Dad with the rifle. "I want to make a real deep impression on him in his final moments of life."

"You going to kill me too?" I whispered.

"You, I'm going to keep."

"Keep?"

My father thrashed against the wall, struggling to stand. Minty heaved himself over on the floor, his eyes gleaming at me. "No!"

Raptor stared at me. "I've been watching you a long, long time, Melinda. Been waiting."

All the adrenaline seemed to wash out of me, my body going limp in his hold. "No. No."

"And if you don't behave, little girl, I'm going to sell you." He gripped my ass painfully. "You want me to be good to you? You keep that in mind."

I twisted in his hold. "And how do you define being good to me?"

He shoved me in the chair and hooked the strap of the rifle over his shoulder. Grabbing a big roll of duct tape from the small table, he ripped a long piece open, and plastered it over Minty's mouth. Going over to Dad, he bound his head with it against the wall, his hands on the floor. "I don't want you to miss a second of this, brother. I want it to burn your fucking eyeballs and boil your ears before I gut you."

The room wavered as Raptor tracked toward me. "Let's see what else your mouth can do other than yap, Melinda." Tipping over the chair, he shoved me to the floor before him. His hands pulled at the thin collar of my T-shirt, ripping it. "That's it. Want to see your tits while I fuck your face."

No

No

No.

He undid his belt, and the room spun. I got up on my knees. "It doesn't matter to you that I'm Emmy's daughter? That I might be your kid?"

My father howled, his body thrashing against the floor. A horrible cry rose from Minty.

"Nothing matters anymore. Nothing." Raptor took out his dick and rubbed it hard up and down as he took in a deep inhale, his chest puffing up. "You know how to blow cock like a good bitch should? Back in the day, me and Pick used to teach 'em how. They'd line up for our dicks with smiles on their pretty faces, didn't they, man?" He laughed, his dick stiff in his hand, his tip red and swollen. I didn't move, didn't react. Dad's desperate cries filled my ears. An ugly scowl furrowed Raptor's face, his lips curling. "Open that mouth."

My neck straightened. "Fuck off!"

Roaring, he slapped me, and I went flying, the wood floor meeting my head. Pain exploded through my skull, and I blanked. Clawing at my legs, he dragged me down the floor. A howl exploded behind me and I craned my neck. Minty heaved himself at Raptor's back and they both fell over. I scurried away from them on all fours.

My gaze shot around the room, for something, anything to use. My hand went to my back pocket where I'd tucked the burner cell phone. Raptor's hand dug into the back of my shirt, and he yanked me back. My arm flew, bashing the phone into his face.

He yelled, slamming me to the floor, and the phone spun away from me. An explosion ripped through the air, and flashes of light burst outside the window. *Boom. Boom. Boom.* The cabin rocked and rattled with force.

The tiny square window high up on the wall at the back of the cabin shattered into pieces, showering over us as I bent my head down. More explosions ripped around the cabin Minty crawled to a corner, and I darted towards Dad. Raptor cursed, a hand over his eye. He'd been hurt.

His rifle. His rifle.

I'd clocked where he'd dropped the weapon earlier. The sofa. I crawled to the sofa by Minty, my hands reaching for the rifle. My fingers found the hard, sleek case of the butt. Clasping it, I hoisted the rifle up and released the safety.

My insides tightened at the weight of it in my hands, the weight of it against my body. Thank God Catch had taken me and his old lady for shooting practice a few months ago and he'd shown me how to use a rifle. I swallowed hard as I glanced at my father, his eyes burning. I'd seen him use his often enough.

In the smoke-filled darkness, Raptor pulled himself up and scouted out the open window frame. Shots exploded in the air, and he slid back against the wall.

Had to be Wes. Let it be Wes.

I wanted this bastard to face me. Look me in the eye. Know it was me finishing him off.

Me.

My arms shook. Steadying my legs on a quick breath, I took aim. "Hey, fucker!" I shouted out. He glanced at me, and I fired, my body jerking with the force. Raptor dropped to the floor.

Fuck yes.

I ran to my father. "Daddy?" Putting down the rifle, I ripped all the tape off of him, and he grunted. "Come on, we've got to get out of here!" I pulled on him.

"Lindy…"

"Now!" I strained to get him upright. Finally, he stood and we got out the door.

A shot rang out and Dad howled, his body popping back, falling to the floor. "No!" Blood slid over my hand.

Raptor yelled, "You're not going anywhere."

THIRTY-TWO

WES

I HAD to get them out of there. After those initial shots were fired, I found Raptor's bike and fucked with it so he wouldn't be able to use it. Then I'd texted Butler a 9-1-1 with our location.

I lit the Molotov cocktails I had in my backpack one by one. The last one blew on the steps of the house, and I waited, my muscles clenched tight.

Pick and Lindy tumbled out of the doorway, and I launched into the smoke toward them.

A shot rang out and Pick fell to the ground. Lindy froze, her hand covered in blood.

"Lind!"

Emerging from the smoke-filled house behind them, Raptor, his face smeared in blood, a gun in his belt, a fire extinguisher in his hand, staggered forward, his shoulder bloody. He'd been wounded. Tossing the fire extinguisher, Raptor trained his weapon on me. "And who the fuck are you?"

"Jump's son, Wes."

His brow furrowed. "Jump? The dead Jacks prez?"

"One and only."

His small eyes widened for a moment. "How lucky can I be in one fucking night? You come here with her and Minty?"

"I followed them. I needed to find you."

"What for?"

I got up from the ground, wiping my hands on my jeans, glancing at Lindy who held onto her dad. "You and Jump were good buds a while back? Business partners?"

"We did some business together, yeah." He gestured at me with his gun. "Hands in the air, Junior."

I raised my hands. Behind Raptor, a figure slowly emerged from the cabin, crawling. Minty, an object in his hand. A pain-filled scowl ravaging his features, blood all over him. He threw something at Raptor, but in that instant, Raptor noticed him and swiveled out of the way. A knife thudded onto the ground in front of me.

"Piece of shit!" Raptor shot at him and Minty let out a savage cry, his body jerking. Lindy wrapped herself around her father's arm as Minty quivered on the ground, moaning.

Raptor pointed his gun at me again. "Why the fuck are you here?"

"Jump left behind accounting of your side hustle."

"What of it?"

"He left behind money, and I got it right here." I pointed to my backpack on the ground a few feet away.

"How much is it?" He lowered the gun, his hand squeezing his bleeding upper arm by a gunshot wound. Had Lindy shot him?

"Forty thousand. Let Lindy go and the money is yours." He didn't move a muscle, didn't crack a smile, nothing. I pushed. "Everyone's looking for you. You need cash, don't you? Things are tough for you now—"

"And what do you know about tough, pretty boy?"

"With Dog arrested, and your little gig blown apart, you've been hiding from the feds and the Flames. I doubt you've been able to run a new gig since."

He erupted into a roaring laugh that drilled into my bones. "You trying to make deals with me, Junior? Just like your daddy. Jump always had a deal up his sleeve to lay on the table."

"I deal in facts. The last thing you need is a kidnapped girl slowing you down, a girl who's going to fight you with every breath, who doesn't want to be with you. That'll only get you noticed, and not in a good way."

"I like girls with fight in 'em." He glanced at Lindy, and something cold slithered through me.

"Take the money and leave her be."

Raptor only chuckled.

"What the fuck is so funny?"

"Here you are, trying to make good on Daddy's promises even though he's dead and gone? If there's one thing about Jump that I did like, it's that he always paid on time and never cheated me. Our account was clear when the Reaper came for him. I got news for you, Junior, that money wasn't meant for me. That was payment for another job Jump had cooking right before he got himself blown to bits."

My pulse thrummed as my gaze shot to the backpack stuffed with the money.

Raptor's eyes flared. He was enjoying this. "Only he didn't get a chance to pay up. Look at that, huh, Pick? That organized son of a bitch had the cash ready to go, and Junior found it."

"Raptor, don't," growled Pick. Lindy's face went pale.

"Kid should know the truth, don't you think?" Raptor spit on the ground.

"What are you talking about?" My voice had gone low.

Raptor's lips slid into a grin. He was eager. Eager to inform me, eager to blow my mind. "That money was supposed to be paid to Pick."

"For what? What kind of job?" Lindy's breaking voice seemed to echo all around me.

"Jump hired Pick to kill Butler," Raptor said.

My heart gonged in my chest, flattening my lungs. "No fucking way. You're lying." My vision clouded.

"Why would I lie? I'm the one who helped set it up. Forty K in cold cash. You disappointed in your daddy now, Junior? Come on, Pick. Tell 'em all about it."

"Dad?"

"It's true." Pick gritted out. "I'm sorry, Wes…"

"You weren't sorry then, were you, fucker? You asked me to pitch your name for the job, and I did it. You wanted that money. Tell them!"

"I needed that money and Jump was offering." Pick's broad chest heaved as he gulped in air.

"Why?" My throat burned, my stomach hardened. "Why Butler?"

Pick's jaw muscle flexed. "Jump didn't want Butler back in his chapter when he'd come back from being a Nomad. Said he'd always be a junkie who couldn't be trusted, no matter what. And when Butler came back, he was disrespecting him in front of the brothers."

"Fool," muttered Raptor.

"Jump was sure Butler had gone behind his back and set up an alliance with Finger and the Flames. He didn't want that, and he told our Prez, who got real pissed about it. Then I went and did some digging on my own, and found out that when Butler was a Nomad, he'd done a few secret jobs for Finger." Pick let out a heavy breath."I brought that to Jump and Notch. Jump was furious. He'd been right about him. Said Butler had to be stopped."

"And our prez agreed," added Raptor.

Lindy staggered to her feet. "Wes?"

My gut churned. "No. No. He wouldn't do that. No fucking way. Not to a brother."

Raptor's eyes gleamed, his tongue rolling over his teeth. "Tell Junior the rest now, come on. Come on…"

Pick scowled as if the memory hurt. "Jump wanted me to make it look like Finger had set it up."

"Your daddy was one sharp fuck, huh? Two birds, one fucking stone. Real sweet," said Raptor.

"We set a time for it to happen, but then Jump got killed, and—"

"He didn't get the chance to pay you," laughed Raptor. "Shit luck, huh?"

"But our prez, Notch, still thought it was a solid idea," Pick's voice wore on. "Butler dead and Finger blamed for it would solve a lot of our problems. So we went ahead with it anyway."

My limbs had gone numb, my insides sinking as if gravity had its claws in me. My heavy gaze fell on the backpack with Dad's blood money in it. Ringing went off in my ears. Everything whirled around me, picking up speed.

Lindy cried out. "Dad? Is that why you were in Deadwood that day when I was with Wes and Butler? You'd told me you'd be on a run to Oregon. I'd figured you'd be gone for—"

"There was no run to Oregon. I was tailing Butler." Pick strained for a breath. "Couldn't believe my eyes when I saw you standing there on the street with him. And I knew you were bull-shitting me about why you were there." Glancing at me, he brushed his hand over his mouth.

"What a fucking shit show you are, Pick." Raptor's heavy gaze landed on Lindy. "First he loses out on Jump's cash, then he goes and cancels his kill because of you. Shit for luck and shit for loyalty. Couldn't get the job done, the job his president ordered him to do." Raptor turned back to Pick. "That asshole Butler led the charge with Finger against us. If you had done what you were supposed to do, things would've gone different for the Blades." Raptor launched at Pick, punching him in the face.

"Stop it!" Lindy shouted as her dad fell to the side with a grunt.

My pulse hammered in my head. "But, Pick, you were the

one who saved me and Butler from that guy who was shooting at us when we left Deadwood. Why would you do that if—"

Pick lifted his heavy gaze to mine. "You were Jump's kid. You were Lindy's…I couldn't let you die. Couldn't."

"You shit!" Raptor raged. "You had another perfect opportunity that came out of fucking nowhere to let someone else get the job you just failed at done for you—by a Flame no less—just what we wanted, and you let it fucking slide?"

"You saved our lives that day," I said.

Pick's shoulders fell. "Lindy did. She knew something was off. She insisted we follow your route out of Deadwood, and sure enough…"

My skin prickled with icy needles. If my mother hadn't figured out I was making explosives to terrorize the Blades and then told Butler to stop me…

If Butler hadn't dropped everything and run up to Deadwood to find me…

If Butler hadn't behaved like a true father to stop me from doing something twisted and, by doing so, protected a young girl he didn't even know…

My skull ached, acid roiled in my veins.

"Wes!" Lindy shouted.

Something heavy shoved at me, and I stumbled. Raptor had ripped the gun from my side and pointed it at me along with his gun. "Story time's over, Junior. Toss the money bag to Melinda."

I threw my backpack at Lindy's feet.

"Open it," he ordered her and tucked my gun into the front of his jeans like a pirate would.

Lindy crawled forward on her knees, and my pulse jerked. A dark bruise marred one side of her face, her lip was cut and swollen, her hair was a mess, and her shirt was stretched out— no, it was ripped. My jaw clenched down on the fire blazing in my gullet.

Fire for my father's sins. Fire for Lindy crawling, for Lindy bruised, abused.

Snatching the backpack, she tore open the zipper, and holding up the bag, turned it over. The bundles of cash thudded to the ground in a heap.

"Bring one over. Let's see if it's real."

Lindy handed him a packet, and he inspected it and gave it back to her. "Back in the bag."

Acid raced through my veins at the sight of her on the ground, following his orders, scooping up the cash and swiftly tucking it back inside the bag. She zipped it up, her hands closing over the exterior pouch. She lifted her gaze to mine, and I raised my eyebrows.

Raptor aimed his gun at me. "You—on your knees." I did as he said, and he glanced over at Lindy. "You lied to me, Melinda. You came with Jack Junior, didn't you? He your boyfriend?"

Still clutching the backpack, Lindy said nothing, her features calm, betraying no anxiety, no panic. Defiant.

Raptor shoved the barrel of his gun into my forehead. Cold, hard metal pressed into my skull, and I froze. "I hated Jump like I hated all the fucking One-Eyed Jacks. He got his, didn't he? And on his club property, pathetic fuck. You trying to be a hero here is real cute, Junior, but that ain't happening."

"Leave him alone!" shouted Lindy.

A smirk creased his face. "Ain't no heroes in real life, Melinda. Not even your own daddies." He traced the gun barrel down my nose, my mouth to my chest and ground it against my hollow heart. "Right, Junior?"

THIRTY-THREE

WES

Raptor shoved me toward Pick and Lindy. "Help her get Pick in the cabin."

Crouching down, I curled my hands in Pick's jacket.

"Wes…" Lindy's raw whisper crackled in the air between us. A plea, a prayer.

Keeping my focus on Pick, I said, "You've got to run, Lindy."

Her hand slid around her dad's arm. We were both making a show of helping Pick stand up. "I can't leave you."

"You got to."

"It's not worth—"

"You're worth everything," fell from my lips, from my heart, my soul.

"Wes, I—"

"Stop yapping and move!" Raptor's voice boomed.

We got Pick on his feet and he leaned his weight on me.

Raptor pointed the gun at Lindy. "You—grab the backpack and stay put out here. Don't you dare fucking move. There's nothing and nobody around here for miles." Wincing, he shoved his gun in his waist. His shirt was seeped with blood down his arm. He tracked over to Minty and on a grunt hauled him into the house by his arms as if he were a heavy sack of garbage. "Let's go, Junior!"

Holding onto Pick, I glanced back at Lindy. *One last time.* She stood tall and stiff as a soldier on watch, my backpack clutched in her embrace. I lifted my chin at her. *Run.*

Pick and I hobbled toward the small house. Images raced through my brain…

Mom's wicked laugh.

Lindy's sensational smile lighting up her pretty face when we first met. "Hey, you."

Butler yelling my name as my bike spun out.

Dad next to me as I got ready for a race, my palms sweaty in my gloves. "You got this, Flash. All you gotta do is feel it and fly like you always do. Just like we do together on the road. We fly, don't we?"

And I'd always respond with: *"Yeah, Dad, we fly."* And that exchange, along with the weight of his heavy big hand on my shoulder, would kick away any tension. The track would clear. My focus would sharpen once more.

The past few years I sure hadn't lived up to Dad's nickname for me. Put everything on hold, put the brakes on everything that mattered. Shut it down.

Then Lindy appeared in Meager, blazing in the sunlight on that sidewalk, and I'd blinked in the fierce and dazzling brilliance of her.

The blinders got ripped off. Everything got tossed up in the air and landed different, felt worse *and* better, because I was feeling. Suddenly there was so much to fight for, breathe for. So much that was sacred. So fucking much to live for.

So fucking much to love.

In the smoke-filled darkness, Raptor tore Pick from my grip and shoved him to the wall, where Minty was crumpled on the floor. His fierce gaze on mine, Pick struggled to stay on his feet. Raptor clawed at my jacket and pulled me, my back slamming against his chest. I willed my muscles to relax. A sense of heightened calm seeped through me that I knew wasn't only adrenaline.

Purpose.

From behind me, his heavy breaths filled my ears as he wrapped an arm around my chest. "Say hi to Daddy for me." His free arm swung out.

Bringing my hands together, I bashed my fist against his injured shoulder. He hollered, his grip on me releasing. I darted forward, but he grabbed me by the arm, pulling me back in. Suddenly, a roar rang out and Pick surged in the darkness, thrusting his weight on Raptor like a football defensive end. Minty was at our feet, pummeling his fists on Raptor's legs.

I twisted out of the way, but a fiery sting tore down my jaw, skidded over my chest, and I shouted out. He'd cut me. I clutched at Raptor's wrist and twisted his arm with all my body weight, yet he still wouldn't let go of the fucking knife. His blood seeped over my hands.

Chaotic punches and curses flew in the darkness. I held on, and my teeth clamped down on his thick hand. Red light flashed around us, fresh smoke filling the cabin, throttling my lungs. The blade finally clattered to the floor, and Minty grabbed it and jammed it into Raptor's leg. A vicious tornado of grunts and punches and curses. Raptor got hold of his knife again.

Heat and flames crackled and fizzed around us. The house was on fire. This was it. The end of the world. And we were all going to Hell together.

A fist jammed the side of my face, and my head swung, my vision darkened, my jaw slackened. Everything tilted and hung on a thread.

Raptor's wide hand found my throat and he pulled me close. His eyes, red and monstrous, gleamed at me through the haze. The medieval assassin. *Fuck you.*

You got this, Flash.

Raptor twisted back under Pick's assault, and my hands raked down his torso. *There.* My sweaty fingers clamped over the butt of a gun. *My gun.* I yanked it back. Pick collapsed, and a fierce sting ripped down my side. My body seized. Raptor's blade had gashed me. My grip on the gun loosened.

Fly!

Gritting my teeth, I willed myself to stay upright. My knee shot up between his legs, and Raptor fumbled. Pain throttled through my chest, I couldn't breathe. I leaned in. One last time.

An explosion rang in my ears.

My body stilled.

Fly.

THIRTY-FOUR

LINDY

When I'd stuffed the money back into the backpack, I'd realized there was something else in the front zipper compartment of the sack. Flares. As Raptor yelled at us, Wes realized I'd found them and raised his eyebrows at me.

Yes, Lindy, use them.

I'd clutched the backpack for dear life as all the men had disappeared into that cabin. Wes glanced back at me one last time.

This is not goodbye. Not now. Not ever. No fucking way.

I raced around the cabin to the broken back window. I took out a flare, removed the plastic lid, twisted off the cap, and scratched the surface of the cap against the black button, careful to point it away from me. It ignited and I threw it inside the cabin. I was either going to burn them alive or force them out. Either way, I had to do it. Had to do something.

Crash. Puff.

I sucked in a breath. A pink-red pop of light flared inside. Shouts and curses and smoke filled the cabin. I ran back to the entrance of the house. "Wes! Wes! Dad!" I screamed through the smoke pouring out of the front door and the broken side window. I lunged toward the entrance, but an iron arm was suddenly around my waist, holding me back. My heart flew out of my throat. "No! No!"

"Lindy!"

The familiar voice had me turning. Butler.

"Let me go! Let me go! They're all in there! They're still in there!" I clawed at him, clawed at the air. The small house glowed with red light, smoke, and flames. My life was in there, the only life I wanted. The life I cherished.

Butler yanked at me. "Wes in there?"

"And my dad and Minty. And Raptor." I pushed at him as wood cracked and flames licked at the exterior of the cabin, but his grip only tightened. "No!"

Footsteps tromped around us. "Lindy?" Catch yelled, grabbing my arm. Finger towered over us.

Letting go of me, Butler darted toward the cabin, but Finger vaulted forward and stopped him. Butler got in Finger's face. "The kid is in there!"

Finger's eyes widened, his head drawing back. On a snarl, he shoved Butler out of his way, and he was gone, running into the burning house. My throat raw, I sucked in air as the smoke enveloped Finger.

Catch and Boner chased after him. Explosions rocked the ground, and shards of glass blew out, raining over us, smoke filling the air.

Oh my God, I did this! I killed them.

"No!" I screamed, my blood turning to ice. "No!"

A large figure emerged from the smoke, a hulking mass. Another emerged. Butler and I ran toward them.

Finger had Wes slung over his shoulder. Catch and Boner dragged my father and Minty out of the building, the four of them stumbling. More Flames ran toward them to help.

"You got them!" My chest heaved. "You got them!" My vision blurred, my heart banging in my chest.

Finger carefully, slowly laid a bloodied, motionless Wes onto the ground before me. "I got him." He wiped Wes's matted hair back from his eyes.

"Wes! Wes!" I touched his bruised face, pale face stained with blood and bruises.

Butler started CPR on Wes as Finger ripped his bloodied and torn sweatshirt out of the way. Open gashes on Wes's side. Raptor had knifed him.

Sour pitched up my throat. "Is he shot too?"

"Just cut. Cut bad." Finger let out an animal-like groan. "Ah fuck..." Blood seeped from Wes's wounds.

My head swam. Gritting my teeth, I took Wes's cold hand in mine and pressed my lips to his flesh. "Wes, Wes, come back to me, come back to me," I prayed, kissing his hand as Butler worked on him, infusing him with air, striving for his body to function.

A heavy hand landed on my back. "Lindy..." My heart beat again at the sound of my father's voice.

"Dad? Thank God. Oh, Daddy..."

"He'll be okay, honey. He'll be okay," Dad grunted as he was lifted by two other Flames.

My fingers raked through Wes's hair. "Please, Wes, please, baby, come back to me. Wes...Wes..."

"Butler—" Finger's sharp voice boomed, and Butler shot him a grim glare, the lines of his face drawn tight as he worked. "I think he might've cut him in the lung. We got to get him to a hospital right now."

"I have Wes's truck." From my pocket, I took out the keys.

Catch caught the keys sliding from my numb fingers. "We got a van too." He ran.

Finger's hands pressed down over Wes's bleeding cuts, hands soaked in blood. "Goddammit..."

So much blood.

Wes's blood.

THIRTY-FIVE

LINDY

Butler's voice boomed, "LET'S GO! LET'S GO! LET'S GO!"

The men heaved Wes up in their arms, and I led them to the truck.

The van doors slammed shut with my father inside, along with an unconscious Minty.

Finger and I climbed into the cab of the truck alongside Wes. I laid down next to him and kept whispering in his ear the whole ride while Finger kept compressions on his wounds. Finally, we got to a hospital.

Stab wound to the lateral torso.

Punctured lung.

Surgery.

That blood-soaked chaos played over and over again in my head as we sat in the hospital waiting room for word about Wes's condition. All we knew was that he'd needed a chest tube to restore negative pressure in his chest cavity and inflate his lung.

Inflate his lung?

"Drink the tea, Lindy. It'll do you good." Tania held out

another cardboard cup filled with dark liquid, and this time I took it and sipped. But the tasteless hot tea did nothing to relieve the ice in my veins. The waiting room was filled with One-Eyed Jacks and Flames. With Catch and Drac on either side of him, Finger stood still like a statue against the far wall, his arms crossed at his chest, his jaw set.

Let's go! Let's go! Let's go!

A punctured lung. A most basic organ that one couldn't live without had been slashed and deflated. Wes was bloodied and bruised and fighting for his life. My stomach churned.

Let's go! Let's go! Let's go!

The heat of the tea spread through my chest as Tania rubbed my back. "Thanks, Tania," I whispered as we both watched Alicia, stiff and pale, sitting with Grace, the two of them holding hands tightly, Grace whispering to her. Ronny spoke quietly on the phone, a hand on Alicia's leg.

My heart screwed tightly in my chest. Alicia was suffering because of me. She'd lost Wes's dad to club violence, and now their only child was hanging on by a thread? And Grace? Reliving her past hell and being strong for her friend.

Wes pull through, pull through.

"He's strong, he'll pull through," Butler muttered as if he'd heard my thoughts. His hands curled into a fist at his mouth.

"That's right, baby, he will." Tania's voice was firm. Her arm slid around her old man's shoulders. "He will."

A nurse entered the doorway, and silence zipped through the room. "The family of Owen Reynolds?"

"Yeah?" All the men moved forward in a wave, and the nurse's eyes widened, her mouth dropping open at the dark tsunami of burly manhood rising before her.

My heart skipped a beat. Wiping at my eyes, I gave the tea back to Tania and darted forward. The men parted for me, and I raised my hand to get the nurse's attention. "I'm Mr. Reynolds's daughter."

The nurse's shoulders eased at the sight of me. "You can see your dad now."

"Tell him we're here, Lind," said Catch.

"I will."

My heart thudded in my chest as I followed the nurse down the hallway to the ER. She updated me on Dad's condition. His finger wound had been cleaned and he'd only been scraped by the bullet to his back. I asked her about Minty, and she told me the two bullets had been removed successfully, his wounds had been treated, and he was now asleep. She came to a stop and pulled back a curtain, revealing my father in bed, hooked up to an IV, his right hand bundled in fresh white bandages. Stitches and bruises marked his face.

"Daddy?"

He raised his head. He was unusually pale, his face ravaged. He reached out to me, and I ran to him, sinking my face into his throat. "Dad…"

"Baby, how you doing? You okay?"

I pushed my hair back from my face. "I'm fine. But you—"

He lifted my chin. "You're anything but fine after what that fuck did to you."

"It's just cuts and bruises. They'll heal. What matters is that you're alive. Minty's alive. And Wes…Wes is in surgery…" My breath hitched.

"Any word on him yet?"

I swallowed past the lump in my burning throat. "Not yet. Hopefully soon." My eyes filled with water, and I looked away.

"Honey. Look at me."

I met his gaze, my lips trembling.

"You love him, don't you?"

"I love him." Tears streamed down my face. "But this is my fault, Dad. I told Wes about the Dip, that I wanted to go see if you were there, and he insisted on bringing me. Now he's having surgery on his lungs. And if he makes it, he'll be hooked up to a ventilator breathing for him and all sorts of tubes and —and—"

My father gripped my arm, shaking me. "Baby, slow down. Come on. It's okay. The doctors are working on him. They know what to do."

I only nodded my head.

"Why didn't you tell Finger? Why did you two go out there on your own?"

"I thought there was a chance you'd teamed up with Raptor to leave the Flames, so I didn't want to say anything until I knew for sure."

Dad's bruised eyes widened. "What are you talking about?"

"You'd disappeared without a trace in Blade's territory, and there was no word from anyone claiming to have taken you. Minty was concerned that it was a possibility, and I had to agree with him. We wanted to protect you. I thought since the Flames had taken off for Kansas City, thinking the Guns had you, I had plenty of time to check out the Dip, and at the very least see if Raptor was using the place, and then I'd let the Flames know..."

His head fell back on his pillow, and he let out a long groan.

I bit my lip. "But that wasn't what happened, was it?"

"No, it's not." His lips pressed into a thin line. "You put yourself in danger, Lindy."

"I had to make sure, no matter what the truth was."

"I'm your dad, and I'm supposed to protect *you*."

"You always have." My voice broke. "This time I wanted to protect you. I had to. I had to..."

"Lindy..." He pulled me into his chest, and my body sagged as I cried. All the worry, all the frustrations, all the questions poured out of me.

I stroked his arm, my watery gaze settling on his bandages. "How's your hand? Was it infected?"

"Almost, but they cleaned it up."

"Fun times."

"Oh, yeah."

I sat up and met his gaze. Not knowing what to say first, all of it a jumble, all the emotions jumbling the words.

He touched the side of my face. "Everything he said about me and your mom and him…"

"You don't need to explain anything. It doesn't matter."

"It does matter. We—"

"You know what matters to me? Just like that fucker said—you raised me. You took care of me and Mom, you kept us safe. You did that. We were a family, and you loved us and you showed us that love every single day." My breath hiccuped in my chest, and I squeezed his good hand. Dad was my rock, always my rock. I cleared my throat. "And I need to tell you that I'm sorry about being distant since Mom died. I didn't know how to handle losing her. I wanted to be strong for you…"

He wiped the wet from my face. "We both miss her. Every morning I open my eyes and I know I got to get up and face another day without her. Don't know I'll ever get past that."

I slid my hand over his. "There's no getting over Mom, but we should try to get past the horrible awfulness of her being sick and her dying." I gave him a watery grin.

He kissed my hand. "Yeah. We can do that."

"I can't lose you, Dad."

Wincing, he shifted his body to sit up more. "Honey, you want to get a DNA test, see who your real father is? We'll do that."

"I know who my real father is, and I don't need scientific data to tell me the obvious. Some piece of paper is never ever going to change that fact or change how I feel about you or how I feel about me. In my blood, in my soul, it's you, Dad. We're a family." I let out a rough sigh. "If once upon a time Mom loved both of you, and the three of you were happy together, that's good enough for me."

"She did. And yeah, it was good once upon a time. But I want you to know, it going wrong wasn't about you like he made it sound. He had his eye on becoming president, and he wanted to make his mark fast, make it deep. It was his choice to leave and go underground."

"And you got on with your lives."

His lips curved in a grin under his mustache. "We sure did. Best thing ever. The very best."

My heart swelled. Dad and Mom had made a conscious choice to love, to bring me into their world. "The very best," I repeated.

"Honey, what he did to you, what he tried to do to you… that's on me…"

"No. That's all on him, Dad. That's fucked up. He's dead now, and me and you and Minty and Wes put him in the fucking ground. He's nothing but ashes, and he can't hurt us or anyone else ever again."

"Never again." His fingertips stroked my cheek. "How did you figure out we were at the Dip? How the hell did you remember? Was it Minty?"

"It was Wes. He found those accounting notebooks of his dad's hidden in their house, detailing Jump's under-the-radar business with Zed and Raptor from years ago. The Dip was a drop-off point for them because Jump had it listed. Wes asked me if I knew what it was, and that's when I realized it would be the perfect hideaway for Raptor. That he could still be using it."

"So why didn't you tell me about it?" Finger's deep, scratchy voice rose from behind me, and my body jerked off the hospital bed.

"Finger." Dad held out his good hand, and Finger clasped it and they shook.

"Good to see you alive, brother."

"Thanks for getting us out of there."

"How is it you got back from Kansas City so fast?" I asked Finger. "Flames of Hell have a helicopter?"

"Lindy…" Dad warned.

'Never went." Finger crossed his arms.

"You never went to confront the Smoking Guns?"

"The message they sent us was too obvious. Whoever had Pick wanted me to go to the Smoking Guns, not only to waste my time so they could gain time but to put salt on that wound for shits and giggles and fireworks. So we pretended to go there and laid low instead. When Minty took off last night, we followed him."

"Leaving Minty in Nebraska and sending me to the Jacks clubhouse was part of the plan?"

"I was sure Raptor had your dad, and that he'd try to get to you somehow. Must sound cold—"

"Makes perfect sense to me, and it's what I asked for anyhow," I said.

"You did." Finger glanced at Dad. "Your girl is something else."

"I'll take that as a compliment," I murmured.

Dad only let out a groan.

"Dad, after I opened that damned box at the shop, there was no time to waste. It was worth looking into the Dip while the Flames were gone to Kansas City."

"Practical." Finger tilted his head. "Yet so fucking dangerous, young lady."

My dad let out a grunt. Alpha man agreement.

"Finger, no matter what I found at the Dip, I was going to contact you right away and let you know."

"I get it," said Finger. "It was a bold move."

"Did you count on me and Wes doing something stupid?"

"I didn't say stupid. I said dangerous and bold. You got a lot of fight in you, Lindy. So does Wes. I figured if someone didn't try to get to you, maybe you knew something you weren't telling and would make a play." He shot a look at Dad and back at me.

"I should've told you."

Finger dipped his head. "Thank fuck Wes texted the cabin's location to Butler."

"He did?" I blew out a breath, my shoulders sinking. "I'm sorry, Finger. You and Lenore took me into your home, you both offered me protection and…and the trust of being with your family. I'm so grateful to you for that, and for not giving up on Dad. And now you probably don't trust me anymore." My eyes filled with water. "And Wes is fighting for his life…I'll never forget seeing you run in there and bring him out."

"Wes is a good man." His lips tipped up ever so slightly. "He may have One-Eyed Jacks blood in him, but he's family."

That word settled over my chest like a thick warm blanket. "He is," I whispered. *My family.*

"Even before that damn package arrived, Butler was sure that you and Wes would come up with some sort of plan to do something."

My face heated all over again. "He did?"

"Butler has good instincts. He put a tracker on Wes's truck."

"Wes found it."

"Wes has got passion. Showed his creative streak years ago when he assumed the Blades killed his dad, didn't he?"

"What are you talking about?" said Dad. "What did he get up to?"

My pulse jammed, my gaze shooting up at Finger. His hand reached out and squeezed my shoulder. Was that assurance? "After Jump got killed, didn't you all have some petty thefts on Blades property and firebombs thrown at your chop shop?

Dad's eyebrows shot up his forehead. "That was him?"

"That was him. When Wes is on a mission…"

I shifted my weight. "This time I was the one on a mission."

"Lindy," said Finger softly, his hand cupping my chin. "*You are his mission.*"

My heart stopped. "I'm going to go back to the waiting room and see if there's any word on Wes. I'm sure you two need to talk anyhow."

"We do, but not here." Finger's hands settled on his waist.

Dad's jaw tightened. He was going to have to tell his prez why Raptor took him and what he gave him, and why he never told the Flames about the Blades' stash to which he'd held the keys, or about the Dip. Would Dad be punished somehow?

My brain couldn't compute any of that now, but what I knew for sure was that Dad and I were Flames of Hell. I was a part of something bigger than me, something solid, real, and true that I finally embraced with all of my heart, not only a piece of it.

Like I could embrace the One-Eyed Jacks too.

The curtain rustled. Tania stood there, her face bright. "Sorry to interrupt. Lindy?"

"Tania? Is there news?"

"Wes is out of surgery. Everything went well." Her gaze met Finger's, and they both grinned.

As my and Tania's quick footsteps echoed down the hospital hallway, I felt that ancient knot of grief and uncertainty, suspicion and wariness, loosen in my gut. Relief flooded through me, lifting me on a euphoric high. Gratitude and a flicker of something else had me smiling.

Hope.

No more looking back. There was only now and moving forward.

I ran.

THIRTY-SIX

WES

My eyelids were heavy and I struggled to lift them. Lift them through the tension and pain in my upper side. *Open.*

My vision was blurry and I struggled to focus. A white blob with black dots

What the hell is that?

The blob took shape and became clearer. Snoopy? The Snoopy I'd given Lindy.

I tried to move, but a dull pain radiated through me.

"He's waking up!"

At the sound of her voice, the most comforting word in the English language burst in my mind. *Mom.*

My mother's hands stroked my arm, her voice murmuring in my ear, pulling me forth. "Hi, Wes. I love you, baby. You're going to be fine. You're at the hospital. You had surgery and everything went well."

My head turned toward her voice, her face coming into focus at last.

"The doctors said you're real strong and you need to rest.

Lindy's here, and she's okay. Pick and Minty are on the mend. All you have to do is rest."

I pushed my lips up into a grin. Pure Alicia. Prepped and primed. The second I'd become conscious, she gave me all the info she knew I'd want in under five seconds. I squeezed her hand. "Mom," I managed, my voice sounding rough. My throat was raw.

"Don't try to speak yet, honey. You've been on a ventilator. They just took it out. You're probably feeling sore."

"Mmm." With my other hand, I grabbed onto Snoopy, my fingers digging into his soft plushness.

Mom receded, and medical staff fussed and hovered over me. Within moments, Mom returned. "Honey, Lindy's here. Do you have the energy to see her now?"

I squeezed my mother's hand and attempted to nod.

Her smile filled my vision. "Be right back." She kissed my forehead and left the room.

Moments later Lindy came in, and my weary gaze swallowed her whole.

She took my hand, her gaze darting to Snoopy. "Hello, Sleeping Beauty. I'm so glad you're okay."

"Lin—"

"Shh. I can only stay for a couple of minutes, so I'll do the talking." My heartbeat picked up speed as she swiped at my hair, her fingers softly stroking the side of my face. A noise rumbled in my throat as I studied the black and blue marks on her face, the cut on her lip. That fucker had assaulted her, left his marks on her.

She kissed my hand. "I'm fine. He threatened me, and I talked back, so he smacked me. Your firebombs stopped him, and I was able to shoot him. In the shoulder, but it was something. All the men showed up, and Finger got you out of the house, and they got Minty and my dad. They're both okay..."

As she talked, I focused on her beautiful brown eyes. Eyes that were so expressive of every emotion, every feeling.

She squeezed my hand even harder, and that rumble went off in my chest again. "Raptor's gone. You shot him in the stomach, and he got burned alive in that fucking cabin." The brightness in her face faded. "But you're suffering because of me and my great idea to go the Dip on our own, and I'll never forgive myself."

"A…live," I managed.

"That's right, we're alive. You, me, my dad, Minty." She planted a quick kiss on my lips. "I haven't said a word to anyone about what was said up there. That's up to you. Must have been an awful shock for you. Are you going to tell Butler about what Jump did?"

My hold on her hand tightened.

She touched my cheek. "Tell him, Wes. It needs to be finished, and you need to finish it. You shouldn't have to hide that terrible secret, because if you do, it will kill you. You can't let it. It's not your sin to hide. It's Jump's. And anyhow, Butler's tough, I'm sure he'll be able to handle the truth. It might do both of you good."

My pulse charged in my veins. My beautiful smart as fuck woman. I nodded.

She stroked my arm gently, careful not to touch the tubes. "Speaking of truth, I found out more about my parents … can I tell you?"

I squeezed her fingers and she told me what she'd learned about her parents' relationship with Raptor, about him. About how he could be her dad and none of them knew for sure. How it didn't matter to her. How she and her dad had talked everything through.

I met her intense gaze, desperate to take her in my arms and ride through this carousel gone amok that we'd been on together. To hold her.

Lindy kissed my hand again. "A lot of secrets got told that night," she whispered. "And we took them in and then they went up in flames and burned to smoke and dust in the darkness. That's good, 'cause they're not ours to keep.

"All the whys and the what ifs, the hows that we've been stuck to? The fire burned those too, Wes. Sure, the truth stings. It's astonishing and ugly, but there's no changing it. There are no more questions and there's no more pushing back for us to do. There's a bright clean in that, don't you think? Such a relief."

Yes.

I clung to every word she uttered. Truth had slashed me, cut me deep, slit me open. Bled me. But I was here. I was alive, and I was with Lindy. And we were free.

"My dad and Minty are back in Nebraska, and I'm going to go there this afternoon to help them both get set up with physical therapy. I'm going to help Dad find somewhere else to live. He doesn't want to be in that house anymore." She let out a sigh and glanced at me. "Fresh, clean start."

My skin tingled with heat, sweat broke out on my forehead. Would she be back? I squeezed her hand.

"You'll be released from here soon and go to a rehab hospital in Rapid. Then your mom's going to take you home with her and Ronny. You hang onto Snoopy for me until I come back."

My pulse jumped, and my muscles tensed, a stinging pressure erupting over my side. "Promise?" I grit out.

She grinned and brought her lips to mine. "I promise, Wes."

And on the glory of her sweet kiss, the relief of her pretty face lighting up once more, my eyelids drifted shut. My muscles got heavier, heavier. Her hand slid from mine, and I drifted.

Soft fingers glided over the side of my face, sending a stroke of warmth radiating over my flesh. Silky softness brushed my cheek. "Wes? You know what the cleanest, brightest feeling ever is?" Her whisper tickled my ear, sweeping through my darkness. "That I love you."

THIRTY-SEVEN

WES

After a stint at a rehab facility in Rapid, I was finally released and returned to Meager, to Mom and Ronny's new home where they'd just moved in a few days before. Their new house was in Beck and Violet's neighborhood and although was smaller than our old one, was full of natural light and seemed more spacious and comfortable. The small backyard was a patch of green surrounded by trees giving the property privacy.

Mom had wanted to put off moving in, but everyone insisted she go ahead with it. And while she stayed with me at the rehab hospital in Rapid, the move had taken place. After the professional movers had done their job, all the brothers and old ladies had pitched in and got everything unpacked with furniture in place, food in the kitchen, and appliances and light fixtures hooked up and working.

Fernando, Ronny's dog, an old German Shepherd he'd had for years and years, lay on the foot of my bed. We'd nap together most of the day. He was always tired, just like me. Whenever I'd wake up and spot him at my feet, a sense of calm eased through me. All was right with the world.

"Honey—" Fernando raised his head at Mom in the doorway. "Butler's here to see you."

Today was the day.

Today was the first day I'd felt I had any kind of normal energy, so early this morning I called Butler to see if he could come over this afternoon. Slowly, I swung my legs out of the bed and sat up, shoving my feet into my Vans slip-ons.

Mom brought over the new thin robe she'd bought me and helped me into it. I grit my teeth at the sting that raced over my muscles. Stretching my arms and chest wasn't easy but getting better. "It's a beautiful day. Butler's out on the patio. I'll bring y'all coffee."

Together, Mom and I and Fernando went downstairs. I had to take a break and catch my breath; luckily, she didn't say any encouraging words. She knew better. She waited, and the moment I took another step, so did she.

Mom took off for the kitchen, and Fernando followed me out onto the backyard patio. Butler shot up from his chair, his pale blue eyes gleaming in the sunlight. "There he is." He came over and squeezed my shoulders with his massive palms. "Sucks I can't hug you. I just want to crush you and never let go." He chuckled, his face reddening. We sat down at the table side by side, Fernando next to me on the grass. "It's so good to see you standing, walking, with color back in your face again. My heart literally stopped when I got there that night."

"Then I'm glad your pacemaker works."

"Not funny." He leaned over on his thighs. "Not funny at all."

"Lindy told me about Finger getting me out."

"I had to stop her from trying first. Then Finger stopped me, and he went in and got you out. Didn't hesitate."

The Jacks and the Flames working together. Brotherhood was a beautiful thing.

"The Flames put the fire out and found a trap door in that

cabin," said Butler. "Raptor had a stash of ammunition, a few weapons, a pile of brass knuckles."

"And Raptor?"

"As the feds have been after him since that shit went down with Trick and Nicole, Finger cut a deal with his fed contact in return for them smoothing things out with the local cops where your, Pick, and Minty's injuries are concerned. He also had Pick give them any info he'd gotten from Raptor on his latest activities and contacts."

"Good."

"Before we left there, Boner found a backpack filled with cash. That yours?"

I met his gaze. "I got something to tell you."

His eyes narrowed. "You want to wait 'til you get stronger? Last thing you need is…"

"What I need is to tell you."

He took in a breath and leaned back in the chair. "Tell me."

"Coffee!" Mom swept in with a tray filled with two mugs, a pitcher of steaming coffee, sugar and half and half, and the corn muffins I loved from the Meager Grand. "I'll leave you to it."

"Thanks, Alicia."

She left us alone again, and Butler poured us coffee. I took a muffin, but I couldn't face eating yet.

"Go on," said Butler, taking a sip of coffee.

I told him my father had wanted to kill him and had hired the Blades, specifically Pick, to do it.

Butler's eyes clouded, his brow furrowing as he stiffly put his coffee down on the table. His gaze darted to the trees at the end of the yard. My insides twisted as I waited in the awful silence, watching his jaw clench tighter and tighter. His hands dug through his blond hair and he cleared his throat. "When I returned to Meager to rejoin the chapter, I'd stopped to eat at this restaurant in eastern South Dakota. Happened to bump into Tania there, who was also on her way home for good, and we ended up sitting together. Guess who showed up and threatened me?"

"Pick?"

"Pick." His stony gaze returned to me. "He told me word was out that I'd been working with people I shouldn't be, and that his president didn't like my 'interfering.' They'd been keeping an eye on me when I was a Nomad. That was way before that day in Deadwood when he showed up." He wiped a hand across his mouth.

"Hit day."

"But Lindy being there stopped the hit. Lindy being there with me and you. And then he chose to take his daughter home." Butler swallowed a gulp of coffee.

"You chasing after me to stop my grand fuckup of a lifetime saved both our lives and Lindy's soul." Uttering those words made my chest ache.

"Does your mother know?"

"I don't want to tell her."

"She knows plenty. Doesn't need to know this."

My shoulders sank. "I'm sorry, Butler. So sorry."

He clamped a hand on my knee, his gleaming crystal blue eyes sending an icy current right through me. "You got nothing to be sorry about, Wes. Not a fucking thing. I knew Jump real well, and you know what? This makes perfect sense."

"How does this make fucking sense?" My breath constricted for a painful split second, and I grit my teeth. "You were his brother!"

"Jump stopped trusting me a long, long time ago, Wes. It started the second I fucked things up for our chapter when I had a crush on Grace back in the day. She was with Dig, but I liked her and couldn't stop flirting with her. So fucking stupid and so fucking careless. One day I got real careless, and everybody saw. Dig was furious, rightly so. He lit into me, busted me up, and I got sent to our chapter in North Dakota in the middle of all this tense political shit going on at the time. I was out of this crucial vote that was going to happen the day after. A vote we'd all been counting on, especially Jump. They ended up losing the vote.

"Eventually, Dig and I became friends again, but Jump? Never forgave me for ruining things. And then later, after my first wife died and I was fucking up with drugs, selling out the Jacks, that was it for him. I fucked up bad, absolutely. And your Dad kept that long list of my sins running fresh in his head.

"But the worst part? He never forgave Grace for it, either. Not ever. She'd done nothing wrong but put up with me, but nope, he blamed her as much as me. And almost twenty years later, he used it against both of us—for the good of the club, of course. That shit came easy for him." He shook his head at the still vivid memory, a memory that burned. "Me, I'd deserved it for the shit I'd done when I was too busy getting high, but it was a vicious and cruel thing to do to Grace."

My back went rigid, "What the hell did he do to Grace? *Grace* of all people?"

"You don't need to know." He cleared his throat. "After I stepped down as President of North Dakota, got clean, served as a Nomad for National, I came back. But he didn't want me back, not in his chapter, and he made that real clear. Then, when he realized I'd been working to revive Dig's idea of creating an alliance with Finger and the Flames, he got even more pissed off. I knew it'd be hard to convince him because he'd been against it from the very beginning. Yeah, I did it behind his back, but I knew it was a good opportunity for us.

"He wouldn't listen. We argued, a lot. I said things I shouldn't have, challenged him in front of everybody. We had to change course back then. The timing was right, so I took that risk and went in, hoping for the best."

"But you were wrong," I whispered.

"Deeply fucking wrong." He let out a rumbly laugh. "I'm glad you told me. Know that I respect and honor how difficult it must have been for you to find out from Raptor, and under those circumstances, and how hard it was for you to tell me.

Leaning back in his chair, he sipped on his coffee. "Jump was set in his ways, stubborn often selfish ways. And in those last years, it had begun to take away from what our brotherhood was meant to be.

"Wasn't like that in the beginning. We had a lot of fun. We worked hard together toward common goals. Most of all, we trusted each other. Every single one of us. But when the trust stops… infection creeps in."

His lips tilted into a soft grin. "I remember when I was a prospect, I'd asked Wreck what the meaning of the gleaming eye on the Jacks skull was all about. Had to mean something, right? I wanted to know."

"I don't know what it means either. Never thought to ask. What did Wreck say?"

"He told me that even in the darkest of times, in despair and death, there's always a gleam of brotherhood to light your way. It's a promise. But it's also a warning to never fuck with that."

A prickle raced over my skin. "As it should be."

"As it should be. You understand that promise, Wes. I know you do. You feel it."

"I do."

Butler cleared his throat. "Was that money in your backpack Jump's payment for—"

I interrupted him. "I want you to give it to the club."

"It's yours, Wes. You found it with the notebooks, right? You should—"

"Don't want it, makes me sick," I muttered. "But it's still money, money the MC can use. The club always needs cash, right?"

"Yeah."

"It's up to you. Use it or burn it."

Butler let out a laugh. His rich and full laugh always set my muscles at ease. "Let's use it for the club. We have a project coming up with the Flames and we need to make a down payment on that investment. Things have been a little tight for us lately so that cash is perfect timing."

I let out a short laugh. "That'll make Dad roll over in his grave for sure."

"Think so."

We both grinned, but our thin amusement quickly faded.

"If I hadn't found those notebooks of Dad's—" I lowered my voice "— and if I hadn't shown them to Lindy, who recognized the Blades' name for the area where the cabin was located, we might never have found Raptor and Pick. He was planning on taking Lindy too—"

"You should have told me, Wes." There was an ache in Butler's voice that squeezed my heart.

"You're right. But after Lindy got that delivery, all I could think of was helping her find her dad."

Butler's gaze lowered to his boots. "I almost lost you on that road in Deadwood. And I almost lost you again now..." His breath caught.

"I'm here, where I'm supposed to be."

He met my watery gaze with his own. "And don't you fucking forget it."

"As for you, no matter how hard two different people wanted you dead *and* tried to kill you on the same damned day, they didn't take you down."

He put a hand on my shoulder. "Not even my weak heart did me in that day. And not even fucking Raptor could stop you and Lindy." His fingers squeezed my flesh. "You and me still got a hell of a lot of living to do."

All the emotions burst in my chest like a volcanic eruption. A noise escaped my throat, and I averted my gaze to the dog at my feet.

Butler's arm slid around my shoulders and squeezed. "Listen to me, Wes. Jump's choices are not your choices. His sins are not in your blood, and they cast no shadow over you. I think you let them all these years, along with guilt and regret." Shifting to face me, he cuffed my neck and I met his gaze. "You gotta listen to me. I've been in those trenches, let that shit weigh me down and blind me. His shit is not your burden to bear. Never was, and never will be. I will not lose the fine man you are to any of this. You hear? We need you, Wes. Me, your mom. Lindy. Even Finger. We need you."

"I always wanted to know how far his shit went. What I did know up until now kept me angry, kept me down."

"Anger's easy, but it can be deceiving. Is that why you haven't wanted to prospect for the club?"

I nodded as I sucked in a breath, my chest aching with it.

"Listen to me. You are your own man, and all of us love you for who you keep showing us you are."

My teeth scraped over my lip. "I feel so much shame..."

"That shows the kind of heart you have. You're feeling the grief for everybody. The responsibility." He clamped a hand on my leg. "Feel it and let it go. It sucks, but you'll come out the other end stronger. You will because that's the person you are, always seeing the best in people. Always being there for them. Those you love, you love hard. See all that in yourself now."

We both settled back against our chairs, taking in the slanting ridge of evergreens in the distance.

"Your dad was a difficult, stubborn, self-righteous fuck. An ordinary man, a smart man, who always wanted his way. He did love you, even if he didn't show it to you the way you would've wanted. He did love you."

"In that cabin, when I thought it was over, I heard Dad's voice calling me Flash, telling me what he always used to tell me at the start of a race to keep me focused. And all the fear cleared, and I knew what I had to do, what I could do, and I was ready to do it. Suddenly, Pick rushed at Raptor, Minty went at his leg, all of us working together to bring him down. And in that split second that Raptor loosened his grip on me, I went for it. He got his cuts in first, but I was able to grab the gun from his belt."

"And you pulled that trigger right when you had to. There

you go, Flash." He shot me a grin, a hand mussing my hair. "How's Lindy doing with this revelation?"

"It's been a lot—for her and her dad. They've also got a lot of family stuff to go through together, stuff that has to do with Raptor. We've been texting, and she's doing good."

"So you're keeping in touch?"

"We are." My lips tipped up.

"Good. I'm glad."

"Are you?"

"The two of you are great together. Best of all, you seem like good friends, and that's real important."

"It is. She'll be back soon. She's helping her dad get settled in a new apartment." I ate a piece of muffin. "Got to say, at the end of the day, no matter what muck Lindy's father was sunk in, Pick always chose his family, like he did that day in Deadwood."

"Mark of a good man."

"You're a good man too, Butler. Your choice to come to Deadwood and stop me from hurting Lindy changed all our lives for the better—even Pick's." I met his fierce gaze with my own. "You and Pick and Finger have shown me what it means to be a father, a friend. A brother. Love you, B," I whispered.

"Love you, too, Westley." He refilled our mugs. "I admit, when Lindy came to town and I saw you two hanging out, I was concerned."

"It was a shock seeing her here, but it forced me to look in the mirror for the first time in a long time. I felt like I'd gotten this second chance to get to know her, to become friends, to make it up to her somehow, but also to deal with my own shit that I'd packed away." I let out a laugh. "And then that spark that has always been there between us blew the fuck up."

"You in love with her?"

"Like crazy."

He let out a laugh. "You told her yet?"

"I'm planning on it. The minute she comes back to Meager."

"Proud of you. Proud of both of you."

"After Deadwood, you told me that I had a burning heart inside me and that I should let it lead me to figure out what exactly I believed in and to stand up for that before it was too late. You were right, B. I let it lead me, and it got me right here."

"Ahh, Wes." He gripped my arm. "When you leave this house, it all begins."

"What's that?"

Grinning, he stretched out his long legs. "A new life worth living."

THIRTY-EIGHT

LINDY

"That was a damn fine dinner, sweetheart." Dad settled into the sofa in the living room of his new apartment.

"Thanks, Dad. I'm glad you liked it." I brought our dishes to the small kitchen.

"You sure do know how to pan sear a rib-eye in a frying pan. A simple thing, but nothing better. That there is a priceless talent."

"If you got yourself a good quality steak, then it's all about the butter, the salt, and the timing."

It had only taken two weeks to find the apartment which was only a few blocks away from the Flames clubhouse. The brothers had moved the few belongings Dad had wanted to hold onto, and the rest I'd donated to a hospital charity shop over in Chadron.

Dad had started occupational therapy for his maimed hand, and although it was painful and challenging, he was determined. A biker had to ride, a biker had to handle his weapon, and that was my dad, through and through. Same as Minty.

Dad gestured at me. "Honey, come here. Leave the dishes."

"But—"

"Honey." His voice had gone firm in that executive, father, command kind of way from my childhood.

I dried my hands on a towel and sat down next to him. "What is it?"

"You don't have to stay here and take care of me."

"I like taking care of you."

"I know you do. But you've been doing it for a long, long time now, and you don't have to anymore." That muscle along his jaw flexed. "Yeah, I needed help to get started on dealing with this—" he raised his hand "—and finding this place and getting set up. But this is a one-bedroom apartment, isn't it?"

"It is."

"We both know you need to be in Meager. I talked with Lenore the other day after our family dinner at the clubhouse."

"I saw the two of you talking, but you didn't say anything about it, so I figured you would when you were ready."

"She told me how great it was having you work with her at her store. How she'd love to have you back. And not just for helping her at the shop, but doing her makeup thing with her. She said she has big plans, and you've been helping her figure that out. She also said she wants to send you to school. There's one in Rapid."

"She said that?"

"She asked me 'cause she wanted to make sure that I was cool with you leaving here and going to Meager." He squeezed my leg.

"Are you?"

"It's your time, baby. It's been your time for a long while." Taking in a deep breath, he pressed his lips together. "That night at the Dip, you were so fucking brave. And while I was so proud of you, and so damned terrified, it made my heart break that you were in the middle of this hell battle where you shouldn't have been."

"Daddy—"

"You fought back at every turn. You're so strong."

"I get that from you."

His brow furrowed. "When you said your mom and I had made a decision and moved on, that was exactly right. Emmy and I knew what we wanted, knew where we belonged. Now it's time for you to figure out the same for yourself. Does it mean working with Lenore? Only you know, and only you can decide.

"You've got the chance to build something new that you care about, something of your own with a woman like Lenore supporting you. Not just making a buck to pay the bills, but doing something you love and leaving your mark." A lopsided grin rose over his lips. "And to keep learning, 'cause I know you love learning. But part of learning is putting all that to use. And with Lenore, you got that chance in a big way, don't you think?"

My heart thudded in my chest. "I do."

"You got smarts and you got energy and talent. Don't waste it, Lindy. Don't squander it. If you do, it'll only make you sad and bitter." He kissed the top of my head. "Your mom would want this for you, too."

I hugged him, my cheek settling on his chest.

His arms tightened around me. "And if you want to be with Wes, be with him and see what happens. You're never gonna know unless you dive in." He blew out a heavy breath.

I lifted my gaze to his. "What is it?"

"Since the day you were born, I've never wanted to have this conversation about my little girl and a man. But here we are."

I chuckled. "How's it feel?"

"Awkward, stomach-churning, but I'm okay." He chuckled, and I joined him in that laughter. "How are you doing, honey?"

"Butterflies, but I'm okay too." I sat up, those butterflies dancing wildly up my chest. "Dad, I want you to know…I love Wes. He's the one for me."

He let out a soft laugh. "Ah, Lindy. From a little girl, you always knew what you wanted and what you didn't want. What you liked and what you didn't. No wondering, no floating, not you. Why would choosing a man be any different?"

"I am stubborn that way."

"Lenore told me that you can keep on staying with her until you find something of your own. And Meager ain't far. Look at Finger and Lenore, and Catch, who's got his little girl over there as well as his mom and sister. They're back and forth all the time. Now, so will we."

"Speaking of back and forth, what's up with my car? You said the guys were working on her, but–"

"They had to bring her to another shop. She needed next-level work. They're taking care of it for you."

"Really? That's so nice."

"We'll bring her to you when she's done."

"Might be a while, huh?"

"Looks that way."

We both sat together in silence.

"Lindy?"

"Mmm?"

"I like us talking like this. Laying it out. It's a shame we didn't do it so much after your mom got sick."

"I like it too, Daddy. And I'm sorry, 'cause I know I didn't make it easy."

"I didn't give you much to go on. We both got stuck."

"Dad?"

"Yeah?"

"Love you."

"Love you too."

My lips tipped up. "Love you three."

THIRTY-NINE

WES

Three weeks had gone by.

I started working at the tattoo shop for a few hours every day as Mom was running around the county shopping with Tania, who was her interior decorating guru for the new house.

I wasn't inking yet but managing from the front desk, handling clients, appointments, and the register. I was thrilled. Anything was better than shuffling around my mother's house all day every day, but I'd been in no rush to go back to my place. I'd decided to wait until Lindy came back to Meager, which was today.

I'd taken the day off from the shop and packed up my stuff at Mom and Ronny's to return to my apartment in town. To say my mother was thrilled would be an understatement. This morning, when I set my duffel bag down by the front door, she'd practically cooed at me while she was getting her shoes on to leave the house with Tania. "I'm so excited."

"You're excited that I'm leaving? What kind of mother are you, Alicia?"

"I didn't plan on you staying here forever."

I let out a huff of air and rolled my eyes. "Because you and Ronny are still in your honeymoon phase?"

"Baby, that phase will never be over. No. It's the guest room. It wasn't intended for you. It's for my grandchildren." She let out her throaty laugh. Tania pulled up the drive and waved, and Mom grabbed her handbag. "Oh, and don't worry, I won't come over to your place unannounced. I promise. But—"

"But?"

"Once you and Lindy get settled, I will be waiting for an invitation."

"Got it." I planted a kiss on her cheek, and she was off, and I got in my truck and went to my apartment.

When Lindy had gone back to Nebraska, we'd texted and called each other regularly. She was coming back to Meager to work with Lenore—and to be with me. We'd decided that she would move in with me at my apartment. As her car was out of commission, she'd been waiting until Catch was free to bring her to Meager in the club van with her stuff. Last night she called me.

"I'm coming tomorrowwwwwwww!"

Now as I waited for her, I walked through my apartment wondering what she'd think of it. It had a big bedroom with a view of the small garden at the back. The owner had recently renovated the bathroom, and although the kitchen was only a tiny strip of counter and appliances, it was clean, and there was even a small dishwasher.

I'd bought a new mattress, and Mom and Ronny had bought us a small round table with four chairs as a gift, which was now on one side of the large bay window in the central living space with my drafting table on the other side.

"There are two of you now, and you need a table to eat together. Something basic to start with," Mom had said earlier in the week when we'd set it up. She helped me clean up and trash stuff I didn't need or want anymore. And, most importantly, make room for Lindy's stuff in the closets and on the shelves. It was good to have a woman's opinion on all that, and it had given me ideas…

Stretching out on my sectional sofa, my gaze darted to the vintage rusty clock on the wall for what felt like the hundredth time today. *Today* would be the best day ever. My phone pinged.

"We're here!"

I ran down the stairs and darted outside as the van came to a stop. The door ripped open, and I pulled Lindy into my arms. "Finally."

"Finally."

We kissed. Her sweet taste pulled me back into the swirl of us —the longing to be together at last.

After Catch and Dreg brought Lindy's stuff upstairs to the apartment, I offered them sodas. They drank, and then quickly took off. Lindy and I fell on my sofa wrapped in each other's arms.

"Wes?" she whispered.

"Yeah?" I whispered back, inhaling the fruity scent of her hair like it was a long-lost favorite perfume. It was.

"I want to kiss you."

"Kiss me. I won't break."

Her lips, silky and soft, pressed against mine.

A noise unfurled in my throat. "Fuck, I missed you so much." My forehead slid against hers. I wanted to appreciate every moment of this, of her, being with her again. There was no more need to rush, no more stolen moments in the darkness. No more wondering, hoping. There was only us enjoying being together.

"I missed you, too." Her hands raked through my hair. "Your hair grew out a little. I like it."

I took her mouth. I breathed her in, my hands stroking, our tongues sliding, tasting, our bodies pressing. Our heartbeats chased after each other.

She let out a giggle. "I almost feel nervous."

"Me too." My hand slid under her T-shirt to stroke the silky skin of her back. As we kissed, she straddled me, her tongue diving deep. Releasing me, she ripped off her T-shirt, ripped off her bra. Taking my hands, she put two of my fingers in her mouth, sucked on them, and put them on a breast, then did the same to the other hand, this time, sucking long and slow, her molten gaze heavy on mine as I twisted a nipple.

"I want to fuck you so bad, Lind."

"Fuck me, Wes. I need you."

"You're going to have to stay on top. I'm still…"

She let out a giggle as she got off me and slid off her jeans, her panties, and then tugged my sweatpants down my legs, giving my dick a swipe of her tongue.

Leaning over, I grabbed a condom from the pack I had put in the drawer of the side table.

"I see you're prepared?" She ripped the packet with a smirk.

"When I got here this morning, I stashed rubbers all over the apartment."

Laughing, she smoothed the rubber down my shaft. "This is something I never got to do…"

I let out a hiss of air at the firm slide of her fingers, her sure hold on me at the root. Straddling me, she took my cock in her hand and brought it to her slick entrance. "And I never got to do this before either…" Rocking her hips, she took me in one long, slow slide, gasping.

The sight of my cock being taken in by her pussy made my heart leap in my chest. "Ah fuck…" Gripping her hips, I met her thrusts with my own, deeper, slicker. In that demanding rhythm our bodies created together, we surged toward something new. "So good, Lind, so fucking good…damn…baby…your pussy taking me in." Her tight walls gripped me and sucked me in with my every thrust.

I flicked at her clit, and her moans filled my chest with heat. I would never get used to that glorious sound. I wanted more. "The neighbors are all at work. Get as loud as you want," I gritted out as I tweaked a nipple.

Her eyes flaring, she rode me faster, her nails digging into my arms. Her beautiful tits bounced and shook with our quick movements. Suddenly, her mouth fell open and her body stiffened in my hold. Shuddering, she cried out loudly, the orgasm ripping through her. "Wes!" She came, she stilled, cries slipping from her lips, her body slick with sweat.

I took her in my arms. "Lindy, I love you. Love you, baby."

She kissed my chest. I embraced her, our wet bodies tangled in each other, my cock still inside her. Our heavy breaths filled the room. "Love you, Wes, so much my heart is bursting. Love feeling you inside me, nothing better, nothing…" She laid gentle kisses on my fresh scars. "I don't want to lose you."

"You'll never lose me."

She hugged me gently.

"Tighter."

"Won't it hurt?"

"Tighter."

She held me tighter, and I breathed her in, the feel of her against me once more sank into my muscles, and my bones, swelled in my veins. We took each other in, worshipped, caressed, the electricity thick between us, the hum of it vibrant and alive. We lay together on the sofa for hours talking, laughing, licking each other.

"I have good news." I wiped back a lock of hair from her face. "My half of the money from the sale of our old house is now in my bank account."

"That's great."

"It is. It's a lot, and there's an investment I'd like to make."

"In the tattoo shop? Eagle Wings?"

"In you."

Her head shot back, her eyes widened. "In me? What do you mean?"

"You told me that it was a dream come true for you to work with Lenore on her makeup business, testing products, packaging, and creating a brand with her."

"It is."

"Now you're going to be working on that with her. See how things go, and maybe you'd like to be a real partner in that business with her. Because with you on board, that business is going to grow."

"I don't know if she'd be into giving up—"

"She wouldn't be giving up anything. She'd gain a business partner she trusts, who knows what she's doing and is passionate about that business. She's already investing in you by sending you to school in Rapid. When the time is right, you've got nothing to lose by asking her. And by then, you'll know if you want to stay with her on it or not. I want you to know that if you want it, you can go for it. And I'd like to give you the money that you'd need to go in with her and expand in the way you'd both want."

"Are you serious?"

"Very."

"But, Wes, I can't just take your money, I—"

"It's our money."

"Our money?"

I sat up. "I'm all yours, Lind. Every grain of me."

"Wes?" Her voice suddenly went fragile.

"You're it for me, baby. I don't want to waste any time. Not one fucking second, never ever again." I reached down under the sofa on my side and grabbed the tiny box. Lindy let out a gasp at the sight of it.

A knot of emotion blocked my throat, but my words blew past it. "Lindy Reynolds, you're my sacred in this life, and I love you like crazy. Will you marry me?" I opened the box and offered her the ring.

She stilled, her eyes wide, her jaw slack.

"Sweetheart, I'd get down on one knee, but that lunge move is still kind of a challenge. I figured us being naked and me having just come inside you works too, but if you need—"

"Works for me," she whispered.

"And..."

"Yes!" She lunged at me, her lips taking mine, her tongue diving, making thrilling promises. She stroked my face, sighed into my soul. "I love you like crazy, and I want to be with you forever, and I don't want to wait either."

The box had fallen between us, and grabbing it, I took out the ring and she gave me her hand that now trembled in my hold. I slid the diamond on her finger, and she let out a gasp. A one-carat princess cut diamond in a simple brushed rose gold setting that Jill had made. It was simple, and the matte finish of the gold gave it an unusual edge.

"Oh, Wes, it's gorgeous."

"It's an original made by Jill."

"I love it."

Grinning, I grabbed my phone and texted.

"Are you texting your mom?"

"Nope."

The response text came back immediately

WOOT! Plan in motion!

I typed back and put down my phone. "Let's get cleaned up and dressed. Because I have things planned for us this afternoon."

"Shouldn't I unpack first?"

"Babe, this is a special day. Unpacking can wait." Rising from the sofa, I shot her a smirk, my hand fisting my cock. "Want to take a shower together?"

Her eyes flared. "Ooo…we've never done that before." That clear ringing laugh of hers filled our home.

FORTY

LINDY

After a quick and fierce sex session in the shower, we got dressed and got into Wes's truck.

"Where are we off to?"

"I have a few surprises lined up for you here in town to celebrate." He pulled out of the driveway.

"Babe, this is the best surprise ever." I took in the glittering ring on my hand. "I can't stop staring at it."

Grinning, he planted a kiss on the side of my face and swung out onto the road, taking my hand in his. We found parking on Clay Street, and hand in hand walked into Tania's antique store and art gallery, the Rusted Heart.

"Hey, guys," Jill greeted us. I held up my hand with my precious engagement ring on it and hugged her. "It's so beautiful. I love it. And I love that you made it."

"I'm so glad. It's perfect on you, Lindy. It suits you. I was so excited when Wes called me and asked about a ring."

Wes spoke with Tania and Willy, who was the eldest member of the One-Eyed Jacks. "Congratulations!" Tania hugged me.

"Congrats, honey," said Willy.

"Thanks, Willy."

Tania and Wes shared a look, and Tania turned to me. "I have a special piece here that Wes asked me about when he came by for your ring, and we thought you might like it for your home." She and Willy moved to the side, and behind them stood an antique vanity table with a large curved three-part mirror attached.

I blinked. "It's…it's gorgeous."

"I found it at an estate sale in Colorado," said Tania. "It's from the thirties, kind of Art Nouveau in the detailing, beautiful solid wood. It has these three roomy drawers on each side along with this wide and shallow drawer up top." She opened the wide drawer, which had small compartments built into it. "This big mirror is what had caught my eye to begin with…I've never seen anything like this shape. It needs some work, and that's where Willy comes in. He's an amazing carpenter who works with me on renovating pieces and custom building all sorts of goodies."

Willy rubbed his hand along the surface of the vanity. "Luckily, her structure is solid, but she's going to need stripping down and sanding, varnish and paint, and then I'd replace the hardware because what's on here isn't true to the period, but that'll be up to you." His hand went to the back of the mirror. "Mirror's in good condition, but I'd like to create a new support structure in the back for it 'cause it's worn out and wobbly."

Tania pointed out a faded cushioned stool by the side of the vanity. "This is the original matching stool, but it needs reupholstering."

Wes's hand squeezed my hip. "What do you think, Lind?"

"It has such personality and character. And it has actual storage space, not a dainty table with one small useless drawer, so it's functional. And I like that it has feminine lines without being fussy or busy. It's sophisticated and elegant. I really like it."

"I agree on all counts," said Tania. "Have you ever had a vanity table before?"

"Never."

Wes's hand stroked my back. "I wanted you to have something special that you could use for work and play. And when I saw this I thought it would be a forever kind of piece that you'd enjoy using and would always remember today. But it's up to you if you like it."

"Baby...." I squeezed his hand, my face heating. This sort of thoughtful gift from Wes was beyond any kind of fairy tale romance happy ever after that I had ever imagined. "I love it."

"Yay!" Jill clapped.

"It's settled then," said Tania. "And this is a gift from me and Butler for your engagement."

Wes shifted his weight. "Tania, you guys don't have to—"

Tania raised a hand in the air. "I'm so pleased this piece is going to Lindy, and you saw it, Wes. You knew. Let us do this for you. Butler and I are so happy for you."

"Now where to?" I asked Wes as we walked down Clay. The setting sun filtered through the orange red and yellow leaves on the trees lining the street. A chilly breeze raced around us, and I snuggled next to Wes. "I swear I can smell pumpkin spice in the air, can you?"

"It's that time of year. Erica's been making all kinds of goodies at the Grand to kick off the season."

"I might need one of her gooey cinnamon buns and a caramel latte in a bit."

We turned the corner and headed into Trash Ink. There they are!" Jet shouted out. "Congratulations!" Jams and Rachel clapped and whistled. Alicia and Ronny greeted us with hugs. Champagne bottles popped open, and the frothy booze was poured, its icy-cold sweetness rushed down my throat and into my veins like an injection of pure joy.

"Such a beautiful ring." Alicia held my hand. "Stunning."

"My fiancé has great taste."

She cupped my chin. "He certainly does, sweetheart. Oh, Lindy…" Alicia's eyes filled with water. "I'm so glad you have each other. I'm so happy for the two of you."

My heart squeezed, and I hugged my mother-in-law-to-be. "I am too."

"Cake anyone?" Lenore burst through the door, holding a big box from the Meager Grand.

"Lenore!" I ran toward her.

"Oh shit!" Jams let out a loud gasp as he plucked the cake box from Lenore before I could smash it with my hug.

"Ah, honey, I'm so happy for you. You deserve this." Lenore squeezed me tight. "Both of you do."

"Look at my ring. Jill made it." I showed her my engagement ring.

"It's gorgeous. Way to go, Wes!" she shouted out, and everyone cheered.

I hugged Lenore again. "I'm so glad you're here," I whispered in her ear, my voice breaking. Lenore was family. Mentor, Flames old lady, a mother, my friend.

Her embrace tightened. "I'm glad I'm here too. Wouldn't have missed this for anything."

"There you go." Jams handed us two dishes with thick slices of cinnamon and toffee buttercream layer cake with pure white frosting showered with gold confetti-like candy on top.

"So pretty."

"Isn't it?" Lenore and I dug into our cake. "Mmm and so good…"

"We ready?" Ronny shouted out, rubbing his hands together.

"Let's do it," replied Wes.

"What are we doing?" I garbled through a mouthful of luscious cake.

Ronny gestured for me to come forward, and Lenore took my dish as Wes took my hand and led me to the front of the store. "I texted Ronny before to let him know you said yes, not only for this little party but because he's got a special gift for us."

"Holy shit, Wes. You plan, you go big. You are your mother's son."

Alicia laughed loudly along with everyone else. Wes grinned. "And proud of it, babe."

On the counter, Ronny laid out a piece of drawing paper with two ring designs sketched out. One said "Wes Forever" and the other said "Lindy Forever."

Wes cleared his throat. "I wanted to celebrate today with a tat from Ronny that marks us forever because for me this is the first day of our lives together. A tatted ring where our wedding rings will go soon."

My heart throbbed in my chest. Lucky, blessed, grateful, that was me. "Let's do it!"

The music flared loudly and everyone cheered. Wes, Ronny, and I went into a back work room and Ronny inked our rings on our fingers.

With every stroke of Ronny's ink, the bond I had with my man embedded in my body, saturating me with our color, curling and connecting like each letter on my skin. As the ink appeared on my flesh, the love that I had for this extensive and extraordinary family of ours—a family Wes had given me—took root deep inside me.

So much deeper than I ever thought possible.

FORTY-ONE

WES

After we got inked at Trash, we all went to Pete's where the club was waiting for us, and we partied until closing.

This morning we woke up late, twisted around each other in our bed, and after I made us coffee, we began to unpack Lindy's stuff and make the apartment our home. We took our time arranging and organizing, and of course, fooling around a hell of a lot in between.

Lindy had an amazing framed photograph of her mom driving the Challenger with Pick holding toddler Lindy in his arms. We hung it on the wall of the living room where the new dining table was, and next to it, I hung the photo I'd taken from my mom's house of me and my parents at the Colorado chapter.

"I like these pics together," she murmured. "We're kind of around the same age, aren't we?"

"I think so. I love that."

"I can't wait to add more photos to this wall."

I kissed her.

After we finished a pizza we'd ordered for dinner, I applied gel to our new ring tattoos. My name on her flesh—that did something to me. Something profound and something erotic. It untwisted old sediment and lodged a burning ember deep inside me. I laid a soft kiss on the top of her hand. "Babe?"

"Mmm?"

"When do you want to get married? We haven't talked about it yet."

"What are you thinking?"

I fastened the top on the gel tube and tossed it on the table by the sofa. "If you want to wait, that's cool with me. We just moved in together, and we need to get used to—"

"Do you need to get used to anything?"

"No." I grinned. "Do you?"

"One thing."

"What's that?"

"Having lots of sex with you all the time. I love everything about it and I don't want it to stop. And I don't want to get used to it or take it for granted. Ever."

Laughing, I kissed her. "I want to give you the wedding you've always dreamed of. That might take time to plan, not that I know anything about that kind of thing. But, come on, don't tell me you don't have ideas of what you want for your wedding day."

She pushed the hair back from my eyes. "Wes, my dream is to be with you, and I know that whatever we come up with for a wedding will be perfect for us in every way. I don't need limos or some fancy venue with a three-course meal. I don't care about flower arrangements or a rehearsal dinner. I'm not hung up on that stuff. I'm hung up on *you*." She brushed her lips against mine. "First and foremost, I don't want to wait."

"Good. Me neither." I threw my arm around her, and we sank back on the sofa. "The essential for our wedding is this: we're going to need a big outdoor space because both the Jacks and the Flames are going to be there."

"The Flames property is big, but…"

"But what?"

Her lips twisted. "It's just so damned …industrial."

"You mean fucking ugly?"

"Very fucking ugly." She burst out into laughter.

I stroked her bare middle under her t-shirt. "The Jacks club-house property is beautiful."

"It sure is."

"And it has the space and—huge plus—privacy."

"Would it be hard for you there?"

"I think it'd be perfect. And you know what else would be perfect? Pretty soon that back area surrounded by the woods is going to be on fire with autumn leaves."

Lindy's fingernails dug into my arm. "That sounds amazing. Let's do it."

"You know what this means, don't you?"

"Alicia."

Grabbing my phone, I put in a call to my mother and told her what we wanted to do. A loud "Oh my God!" and whoops filled the line, and Lindy fell back on the sofa laughing. I put my phone on speaker so the three of us could talk.

"Alicia, can you come over tomorrow for lunch, and you and I can sit down and go over everything?" said Lindy.

Grinning, I squeezed Lindy's knee. There was something to be said for the two most important women in my life getting along and working together.

"Is twelve-thirty okay?"

"Perfect! See you then."

"Bye, Mom." I clicked off the call. "You don't know how happy you made her."

"It makes me happy too, baby. I love Alicia, and I want your mother to be a part of this. Plus, she's the only woman for this job. Now call the club and get their official approval so we can get this ball rolling."

I rang up Kicker, the Jacks prez, and asked him if Lindy and I could get married on the property.

"Wes, it'd be an honor, son. A real honor."

We discussed which dates would be convenient for the club, and we settled on a Friday night six weeks from today.

I got off the call and quickly scrolled through my calendar, which I hadn't checked in a while. "Lind? Do you want to call your dad now? Or Lenore?" There was no reply, and I lifted my gaze and did a double take. Lindy was sitting on the kitchen counter. Naked.

My heart stalled and shot forward in a gallop like a runaway mustang. "Baby?"

"Right now I would like my husband-to-be to fuck me."

More glorious words had never been spoken to me before. I tossed the phone. "Lie down."

Grinning, she pushed away the napkins and the empty pizza box and they fell to the floor. She laid back on the counter, her knees up, and I spread her legs. I took a lick of her ankle gently, a wet whisper, and she let out a sigh, her luscious body relaxing.

I wanted more of those fucking sighs. Sighs of longing, aching, anticipation. All for me.

My tongue lashed up her calf to her thigh and I bit her skin. "I got to get that vine tattoo done on your leg right there. Get a wedding dress with a long slit, because I want to see my ink on this gorgeous leg when you walk down the aisle. Plus a slit should make fucking you in that white dress real easy and real hot."

"Oh God..."

"And what's that tattoo going to say, baby?"

Her head shot up from the counter. "Hell Yes!"

My tongue dove into her pussy for one long, slow stroke, drawing out a raw moan from Lindy. I pulled back as her body twisted with hunger on the counter.

"Don't stop..."

"Don't move." I opened the freezer and got out the strawberry ice cream we had planned on eating later.

Her eyes widened. "Wes..." she bit her lip.

I ripped open the carton, grabbed a spoon, scooped out a

spoonful of the pink ice cream, and dropped it on her lower belly, which trembled under my icy assault. I brought it to her mound and swirled it down around her.

Her body jumped, and her hips twisted. "Wes!" she hissed.

My fingers swirled through the ice cream, through Lindy. "All this silky, melty pink…this fucking beautiful creamy cunt just for me…"

Her head knocked back. "Fuck, Wes. Fuck…"

I bit her knee. "Baby, first I eat you, then I fuck you."

My mouth sank over the cold and sweet velvety ice cream melting down between her legs. Her pelvis raised and rolled impatiently. Gripping her ass cheeks in my hands I suckled and kissed, and nipped and sucked, pulling her plump clit in my mouth. My ice cream-covered fingers went to a breast and squeezed a hard nipple, kneading her tits.

Her hips bucked against me and she screamed as the orgasm shot through her, my cock throbbing in my shorts. Lifting her off the counter and turning her around, I steadied a wobbly Lindy facing the counter. "Hang on tight…"

I ripped off my shorts and spread her legs as she gripped the counter. Grabbing a condom from the kitchen drawer, I ripped it open with my teeth, and the sound of the packet ripping along with my grunt had Lindy moaning.

Fitting on the rubber, I snapped the elastic on the base of my dick on purpose, and she let out a gasp. My hands skimmed down the smooth damp skin of her back to the lush curve of her ass, and her body trembled under my soothing strokes. I smacked her ass cheek and she let out a gasp, her body jerking. The red flush on her skin had my balls tightening. Crouching down, I licked at her ass and nipped a sensual curve, a bruising kiss that elicited a raw moan as her legs stiffened, her toes lifting. I stroked the length of my shaft from her puckered hole down to her juicy slit. Nudging, teasing.

"You need me, baby?"

"Wes!"

Gripping her hips and tilting them, my every muscle on fire, I buried myself inside her in one thrust and pounded. Lindy swelled and tightened around me, everything tightened. She cried out at my every thrust, her body quaking in my grip. The sound of our flesh slapping together was a heady rush that fed my strawberry-swirled lust.

A raw grunt fell from my lips as my senses exploded. Buried deep, my cock jerked inside her as she tightened and pulsated all around me, her sharp cries filling every crevasse in my soul.

A silky dream, a carnal feast. The beginning of us.

FORTY-TWO

LINDY

"Wes, it's even more beautiful than when you first showed me your sketch and told me your idea. My man's an artist."

Wes made sure the bandage on my thigh was secure, and I lowered my long skirt down my legs over my boots. He had just completed the final coloring details on his thorny vine. The Hell Yes he'd finished a couple of weeks ago.

He cleaned up and organized his workstation. "You ready?"

"I'm ready."

We said goodbye to everyone at the shop and got in Wes's truck parked out front. He pulled out onto Clay. "Before we go to the Grand, I need to stop by Eagle Wings, got to pick something up."

"Okay."

"How's the wedding dress coming along?"

"The way Lenore works is so inspiring to me. She's very instinctual with fabric. She knows how it will fall over your body—if she just tucks it here or lets it out there, it changes everything. Every minute detail builds on the next. Her creating a piece *on* me and *for* me is the greatest gift. Oh hey, she mentioned something about Beck having found your suit?"

"He called me earlier. Said it's perfect."

"Dude, you got yourself a top-notch celebrity stylist for life, what luck."

"I'm still not going to wear his boots."

I laughed. "Violet said he's hoping you would this time."

"Butler has successfully waylaid Beck's plans. He's taking me shopping at Pepper's tomorrow for a new pair of boots. A special gift from my other best man."

"Ah!" I clapped my hands together. "Can't beat that."

He let out a laugh. "And I saw Jill this morning on Clay and she told me our rings are ready, and she's making some final adjustments on your headpiece thingy."

"Mmm."

"Come on, you still don't want to tell me about it?"

"Mmmhm."

Jill had not only made our simple thin white-gold bands (thin so that our tats would be visible underneath them). She also insisted on creating a special headpiece for me. A silver plated wreath with crystals as a wedding gift, and it was incredible.

I also asked Jill to make a necklace for Wes that matched my angel, which I planned on giving him the night before our wedding.

My fingertips brushed Wes's arm. "Today I showed Lenore photos of the house in Malibu that Violet sent me. She flipped out."

"I flipped out when I saw those photos. I still can't believe that's happening."

"It's happening."

Beck and Violet not only gave us the gift of our wedding photos, but our honeymoon too. They were flying us out to L.A. on a chartered plane and had rented a house for us on the beach in Malibu for three weeks, complete with a chef and a driver on call.

We'd hole up on our own at the beach house for the first week. But then the next two weeks, I would be working with Violet on a music video shoot, where I'd be assisting a makeup artist who she usually worked with. I'd been following this makeup artist on social media for years and was a huge fan of her work. This opportunity was beyond a dream come true.

"And Lenore set up an appointment for me to visit the cosmetics lab in L.A. to go over the latest samples and discuss a few other details. I can't wait to learn up close how product development works. Is everything set with the shop in L.A.?"

"Ronny confirmed with me this morning."

"I'm so excited for you, baby."

"I'm excited for me. It's a once-in-a-lifetime opportunity to work with a tattoo artist like Tommy LaCrosse."

Ronny had hooked Wes up with a good friend of his, a fabled tattoo artist in Los Angeles. Wes was psyched to not only meet the legend but to learn everything he could by working for "The Cross" and his experienced staff at their landmark shop for two weeks.

"Lind, you sure you don't want to go on a Caribbean cruise instead of a working honeymoon in Malibu?"

"Hell no. We're going to be together in this amazing luxurious house on a beach on the Pacific, *and* we get to work our dream jobs *and* hang out with Beck and Violet in L.A.—which, by the way, will also include me and Violet shopping. Are you kidding me, Westley?"

"Just checking." He laughed, taking my hand in his as the truck entered the small twisting road that led to the clubhouse. Within moments, we parked in front of Eagle Wings.

I checked my phone for the time. "Baby, don't be too long. We've got people waiting on us at the Grand."

"Why don't you come in with me?"

"Why?"

He pressed his lips together, his gaze darted away. "Just… come with me."

Something was up.

We got out of the truck as Lock and Trick tracked out of the bay, their chests puffed, grins on their faces. Lock and Wes embraced. "Good to see you guys. Hey, Lindy."

"Hi, Lock. Hey, Tricky."

All three men shared pointed looks and we-got-this alpha man chin lifts. I shifted my weight. "What's going on?"

Lock let out a chuckle. "Follow me." We followed him to the side of the shop, the new outdoor workshop, where a bike and a few vintage cars were being worked on under a series of canopies.

I stopped in my tracks, my heart bonging in my chest. "Oh my God. Are you serious?"

Lock's hand rested on a car whose lines I'd recognize a zillion miles away. "Get over here, Lindy." My baby, my mother's precious 1974 Challenger, was being revived. Repaired and rejuvenated. New life, new era, the Eagle Wings way.

Tugging on my hand, Wes led me over to my car. "What do you think, Lind?"

"This is where my car's been all this time? Which means my dad was in on this?"

Tricky grinned. "I went down to Nebraska and brought her up here. We cleaned her inside and out. She had some major rust issues that took us some time to deal with, and we still got some more work to do on her insides. Brand new custom-made cushioned seating is in the works, and her new engine should be here in a week. Soon enough, I'll have her riding smooth as silk and wild as fire."

"Oh, man…" My hands flew to my mouth, my eyes filled with water.

"After that, we got the detailing up," said Lock. "This is your baby, Lindy, and it's up to you to decide on the colors you want, choose the—"

I burst into tears and grabbed Wes, smashing my face in his chest. His arms tightened around me. "Sweetheart?"

I wiped at my eyes, hiccuping in breaths. "This was my mom's dream car, and my dad had gotten it for her as a birthday present, and she loved it. She always wanted to give the Challenger this kind of special treatment, but she never got the chance. When she became my car, it was such a thrill, but over the years she had so many issues—real expensive, complicated ones. It was endless as if she was slowly giving up, and I didn't want her to. The guys at the club did what they could to keep her running, but …" I hiccuped another breath. "Then…then she crapped out on me the day Dad disappeared."

"Oh, Lindy…" Lock shifted his weight, his hands on his hips.

"Now to see her like this, getting all the love and attention she deserves, is beyond. And to have Eagle Wings working on her?" Emotion overwhelmed me once more, and I launched myself at Lock. His arms flew around me. "Thank you so much. Thank you."

"You're welcome, Lindy." Lock's gleaming dark silvery gaze met mine, drilling into my chest. "And thank you for sharing that with us. Believe me, I understand how special she is to you. I really do."

I believed him.

I went over to Tricky and hugged him. "Thank you so much."

"My pleasure, Lindy."

"Thank you, everybody!" I shouted out to all the men working on the cars and bikes, and they all grinned back at me.

Tricky showed me the other cars and motorcycles the guys were currently working on. The racing stripes, the gloss, the variety of colors and tones, and the custom graphics were out of this world. I knew Wes had worked on a couple of these projects as he'd mentioned them to me.

Lock slung an arm around Wes's neck. "Your man is our up-and-coming paint detailing specialist, so you tell him what you want for color and styling, and he'll work his ass off to make it happen, won't you, Wes?"

"Absolutely." A smile slashed over Wes's handsome face.

"All the sparkle I want?" I asked my man.

Wes took my hand in his. "All the sparkle and more."

FORTY-THREE

Lindy and I sat at a table at the Meager Grand with a cappuccino for her and an espresso for me. The sun had just set and the votive candles decorated with wheat leaves were lit on the tables. In walked Zoë and her two moms.

I stood up. "Gail, good to see you." I extended my hand, and Gail, Zoë's mom, shook it while Lindy hugged Zoë and then Lenore.

"Wes, so good to see you. And you must be Lindy?" Gail extended her hand, and Lindy took it.

"So great to finally meet you, Gail. I've heard so much about you from Zoë and Lenore."

"Good to meet you too, Lindy." Smiling, Gail turned to Zoë. "Honey, you're going to sit here with Wes and Lindy, and Lenore and I will be right over there, okay?"

"Okay."

Lenore and Gail grinned at us and went down to the counter to place their order.

Zoë took a seat at our table as she scanned the room. "I've never been here at night before. It's pretty with the candles."

"I think so too," agreed Lindy. "The Grand is only open this late on Thursday night. It's special. Which is why we invited you here tonight."

Wes waved his hand at Erica down at the front, who had been waiting for Zoë to arrive. Within moments she brought over a tray filled with six different slices of cake and three spoons.

"Enjoy, you guys. Take your time. And, Lindy, call me tomorrow and let me know."

"I will, thank you, Erica." Lindy handed Zoë a spoon and a napkin.

"So much cake, which one should I take?" asked Zoë.

"Zo, tonight we get to try *all* the cakes." I grabbed a spoon.

Her mouth dropped open. "All of them?"

"These are all the different cakes that Erica makes here at the Grand, and we want you to help us choose our favorite."

Holding her spoon in the air, Zoë eyed us both. "Why?"

Lindy pressed her leg against mine under the table. "I have wonderful news, Zoë. Wes and I are getting married."

"You are?"

"We are," I said.

"Finally!" Zoë's voice was loud with excitement. Lindy and I burst out into laughter, as did Lenore, Gail, and Erica across the café.

"Look at the ring Wes gave me." Lindy showed Zoë her ring.

Gasping, Zoë grabbed Lindy's hand and brought it close, her lips parting as she studied it. "It's so pretty. Good job, Wes."

"Holy cow," I chuckled. "Lenore said the same thing to me."

Zoë blushed, her hands still gripping Lindy's.

"And I'd like you to be a bridesmaid at the wedding. Would you like that?"

"Oh yes, please!"

"Yay!"

Zoë's features grew serious. "You see, Lindy, just like I told you. The love didn't leave. It couldn't. It was too big, too true."

I stilled at her words.

"You were right, Zo," Lindy whispered as she leaned in and planted a kiss on Zoë's cheek. "The love was right here all along. And you helped me see that."

The emotion in their voices made my heart swell. The girls still held hands. This was family, this was connection, and Lindy craved it and honored it as much as I did, as much as Zoë did. My leg pressed back against Lindy's under the table.

"Now we're going to be sisters for real," whispered Zoë.

"For real," Lindy whispered back, her lips trembling, a tear sliding down her cheek. I wiped it away with my thumb.

Letting go of Lindy's hand, Zoë's face lit up. She adjusted her glasses on her nose. "One big perfect circle."

Just then the door to the Grand swung open, and Finger entered the cafe, greeting Gail and kissing his wife. Turning, he spotted us, a thick eyebrow lifting. He raised his chin at me, his lips tilting into something resembling a smile that shot warmth in my veins.

Lifting my chin, I smiled back at him. "You're right, Zo. Together we're one big perfect circle."

Zoë dug her spoon into a thick slice of chocolate cake layered with caramel buttercream. "Time for cake."

FORTY-FOUR

WES

Up on the hill at the edge of the Jacks property, the big wooden arch draped with muted orange fabric and dark flowers and wheat was embraced in an explosion of vibrant yellow, glowing orange, and fiery red from the trees around us. Our own autumn chapel.

My mother and Lindy had truly transformed the site of our wedding celebration into an autumn wonderland.

Wooden lanterns of all shapes and sizes with thick LED candles glowing inside along with pumpkins were everywhere. The tables were decorated with more candles, tiny sparkling lights, and arrangements of dark flowers and sheaves of wheat. Instead of flower petals, colorful dried autumn leaves were strewn up the aisle, and they shifted in the crisp breeze around me and my two best men, Beck and Butler.

Just beyond us stood Mom and Ronny along with the Jacks old ladies. All the Jacks had their bikes on one side of the aisle and the Flames's bikes starting with Finger's were lined up on the other. The local pastor, who had married Finger and Lenore waited with us.

My fingers stroked the silver charm of a small angel with big wings on a chain that Lindy had given me last night as a present. My necklace matched hers, and I loved it because Lindy was my guardian angel who had saved me over and over again in so many ways.

I pressed the cold silver against my hot skin just below my pec where Ronny had inked Lindy's name over my heart. I kept my dress shirt unbuttoned because I knew my woman liked it, and I wanted her to see the necklace on my chest when she came up the aisle. Lindy was the one and only woman I'd ever loved, and in a few moments, we'd be united as one forever.

Butler hooked an arm around my neck pulling me close. "Still can't believe I'm standing here with you as we wait for your bride. This means the world to me, Wes, and I want you to know that."

"B, it's an honor for me."

"I'm so proud of you." His voice got rough and he thumped me on the back. "You're going to make a damn fine husband."

"And you're going to make a damn fine grandpa."

His body went rigid. "Are you trying to tell me something? Are you two—"

"Not yet. Soon. When it happens, be ready."

"Oh, I'm ready." Grinning, his gaze shot down the aisle. "Ahhh...." Butler cupped his hands around his mouth and shouted out, "Here we go, y'all!"

Whooping out loud, Finger revved his bike, and everyone else revved and roared in response. In the distance, the two young daughters of the Jacks' prez, Kicker, along with Jill and Catch's daughter, Becca, and two other little girls from the Flames threw red rose petals in the air. After them, Tania, Violet, and Zoë dressed in long black dresses holding small bouquets of red roses came up the aisle.

Zoë laughed at the noise of the roaring bike engines. Right after her came Grace and Lock's son, Thunder, his long shiny hair in a braid, wearing a black formal shirt with black jeans and boots. He was holding a small antique jewelry box made of mother of pearl, a gift to us from his parents, that had our rings in it. Thunder held onto little Nic's hand, who ambled alongside him, dressed in the same way, a finger in his mouth.

Following the boys was Lenore, Lindy's matron of honor, looking like a fearsome modern Greek goddess in a long black dress that was draped around her figure. The Flames cheered even louder as their Prez's old lady planted a kiss on her husband's mouth.

My breath cut, my body stilled, all the noise faded. *There she is.*

My heart pounded out of my chest as my vision filled with my bride and her father walking arm in arm. Pick cheered loudly with the brothers, once in a while wiping at his eyes. My Lindy kept her gaze on me. A princess.

My queen.

Her red and black hair was down past her shoulders in thick waves with a wreath of delicate silver leaves with crystals around her head that gleamed in the sun. She didn't wear a veil, but her sleeveless, V-front, white dress had long scarves of fabric streaming from her shoulders, creating an elegant flow of white behind her, which joined the long train of her gown.

I blinked, my insides tightening. She was an angel.

The closer she got to me, her bold red lips curved into a big smile that lit up her beautiful face. She and Pick stopped at the head of the aisle, and Lenore took her flowers. On a grin, Lindy gestured at Minty, and he limped forward and the two of them hugged. Minty let go of her, and Finger took Lindy's hand in his and kissed it, and they exchanged brief words, the two of them smiling.

Turning to her dad, Lindy gave him a great big hug, and he rocked his daughter in his arms. At last, Pick led her over to me and placed her hand in mine. "Treasure her, son. Don't ever let go of what you're feeling right this very minute. Honor it every day."

"Always," I murmured, squeezing her hand.

"Lindy," Pick continued, "be good to your old man. Listen with your heart. Hold on."

"Always," she whispered, squeezing my hand back.

Vows for a lifetime if ever there were.

We faced the pastor, and roars and whistles exploded once more. Raising his arms high, Butler waved down the crowd as Finger and Kicker let out long sharp whistles. Everyone settled down at last.

Lindy and I held onto each other for dear life. For our new life. Our life together as one.

Blessing. Union. Forever.

Words I'd heard a zillion times before. But now, each one pressed into me fresh and sharp. Into my heartbeat, into my flesh, my blood. Seeped into the very lining of my soul.

Constant faith. Abiding love.

Through the good and the ugly, they will carry us.

Cherish.

Oh, how I cherish.

To love. To honor. To comfort. To keep.

Always.

Do you, Melinda…

Do you, Westley…

We do, we do, we do.

Thunder moved forward and opened the jewelry box for us.

A pledge. A promise.

Both of us teared up as we slid the rings on each other's fingers. Thunder remained close, making sure we got them on right. He dipped his chin in approval.

"Thanks, bud." I winked at him, and he grinned back at me.

"I now pronounce you…"

Lindy and I stared at each other. Stunned. Ecstatic.

We got here, baby. You and me. Together forever.

"…husband and wife!"

She launched at me, and I lifted her in my arms as we kissed.

Dready and Dawes's sharp whistles split the air. Bear's whoops boomed. Claps and cheers surged around us. Pick, Boner and Jill, Lock and Grace, Kicker and Mary Lynn, Tania and Butler, Mom and Ronny, Trick and Nicole, Finger and Lenore, Drac and Krystal, Catch and Nina, Beck and Violet all circled us. Holding hands, Zoë and Becca and Nic and Thunder jumped up and down, hooting loudly.

Our family's wild cheers and whistles and the roar of their engines resounded around us, melding with the vibrant pulse of our heartbeat.

EPILOGUE

TWO MONTHS LATER - WES

"You sure about this?" Kicker, the Prez of the One-Eyed Jacks, eyed me as he crossed his arms.

"I'm sure."

Lindy squeezed my hand as Lock and Butler exchanged a look and grinned.

Grace stepped outside the office and joined us in the court-yard of Eagle Wings as the Prez, Butler, Lock, Boner, Lindy, and I took a long look at my father's Panhead with the Jacks gleaming eye skull, and "JUMP" flickering in a silver cloud of smoke on the tank.

A thick silence fell.

Were they reminiscing in their heads about shared adventures with Dad on this Harley? Good days, shitty times, wild adventures, close calls?

My first time riding a motorcycle as a toddler was on that bike with Dad. I could still see clearly in my mind's eye Dad and Mom cruising down Clay with the club when I'd be hanging out in town after school. Or the two of them leaving the house together on this bike to take off on club runs. A sight to behold. Closing my eyes, I let out a breath.

Since Dad's death, I'd held onto his bike. I'd ridden it here and there. Kept it clean. Clung to it, gripped it tightly because it had meaning and significance. It had to, didn't it? Because it fed my anger and my regrets. Such an inheritance.

After Lindy and I had gotten back to Meager from our three weeks in L.A., the decision came over me when I spotted the old Harley in the garage where I kept it. A bright light had gone off in that dim shed. My body had seized with the clarity of it. No murkiness, no maybes, no pushing it off, curling it away. None of that. Only *yes*.

Yes to so much more. Yes to our future that we were living *now*.

Donating it to Eagle Wings was the right decision. Lock and Boner and the crew would rebuild it into something great. They would either use it as a showcase piece for the shop or sell it and use the money to reinvest in the business. A business whose future I was a part of.

My lips tipped up as my back straightened, taking in the gleam of the sun over the shiny metal of the Panhead. I handed Grace the registration papers, "Do with it what you will, Eagle Wings. She's all yours." I lowered my head in a dramatic bow. Grinning, she took the folder of documents and hugged me. I hugged her tighter. "Love you, Grace."

"Love you too, Wes."

Lock shook my hand and gave me a great big bear hug. "Thank you."

"Thank you, man," I murmured. "For everything." Letting go of me, Lock slid an arm over his wife's shoulders and they headed back into the office.

Boner and I high-fived and hugged, and he took the bike inside the bay, where he and Tricky led the Harley up a small ramp deeper into the shop. The Panhead faded from view, and I let out a tiny breath, my muscles easing.

The sun's heat seeped through my flesh as Finger's words came back to me: *"Make your bridge out of what your father gave you along with your own vision 'cause that's what you got. May be good, may be dark, doesn't matter. Bright spot, your mother is a hell of a strong, straightforward woman, and you got the Jacks in your corner. All of that is the truth of who you are, and that's powerful. You want better? Use it and cross that bridge."*

He was right. Everything I'd learned from my dad, my mother's infinite support, the love and loyalty of my Jacks family—that was the truth of who I was, and I revered that truth, always had, and it was so powerful.

Now I could finally let go of the dark web of pain and regrets and the shadows of so many sins. They no longer owned me. And in that surrender I moved into creating what I felt was better because I did want better. Better for me, for Lindy, for the Jacks. Finally crossing my bridge on my terms to make it happen.

Lindy's arm went around my middle. "You good, babe?"

"Very good." Grinning, I kissed her.

Butler came over to us. "You guys ready for tomorrow?"

"I'm ready," I said. "I'll be here bright and early."

"Glad to hear it. Every detail counts when you're prospecting."

Lindy and I shared a look. I'd have to live at the Jacks clubhouse for the next two weeks and probably more to fully immerse myself in club doings. I'd taken time off from Trash Ink for this, too.

"You going to be okay on your own, Lindy?" asked Butler.

"Keeping busy. Tomorrow night I'm flying to L.A. on a job with Violet for a week, then when I get back, I start school in Rapid and work at Lenore's in between."

"Huh." I frowned at my woman. "Are you saying you're not going to miss me?"

"Oh, I'm going to miss you all right. When I get back from L.A., I better get conjugal visits or I'm going to have to sneak into this clubhouse like some groupie—just so you both know."

"Damn, baby, that might be fun though…"

Butler let out a loud laugh. "No worries, Lindy. This won't be for long. Being made a member isn't a matter of time. It's a matter of commitment." Holding my gaze, he put a hand on my shoulder and squeezed.

I was becoming a One-Eyed Jack because I wanted to be for me. Because I esteemed this brotherhood, this family of mine and Lindy's that meant so much to the both of us. We had a lot to give to our family. Both here in Meager and Nebraska, our lives were rooted in it, pulsed with it, and always would.

"How's the new bike running?" Butler glanced at my gleaming new Softail Deluxe in the parking lot.

"She's a dream," exclaimed Lindy.

We said goodbye to Butler, and I got on my bike and started her up. My heartbeat jerked at the guttural roar of my Harley growling back at me. Would I ever get used to this intense feeling surging through me at that sound? Never.

My dick throbbed at the sight of my old lady in my faded club T-shirt that she'd ripped at the collar to be an off-the-shoulder T along with her tight faded jeans, the new black riding boots I'd bought her at Pepper's, and her old leather jacket with loads of buckles on it. "Come on, Lind. Get on."

"In a rush, are we?" She secured the lid on her head.

"After we go swimming, I got to get my hot wife home and make hot crazy love to her all night long."

"Ahh, great answer. I like that plan." Laughing, she climbed on the back of my bike and slid her arms around my middle. We sped out of the Jacks property.

Although fall had begun weeks ago with a cold sweep, today was an unusually warm and sunny day and we'd decided to take advantage of it. We descended the hill through the dense forest, the air brisk over us. The crisp scent of pine and aspen filled my senses as we tore around the curves that led out of Meager.

Cutting through a dark golden field of sunflowers which was being harvested, I got us on the road to the Hippie Hole, a classic Black Hills swimming spot. I hadn't been in a long time, and I wanted to share it with Lindy.

Cutting through the crisp wind, we swept past the ancient granite hills, through the evergreens. Those trees whose colors had changed to rich yellows, oranges, and reds for the season shimmered in my vision. I remembered the roads that led to this hidden paradise and made the turns and parked the bike.

Lindy grabbed her tote bag, and together we hiked up the path and finally got to the swimming hole. "Wow," she exclaimed. "This is incredible."

"When I was little we'd come here a lot with the club."

There were plenty of people here enjoying the surprising heat, and we finally found a spot to stash our bag filled with towels, water, grapes, and cookies. We already had our swimsuits on underneath our clothes.

Quickly, we got into the water and swam and dove. Holding onto each other, we bobbed in the cold water and kissed, laughing as we splashed at each other. It felt good to horse around like the kids swimming next to us who seemed to have no cares in the world.

I had no cares in the world.

When we got back up to our perch in the stone and relaxed on our thick towel, our wet skin gleaming in the afternoon sun, I drew Lindy close to me and grabbed my phone. Raising it high I got the the two of us with the swimming hole behind us in the frame. "Ready?"

Giggling, Lindy pressed herself against me, her arms holding me tight around my middle. "I'm so happy, honey." She smashed her lips against my cheek as my thumb pressed the camera button. Laughing, we stuck out our tongues at the camera, at each other.

I wiped back strands of wet hair from her beautiful face. "Love you, Lind," I whispered against her smiling lips and snapped another photograph.

———

On the back of my bike, Lindy let out a whoop, her hands high in the air. Heat filled my chest as I led my Harley over the blacktop through the drenched with color trees, our very own jewel-filled magic kingdom, toward Meager. Toward home.

On Clay Street, now decorated with colorful banners celebrating autumn, traffic was light, and I sped through town as I'd done a thousand times before. But now, it felt different. I was married to the love of my life who was on the back of my bike.

Slowing down at the Rusted Heart to make a turn at the next corner, Jill and Boner's son, Nic, stood on the sidewalk holding hands with Willy. Lindy waved, and Nic hopped up on his toes as he and Willy waved back at us. I made a right turn at the corner. Up three blocks, over another two. Pulled in the drive.

Home.

Home for now.

We looked forward to getting our own house one day, probably after I finished prospecting. But my mother and her realtor friend were on the hunt for us from now because, as Alicia had pointed out, you never knew what might come up, and if we found "the one," we should be ready to make a definitive play for it.

The minute I locked our apartment door behind us. Lindy attacked me. We kissed as we peeled off our jackets, our boots, our clothes. My bathing suit trunks. Her bikini top. Embracing we fell on the sofa together, laughing. My hands slid over her breasts, down the curve of her hip memorizing every silky curve and dip of her flesh. "I'm going to miss you so much."

"Me too."

She yelped as I ripped off her bikini bottom and slid my fingers inside her wet pussy on a groan.

"Fuck, I'm going to miss this..." I nuzzled the underside of a tit.

Her fingertips dug into the sides of my face. "Babe, there's something I want to say."

"Say it while I make you come."

Her hips ground down on my hand. "No condom. I want us to make a baby. I don't want to wait. I want more of us, more of this."

My heart pounded in my chest at her words. "Hell yes."

"Was that for the no condom—" Her back arched as I nipped at her breast. "—or the baby?"

I laughed as my fingers slowed their pace inside her wet heat. "For both."

Her head knocked back, and the moans that fell from her lips filled my insides with even more molten heat. I loved making Lindy come, watching her come every fucking time.

"I don't want to wait either, Lind. No time is ever "perfect." It's what we make of it, how we handle it. I want everything with you. That's how I love you." My fingers churned and her body trembled. "You feel that, babe?"

Her molten gaze found mine. "I feel it...I feel it..." Her hips squirmed against me, her fingernails grazing down my upper arms, over the tattoo I'd gotten in L.A. of an angel's wing with the word "SACRED" inked inside it.

Lindy was my sacred. We had that sacred together—the trust, the belief, the satisfaction, the tears and the laughter, our fucking, the honesty. All of it, sacred.

Her breathing deepened, her legs stiffening, spreading wider. "Make love to me, Wes."

On a groan I brought my aching cock to her wet entrance, stroking my swollen tip in her slickness.

"Wes!" Her hips lifted.

I thrust inside my wife's luscious body in one long stroke.

Her back arched and I licked at her tits, her nipples hard, begging for my attention. Bringing one of her silky thighs over my shoulder, I slid back slightly and thrust deeper, picking up my pace. I let out a hiss at the throbbing pressure of her around me, nipping at the tattoo of thorny vines I'd finally finished on her leg.

She let out a low moan as her greedy-for-me pussy stretched around me, clenching my cock in a way that blew my brain cells apart.

"Hell yes…" she grit out, her thrusts meeting mine.

Heat blasted through me, pleasure building. I wanted to brand every sensation in my memory to last me until the next time I made love to her.

"Lind…love feeling you on me. Gonna fill you up with my cum."

Her face streaked with red, lips parted, she met my gaze with her steely one. Her hips lifted against mine as her fingers slid in the slickness between us to her clit and down over my thrusting cock. "Do it, baby. So good, Wes…so fucking good."

"This is how I love you, Lind. Hard and fast, gentle and wild. With everything I got, 'cause you're everything to me. Every fucking thing."

"Everything, Wes." The pleasure swelled and surged, taking us with it on its tide. "Everything."

LINDY

The next morning, I kissed my husband goodbye and good luck as the orange ball of the sun rose in the mellow, tender sky over us.

A new day, a new era.

He wiped at the tears welling in my eyes, and my lips tipped up. I pressed my lips against his, and he smiled. "Love you, baby."

"I love you, Wes."

Life wasn't perfect. Our lives hadn't been and never would be. But they were beautiful to live just the same. There was so much goodness here. Precious goodness that Wes and I cherished and held onto, not only to preserve but to nurture. To create more, give more. That's the true strength of love.

My hand slid to my tummy. *Always more.*

The blazing ball of yellow-orange sun rose steadily and brightened the sky over us as Wes took off down the road, a hand in the air as he and his bike zipped out of sight. I raised my hand in response, my heart skipping a beat.

Through fear and blood and smoke, we fought hard to hang onto love, and we gained more than we'd ever imagined. Home. Family. Truth.

And that truth–be it ugly, painful, messy–was a beacon in our darkness. A measure. It would never twist or buckle. Truth and true family stand mighty and steadfast through harsh winds and merciless storms. In the unrelenting heat of the sun.

Inhaling the fresh crisp morning air, I grinned as I pulled Wes's hoodie jacket tighter over my chest. The rip of Wes's bike growled in the distance, and my heartbeat picked up, warmth sweeping through my soul as I lifted my face to the first bright rays of the sun.

THE END

ALL IS BRIGHT

CHRISTMAS BONUS EPILOGUE

I unlocked my apartment door. "Lind? Babe?"

"Wes?" Lindy peeked out from the kitchen. "What the—"

Rushing my old lady, I swept her up in my arms, squeezing her tight. I took my wife's mouth and our tongues eagerly dove and slid, and a rumble rose in her throat. She nestled her face in my chest. "Baby, what are you doing home? Did you escape the club for a quickie?"

"Shh, wait. Let me enjoy this moment. Been too fucking long." My entire body wrapped around hers even tighter, holding her firmly against mine. Burying my face in her neck as she let out a sigh, I inhaled the sweet scent of her favorite perfume, something between lilacs and wood, a unique blend made for her by Lenore. That contrast of subtly sweet with a dry edge was pure Lindy.

How I'd missed this, holding her, inhaling her. Feeling her body against mine. Listening to her breathing and all the little sounds she made like right now. These small, quiet moments between us that I couldn't name but knew I needed. Living apart from her at the clubhouse had been difficult in ways I hadn't realized.

My hand gripped a full ass cheek. "Damn, I missed you, wife."

Letting out a squeak, she giggled. "Damn, I missed you too." Pulling back, she grinned at me, her cheeks flushed. "I thought you were getting out tomorrow on Christmas Eve?" She caressed the stubble on my cheeks.

"Butler took pity on me. Told him I had to go shop for my wife before we all go to Pete's tonight. That I had to find her the most special Christmas present ever."

Her head tilted. "You left such an important mission to the last minute? That's unlike you."

I only shot her a grin. I loved teasing her. Of course I already had a gift for her.

Over her shoulder, my gaze landed on a wrapped package of food from Meager's Italian restaurant, the Bay Leaf on the kitchen counter. Suddenly the mouthwatering scent of my favorite sandwich filled my senses. "Tell me that's a veal parm with pesto—"

"It is. I was about to bite into it when you came home."

"Lord, I'm starving." I darted to the counter and ripped open the wrapping of the huge sandwich. "You've never liked this sandwich. I'm always the one ordering it." I bit into it and groaned at the blast of luscious flavors filling my mouth.

A hand on my back, she let out a laugh. "I was so hungry today. When I got off work, my feet magically led me to the Bay Leaf, and before I knew it I was ordering." Her arms went around my waist. "Why don't you get cleaned up, and I'll set plates for us to eat. Don't get me wrong, baby," she chuckled. "Dirty is a good look on you…"

Putting down the sandwich, I glanced at my soiled T-shirt and dirty fingers. "I am covered in motor oil. Be back in a sec." I ripped off my hat and my leather jacket, and planting a quick kiss on her warm cheek, I went into our bedroom and tore off my work clothes and found a clean pair of jeans and a fresh long-sleeved T-shirt. The scent of our favorite fabric softener filled my senses. Nothing better than being home.

Grinning, I grabbed a sweater, and my gaze snagged on Lindy's antique vanity table. She'd had Willy paint it a glossy dark purple, and it was full of bottles and potions and compacts. A photo of us with Beck and Violet in L.A. was stuck in the edge of the mirror. They'd be here next week in time for New Year's.

I went into the bathroom and washed my hands and face with Lindy's fancy skincare soap. I'd even missed that while I was staying at the clubhouse. As I put the big tube of gel soap back in its place on the counter, my fingers brushed over a plastic stick. It slid into the sink, clattering.

I blinked. A pregnancy test stick.

Oh my fuck....

My chest tightened as I picked it up.

It was positive. POSITIVE. My lips parted, my breath burning in the back of my throat. We were having a baby.

Lindy was pregnant.

Staring at myself in the mirror, my heart thudded in my chest. I was going to be a dad. A father.

Had Lindy taken the test and then forgotten it in here when I came home unexpectedly? I tucked the test stick in the back pocket of my jeans.

Back in the kitchen I watched Lindy take a bite of the sandwich. Lindy, a mom. Lindy, the mother of my children. Lindy and me...*parents*.

A prickle raced over my skin. My surprise couldn't be better timed.

She wiped at her hands with a napkin. "Honey, what are you staring at? Come sit down and eat or I'm going to eat it all, I swear."

"Forget the sandwich, Lind, there's something I want to show you." I wrapped the sandwich back in its packaging and popped it in the fridge.

Her lips twisted. "Does it include food?"

"Yep."

She got up from the table. "Here in town?"

"Right here in Meager." I threw my leather jacket and beanie hat back on. "Bundle up and let's hit the road."

"This better be good…" She put on her hat and scarf, her gloves and boots, and her puffy winter jacket.

"It's real good."

We locked up, got in the Charger, and headed down Clay, which was a holiday wonderland. Snowflakes and stars made of tiny lights twinkled over Meager's main street, and each and every store was decorated for Christmas. The wreaths and red ribbons which festooned the street lamps rustled in the breeze. It had snowed yesterday, and now, in the mellow haze of twilight, the town looked more sparkly and fairy tale-like than ever before.

Passing the town Christmas tree, I crossed over to the other side of Clay and headed past the street where Beck and Violet's house, Whisperwind stood. Rounding a corner and down another street, I finally parked the car, my heart beating hard in my chest. "We're here."

"What's going on?" Lindy's breaths were visible puffs of air in the biting cold as we got out of the car. "Why are we here?"

Pressing my lips to her cold cheek, I took her hand in mine and led her down the stone pathway to the door of the house.

"Wes?" Squeezing my hand, she stopped us. "Tell me now."

"Babe, let's get in the—"

"Wes!"

My chest filled with air as I took her other hand in mine. "Mr. Ryan wants to sell us the house. It can be ours if you want it."

Lindy's eyes widened. "Are you serious? It's beyond our budget, and anyhow, when we tried, we got ridiculously outbid. What happened to—"

"Deal fell through, and Mr. Ryan needs it sold yesterday. Also helped that Violet's grandma, who lives down the street and grew up with the Ryans, pestered him non-stop about letting us have it."

"Gigi did that for us?"

"She sure did, and he called me two hours ago and offered it to me at our original bid. That's why I got out early. He wants to know now before Christmas."

"Now?"

"Now. Gigi had the keys, and on the way home I swung by her house to pick them up so we could take a look again. Bonus, there are no realtors involved on this, so we'd all save big on the fees."

Lindy let out a gasp. "Honey, this is…"

"Our dream house."

"Our dream house," she whispered, her eyes filling with water as a smile trembled over her beautiful full lips. "Is this for real?"

"It's our real, baby. Our dreams are coming true. My other big news is that I'll be made a member of the club right after New Year's."

"It's official?"

"It's official."

"I'm so proud of you, Wes!" She threw her arms around me.

"Lind, we did this together, all of this. You and me. Wouldn't have happened without you."

Her hand stroked the side of my face. "So much wouldn't have happened without us together, Wes."

I took out my cell phone. "Mr. Ryan's waiting on my call. Do you want this house for us?"

"Do you?"

I let out a chuckle. "Babe."

Tears ran down her cheeks. "Yes!" she shouted, hopping up and down. "Yes! Yes! A thousand times YES."

———

I UNLOCKED the massive wood door, and Lindy and I entered the house we'd fallen in love with a few weeks ago.

"It's beautiful, and it smells of fresh wood in here. I love it," murmured Lindy, wandering into the open plan living area as I called Mr. Ryan with the good news. He was thrilled.

Mr. Ryan had grown up in Meager and eventually landed in Denver as a very successful corporate lawyer. After his parents had passed on, he tore down the old house and custom built his fantasy contemporary, which was out of tune on this block of older and smaller family homes. But because his front property was long and bordered by tall trees, and the house was tucked away in the back by more evergreens, the sleek structure was not immediately visible from the street, giving it privacy.

Four bedrooms, a large living room space with a stone fireplace, a kitchen and dining area, and in the back, a patio and an unfinished small swimming pool. On one side was a three car garage as Mr. Ryan was a collector of muscle cars. He was a client of Eagle Wings, where I'd first met him two years ago when he'd bought a refurbished Mustang from us.

Once he'd finished building the house, he'd gotten a divorce. But now he was about to marry another woman, who wasn't interested in spending time in a small sleepy town in South Dakota, so he'd decided to sell and upgrade in Denver. He'd had two deals on the house fall through and he was done waiting. Throw in Gigi's relentless prodding, and he accepted our offer.

"What's all this?" Lindy's voice echoed in the vast open space from the kitchen area.

Grinning, I tracked into the kitchen, where Lindy held up a bottle of champagne. On the counter stood two glasses and the cake I'd ordered from the Meager Grand with "Our Home Sweet Home" written in pink icing on top of chocolate ganache.

"You planned all this?"

"Just in case you said yes. Wanted to make the moment special. Gigi and I worked it out."

"You make everything special, baby. God, I love you." She

took my mouth, her arms wrapping around my middle, holding me close.

"Love you too." My tongue dove deep, eliciting moans from her chest and throat. I lifted her up on the counter and she grabbed one of the forks, dug into the cake, and fed me the luscious piece. I opened the champagne and poured. We held up our glasses. "To our new forever house. To living our dream life."

"To all of it, Wes."

We clinked and I drained my glass of the cold sweet and fizzy liquor. Lindy only took a quick sip and pressed her lips together as she put her glass on the counter. Her eyes widened, her neck stiffening. Had she now remembered leaving the test stick back in our bathroom?

The pregnancy test stick burned a hole in the back pocket of my jeans.

I licked at my lips as I stroked her sides. "This house surprise is only part of my Christmas gift to you. I already shopped, but you're going to have to wait until Christmas morning for that."

"I knew it." She grinned tightly.

"But I do have something else to share with you now. It's your gift to me. Or our gift to us."

"What are you talking about?"

I took out the stick. "I found this in our bathroom." I held it out to her.

Her mouth dropped open, her gaze glued to the stick.

I kissed her forehead. "We're going to have a baby, Lind."

She took the stick from me. "I took the test right before you came home, then….oh, Wes. Our baby is here!" She lunged at me and I held her fast and tight and hard, our hearts beating furiously.

"Think of it, Lind. We'll be living within walking distance of Beck and Violet, Gigi, my mom and Ronny. Not far from Lenore and Finger. We're going to fill this house with family, friends, all our kids."

She wiped at her eyes. "You bet your sweet cock we are. Take all the vitamins, big man, you're going to need them."

"What I need right now is to make love to my fucking amazing hot and sexy wife." My lips nuzzled her throat, and I let out a growl.

"I love it when you say that."

My fingertips dug into her waist. "Shit, can we? Is it okay?"

"It's fine." Chuckling, she moved the cake and champagne to the other counter, came back to me and undid the buttons on my jeans. Her hand slid down into my briefs, curling over my already stiff dick as she let out a groan.

"Fuck me…" I met my wife's gleaming gaze, my head slanting as my breathing shallowed. She was on fire. "Your hormones are flying, aren't they?"

"Mmm." Her hand rubbed at my shaft, and my muscles tightened. Her expert hand job had my tip wet, and my now very hard cock twitched for satisfaction in her firm hold.

My old lady already had a healthy sex drive. Damn, I was in for it.

Lucky me.

Her eyes narrowing, she grinned at me. "Promise you'll never say no to me?"

"Me say no to you?" I let out a laugh. "Not a chance. No way. Never. Now get rid of the leggings."

Her hand released me, and she got out of her boots and leggings. I lifted her back on the counter and spread her legs, pulling her to the edge. Two of my fingers slid through her wet slit. "Fuck me, your juicy, silky cunt is my happy place." My mouth sank between her legs, and she let out a loud gasp as her hips rocked against my face.

"It's been too long…" she whimpered, leaning back on her arms.

Lindy's taste, her scent, her flesh, her moans were home to me. I feasted on my wife on our new black granite kitchen counter. Her body jerked, her long red hair flying as she yelled out my name. My wife's beautiful rich voice echoed through our forever home.

I got her off the counter, turned her around and, gripping her hips, filled her with my cock. "Our house, Lind, our dream," I gritted out with every long, slick thrust. "Together."

"Always…" Her body slammed back against mine as I pounded into her. Every cell in my body detonated as we came.

After, we got dressed and cleaned up, and Lindy brought the cake back to the kitchen island. "This cake needs to be enjoyed. Let's call everyone to come over and tell them our good news."

I wiped her hair back from her flushed face. "Got the urge to share the joy, huh babe?"

"I do. 'Tis the season, and I want to celebrate our house, our baby, your becoming a One-Eyed Jack with our family. We'll start the holiday party here and then we can go on to Pete's together as planned."

My insides burned. How I loved this woman. "Let's do it."

We both got on our phones and made the calls. Within twenty minutes, our new house bustled with noise and laughter and music, soda, booze, and pizza.

Ronny and Mom brought a small tree decorated with red and silver balls and loaded with tinsel and put it down it by the hearth as Butler set a fire in the fireplace. Erica and Gigi brought over hot chocolate and holiday cupcakes from the Grand which Thunder, Becca, and Nic were chomping into.

"The house is gorgeous. So happy for you," said Nicole as she admired the kitchen cabinetry.

"The bedrooms are so roomy," exclaimed Grace as she came down the staircase with Tania and Erica.

Lindy hugged Gigi. "We can't thank you enough, Gigi. Means so much to me that you spoke to Mr. Ryan for us."

"This house needs you and Wes," replied Gigi. "And we're family. Welcome to the neighborhood, honey." They hugged again.

"Everybody! We have an announcement to make!" I shouted

out lifting my glass of whiskey in the air. Now for the best news. Everyone quieted down, and Lindy wrapped an arm around my middle, squeezing tight. I kissed the top of her head. "You tell them, Lind."

Lindy's face was flushed with excitement. "We're having a baby!"

"Oh my God!" my mother shrieked.

Whistles and cheers broke out as Mom rushed at us hugging us both. Grace and Jill and Nicole clapped and hooted, hugging Lindy. Tania and Butler embraced each other, and Trick and Boner slapped me on the back.

Willy slid a burly arm around my shoulders. "Look at you, you little shit. Still remember you riding around the clubhouse on your tricycle. Where did the fucking time go?" His eyes glimmered, and I hugged him tight.

Lock slapped a hand on my back, "So happy for you guys. Best thing ever."

"It really is, man." I hugged him.

Butler and Tania came over and swept us up in a group hug. "Santa did good this year, huh?" Butler laughed.

"He sure did," agreed Lindy.

With Bear and Dawes hoisting them up, Thunder and Nic stood on the island counter wearing Santa caps on their heads as they sang along with the Christmas carols Dready had put on a speaker. "Fa la la la la la la la la!"

Boner and Becca danced a tango, and he twirled his stepdaughter over the sleek wood floor of the living room as she giggled loudly.

Lindy got up on her toes and whispered in my ear, "I love you Wesley, for giving me this full life in this wonderful town with this extraordinary family. For giving me the gift of you. For our baby. All my dreams and so much more keep coming true."

I held my wife close as my heart spun and burst. "So much more."

Outside snow was falling once again, and Lindy leaned her

head on my chest as we took in the snowfall frosting the tall, proud evergreens on the property through the big living room window.

Silent night. Holy night. All is calm. All is so damn bright.

Lindy let out a sigh. "Shame my dad and the Flames are in Florida for the holidays this year."

"Next year, we'll insist they come here to celebrate our baby's first Christmas, all of us together."

Her eyes gleamed, a smile lighting up her face. "Oh Wes, won't that be wonderful?"

I tipped her warm face to mine, and my lips gently brushed hers. "Merry Christmas, baby."

THE END

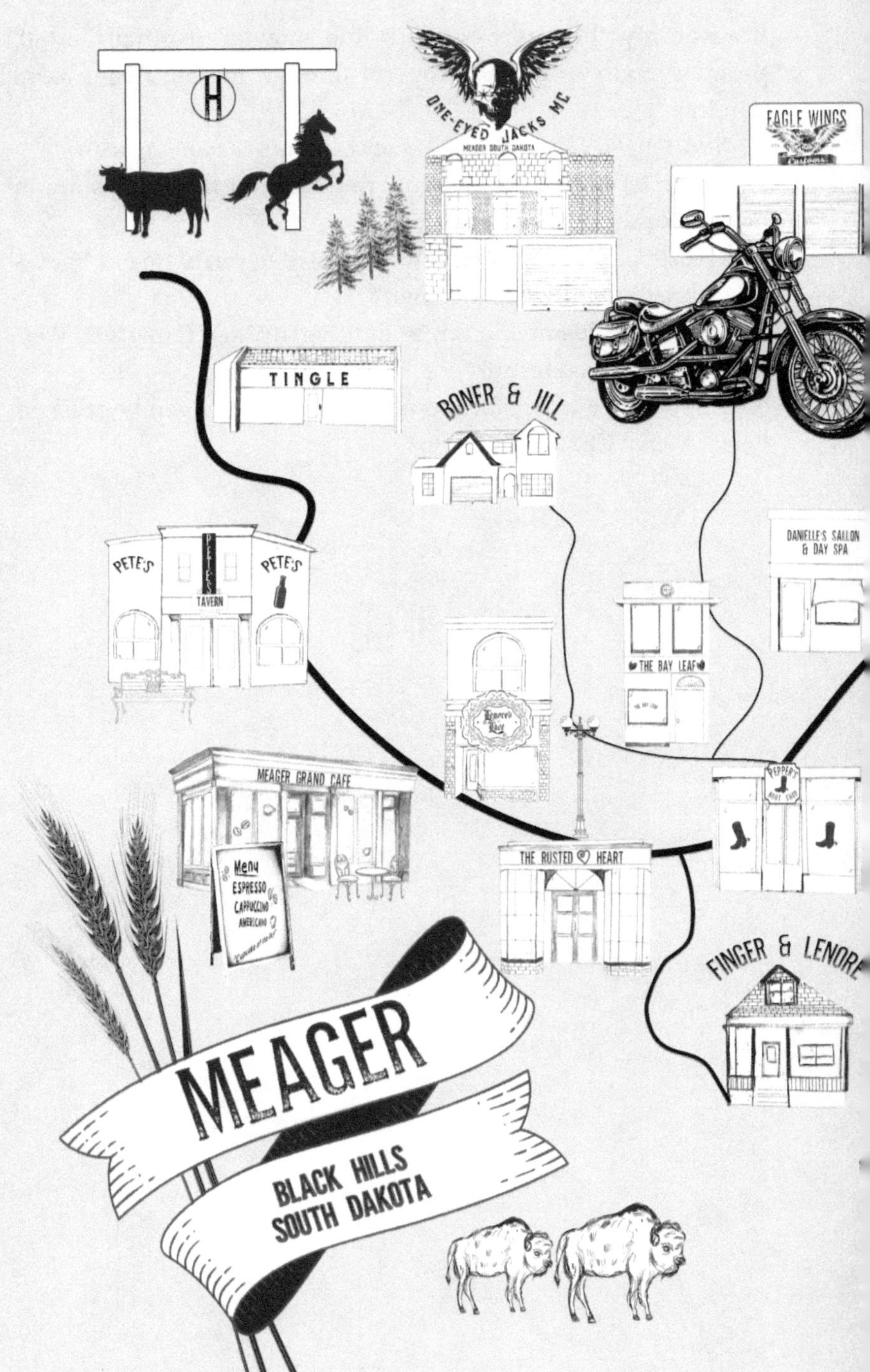
ONE-EYED JACKS MC
MEAGER SOUTH DAKOTA
EAGLE WINGS
Customs
TINGLE
BONER & JILL
DANIELLE'S SALLON
& DAY SPA
PETE'S
TAVERN
PETE'S
THE BAY LEAF
Lenore's Diner
MEAGER GRAND CAFE
Menu
ESPRESSO
CAPPUCCINO
AMERICANO
PEPPER'S
BOOT SHOP
THE RUSTED HEART
FINGER & LENORE
MEAGER
BLACK HILLS
SOUTH DAKOTA

TRICKY & NICOLE
LOCK & GRACE
ROCK HILLS CEMETERY
ORGANIC DELIGHTS CO-OP
BANK
HILDEBRAND & HILDEBRAND
TIBBET'S GROCERY
VERONICA'S
VINTAGE CLOTHING
TRASH INK TATTOO
TRASH INK TATTOO
FITSMASH STUDIO
POST OFFICE
POST
PRAIRIE PUMPER
WHISPERWIND
WES & LINDY
GIGI
UNNY & ALICIA

BOOKS BY CAT PORTER

- LOCK & KEY SMALL TOWN MC ROMANCE SERIES -

READING ORDER

1 - LOCK & KEY - LOCK & GRACE

2 - RANDOM & RARE - DIG | LOCK & GRACE

3 - IRON & BONE - BONER & JILL

4 - BLOOD & RUST - BUTLER & TANIA

5 - FURY - FINGER & LENORE

6 - LOCK & KEY CHRISTMAS - LOCK & GRACE

7 - THE DUST AND THE ROAR - WRECK & ISI

8 - THE FIRE AND THE ROAR - MORE WRECK & ISI

9 - THE YEAR OF EVERYTHING - EVERYONE IN HIGH SCHOOL

10- THUNDER & FLARE - TRICK & NICOLE

11 - SPARKLE - ALICIA & RONNY

12 - SIN & SURRENDER - WES & LINDY

THE LOCK & KEY MC ROMANCE SERIES BOXED SET: BOOKS 1 - 3
Books 1-3 in one e-book

- THE WIND & THE ROAR DUET -
Beck & Violet - Friends-to-Lovers Rockstar Romance

*(*Same small town as Lock & Key MC Romance series*)*

1- WHIRLWIND

2 - WHISPERWIND

DAGGER IN THE SEA - TURO & ADRI
Mediterranean Romantic Suspense Adventure

ABOUT THE AUTHOR

Cat Porter was born and raised in New York City, but also spent a few years in Europe and Texas along the way, which made her as wanderlusty as her parents. As an introverted, only child, she loved reading and going to the movies, and had very big, but very secret dreams for herself.

She graduated from Vassar College, was a struggling actress, an art gallery girl, special events planner, freelance writer, restaurant hostess, and had all sorts of other crazy jobs all hours of the day and night in New York to help make her dreams come true.

She has two children's books traditionally published under her maiden name. And yes, she loves writing contemporary romances as well as historical romances.

She now lives on a beach outside of Athens, Greece with her husband, three children, and five huge Cane Corsos, freaks out regularly, still daydreams way too much, and now truly doesn't give AF.

She is addicted to reading, classic films, cafe bars on the beach, the Greek islands, Instagram, Pearl Jam and U2, bourbon she brought home from Nashville and whiskey she brought home from Dublin, and realllllly good coffee.

Writing has always kept her somewhat sane, extremely happy, and a productive member of society.

www.catporter.com

Email - catporter103@gmail.com

amazon.com/author/catporter

bookbub.com/authors/cat-porter

instagram.com/catporter.writer

x.com/catporter103

pinterest.com/catporter103

tiktok.com/@catporter_writer

facebook.com/CatPorterWriter

bsky.app/profile/catporterwriter.bsky.social

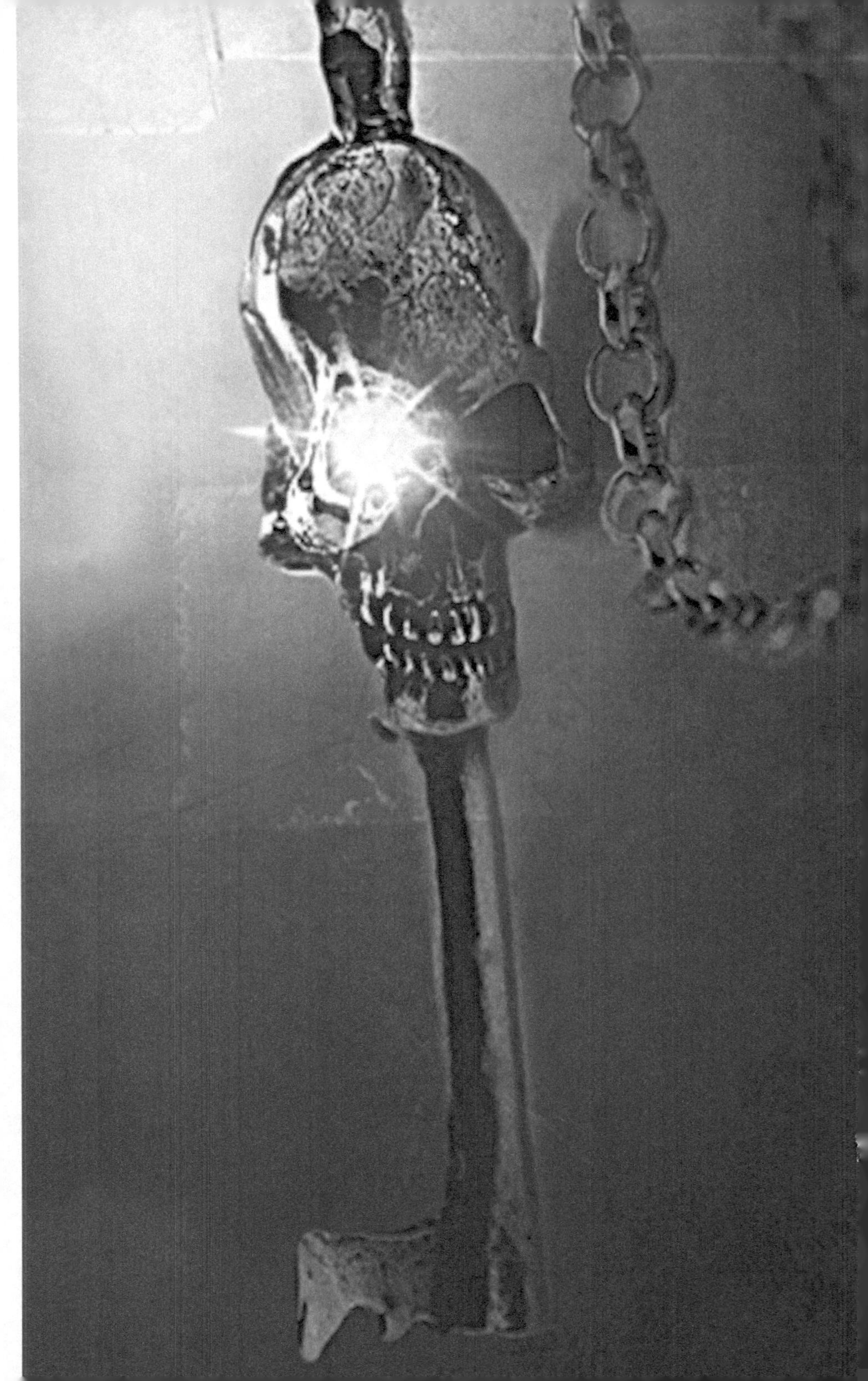